HOLLOW WORLD

By
Michael J. Sullivan

Hollow World

Cover Illustrations: Marc Simonetti & Michael J. Sullivan
Cover Design: Michael J. Sullivan

Tachyon Publications
1459 18th Street #139
San Francisco, CA 94107
(415) 285-5615
tachyon@tachyonpublications.com

smart science fiction & fantasy
www.tachyonpublications.com

Series Editor: Jacob Weisman
Project Editor: Jill Roberts

ISBN 13: 978-1-61696-183-1
Printed in the United States by Worzalla

General Release First Edition: 2014

9 8 7 6 5 4 3 2 1

Learn more about Michael's writings at www.riyria.com.
To contact Michael, email him at michael.sullivan.dc@gmail.com

Praise for Hollow World

"This is a clever and thought-provoking story, with loads of interesting ideas, some adrenalin-pumping action and plenty of humour...overall an entertaining read with Pax being one of my favourite characters of the year."

— Pauline M. Ross, *Fantasy Review Barn*

"This is social science fiction that H.G. Wells or Isaac Asimov could have written, with the cultural touchstones of today. A modernized classic, *Hollow World* is the perfect novel for both new and nostalgic science fiction readers."

— Justin Landon, *Staffer's Book Reviews*

"This book made me laugh. It also made me cry. And in the end, it made me think. I highly recommend *Hollow World* for anyone looking for a book that brushes on and plays out some political and social issues we face today."

— N. E. White, *SFFWorld.com*

"I fully expected this to be a good speculative read, I had not expected it to be one of those rare literary gems that exceed the speculative genre to become worthy of any English literature class."

— Stephan van Velzen, *Ranting Dragon*

"I'm happy to report that not only does *Hollow World* establish Sullivan as a force to be reckoned with in any genre he chooses to ply his talent to, it also is a prime example of one of the reasons speculative fiction is so important...Sullivan questions our assumptions about our society as a whole that makes this one of the best novels, I've read this year."

— Matt Gilliard, *52 Reviews*

"*Hollow World* is a character-driven story packed with intensity and emotion... *Hollow World* was easily one of my top reads of 2013."

— Stephenie Sheung, *Bibliosanctum*

Free Ebook for Print & Audio Purchasers

When publishing *Hollow World*, I retained the ebook rights. This was done to provide me the most distribution flexibility. I'm a firm believer that digital rights management controls do nothing to prevent piracy and only end up inconveniencing legitimate buyers. I also believe that if you've bought a royalty-producing print copy, then you have already compensated me for my efforts and as such you should be able to read the book in any format you desire. I love having books on my shelf, and yet I can't deny the convenience of my ereaders. It shouldn't be a matter of one or the other, and I'd rather have you buy more books (by myself or other authors) than have to buy the same book twice.

So, if you buy a print copy of *Hollow World*, you can receive a DRM-free ebook at no cost. If you purchase from Amazon, your free ebook will be delivered through their MatchBook program. For purchases on other venues, simply email me a copy of your electronic order, or a picture of your bookstore receipt, and I'll send it out to you. Please keep in mind this is something I want to do for my readers, but it will be a manual process, and there may be quite a few of you who might want this. I'll do my best to send the ebooks promptly, but it could take some time, so please be patient. Here is all the information to ensure the fastest delivery:

To: Michael.sullivan.dc@gmail.com
Subject: FREE HOLLOW WORLD EBOOK
Body of email: Please indicate what file format (or formats) you would prefer: pdf, mobi (Kindle), epub (NOOK, Kobo, and iPad), .lrf (Sony Reader), etc.

This book is dedicated to the people at Tachyon Publications who are leading the way in publishing done right. I hope more organizations follow in their footsteps.

Michael Sullivan's Works

The Riyria Revelations
Theft of Swords (contains *The Crown Conspiracy* and *Avempartha*)
Rise of Empire (contains *Nyphron Rising* and *The Emerald Storm*)
Heir of Novron (contains *Wintertide* and *Percepliquis*)

The Riyria Chronicles
The Crown Tower
The Rose and the Thorn

Standalone Novels
Hollow World
Antithesis (forthcoming)
A Burden to the Earth (forthcoming)

Anthologies
The End—Visions of Apocalypse
Triumph Over Tragedy
Unfettered
Help Fund My Robot Army

AUTHOR'S NOTE

Time travel as described in this novel isn't possible. It's important to mention this up front. I'm not saying, "Don't try this at home." I'm simply clarifying that this is as much a work of fantasy as it is science fiction—but, then again, most science fiction has a dash of fantasy thrown in, that artificial *what if* spark that ignites the chain reaction that propels everything forward.

In the classic *The Time Machine,* H. G. Wells's high-tech explanation for how his device was able to skip through years was: "Now I want you to clearly understand that this lever, being pressed over, sends the machine gliding into the future, and this other reverses the motion." That's pretty much the extent of his hard science. Of course his story, while named *The Time Machine*, really wasn't so much about the machine or the science behind it, but rather speculations on the future of mankind.

So is *Hollow World.*

The Time Machine was first published in Britain in 1895. Apparently, back then, you could get away with stating that pressing a lever resulted in doing something otherwise known as impossible. Of course back then, they didn't have the Internet. The average reader today knows that you can't travel faster than the speed of light, or through a black hole. This education may be due more to the success of science fiction entertainment such as *Star Trek* than to high school teachers, but here we are. The modern-day reader is better educated and demands plausibility.

To this end I did research into time-travel theory, and I drew inspiration from a handful of sources, most notably *Time Travel in Einstein's Universe: The Physical Possibilities of Travel Through Time* by renowned astrophysicist J. Richard Gott. Mr. Gott provided a plausible explanation for how a stationary object could move significantly forward in time by overcoming the g-force restriction of linear travel by moving interdimensionally. This is theoretically possible if you could put yourself in the near-center of a black hole while maintaining a defensive shell using electrostatic repulsions of like charges. That's the theory, but as I said, time travel of the sort required for this story isn't possible—at least not in an urban garage. I fudged the math—a lot. I aimed for a dramatic blend of façade, plausibility, and smoke-and-mirrors illusion so that if you don't look too closely, you can *almost* imagine it working.

Like H. G. Wells's tale, *Hollow World* really isn't about time travel any more than reality television shows are documentaries. I hope you won't allow a little creative license to get in the way of enjoying the ride. I felt providing a good reading experience superseded an adherence to strict probability. *Hollow World* isn't a story about the science of time travel.

So, what *is* this story about?

Read on—a world awaits.

—Michael J. Sullivan
July 2013

CONTENTS

HOLLOW WORLD

Running Out of Time

When she said he was dying, and explained how little time he had left, Ellis Rogers laughed. Not a normal response—the doctor knew it, Ellis did too. He wasn't crazy; at least he didn't think so, but how does anyone really know? He should have seen visions, flashes from his life: kissing Peggy at the altar, graduating college, or the death of their son, Isley. He should have fixated on all of the things that he'd never done, the words he had spoken, or the ones he hadn't. Instead, Ellis focused on the four-letter word the doctor had said. Funny that she used *that* word—he never told her what was in his garage.

The pulmonary specialist was a small Indian woman with bright, alert eyes and a clipboard that she frequently looked to for reference. She wore the familiar white lab coat—stethoscope stuffed deep in one pocket. She sat, or more accurately leaned, against the front of her desk as she spoke. At the start of her speech, the doctor had begun with a determined, sympathetic resolve, but that train had been derailed by his inappropriate outburst, and neither of them seemed to know what to do next.

"Are you...all right?" she asked.

"First test I ever failed," he said, trying to explain himself, hoping she'd swallow it and move on. Given the news she had just delivered, he deserved a little slack.

The doctor stared at him concerned for a moment, then settled back into her professional tone. "You should probably get another opinion, Ellis." She used his first name as if they were old friends, though he'd only seen her the few times it had taken to get the tests performed.

"Is someone working on a cure for this?" Ellis asked.

The doctor sighed, keeping her lips firm. She folded her arms, then unfolded them and leaned forward. "Yes, but I honestly don't think anyone is close to a breakthrough." She looked at him with sad eyes. "You just don't have that much time."

There was that word again.

He didn't laugh, but he might have smiled. He needed a better poker face. Ellis shifted his sight away from her and instead focused on three jars sitting on a counter near the door. They looked like they belonged in a kitchen—except that these contained tongue depressors and cotton swabs instead of sugar and flour. He couldn't tell what was in the last one. Something individually packaged, syringes, maybe, which reminded him to double-check the first-aid kit to make sure it had a good supply of aspirin. Not all of them did.

The doctor probably expected him to cry or maybe fly into a rage cursing God, bad luck, the industrial food complex, or his own refusal to exercise. Laughter and smiles weren't on that menu.

But he couldn't help being amused, not when the doctor was unwittingly making jokes.

No, he thought, *not jokes—suggestions. And she's right, there's nothing stopping me anymore.*

He was dying from idiopathic pulmonary fibrosis and she had given him six months to a year. The *to a year* portion of that sentence felt tacked on in an overly optimistic manner. Anyone else might have focused on that part of the equation—the dying part—and thought about trips to Europe, safaris in Africa, or visiting neglected friends and family. Ellis was planning a trip of a different sort and began running a mental checklist. He already had most everything. Flashlight batteries, he should get more of them—can't ever have too many batteries—and some more M&M'S, why the hell not? It wasn't like he had to worry about his weight, diabetes, or tooth decay. *I'll buy a whole box! The peanut ones, the yellow bags are always the best.*

"I'm going to set up an appointment for you to come back. Two weeks should give you enough time to see someone else and have the tests repeated." She stopped writing and stared at him with her big brown eyes. "Are you sure you're all right?"

"I'm fine."

"Is there someone I can call?" She flipped through the pages on the clipboard again. "Your wife?"

"Trust me, I'm good."

He was surprised to realize he was telling the truth. The last time he felt that way was thirty-six years ago when he had sat across from the loan officer's desk and learned he'd qualified for the mortgage that allowed him to move out of his parent's home. Fear mingled with the excitement of facing the unknown. Freedom—real freedom—had all the rush of an illegal drug.

I can finally press the button.

She waited a beat or two longer, then nodded. "Assuming your second opinion concurs with mine, I will add your name to the registry for a transplant, and I'll explain the process in detail at your appointment. Aside from that, I'm afraid there's nothing else we can do. I'm really very sorry." Reaching out she took his hand. "I really am."

He nodded and gave a slight squeeze. Her smile appeared less forced then. Maybe she was thinking she'd made him feel better, made some emotional connection. That was good, he needed all the karma he could get.

"What'd the doctor say?" was the first thing out of Peggy's mouth when Ellis walked through the door. He couldn't see her. He guessed she was somewhere in the kitchen, shouting over the television she'd left on in the living room. Peggy did that a lot. She said it made her feel less alone, but she kept it on even when Ellis was home.

"She said it was nothing to be concerned about." He dropped his keys on the coffee table in the candy dish their son had made years ago.

"She? Wasn't your appointment with Dr. Hall?"

Dammit! Ellis cringed. "Ah—Dr. Hall retired. I met with a woman doctor."

"Retired? That sounds sudden. Is he okay?"

"Yeah—yeah he's fine."

"Well good for him. I'm surprised, though. He really isn't much older than we are, and I always thought doctors retired later than other people. So this other doctor, she wasn't concerned about your cough?"

Ellis found the remote and turned down the volume until the gaggle of women arguing on the television was nothing more than a low hum. He wondered if it was the same show he always walked in on or if all the shows she didn't watch were the same.

"Not really. She said it was just a virus," he called back.

The living room was a milestone showing how far they had come. Two Williams-Sonoma mohair couches faced a big screen television as wide as the bathroom in their first apartment. On shelves near the fireplace sat his M.I.T. textbooks alongside dissertations he had bound in genuine leather. Above those were a pile of thrillers and murder mysteries by the likes of Michael Connelly, Tom Clancy, and Jeffery Deaver—his mind candy.

Photos were everywhere: hanging on the walls, propped on end tables, balanced atop the television. From each frame a sandy-haired cherub with freckles and a varying number of teeth smiled back. The one taken at Cedar Point commanded the centerpiece of the granite coffee table. All three of them had been in that amusement-park photo, but a strategic fold had left only Ellis's left hand visible where it rested on his son's shoulder.

"Did she even give you anything for it?" Peggy asked. She entered the living room still wearing her work clothes, what she called her "three Ps": power pantsuit and pearls. She glanced at the television, perhaps checking to see if she was missing anything important, then turned back to him.

For a moment he considered telling the truth, at least about his prognosis. He wanted to see what she'd say. What she'd do.

He couldn't say yes. She might ask to see the bottle. "She gave me a prescription. I just haven't filled it yet."

"Well, you better do that soon. The drugstore will be closing—at least the pharmacy counter will." She pulled a fresh pack of menthols from the pocket of her jacket and began to tap out a cigarette, then paused, looking at him. "Oh," she said with a disappointed tone and a little frown. "Aren't you going to the garage?"

"Actually, I'm meeting Warren. Just came home to get my coat. It's getting cold."

"Well, if you take any pills, look at the bottle before you start drinking."

Ellis grabbed Peggy's keys off the hall table as quietly as he could, but instead of heading out the kitchen door he climbed the stairs to their bedroom, and once inside, locked the door. His heart was pounding so loud he hoped Peggy couldn't hear it. Taking this first step made it real for him.

Jesus, I'm actually going to do it.

He crept to the closet, put on his coat, then began excavating. The left side of the walk-in had always been Peggy's territory. Stacked on the floor were old shoes, the wedding photos, and God knew what else she had stuffed back there in an assortment of cardboard and plastic containers. Ellis knew what he was looking for, and after carefully disassembling a tower of shoe boxes, he uncovered the treasure-chest-shaped jewelry case. She kept it locked. The key was on her ring along with a bottle opener, flip-out nail file, coin purse, rape whistle, penlight, laminated photo of Isley, silver medallion of a camel or llama, another of a soccer ball, and a big plastic plaque that read: PEGGY. The ridiculous thing was that the Nissan had a keyless entry system and a push button start.

The jewelry box opened like a cash register with the top popping up and the drawers pushing out in tiers. The thing was packed with memorabilia. He spotted a Mother's Day card Isley had made when he was around six. Just a bit of folded poster board with the word MOM scrawled in crayon. There were a bunch of letters, a few photos of Isley, ticket stubs to a play called *No Parking* that he didn't remember, and a bunch of poems Peggy had written before they got married, back when she was learning to play the guitar and planned on being the next Carole King.

And, of course, there was jewelry.

Old clip-on earrings, and the newer pierced ones, some dangled like Christmas tree tinsel, others were just studs. She had two strings of pearls, a choker with what looked like an ivory medallion, and a host of rings. Most of it was costume. Four pieces were not.

Peggy's engagement ring and wedding band were there, but he wouldn't touch those. Ellis was only interested in a pair of diamond earrings he had inherited from his grandmother. The jewelry was at the bottom, buried under the memorabilia.

Downstairs he heard Peggy move. Her footsteps crossed the living room, heading toward the stairs. He froze.

Ellis imagined her coming up and reaching for the door.

Why is the door locked? What are you doing in there, Ellis?

What would he say?

What are you doing with my keys?

He paused, listening. She had stopped.

What the hell is she doing? Just standing in the middle of the hall? Screw it.

Ellis reached in and grabbed everything in the way. He stuffed the pile in his coat pocket, then felt for the earrings.

He heard Peggy starting up the steps, and scooped up the jewelry on the bottom. He closed the closet and raced his wife to the bedroom door, opening it just before she touched the knob.

"Still here?" she asked.

He smiled. "Just heading out."

His heart was pounding as he went down the steps. He gingerly set her key ring back on the little table near the coat rack and walked out. On the porch he put his hand in his pants pocket and felt for the jewelry. Ellis sighed. He'd accidentally grabbed Peggy's rings along with his grandmother's diamonds. He'd leave them on the kitchen counter when he got back from the bar, although they obviously didn't mean anything to her anymore. She'd worn them for eighteen years but stopped about the time she started taking the real-estate seminars. Peggy mentioned that an article had said women Realtors without wedding bands consistently outperformed those who wore them regardless of whether or not they were actually married. Ellis never argued, never put up a fuss because he knew the real reason. She had put away her rings and started her career the same summer that Isley had hung himself in the garage with one of his father's belts.

Brady's was a nearly invisible bar on Eight Mile Road. Sandwiched between a video-rental store and a Chinese restaurant in a neighborhood of liquor stores and bump shops, it was the only building without bars on the windows. Brady's didn't have windows. The place was just a brick front with a white-painted steel door that clanged on a tight spring.

Ellis stood outside the bar, coughing. He always had trouble going out in the cold, not that it was all that cold yet. November in Detroit, with the moisture coming off the Great Lakes, was just the prelude to six months of bone-chilling misery. Still, his lungs didn't like the change in the air. These days his lungs didn't like much of anything, and the coughing came in fits of chest-ripping waves that left him feeling battered. He waited until the wheezing stopped before heading inside.

The interior of Brady's was about what the exterior suggested: a no-frills bar that smelled like fried food and still reeked of cigarette smoke years after the state ban went into effect. The floor was sticky, the tables wobbled, and the corner-mounted television showed muted football highlights while hidden speakers played vintage Johnny Cash. Without windows, the only light came from the television and a few old-fashioned ceiling lamps, leaving the place a flickering cave of silhouettes.

Warren Eckard sat at the bar, looking up at the television screen and swirling what was left of a Budweiser. Supported by his elbows, he was hunched over the bottle, one foot bouncing to the rhythm of Cash's "Folsom Prison Blues." Warren was wearing a T-shirt that read: I LOVE MY COUNTRY. IT'S THE GOVERNMENT I HATE. The 2XL shirt was still too small, leaving an exposed band of pale skin muffining out of his jeans. Ellis was just thankful Warren wasn't letting his waistband droop any more than it already was.

"Warren," Ellis said, clapping him on the back and taking a seat alongside him.

"Hey! Hey!" Warren turned, grinning at him with an overacted look of surprise. "Well, if it ain't Mr. Rogers. Wonderful day in the neighborhood to ya, old man. How ya been?"

Warren held out his hand, and Ellis took it, his own disappearing inside that big mitt. It had been decades since the accident, but he couldn't help noticing Warren's missing fourth and fifth fingers.

"Who's the kid behind the bar?" Ellis asked, trying to catch the eye of the bartender—some young fella in a black T-shirt with a toothpick in his mouth.

"Freddy," Warren said. "He's Italian. So don't make any dago jokes, or we'll both be swimming *wit da fishes*."

"Where's Marty?"

Warren shrugged. "Day off, maybe. Laid-off likely. Who knows?"

"Freddy?" Ellis called to the kid, who was leaning back on his elbows, fiddling with the toothpick between his teeth. "Can I get a Bud?"

The kid nodded and popped the top off a tall, brown bottle frosted from the cooler. He slapped a square napkin on the bar in front of Ellis, set the bottle on it, and then went back to his elbows and his toothpick.

"Lions playing tonight?" Ellis asked, nodding at the television as he peeled off his coat.

"Against the Redskins," Warren replied. "Gonna get creamed."

"Way to support the home team."

"Well, it'd help if they had any decent players." He drained his bottle and clapped it on the bar loud enough for Freddy to take notice and pull him a new one.

"Maybe you can try out after the baby comes. What are you eight, nine months, now?"

"Very funny, you're quite the comedian. You know damn well that"—he switched into his best impersonation of Marlon Brando, which sounded more like a sickly Vito Corleone than Terry Malloy—*"I could have been a contender."*

"Yeah, well, shoulda, woulda, coulda. Speaking of which..." Ellis withdrew a stapled stack of paper from the inside pocket of his coat. The pages were creased, stained with coffee, and had notes jotted in the margins. The bulk of which was a lot of small text in two columns—much of it equations.

"What's this?" Warren asked. "More of your geek leaking out? You bringing your work to the bar now?"

"No, this one's all mine. Been working on it for years—sort of a hobby. You know anything about the theory of relativity? Black holes?"

"Do I look like Stephen Hawking?"

Ellis smiled. "Sometimes. When you're sitting up straighter and speaking more clearly."

Warren fake-laughed. "Oh you're hot tonight." Turning his attention to Freddy he added, "You hear this guy?—a regular Moe Howard."

Freddy was pulling a pair of Miller Lites and a Michelob for three women, who had taken seats at the far end of the bar. He looked over, confused. "Who?"

"You know, the Three Stooges."

Freddy shook his head.

"Jesus, are you shitting me? Moe, Larry, and Curly. Nyuk, nyuk, nyuk. The greatest comedians of our time."

"What time would that be exactly?" Freddy asked, with a smile that both insulted and charmed.

"Never mind." Warren had his disgusted-with-the-younger-generation expression on, which never ceased to amaze Ellis, because he had known Warren Eckard when they *were* the younger generation.

Warren flipped through the pages, shaking his head the way a cop might at a particularly gruesome crime scene. "I can't believe you do this shit for fun."

"You watch football," Ellis countered. "I play with quantum—"

"Football's exciting."

"So is this."

Warren pointed at the television where a blimp's-eye view revealed the mammoth FedExField in Landover, Maryland. "There's more than eighty-five thousand people in those stands, and a hundred million watch the Super Bowl every year. That's how fun it is."

"Five hundred million watched Neil Armstrong step on the surface of the moon. How fun is that?"

Warren scowled and sucked on his beer. "So what's with the egghead papers? Got a point or just showing off?"

"Showing off?"

"You're Mr. M.I.T and I'm Mr. G.E.D, right?"

Ellis frowned. "Don't be an ass."

"Fifty-eight years of practice, my friend. Hard to turn off." Warren took another swig.

Ellis waited.

Warren looked at him and rolled his eyes. "Okay, okay—skip it. What's this all about?"

Ellis laid the papers on the bar. "So, there was this guy in Germany back in the thirties, Gustaf Hoffmann, who published a theory reviewed in *Annalen der Physik.* That's one of the oldest peer-reviewed scientific journals in the world. It's where Einstein published his theories, okay? I'm talking important science here."

Warren's expression was one of labored patience.

"Anyway, it didn't get much attention. Mostly because the math didn't hold up, but basically he tried to show that time travel is not only possible but practical. I did one of my theses on Hoffmann, applying modern quantum theory on top of his concepts. Even after I turned in my dissertation, I continued to play with the idea and tweak the math. About two years ago I figured out what Hoffmann did wrong."

"That's...that's great, Ellis." Warren nodded robotically. "Twisted and sad, but if you're happy, I'm happy."

"You don't understand. This theory—it's really simple. Not the math—that was a bitch—but the final equation was like all good physics—simple and perfect. The best part is that it's applicable. I'm talking about applied science, not just theory and conjecture. You know, like how Einstein came up with a theory and the guys on the Manhattan Project built the A-bomb. Well, that took years of research and development and tons of infrastructure and resources to make it a reality. This"—Ellis tapped the stack of pages—"is much easier, much simpler."

"Uh-huh, and so..." Warren was quickly losing interest, although Ellis doubted he had much to begin with.

"Don't you get it? This right here is a blueprint for a time machine. Wouldn't you like to see the future?"

"Hell no. I've seen enough of the present to know what'll happen. The last good thing society did together was kill Hitler." Warren took another swallow and wiped his mouth.

"C'mon, are you telling me you don't want to see how everything turns out?"

"That's like wanting to stick around to see how jumping off a cliff turns out." Warren smirked, shaking his head. "World's going to shit. America's like that old Buick of mine. The old gal is rusting out. China is gonna kick our ass. Everyone's gonna be eating rice and carrying little red books."

Now it was Ellis's turn to smirk.

"You don't think so, huh?" Warren said. "The problem is, we've gotten weak. The baby boomers and their kids have had it too easy. Spoiled brats, really. And they're making the next generation even worse. Everyone wants their big houses and fancy cars, but no one wants to work for it. Hell, the only ones willing to work these days are the damn wetbacks."

Ellis grimaced and looked across the bar at a table of Hispanics near the door. They either didn't hear or didn't care.

"You wanna use your indoor voice, Mr. Bunker? And you might consider joining the rest of us in the new millennium and use the revolutionary new terms of *Hispanic* or *Latino*."

"What?" He looked toward the table near the door, and in a louder voice added, "I'm complimenting them. They're good workers. That's what I said."

"Never mind." Ellis rubbed his face with his hands. "We were talking about the future, remember?"

"Screw that shit. It's gonna be some sort of apocalyptic hellscape or, worse, some kind of oppressive prison-world run by Big Brother from that Orson Welles story."

"*Nineteen Eighty-Four* was written by George Orwell. H. G. Wells wrote *The Time Machine,* and Orson was a director and actor."

"Whatever. I'm just saying the future don't look bright, my friend."

Ellis wondered if Warren realized he was part of that same baby-boom generation he was pinning the downfall of civilization on. He didn't think Warren would throw his own name in the spoiled-rotten hat, and maybe he was right not to. They both came from blue-collar families whose fathers had worked themselves into early heart attacks. Ellis had been lucky, Warren hadn't.

Warren's dream of playing professional football had died for good when he lost his fingers. He'd cut them off in the die-stamp press at work after removing the safety cover because it *was in the way*. Warren won a lawsuit on the grounds that the cover shouldn't have been removable. Apparently Warren felt as entitled as the next guy—felt he deserved something after losing his fingers. His friend's personal responsibility had evaporated with the lure of a big check.

"Now, if you can send me to the past, okay then," Warren said. "Shit, the 1950s were a fucking paradise. America ruled the world and was a beacon of hope and freedom for everyone. Anyone who wanted to could achieve their dreams. People knew what they were supposed to do. Men worked; women stayed home and raised the kids."

"Can't go back. It doesn't work that way. This Hoffmann fellow says you can only go forward. Well, you don't actually *go* anywhere. You pretty much stay put and let time pass you by. It's like when you go to sleep. You lie down, close your eyes, and *poof* it's the next day. You just skipped over those seven or eight hours. But even if it were possible to go either way I'd still like to see the future."

"And you will. Part of it, at least. We aren't dead yet, right?"

Ellis took another swallow of his beer, thinking how strange it was that Warren had chosen those words—almost like a sign from God. He considered mentioning his pink slip from the Almighty, but when playing out the scenario in his head, he decided to keep quiet. Life in the Motor City didn't invite men to be lippy with their feelings. One recession piled on another created strata of cold steel in the spines of its people. Like those who came before, rust-belt folks gritted their teeth, smoked, drank, and got by. They didn't hug; they shook hands. And Ellis didn't see the point in telling his best friend that he was dying. Bad enough that he had to walk around with that depressing bit of trivia.

"Anyway." Ellis picked up the stack of papers and handed them to Warren. "I want you to keep this."

"Why?"

"Just in case."

"In case of what?"

"In case it works."

"Works? In case what works?" Warren's eyes narrowed, then widened. "Oh, wait—so what are you saying? You're thinking of doing this? Making a time machine?"

"More than thinking. I started building it right after I figured out Hoffmann's mistake. I have it in my garage."

It would be more accurate to say it *was* his garage, but he thought it best to keep this simple. Warren already had that knot in his brow like he was looking at a Magic Eye image and trying to see the three-dimensional object in the pattern.

"Is it—it's not dangerous, is it?"

When he didn't answer right away, Warren's eyebrows went up. "Ellis, you're a bright guy, the smartest I've ever known. You're not thinking of doing something stupid, are you?"

Ellis shook his head. "Don't worry. Probably won't work. It's just that...you know how you feel about not playing on the big fields?" He motioned to the game still on the television. "Well I never got my chance to be an astronaut, to reach space, walk on Mars. This could be like that, but I'm getting old and don't have a lot of time left to do anything *important*—anything adventurous."

"What about Peggy?"

Ellis drank from the fresh beer that had been making a puddle because Freddy had failed to put down a new napkin. He was tempted to ask, *Peggy who?*

"It might be for the best. I honestly think she'll be relieved. A few years ago I mentioned we might consider moving to Texas. There was a great position opening up down there, and it would have meant more money and a big promotion for me. She said she couldn't leave what little she still had left of Isley, but I could go if I wanted. She seemed disappointed when I stayed."

"She still blames you?"

"With good reason, don't you think?"

"Don't beat yourself up. I would have done the same thing, you know." Warren shook his head, his lips pursed like he just bit into a lemon. "Any man would."

"Drop it, okay."

"Sure. Sorry. I didn't mean—"

"Forget it." Raising his voice Ellis called to Freddy. "Hey, set me and my friend here up with a couple of shots of Jack. I feel like celebrating."

Freddy poured, and when he was done, Warren raised his glass. "To a long life."

Ellis picked up his. "To the future."

They kissed rims and drank.

Time to Go

By the time Ellis got home, the reality of exactly what he was about to do had settled in, spoiling his initial excitement. He couldn't just leave. It wasn't right to walk out on Peggy like he was going for the proverbial pack of cigarettes. So they had drifted apart, so what? They still shared thirty-five years together and the woman deserved a proper goodbye. What if he made a mistake, if the wiring or Hoffmann was wrong and he—

What if she stumbles upon another *body in the garage? I can't do that to her! Oh Jesus Christ! What am I thinking?*

He needed to tell her, to explain. Maybe if he did, if she knew what it meant to him and how there might be a cure in the future, she would give him her blessing. Ellis was formulating his arguments when he realized the lights in the kitchen were still on. The grandfather clock in the hallway was just chiming eleven times. He was home earlier than usual, but for the last six years his wife had gone to bed every night by ten thirty.

So why are all the lights on?

They were on in the hall and living room too. They were on, and the television was off. *This is weird. Eerie even.*

"Peggy?" he called. He peeked in the empty bathroom. "Peggy?" he called louder, and began climbing the stairs.

Strange and eerie turned into scary when he entered their bedroom, and she was still nowhere to be found. When he caught sight of the open jewelry box lying on the bed, everything finally made sense. She had discovered his little raid. Of course she had; he'd left everything out. The moment she went to dress for bed she would have seen the open box.

Oh shit! She thinks we were robbed! She's probably terrified and didn't want to be home alone. I hope she hasn't gone to the police. She wouldn't do that before talking to me, would she?

He pulled out his phone. There it was, a voicemail from Peggy. He tapped the icon and put it on speaker.

"El? Oh goddammit, El, pick up! Please pick up." Her voice quivered, and she was loud—not screaming, but frightened. *"I need to talk to you. I need to know what you're thinking."* A long pause. *"I'm sorry, okay? Seriously, I am, and that was years ago. I don't even know why I kept the letters. Just stupid is what it was. I'd honestly forgotten about them.*

"I know I should have told you. Jesus, I wish you'd just pick up. Listen, are you still at Brady's? I'm driving over. I'll be there in twenty minutes. We can talk then, okay? Please don't be mad. It wasn't Warren's fault. It wasn't anyone's fault, really. It just happened, and I know we should have told you, but...well...If you get this before I get there, don't go anywhere or do anything crazy, okay?"

The message ended.

Ellis stared at the phone, his mouth open.

I don't even know why I kept the letters.

He walked to the bed and the open jewelry box, remembering the Mother's Day card, the ticket stub, some photos, poems, and letters. But they weren't in the box anymore. The box was empty. He stared at it a moment, then realized he'd taken them.

Just stupid is what it was.

Ellis reached into his coat pocket.

I know I should have told you.

He took out the pile, letting the poems, photos, and even the ticket stub fall to the carpet. All that remained were the envelopes. The postmarks were from 1995, a few months after Isley's death; the address was Peggy's post-office box—the one she'd gotten for her business correspondence; the handwriting was Warren's.

It wasn't Warren's fault.

Ellis continued to stand there, stunned. After hearing a car, and thinking it might be Peggy, he took the letters and headed for the garage. Detached and set back against the rear fence of his yard the garage was a little house onto itself, the one place completely his. Since Isley's death, Peggy never went there. Ellis needed time, and the garage was his own personal Area 51.

The interior didn't look like a garage. With all the cables, it resembled an H. R. Giger sculpture. In the center sat the driver's seat, which he'd torn from their old Aerostar minivan. The captain's chair was mounted on a black rubber box with hoses snaking out of it, and the whole thing was surrounded by plastic milk crates. A dozen thick cables radiated from the shell like a spiderweb connecting copper plates, breakers, and batteries mounted on the walls and ceiling. What once had been a home for two cars now resembled the interior of the CERN Hadron Collider.

Despite all the equipment, a portion of one wall was left in its original condition where two ordinary-looking items hung. The first was a 1993 Ansel Adams calendar displaying black-and-white photos of Yosemite Valley. Isley had given it to Ellis for Christmas when his son had been just fifteen. Although filled with amazing pictures of waterfalls and mountains, Ellis had stopped turning the pages at September as that one was his favorite. September was also the month that Isley had died.

The second was a poster of the Mercury Seven. He'd had it since he was a boy, when it used to adorn his bedroom along with similar ones of the Apollo crews. When he found it in the attic while looking for more cabling, he couldn't help pinning it up. A little faded, the picture showed the original seven astronauts introduced to the world on April 9, 1959, when Ellis had been almost three years old. Two rows of determined men in tinfoil spacesuits with white enamel helmets stared back. John Glenn and Alan Shepard were his favorites, with Shepard winning out not only because he was the first American in space, but also because he'd managed the feat on Ellis's fifth birthday.

After entering the building, Ellis locked the door. He was having trouble breathing; the crackling rustled in his chest again, only this time he wasn't certain if the difficulty was just because of his lungs. It felt like something else had shattered.

If someone asked Ellis if he loved his wife, he would have said yes, even though he wasn't exactly sure what that meant. Like trying to envision heaven, thoughts of love turned cheesy whenever he tried to focus on specifics. All those movies and song lyrics made it schmaltzy with overuse. Words like *wind beneath wings* and *completing one's self* were nice one-liners, but did anyone really feel that way? He didn't feel that way about Peggy, and he was pretty sure she didn't feel that way about him.

He had met Peggy at a party held by Billy Raymond, a friend of Warren's. They were six years out of high school, and Warren convinced him to go. His friend had been working at the assembly plant in Wixom, and Ellis just finished his first master's degree. Warren never had any problem getting girls, but Ellis always had a better chance of attracting lightning. So he was floored when Peggy talked to him. She was attractive, and it was good just to be noticed. They had seen each other on and off for a few months, then Peggy told him she was pregnant. She also admitted she was scared he would abandon her, the way Warren had left Marcia. Ellis didn't. He did the right thing—at least what he had thought was the right thing.

He and Peggy had never talked much. Ellis was working at GM, improving solar cells and battery efficiency, and Peggy devoted herself to Isley. He had been their common ground, a shared interest. But after he died, they were little more than strangers in the same house. So it came as a shock that her betrayal hurt so much.

Peggy might not have been his soul mate, but she had always been there. They counted on and trusted each other. If gravity failed, the speed of light was broken, and death and taxes disappeared there would still be Peggy, telling him to be home on time because it was Tuesday and they were having salmon for dinner. The letters in his hands were notices that the sun wouldn't be coming up anymore; the world was no longer spinning, and time had stopped.

Except it hadn't.

Peggy would be back to *talk*. He didn't want to talk to her; he didn't want to talk to anyone. He didn't want to see anyone. If anything, he wanted to disappear.

He looked over at the disembodied van seat surrounded by milk crates.

Time hasn't stopped, but it could—at least for me.

Ellis stood up, moved to the fuse box, and flipped the new custom-built breakers for each line—setting them to bypass. He could pull all the power he wanted from Detroit Edison, and it would flow until the wire melted or he tripped a safety switch at the substation, which he would do pretty quickly, but not before he sucked the needed megawatts. The overhead lights dimmed noticeably as he drew power from the house's AC current. The garage hummed with a buzz similar to the noise heard when standing under a high-tension wire.

He took off his coat and stuffed it under the wrap of bungee cords. Everything else he needed was already there; it had been packed for months. He paused, looking around the garage, at the calendar—at his world. He felt alone, as if he stood in a desert; there was nothing anymore but the time machine—a single door at the end of a one-way corridor.

Ellis sat in the chair and set the milk crates in place. Through the grates, he could still make out the Mercury Seven poster. Was this how they felt climbing in the capsule and preparing to enter the unknown? They must have known nothing would ever be the same afterward, for them or the rest of the world.

He fastened his seatbelt.

Ellis picked up the tablet, turned it on, and swiped past the lock screen. He found the custom app he'd built and double-checked his numbers.

Don't go anywhere or do anything crazy, okay?

Why not? As Janis Joplin once sang, "Freedom's just another word for nothing left to lose."

The button on the control panel was glowing red—all powered up and ready to go. His Atlas rocket was locked and loaded. His *Glamorous Glennis* was in the bomb bay of a B-29 Superfortress, awaiting history.

People time traveled every day without realizing it. Some moved faster, others slower, because a body at rest moved through time at one rate, while a body in motion traveled slightly slower. Einstein had discovered that time and space were related, the two connected by a sliding scale—just as the more effort a person puts into making money, the less time they have to enjoy themselves. The reason no one noticed was that the difference was infinitesimal. But send a person in a rocket to the nearest star and back, and if the trip took him twenty years, centuries would pass on earth. Of course most people lack spaceships, but there was another way to affect time—by altering its relationship to space.

Instead of traveling, all that was needed was the equivalent mass of Jupiter compressed down until it was nearly a black hole so that it would generate an enormous gravity well. This would warp space and slow time. Then the traveler simply needed to sit in a spherical mass shell, sort of like the eye of a hurricane where the winds of time didn't blow, and wait the allotted duration. When he climbed out, he would be in a different time. There were obvious problems with this method—or there had been until Hoffmann discovered the means to generate a *contained* artificial gravity well that wouldn't devour everything around it, while at the same time protect the person sitting in the middle.

To insulate the time traveler, an electromagnetic field could be used to create an electrostatic repulsion of like charges, protecting him from the critical mass. If anything went wrong, and the gravity well started consuming its surroundings, the power supply would be destroyed first and shut everything down—a perfect fail-safe. Still, this was essentially Wilbur-and-Orville-style science. A lot could go wrong and Ellis could easily be squished out of existence.

The really scary part would come near the end. Ellis had programmed the tablet to track his position in both time and space, so, no matter how long he remained in time's hurricane eye, he would come out of stasis at the same physical location that he had started. Those calculations were the most difficult. Not only did he have to take in consideration the rotation of the earth, but also the movement of the planet around the sun and the universe and galaxy spinning through space. If he calculated wrong, he could materialize inside a star or, more likely, into the immense vacuum of space.

Ellis had set his destination for two hundred years and eight months. The eight months would allow him to arrive in summer rather than fall. The calculation might not be that precise. Several variables might affect the exact time lapse. The power drawn, the batteries' storage capacity, the wiring used, even the humidity in the air could cause the arrival date to shift by a few years.

Ellis raised his finger and noticed it was shaking. He stared at the glowing ignition. Then it finally happened. His life did flash through his head. He saw his mother, saw his father, saw himself at college, then him holding an eight-pound Isley followed by teaching his son to ride a bike. He saw Peggy in the snow at Mt. Brighton, flakes on her eyelashes, cheeks red, holding on to him for dear life and laughing. They were both laughing. They hadn't laughed together like that in...

Sadness, regret, anger, and frustration—the pain reached into his chest, squeezing his heart. Ellis took a labored breath. "Say goodnight, Gracie," he said, and pressed the button.

No Time Like the Present

The first thing Ellis noticed was that the overhead lights went out with a pop, signifying he'd just killed the breaker at the substation and possibly taken out the power to his part of the grid. Nothing else happened.

His heart sank in disappointment, but then he noticed that the light illuminating the ignition button was still on and the humming was growing louder. The Aerostar seat started vibrating like a coin-operated Magic Fingers bed, and everything was blurry. As much as he wanted to believe that the time machine would work, his rational mind knew it wouldn't. His brain was the *Chicago Daily Tribune* running the banner: Dewey Defeats Truman even while his senses told him something was happening.

Peering through the webbing of the milk crates, Ellis could still see the poster of the Mercury Seven, only it didn't look the same. It appeared to change color, turning bluish. The streetlight shining in the window was spreading out in the color spectrum. Then he noticed movement. He watched shadows crawl slowly, advancing like a time-lapse film. They didn't race; they didn't flash by; they barely moved, but it was noticeable. Time was advancing outside the crates more rapidly than on the inside. He had achieved the gravity well, and it was self-contained, stable, and he was insulated. He knew this by the simple virtue of still being alive.

He looked at the tablet, and saw the numbers scrolling by, faster with each passing second. The program should auto kill both the gravity well and the electrostatic shell the moment the clock timed out, but what would happen after?

There was no going back now.

He'd been sitting in the time machine for about five minutes, and Ellis was concerned about Peggy coming home. He didn't know if she'd be able to see him. He should already be moving interdimensionally, but since he could still see the garage—as distorted as it was—he imagined she might be able to see a ghostly, unmoving image of him, still caught in the instant he pressed the button. Once he reached a certain threshold he imagined he would vanish in a burst of light like the starship *Enterprise*.

How long will that take? I need to go.

As if on demand, there was a jolt and a sound like a freight train. Everything went bright blue and then white. When the sound stopped, he felt as if he were free-falling. He might have screamed, but he never heard it. His mind focused on to just one thought.

So this is what it's like to die.

Ellis wasn't sure if he had lost consciousness or if the term consciousness even applied. He was certain the human mind, whether built from evolution or the will of God, wasn't designed to handle what he'd just done. Human perception of reality could only bend so far. There were limits to comprehension, and without reference points his trip through the world of looking-glass physics remained nothing more than a blur.

Even the duration was hard to judge. So much of human understanding depended on the surrounding environment that even time lost meaning in its absence. If he'd thought about it sooner, he might have counted his breaths or tapped a finger to an internal beat like a clock, but such thoughts were far too reasonable for what he had experienced. Ellis wasn't an astronaut trained to react to the abnormal with calm indifference. Dropping the tablet, he gripped the armrests of the chair, gritted his teeth, and prayed while years streamed past in the form of sheering light and tearing thoughts.

Ellis believed in the Bible and the Methodist God, not that he'd read the book or had a personal come-to meeting with the Almighty, as his mother had liked to put it. Such things didn't matter. He hadn't visited France or read *Les Misérables,* either, but he was pretty certain Paris was out there. He'd gone to church with Peggy regularly when Isley was alive, less so after, hardly at all in the last decade.

Like with Peggy, he and God had grown apart, yet there was something about riding a bolt of electricity and two hundred solar masses through a twisted reality that got him to make the call. God, he imagined, got a lot of late-night drunk dialings. *Aw shit, God, I need your help. I really fucked up this time—damn. I'm sorry I swore just then—fuck, I did it again!*

Ellis found it strange that he hadn't prayed for his life before that. A death sentence should have provoked it, but Ellis had gone to visit Warren at a bar instead of a priest in a church after getting the news. He figured God knew his situation already. What a lousy job that must be, listening to the daily sob stories of everyone on earth. All of them begging not to die or for the life of a loved one, as if everyone didn't know the deal. Still, no matter how much he loathed the idea, fear overrode pride, and at that moment Ellis was terrified. All he had left was God, and for the first time in years he prayed.

Sound was the first thing to come back, a buzz that grew to a ring that hurt Ellis's ears. He dug his fingers into the cushioned velour, sucked air through his teeth, eyes squeezed shut. Finally, a booming crack like thunder exploded, and he felt a final jerk.

Then silence.

The vibrations stopped too. The aftermath left him numb, similar to how he felt after shutting off a car engine following a long stint behind the wheel. He opened his eyes. He didn't know what to expect—a hellish landscape of obliterated ruins, a megalopolis of towers and lights with flying cars screaming by, or the pearly gates and St. Peter shaking his head and sounding like Foghorn Leghorn stammering, "I say—I say—I say you're early, boy." What he saw instead surprised him, though it shouldn't have.

He saw the milk crates.

They were still there. He likely would have died if they hadn't been, although they looked odd now—warped the way his garage had looked just before things went white. He wondered if time was still bending and it took a moment to realize the plastic had just melted some. All the crates were fused, squeezed down, and listing to one side. They were also smoking. It smelled as if he were back in his high school shop class making polymer paperweights. Beyond the crates he could tell everything had changed. He wasn't in his garage anymore. He was outside. A breeze brushed past, carrying away much of the smoke with it. He could hear the rustle of leaves, a soft soothing sound.

The trip was over. He'd done it, though exactly what *it* was, he had yet to determine. He popped the seatbelt and pushed on the milk crates, which all moved as one now that they'd been fused. He was forced to kick several times. When he crawled out, Ellis, who was wearing a flannel shirt, jeans, and a sweater, realized he was overdressed for the climate.

All of the woods Ellis had ever been in were young-growth patches, usually of birches or maples. In school he'd been taught that all the trees in Michigan had been clear-cut back in the nineteenth century—most forests had. Trees were a commodity farmed like corn and cows, and outside of some national parks, few Americans had ever seen old-growth forests. Once, his father had taken him camping up north near Grayling—*that* had been a forest—massive groves of eastern white pine, creating an endless series of trunks standing solemnly in a bed of ferns. Ellis had imagined that the trees went on forever and had been frightened he might get lost in that real-life version of *Where the Wild Things Are*. Still, the trees hadn't been very big, and there had been a systematic spacing of their placement.

Stepping out of the milk crates, Ellis realized the piney woods of northern Michigan had been an overgrown vacant lot compared to where he now stood. He felt insect-small as all around trees of unfathomable height soared into the darkness of a leafy canopy, the same way skyscrapers faded into low clouds. Brooding on hunches of gnarled roots the size of Volkswagens, the goliath trees were spread out, the undergrowth sparse and stunted—mostly moss and ferns. He popped into the right spot. Twenty feet to his left and he would have literally been one with nature. The reentry algorithm was supposed to shift the final location to avoid preexisting objects, but then again the GPS in Ellis's car once took him to a lake that it said was a gas station. Whether the calculation worked or he just got lucky, the result was appreciated.

The air was filled with a damp mist that a pale moonlight couldn't penetrate but instead illuminated, providing a soft-hazed light. Velvet moss blanketed the ground, making pillows out of shattered logs and boulders. Vines drooped in lazy loops, leaves gathered in crevasses, and ivy climbed. In the distance, he heard squawks and peeps he didn't recognize, cutting through the familiar chirps of crickets.

I'm Luke Skywalker crashed on Dagobah.

For a long moment, Ellis just stood still, staring out into the haze, breathing in the thick moisture. *What happened? Did I screw up? Am I back in time? Are there dinosaurs?* Everywhere he looked resembled one of those dioramas in a natural history museum that often showed a triceratops fending off a Tyrannosaurus rex. Hot and humid, too, like a rain forest, but that could also describe July in Detroit.

Have I moved? The synchronization calculations might have been off. Theoretically he could have been anywhere, even another planet, but doubted that on sheer odds. Since he wasn't in the vast vacuum of space, he considered that part of the experiment a success. Any landing you can walk away from, as they say, is a good one.

If he was still where his garage had been, only one question remained: *When* was it? Hoffmann said it wasn't possible to go back in time, so this had to be the future—but when? *Can this really be Detroit in only two hundred years?*

Ellis leaned back on the plastic crates that were still warm and thought of the old Zager and Evans song: *In the year 9595, I'm kinda wonderin' if man's gonna be alive.* Maybe something awful had happened; maybe he was alone, completely alone, the last human in existence.

The absurdity caused him to let out a stress-induced laugh.

Then he coughed.

He didn't want to make noise in this alien place; he didn't want to alert anything, but he couldn't help himself and launched into a series of hacks.

Something moved. He heard it. A great crack and snap of branches—a thud and slap of the earth, then more cracks. Ellis sucked in a breath and held it. The sounds were moving away, growing fainter. One more distant snap, and then he waited for the length of several minutes but heard nothing more. An animal perhaps?

His throat ached from the coughing, and, tasting blood, he spat.

What am I going to do?

If it had been possible, Ellis would have gone back. This wasn't what he had expected. The future was supposed to be more advanced. He was looking for flying cars and moving sidewalks, jet packs, and nonstops to Saturn's moons. That had been his hope, but he also considered that he might touch down in some chaotic post-apocalyptic world complete with bloodthirsty Mohawked gangs of roving bikers. Not that such a thing would be better, just understandable.

"Relax," he whispered. Saying it, hearing it spoken aloud, helped.

I don't know anything yet. I can't judge a whole planet based off one spot.

Ellis waited a few minutes, listening—just crickets and a few distant squawks. He'd have to travel. He wasn't surprised. That's why he'd brought the gear. He just imagined things differently. Ellis had expected to be walking along some superhighway and ducking flying cars—not hacking his way Indiana Jones-style through a primordial forest.

He moved to the back of the time machine and unhooked the cooler and his other gear. He'd brought two backpacks and opted for the smaller JanSport one, the kind kids took to school. He left his sleeping bag and tent as this was good enough for a base camp, for now. He planned to take only what was needed and travel light.

He put a small notepad in his breast pocket, along with a pen, and put the compass in his pants pocket. To the pack he added a handful of energy bars, two cans of Dinty Moore stew, matches, and the rain gear—still in the compressed plastic bag that he'd bought it in. He also included a few bags of peanut M&M'S, his water purifier, jacket, and first-aid kit. He considered flipping on the Geiger counter he'd purchased from Geigercounters.com to take a reading, but he didn't think it was necessary given the abundant life around him. He left it, but added the sunscreen and aspirin. He slung a canteen over his head and slipped the hunting knife onto his belt, then he took out the gun.

This one was a pistol, which, he had discovered while shopping, was not another name for a revolver for reasons so obvious he felt stupid. This pistol was an M1911 that the balding guy behind the gun case had explained was a classic single-action, semiautomatic model that was originally designed by John Browning. He went on and on about the gun's pedigree, its weight, ruggedness, and caliber. What sold Ellis was that it looked exactly like the ones he'd seen spies or military officers using in movies, the nickel-plated

.45 that they would slap a clip into and fire more rounds than any handgun could possibly hold. He'd only shot it a few times at a practice range where they outfitted him with goggles and giant noise-canceling headphones. Turned out not to be nearly as scary as he thought—fun, really. He'd bought a belt holster that he slipped on and tucked the gun into, double-checking to make sure the safety was set right. He didn't want to plug himself in the leg—not much chance of finding a cell for a 911 call.

He felt better the moment he had the gun on. He wasn't a gnat anymore.

Pulling his sweater off and the backpack on, Ellis felt the weight center on his shoulders and didn't think it was too bad, although that assessment might change after a few hours of walking. He had no idea where to go. He had his choice of up- or downhill. Going uphill might afford a better view, but given that he was in a forest at night, what could he really expect to see? Given his physical condition, which was definitely short of Olympic athlete, he guessed downhill was better. Flipping on his flashlight, he panned around, but it didn't help much. With the mist, he could almost see better without it, and he also didn't like the creepy slasher-movie vibe the solitary beam conjured. Before switching off the lamp to save the batteries, he took a compass reading, made a notation in his notepad regarding his direction, and then set off. Every ten or fifteen feet he stripped away a patch of bark, marking the way he had come.

At the bottom of the little valley, everything was pretty much as it had been higher up, only with fewer leaves and more moss. Then he noticed the sound of water. Water was good, he figured. Explorers always followed rivers. He checked and noted his new direction, then walked toward the sound, continuing to mark the trees as he went. Once he found the river, he walked downstream along its bank.

The stream entered into a clearing that provided a break in the vast canopy, granting him access to the sky and stars. Even with the mist, he could see a dazzling array of bright lights and the dust of the Milky Way. He'd never seen anything like it outside of a planetarium, and he stared in awe. As he watched, he caught sight of a falling star. Just a brief glimpse, but it made him smile.

I'm dying all alone on a dead world, but a shooting star amuses me.

The thought was liberating in an unexpected way. He had lived like George Bailey trapped in Bedford Falls, longing for adventure. And there he was, having gone where no man had gone before. It didn't matter that it would all likely end too soon, probably from starvation, some parasite, or, failing all else, his illness. But none of that mattered. Despite everything, he felt good, better than he had in his entire life. He had accomplished something amazing—something wondrous.

He was still alive and completely and utterly free.

The light caught Ellis by surprise. It shouldn't have. He had never known a day that didn't have a dawn, and yet it still startled him. He almost had it in his head that he was on another world, a distant one with different rules, and he'd simply forgotten about the sun. When at last it crested the horizon, he stood staring, grinning. The trees were strange, the mossy land alien, but the sun was an old friend, and she looked no different from the last time they had met.

Ellis had reached a broad clearing, a downward-sloping hill where the river met another tributary and widened. He was finally out of the pages of the Brothers Grimm and, with the first golden rays of dawn, into a Winnie-the-Pooh watercolor. The mist that had plagued him retreated to pockets and with the sun conveyed a serenity to the pastoral landscape. Dew glittered on green grass speckled by golden flowers, while overhead a blue sky emerged and through it darted flights of birds, who sang until they drowned out the crickets.

Finding a log, Ellis sat to watch the show and, realizing he was famished, tore open a bag of peanut M&M'S. The hard-coated candy had always been an indulgence for him—his one extravagance during the lean days at M.I.T. while putting himself through college and stretching every dollar.

Down the slope he spotted three deer emerging from the fog that followed the river's course. Not much later he saw a red fox trotting, and something else he hadn't caught a good enough look at, which scurried among the heather along the forest eaves. Despite the birds, deer, and bumblebees, Ellis was impressed with the stillness. Inside the security of his own home, even late at night, there were always noises: trucks, horns, sirens. The quietest he had ever experienced the outdoors was in that forest near Grayling, a haunting lack of sound in the gray-shadowed world that pines, with their carpet of brown needles, could create. Still, he had always known he was never too far from a road. Some two-lane blacktop would always be there, offering the promise of a car to come. Yet as Ellis ate his M&M'S, he looked out over the gradual slope and realized he could see for miles, perhaps tens of miles. In all that open expanse, he saw no evidence of mankind. He appeared to have the planet to himself.

In a moment of arrogance that took place between the time he filled his mouth with water from his canteen and the time he swallowed, he considered how he'd won by default, how the entirety of the world was his. What Alexander the Great, Napoleon, Hitler, and a slew of Caesars had spent lifetimes trying to accomplish was his just by showing up.

"I'm king of the world, Ma," he shouted. No one heard. A hollow victory.

The moment passed with the realization that he was instead just one more organism in competition to survive. He wished he were younger, wished he wasn't dying and alone. Ellis had never faced a challenge like this. Few had, he imagined. Still he thought he might enjoy it—some of it.

Winter would be horrific trapped inside whatever shelter he might manage to build, shivering and eating nuts and bark like they had in Roanoke. Ellis felt better about bringing his flannel and sweater. But people back then knew how to survive. He wondered if he could build a cabin by himself, then realized it would take forever to chop down even one of those monster trees using the tiny steel-headed hatchet he'd brought. And he had no idea what day of the year it was. Summer, certainly—he was convinced of that—but was it June, July, or August? How long did he have? Best to try and find some natural shelter, like a cave or he'd have to resort to making a lean-to from branches to help protect his tent. He might be able to do that much. Then he'd have to set his mind toward food.

Plenty of animals were around, and he might be able to shoot some, but he only had so many bullets, and he'd need a longer-term solution. With a spear, he might be able to stab some fish. A net would be better, but somehow he had forgotten that. Could he make one? Ellis felt like a domesticated dog turned loose in the wild.

He continued to stare at the valley. Everything was so pretty—just lovely the way the hills sloped down, the river being joined by another stream that widened again and—Ellis squinted. Something lost in the fog was standing out. Being square, it didn't fit. Nature so rarely made sharp, regular angles. Looking closer, he saw other similar shapes peeking out of the mist—buildings. He was seeing the roofs of houses!

He was looking down on a small village. His heart sprinted; maybe he wasn't alone. One more swig of water and he pulled his pack back on. His muscles were stiff. He felt a little lightheaded and once more cursed his age and illness. He stood and took bearings. All he needed to do was follow the river and it would take him right near the buildings. He'd know he was close when he reached the confluence.

With a new purpose and his friend the sun smiling, he walked on, scaring a pair of rabbits that darted across the field. He was making good time that morning and was well down the slope when he realized he knew where he might be. If he really hadn't moved, if he had merely shifted time, then he must be following the upper branch of the Rouge River. He was traveling south, and it had already joined with another river, which would have been the Middle Rouge. So that would put him in Dearborn somewhere. He bent down and looked at the river as the sun played through the ripples. He could see the sand-and-pebble bottom just as if he were looking through glass, and there were fish, lots of good-sized largemouth bass and walleye snapping their way along.

The sun was rising toward midday by the time Ellis got his second glimpse of the buildings. He guessed he was only a mile away and could see a brick wall over which the roofs of several houses rose. He had expected futuristic plastics, steel, and glass creating fantastic geodesic dwellings, and once more he was disappointed. The buildings were old-fashioned two-story Colonial-styles. Not just old-fashioned, but genuinely old. They looked like the back lot of a period movie set in the nineteenth century. Climbing out of a gully, he spotted the clock tower rising above the trees that was a perfect replica of Philadelphia's Independence Hall. Only Ellis wasn't in Philadelphia, but he did know where he was—Dearborn, Michigan, and he was looking at the Henry Ford Museum.

He hadn't been there since his sixth-grade class had visited on a field trip. They had toured the largest indoor-outdoor museum complex in the United States in a matter of hours. All he could remember was the Wright Brothers' shop, a replica of Edison's Menlo Park lab complex, and the fact that Anthony Dunlap had lost Ellis's favorite Matchbox car and offered to replace it with one of the crappy new Hot Wheels. He also remembered a parking lot, and the roads to get there, none of which appeared to exist anymore. Ellis didn't know the area well, but he was certain Michigan Avenue had come in there somewhere. A major six-lane divided freeway was gone without a scar, but the turn-of-the-nineteenth-century wooden buildings of Greenfield Village were still perfect. Something was out of whack, but Ellis was glad for it. If nothing else, he'd have a house to live his final days in.

The brick wall that circled the museum—that sealed off the attraction—was formidable, and Ellis walked around it, looking for a gate. He was hot but not sweating anymore. His feet were sore, his legs tired. His shoulders ached with the press of the pack, and he had a terrible headache. He wasn't hungry, which surprised him. Most days he ate little, but most days he didn't hike five miles. He also had a bad case of time-machine lag, and if no one was home, he hoped to find a nice house where he could put down his pack and perhaps take a nap. He was still circling the wall when, for the first time since he'd left Warren at the bar, he heard the sound of voices.

KILLING TIME

The voices came from the other side of the wall, which was too tall to climb or see over. Ellis stopped to listen and was pleased to discover they were speaking English. Well, sort of—the voices exhibited an odd accent, but it was most certainly English and surprisingly easy to understand. Only two hundred years had passed, but Ellis had anticipated more differences. He even thought there was a good chance that Spanish or even Chinese would dominate.

"...to put it bluntly."

"I don't care about that."

"So why did you ask me here then?"

"To show you the future."

The two voices were oddly similar, almost as if one person was speaking to him or herself. The pitch wasn't high enough to clearly indicate women, nor low enough to ensure men.

"You're lying. This is all about the Hive Project."

"What makes you say that?"

"I've done research. I know who you are—or rather *aren't.*"

A chuckle. "Then why did you come?"

"I came to find out why—why me?"

"You don't know anything—or you never would have come here...alone."

"What do you mean?" The voice was less confident.

"You see, I asked you here to get you to help me."

"That's not going to happen."

"Are you sure?"

"Positive."

A pause, then. "What are you doing?"

Ellis felt the hair on his arms rise. The words were spoken in fear.

"This is also part of the future."

The screams that followed were the worst sounds Ellis had ever heard. High-pitched and horrible, they went from cries of fear to shrieks of terror, and littered in the middle were desperate pleas for it to stop. Only it didn't stop. Ellis heard sounds of a struggle, grunts, and the thump of something falling.

Ellis wasn't a hero. For the most part he preferred to steer clear of trouble. About the closest he ever got was stopping to help people with disabled cars. Peggy used to warn him that he would get shot by some lunatic, but he couldn't just drive by.

After hearing the screams on the other side of the wall, his first instinct was to call 911. His hand actually moved to his phone before he realized his stupidity. Maybe it was the gun on his hip, or perhaps the chilling effect of the screams, but it certainly wasn't a conscious thought that sent Ellis running to find the gate.

The screaming had stopped before Ellis reached the entrance, which was unattended. He navigated around a big oak tree and trotted past a pretty clapboard farmhouse with a split-rail fence and a prairie-style weather vane. Already Ellis's lungs were giving out. He could feel the crackle, like breathing through broken glass. He slowed down, dropping back to a walk, realizing he'd overextended himself. The all-night hike, the heat, and finally the sprint was too much. He wanted to fall where he was, but he forced himself to keep going. When he cleared the house, he could see the inside length of the wall. His blurring eyes caught movement—two people on the ground. Only one was moving.

Ellis didn't find what he had expected. The voices had sounded youthful. He had imagined teens with leather jackets, chains, spiked hair, nose piercings, tattoos, and drooping pants. Dated images, he knew, but he had no idea what else he would find. What he did see wasn't on the list.

They were both naked.

Neither wore so much as a bandanna, and both were bald—not just bald, hairless. Such a sight would normally have been the focus of Ellis's attention if not for the blood. Blood had a way of making anything else trivial—and there was a lot of blood. Both were covered, sprayed and splashed with rivulets dripping. One was crouched over the other, who lay prone, twitching. The one on top worked intently with a blade on the other's shoulder, cutting it apart, butchering the meat with both hands. The knife wielder grinned, then stood up.

Their eyes met.

Ellis, working to fill his shattered lungs, reached for the handle of his gun but didn't pull it. The naked, hairless, blood-covered butcher made no move. They peered at each other for an instant. Ellis still couldn't tell the person's sex. The killer had no genitalia—no breasts, no obvious curves. Slender and willowy, a perfectly androgynous figure like a prepubescent boy or a 1970s supermodel, except that the face was dripping in gore. Their expressions were a mirror of shock and puzzlement. Without a word, the murderer reached out and picked something up off the grass. Ellis spotted only three fingers. He thought of all those alien movies where extraterrestrials groped with three bulbous digits, but then noticed the two stubs where the pinky and ring fingers ought to have been. A spark of light appeared beside the figure like the flash of a camera, making Ellis blink. Then the murderer stepped through a hole in the air and both the killer and the hole disappeared with a snap.

Ellis was stunned for a second and just stared, wondering what he'd seen. Then movement on the ground caught his attention. The one on the grass continued to twitch. Cuts and puncture wounds were visible along the torso, and a vicious slice had cut away a large section of the victim's shoulder. Ellis couldn't tell if this one was male or female either, being as indistinct anatomically as a Ken doll. More than that, Ellis was surprised to notice that aside from being wrenched in pain, this person could have been the twin of the killer.

Ellis dropped to his knees beside the victim and searched for a pulse. He didn't find one, and there was no chest movement, no sound of breathing beyond Ellis's own labored efforts, which were desperate enough. Ellis needed oxygen but couldn't pull in a deep breath. Efforts to draw in more air threatened a cough, and he knew he couldn't afford that. He was already dizzy, the world blurry, and a strange darkness gathered at the sides of his vision. Ellis planted his palms on the grass and lowered his head between his knees. He struggled to block out the blood and the body beside him and focused only on sucking in air.

Relax, goddammit!

In and out, he felt like he was trying to inflate a new pair of balloons and growing light-headed with the effort. He squeezed his eyes tight and realized he was rocking slightly. His whole body was in the fight, struggling to bring oxygen to his brain. Maybe this was it—respiratory failure had won. What an odd moment to go.

~

"Everyone just stay back."

"Darwin—has to be."

"Anyone see the attack?"

"No. I was the one who reported it—who requested help. We didn't see it, though. They were like that when we found them."

"And you're part of the same group?"

"Gale University—I'm leading a class in ancient history. We were on a field trip."

"All right, you can do us a favor and just continue with that. Stay clear of this side of the park, okay?"

"Is it really a Darwin?"

"We don't know what we're dealing with yet, so please give us room."

Ellis opened his eyes and found the blue sky, now decorated with pretty balls of white cotton. The light was different, the sun having moved well to the west so that the trees and farmhouse were casting long shadows. His chest was better. He could breathe again, yet everything else felt sore.

"Pax—open eyes here."

"Okay, everyone just relax." The person speaking was the closest of those around him, but still about thirty feet away.

A dozen people had gathered near the old farmhouse, two standing closer than the rest and all looking identical. Each shared the same soft face with big, dark eyes, short noses, and tan-brown skin as if some Middle Eastern mother had popped out an Irish Catholic-sized brood of identical duodecaplets.

They were all dressed oddly, with several not dressed at all. Some just wore hats, or scarves, or coats. One was dressed all in bright yellow. Another had a full ensemble of red and white stripes—right down to shoes, which made Ellis think of Dr. Seuss. None of them had a single strand of hair, and just like the first pair of androgynous manikins, these new visitors also appeared to have been made by Mattel.

Ellis wondered if he was having a dream of *The Wizard of Oz* variety. Everyone looked vaguely like a bald version of the lady doctor who had told him he was going to die. Maybe he had never time traveled at all. Any minute he could wake up surrounded by Warren, Peggy, and the doctor so he could say, "*And you were there, and you, and you.*"

"We should get more help," said one of the two nearest, who wore just a satchel hanging from one shoulder, a frightened look, and a decorative tattoo. Both spoke in the same fashion as the others.

"Give me a minute, okay," the closer of the two replied. He, she, or it wore a full set of clothes, at least. Some strange getup pulled from a Sherlock Holmes story consisting of a long black frock coat, silver vest, white trousers, wing shirt, gray tie, and a bowler hat. Maybe Ellis had accidentally crashed a wedding or really *had* gone back in time. So what if Hoffmann didn't think it was possible.

"Pax! Don't go near it. If that's a Darwin, we don't know what it'll do. It's already killed one person."

That jarred Ellis's foggy memory, and he glanced over at the blood-covered corpse beside him. Everything came back. *I've been sleeping next to that!* He pulled himself up and quickly shifted a few feet away. He was only up to his knees, but he was still light-headed. The landscape wobbled like he'd been drinking.

All around him Ellis heard a series of gasps and the rustle of feet on grass moving away, a herd of cats retreating.

"Storm it all, Pax! Get back! It's dangerous."

"I didn't kill anyone!" Ellis yelled. The effect of his voice froze everyone.

"You can talk," Pax said. "You speak our language."

"Actually, I think you're speaking mine."

The two looked at each other amazed.

"What are you?" Pax asked.

He reached up to wipe his eyes. This caused more shuffling from everyone except Pax, who didn't flinch. "My *name* is Ellis Rogers."

"But what *are* you?"

"I'm a man—a human. What are *you*?"

This brought a round of whispers from everyone except the one in the bowler hat, whose eyes never strayed. "Human," Pax replied, absently discarding the word and moving on to more important matters. "But you're different—are you a Darwin?"

"I don't know what that is." Ellis didn't like the way he was feeling, sweaty, dizzy, and a tad nauseous.

Pax glanced back at the others, and Ellis noticed a look of embarrassment. "It's a legend. Rumors about natural-borns living in the wilds. Nutty things about people who never joined Hollow

World, who stayed on the surface and survived. You're not one... are you?"

"No."

"You're an old pattern, then?"

Ellis shook his head. "Don't know what that is either."

Pax looked surprised and took three steps forward.

"Pax!" the other one snapped.

Pax stopped, looking irritated. "You say you didn't kill that person next to you. Can you tell us what did happen?"

"I heard two people—arguing, I guess—then one screamed. I was on the other side of the wall at the time. I ran around and saw one on top of the other." Ellis pointed at the body without actually looking at it, trying to avoid seeing the mess again while at the same time wondering if the dampness in the seat of his pants was his sleeping buddy's blood or his own urine. He was far from certain which he was rooting for. "Then the one on top got up and..."

"And then what?"

"I don't know exactly. Just sort of disappeared, I guess."

"Disappeared?"

Ellis shrugged. "Went through a hole of light. That sounds craz—"

"The killer used a portal."

Ellis had no idea what that meant, but the confidence in Pax's words left little doubt, so he nodded.

"You're not actually listening to it, are you?" the one with the tattoo said with an even mixture of disgust and disbelief.

"It's the truth," Pax replied, and even Ellis wondered at the level of confidence. After the story he had just told, Ellis wasn't sure he'd believe himself.

"It's a Darwin—you've heard the stories. You can't believe anything they say. They're cannibals."

Pax gave the other an appalled look. "Ellis Rogers is telling the truth."

"Are you *absolutely* sure?"

Pax sent off another look that could only be interpreted as *seriously*? Which caused the other to scowl in reply.

"Are you a cop?" Ellis asked. "I mean, a police officer?" The pair of eyes beneath the bowler hat peered at him intently, as if Ellis were a book with very fine print. "A law-enforcement official? A servant of the government? A peacekeeper?"

The last title registered a smile, and Pax nodded. "I suppose—yes. My name is Pax. I'm actually an arbitrator. This is Cha, a physician who would really like to get a closer look at the person next to you. Would that be okay?"

"Sure."

Cha hesitated. "Tell it to move away."

"I'm pretty certain Ellis Rogers can hear you, Cha. You don't need me to translate."

"It's okay." Ellis pushed to his feet, still feeling woozy.

"Are you injured, Ellis Rogers?" Pax asked.

"I have a respiratory illness. The exertion of running aggravated it. I think I passed out."

"Are you all right now?"

"Dizzy."

Ellis moved away from the body and leaned on the brick wall. It felt cool and reassuring against his back. Cha moved up, knelt beside the dead body, and opened a satchel. Several members of the crowd spoke in whispers among themselves.

"Where are you from, Ellis Rogers?" Pax asked, moving nearer to him and drawing a concerned glance from Cha.

That bowler hat made Ellis think of Alex DeLarge from *A*

Clockwork Orange, but Pax was nothing like him—too cute. If anything, Pax was more like Charlie Chaplin's little tramp, except for the missing greasepaint mustache.

He wondered how to answer. Could he say he was from another village? Was there another village? He knew so little it was impossible to make even a bumbling attempt at a lie, and he felt deceiving a police officer wasn't the best way to start a new life, no matter how short-lived it might be. "I came from the city of Detroit." He paused for effect, then added in a soft tone, "From the year 2014."

Ellis had no idea what to expect. They should pack him off to a psychiatric ward, but times had changed. Anything might be possible now. Ellis guessed the plausible reactions ranged from him being worshiped like a god to a dismissive nod, as everyone was likely time traveling nowadays. It would explain the disparity in clothes, and that portal could have been Time Machine 2.0. If computers could go from room-sized vacuum-tubed monsters to tablets in eighty years, time travel had to be a whole lot slicker than a bunch of plastic milk crates and a car seat.

Pax just stared at him a moment, looking puzzled. Slowly he watched as Pax's eyes widened. "You're from the past...*way* in the past."

Cha made a dismissive huffing sound.

"Where is this time machine?" Pax asked.

"I left it up in the woods. Five—maybe six miles north along the river, not sure. I hiked a long way. Isn't much to see, really."

"Oh sure," Cha said. "Bet it's even invisible."

"Cha, please."

"You're being ridiculous," Cha replied.

Pax scowled.

"Time travel isn't common then?"

"No," Pax replied.

"It's impossible," Cha said.

Can I really be the only one? Why haven't there been others? "So I'm guessing you don't believe me."

Pax looked at him with intense eyes. "I believe you." The statement was flat, no underlying tone, no sarcasm, and spoken so quickly and loudly that it left no room for argument. Pax continued to stare deeply into his eyes, no glances away or awkward shifts in stance.

If that's a lie, it's a damn good one, Ellis thought.

"The PICA has been cut out." Cha looked up from the body, first to Pax and then accusingly at Ellis.

"Ellis Rogers didn't do it," Pax said firmly. "Ellis Rogers is telling the truth. Look—do you see any blood? Whoever committed the murder would be drenched."

Ellis wasn't certain of a lot of things. He didn't know if the people around him were really human or the result of some android manufacturing plant. He didn't know what year he was in or if technology was ahead of or behind his time. He had no idea what had happened to the city or the world. And the envelope had yet to be opened on whether he'd made a mistake or not, but he was certain of one thing. He was starting to like Pax.

So far everyone he'd seen had the same features, perfect copies of one another, but they weren't the same. Ellis didn't care much for the way Cha shared the same suspicious expression as the others in the crowd, but Pax was different—more gentleness around the eyes, more concern in the line of the jaw and the angle of the mouth, which appeared on the verge of a smile. Hair would have helped. Ellis had never known too many bald people, and the lack of eyebrows was disturbing. Their absence made Ellis uneasy, like he was in a cancer ward, but Pax impressed him as a person he might trust.

"Is there a Port-a-Call?" Pax asked Cha. "There would be an ID stamp on that, and we could trace the jumps."

"I don't see anything. Not even a tattoo—completely clean. Not much of an individualist. There's nothing personal here at all."

Pax turned back to Ellis. "Do you know who the victim was?"

Ellis shook his head, and he wished he hadn't. The world swam. "I just told you I'm from—"

"Yes, I know—I just thought you might have heard a name or something."

"Oh—no." Ellis tried to remember, but he was feeling terrible. "I'm pretty sure neither said a name."

"What were they talking about?"

"I really didn't hear much. Something about a Hive Project and the future. That's about all I remember."

"See," Cha said with a superior tone that irritated Ellis. He had no idea what Cha meant by the single word. It sounded like a continuation of a previous argument, but all he knew was that he didn't like it. He also decided he didn't like Cha's tattoo. Ellis never cared for tattoos, they always made people look cheap—human graffiti—but he made exceptions for statements of honor like military insignias, the name of a loved one, or a quote from the Bible. But Cha's was just strange swirls, like some Aztec art.

"I'm going to sit down, is that okay?" He was going to sit down even if it wasn't. Ellis was feeling nauseous in addition to dizzy, and he let himself slide down the wall to the grass.

Pax nodded. "Nothing at all, Cha?"

"Sorry."

"Concrete! I can't report another anonymous. It'll just make things worse."

"There's nothing here."

Pax looked angry, but Cha only shrugged.

"Can't you run tests?" Ellis asked. "You still have forensic sciences, right?"

They both looked at him, confused.

"You know, fingerprints and DNA samples." He was about to say hair samples but caught himself.

"Those won't help, Ellis Rogers," Pax told him. "We all have the same."

"Same what? DNA? Fingerprints? You can't all—oh." Not androids then—genetic engineering. Ellis finally understood the Darwin reference. So maybe he *was* a Darwin, at least in the strictest sense. *Is everyone here born in a test tube?*

"Without the chip we can't identify the victim," Cha said.

"Really?" Ellis asked. "So you all have chips in your shoulders to tell each other apart? C'mon, there has to be another way. I mean, what happens when those things stop working? Don't they ever fail?"

"Not really."

"In a case like that we could verify identity just by asking questions," Pax explained. "Or run a neural scan. But being dead, those won't work."

"But you must have had this problem before."

The two shook their heads. "Until recently, it's never happened."

"Seriously?" Ellis was amazed.

"What do we do now?" Cha asked.

"Like *I* have all the experience with dead bodies," Pax replied, staring at the corpse with an expression that mirrored how Ellis was feeling.

"You've at least seen one before," Cha said.

"Contact the ISP. They'll want to look it over."

"You two are homicide cops, and this is only the second dead body either of you has seen?" Ellis asked.

"First *I've* seen," Cha corrected.

"What's a *homicide cop*?" Pax asked.

"Police that deal with murders."

With widening eyes, Pax pointed a finger at Ellis. "That's right! You're from the past! *Way* in the past. You know all about this—this sort of thing...about murders, right?"

"Not really. I wasn't a cop. I used to design cars—parts of them anyway—worked on energy and alternate fuel. This village was a museum that was built by the Henry Ford Motor Company, and I—"

"Still is a museum," Pax corrected.

"Okay, well—see, I used to work for another car company, trying to improve the capacity of batteries. I wasn't a detective or anything."

"But they had murders then, yes?"

"I lived in Detroit—they had plenty."

"And you know that they used DNA and fingerprints to find the killers."

"Everyone knows that."

"Maybe everyone in 2014 knows about such things—not so much these days." Pax took another step closer, until they were only an arm's length apart.

Nice eyes, Ellis thought, *something innocent and childlike about them.*

"We don't have this sort of thing anymore," Pax said.

"Murders?"

"Death," Pax replied.

Ellis just stared, certain he wasn't getting everything. He was still trying to understand what Pax meant by him being from *way* in the past. How long ago was *way*? Then it sounded like Pax had said there was no more death. "What did you say?"

"Listen," Pax began in a softened tone. "I'm sorry about all this. You've just been through a traumatic experience. You're tired and not feeling well. You're clearly a pioneer, a great scientist of some sort who's accomplished something astounding. You're a new Charles Lindbergh or Network Azo, and trust me, I'll see you're taken care of. Your very existence is amazing—"

"Impossible actually," Cha added with disdain.

Pax went on without pause. "You should be welcomed with a parade, and a party, and I'm certain a great many people will wish to speak with you. I know you have all sorts of questions, but you need to believe me when I tell you I'm not a *cop*. I'm an arbitrator. I deal with general disputes between people—help them settle their differences with the least amount of bad feelings. And I help people who have experienced painful events in their lives. I was called here to see if I could help these students deal with the trauma of witnessing a dead and brutalized body. But this...is there anything else you could tell us?"

"Are you serious?"

"Right now you're the foremost living expert."

Ellis had never been the foremost anything. And whether he really was or not, he liked that Pax thought he might be. "I don't know what I can offer. I don't know anything about how things work here. All I know comes from reading crime thrillers and watching TV." He said this even as he moved toward the body, crawling now, as standing was too much effort to consider. Cha quickly stepped back, but not as frantically as before.

The corpse looked like the bystanders, who were still shifting around to get a better look at him, except the dead person was covered in blood, cuts, and puncture wounds. Looking down, Ellis felt his dizziness rise a couple of notches. He also had a headache. He'd never seen a brutalized body before. All the dead people he'd been near were thick with makeup and tucked neatly in boxes surrounded by flower arrangements. Luckily, with the exception of the blood, which had already mostly dried, it wasn't a very gruesome scene. No guts hanging out, no bones showing—just the mutilated shoulder, which wasn't as bad as he had expected. The killer had dug in like a doctor to retrieve a bit of shrapnel. He knew he wasn't going to puke, which surprised him, because his stomach had been churning for some time. He tried to focus and apply what he knew from the novels of Patricia Cornwell, Jonathan Kellerman, and the occasional episode of *Law & Order* or *CSI*. "Looks like he was stabbed to death and the killer didn't seem to know what he was doing."

"Why's that?" Cha asked this time.

"Well, unless you've moved things around since my time, the best places to kill a person, according to most of the crime novels, would be a slice across the throat to cut the carotid artery, an upward stab under the ribs to the heart, or a stab to the base of the skull. This person was just jabbing anywhere, straight in and out. See all the puncture marks on the stomach? All of them have small openings, like he was just going for the soft spots. There was no twisting of a blade or attempt to open the wounds wide. And the victim didn't fight back...just defended. See the cut on the arm there? Probably from trying to ward off the knife. And see the blood pool? That wound caught a larger artery there, and I bet that caused the bleed out. These others might have damaged intestines, and maybe eventually done the trick, but not nearly as fast. Might have been saved if not for that arm cut."

"Does that make sense?" Pax asked Cha.

Cha nodded, and Ellis thought there might be reluctance there, but "Aztec Tattoo" got points for being honest.

"So the killer isn't an expert."

"I wouldn't think anyone alive these days is an expert," Cha said. "So you haven't narrowed anything."

"Is there more you can tell us?" Pax asked.

Ellis got up on his knees. "Yeah—this fella's eyes were bad. He wore glasses."

"What did you say?"

"He or she—ah, I mean—well, I don't really know what to... never mind. This *person* wore glasses. See the pinch marks along the bridge of the nose, and the little half-moons on the cheeks? Glasses do that."

Pax looked at Cha. Both were puzzled.

"Hang on." Ellis set down his pack, unzipped a side pocket, pulled out his reading glasses, and set them on his nose. "See. Glasses. I take them off and you can see the divots left—the little impressions."

"I understand what you're saying, Ellis Rogers," Pax explained, "but no one wears glasses."

Cha had found the courage to inch closer to peer down at the body. "I hadn't noticed that. Something did pinch the nose, and there's a crease along the forehead too."

"Like a hat," Ellis said, and pointed at Pax. "Some people still wear those, at least."

Pax offered him a smile, and he responded with one of his own.

"So where are the glasses and hat?"

Pax and Cha looked around but found nothing.

"Killer might have taken them—but no, I don't remember anything in his hands—oh!"

"What?" Pax asked.

"The killer—I just remembered—was missing two fingers. Right hand, I think."

"So, whoever did it was interested in the Hive Project, had likely never killed before, and is missing two fingers. And the victim wore glasses and a hat."

Ellis shrugged. "I told you I wouldn't be much help." He was feeling worse and reconsidering whether he might vomit after all.

"Actually, that's much more than we knew five minutes ago. Thank you."

"You're welcome. And speaking of time and knowing things, what year is it?"

"Oh right." Pax looked embarrassed. "This is the year 4078."

"4078? That's...that's more than two thousand..." Ellis wavered, and Pax reached out, grabbing his shoulders.

"I'm sorry," Pax offered. "I didn't realize it would be such a shock."

"No—no—well, yes, it is, but really I—I'm not feeling very well. I think I need to lie down." He settled to the grass, lying on his back.

"What's wrong with you?" Cha asked.

"I told you I have a respiratory problem," he said, looking up at the sky. "It's called idiopathic pulmonary fibrosis. No one in my time knew what caused it or how to cure it, and in my case it's terminal."

Cha drew closer than ever before and studied him. "Are you feeling better right now?"

"Lying down, yeah. A little bit."

"Stand up."

"I'd rather not."

"Do it anyway," Cha insisted.

Ellis looked at Pax, who nodded. "Cha is a very good physician."

Ellis pushed up and staggered, as the world swam more than before.

"Okay, okay, sit down," Cha told him and gave up his security distance to touch Ellis on the neck. "Your skin is hot and dry. When was the last time you had something to drink?"

"Early this morning, I guess—a couple swallows."

"And did you say you traveled down out of the forests? Five or six miles, right? That's what you said."

"Yeah."

"And then passed out in the sun here?"

"Uh-huh." He nodded.

"You may have a respiratory illness, but right now you're suffering from sunstroke and dehydration."

"Really?"

"Trust me, I see a lot of it. People come to the surface and don't realize the difference a real sun makes."

"A real sun?"

Cha ignored him and turned to Pax. "We need to get the Darwin out of the sun, into a cool place, and reintroduce fluids and electrolytes." Cha pulled Ellis's canteen from around his neck, unscrewed the cap, and smelled.

"It's just water," Ellis explained.

"Then drink," Cha ordered.

"I'm actually feeling nauseous now."

"Of course you are, and soon you'll start to have trouble breathing if we don't fix you. Now sip. No big gulps, just sips."

Pax stood up and drew something out of the frock coat.

"Where are you going?" Cha asked.

"My place. You call the ISP and wait for them."

"You sure? You don't know anything about this Darwin."

"Are you offering to take Ellis Rogers home with you instead?"

"Forget I said anything."

A burst of light and a hum, and Ellis saw another portal appear. Through it he could see a room with a bed, pillows, and blankets.

"Grab him," Cha said, and they lifted Ellis by the arms. The world spun, far worse than before. He heard a ringing, and, as he was half dragged into the opening, darkness came again.

Times They are a Changin'

Ellis woke up sporting a hangover without the benefit of a binge. He'd been awake for some time but resisted the temptation to get out of bed. He had no real idea what had happened or where he was but appreciated the time alone after having ridden the tornado to Oz. How long had he been asleep? How long had it been since he'd left the doctor's office? Only a matter of hours in one sense but more than two thousand years in another.

Two thousand! How is that possible? Hoffmann was off by a factor of ten! Had he dropped a zero somewhere? The whole thing was hard to believe despite having achieved his intent. This must be the feeling that gave expressions of wonderment to Olympic athletes when they took the gold, the look of shock on Academy Award winners even as they took out the speech they had carefully prepared. Some part of them never really believed it was possible until after it happened, and even then such miracles were hard to accept. He'd done it; he'd traveled through time—but Hoffmann was way off on the number of years.

Ellis had expected to jump forward about the same distance as the founding of the United States was back. Life would be very different, but not too alien, and he expected the world would still be fundamentally the same. Instead, he had jumped the same span of years dividing the time of Christ from the age of the Internet. He was the equivalent of a Roman citizen used to slaves, the luxury of horses, and the labor of carrying water—plopped down in the age of computers and fructose corn syrup. Faced with such a shift, Ellis was grateful for the chance to wade in slowly.

Lying in a very comfortable bed, he could tell it didn't have springs, like one of those space-age sponge beds he used to see advertised. He had pillows and sheets, not cotton though; these were softer. He spent little time pondering the bed covering given his surroundings. He'd seen *2001, Blade Runner*, *Logan's Run,* and *Star Trek*. He knew the future was supposed to be stark, cold, and clean—or grease-stained and grit-covered. Maybe it was, but this room wasn't.

He lay in a massive canopy bed nestled in a cathedral of carved wood and luscious drapes. The décor of the room was castle-Gothic, with walls half clad in dark, eight-panel oak and uppers decorated in vibrant murals of medieval ladies and men on horseback. Lions, swans, crowns, and lilies abounded—carved in wood or sculpted in plaster. Above loomed a ceiling painted to look like the sky, with puffy clouds and hilltops around the edges. Light streamed in through a series of peaked, two-story windows with crisscrossed latticework, which cast spears of radiance across the foot of the bed. A breeze fluttered the edges of curtains, and Ellis could hear birds and a distant trickle of water. He smelled flowers as well as something exotic, like cinnamon or nutmeg. Besides the distant birdsong and splashing of water, he occasionally caught a distant voice calling out or laughter rising from far off.

When he finally touched the floor, he found wide-plank hardwood with thick Persian-style rugs welcoming his bare feet. Naked, he kept the sheet around his waist. His pack was on the floor beside the bed, and his clothes were folded and resting on a soft chair. His knife, as well as the still-holstered pistol, remained on his belt.

"Oh, good morning, Ellis Rogers! I thought you'd sleep the day away. Are you feeling better?"

Ellis jumped. He didn't see anyone but pulled the sheet tighter.

"Who's there?" he asked, peering out toward the open archway that led to another room.

"I am Sexton Alva. Pax's vox. They told me you might be disoriented and thoroughly grassed, so I needed to go easy on you. But honestly I find the whole matter utterly amazing!"

This voice was different from all the others: decidedly female, but he couldn't tell where she was and kept the sheet tight.

"Where are you?"

"What's that, dear?"

"Where are you? I can't see—"

"Oh, Pax wasn't kidding. You are completely sonic. Fantastic! Of course you can't see me. I told you. I'm Pax's vox."

"What's a vox?"

"Ha! Utterly magnetic. Really it is—you have no idea. And the way you talk! You really are grassed—real grassed like with spears and bows and arrows and such. I don't think I can explain what a vox is to you—no point of reference, really. You probably think I'm some sort of spirit. You worship rivers and rocks, right? Have a god for everything? You can just consider me the spirit of this house. But don't worry. I'm a good spirit. Just call me Alva, honey."

Ellis continued to turn his head, trying to locate the source of the voice without luck. It seemed to come from everywhere at once. "I'm not from that far in the past."

"What's that?"

"I'm not from that long ago. We didn't have spears and bows. We had cars and planes and computers and—"

"Computers! Yes—that's me."

"You're a computer?"

"No, but it is certainly better than a spirit, isn't it? I'm about as much like a computer as an abacus is. I'm Pax's caretaker. I keep the place running, keep everyone happy and safe. Tell them what to eat in the mornings, relay messages, arrange parties, water plants, entertain everyone, teach them, advise them, watch out for them—more Pax than Vin, of course. Pax is always eager to learn; Vin apparently knows everything already." This last comment came with a heavy dose of sarcasm. *"I've looked after Pax for centuries. Wonderful, wonderful person, and not at all crazy, you understand. You'll do well to remember that if you stay here—or you'll find too much pepper in your meals, and your bath will always be a tad too cold or too hot. I'm sorry. I don't like making such vile threats, but when it comes to protecting Pax, I'm an animal."*

"Where *are* you, exactly?"

"Oh, my physical installation is built into the foundations of the complex, on the sublevel."

"So—you're like a furnace or a water heater?"

"Ha! You're wonderful. In seven hundred and eighteen years no one has ever called me a furnace or water heater. That's very clever. You don't know how hard it is to be original these days. But you're original, aren't you? I mean, truly original. No others like you at all—ever. That's just amazing. You're like a tree, but you can talk!"

"Speaking of that. Alva, I have a question."

"Wonderful! I'm great at trivia."

"I was wondering why we understand each other. After two thousand years I would have expected language to change more than it has. And why English?"

"Oh, you can thank the British Empire for that. Imperialism in the eighteenth and nineteenth centuries established the English language as the dominant common tongue the same way that the Roman Empire had established Latin as the previous international language. The dominance of the global economy by such English-speaking countries as the United States further required all the world's nations to view English as the necessary international language of commerce, which—"

"Okay—okay, so that explains why English survived, but why is it still so—I mean, people in the Middle Ages didn't talk the way I do, even though they spoke English."

"That's because the Middle Ages didn't coexist with a post-globalization environment. Most linguistic changes are the result of assimilating other languages or because isolation causes the independent evolution of a dialect. By 2090, the impact of variations had been reduced to negligible levels as non-English languages were abandoned—wiped out by lack of use. If you wanted to compete economically, you adjusted to the language of commerce. Sure, there are fads and fancies, but the sheer size of the consistent user base and the tendency of humans to prefer familiarity led to a relatively stable form of communication. The longer life spans of humans also reduced trends of change."

Ellis wondered if all that wasn't a pleasant way of saying that Hollow World had a militant Ministry of Grammar Nazis.

"Alva, I have another question."

"I would suspect you have more than one, but go ahead, dear."

"Is this Pax's home?"

"Yes. Beautiful, isn't it? You need to go out on the balcony. Everyone loves the balcony. I'm so glad Pax brought you here. I'm sure Pax is just as happy. Pax loves old stuff."

"Is anyone else here?"

"Just you and me, honey. Pax and Vin went out—but don't be upset. They expected you'd be asleep longer, and they'll be back soon. I've already told them you're awake. Besides, I'm here. Is there anything you'd like? They pumped you full of liquids, but I was told to keep you drinking. Would you like tea? Lemonade, Cistrin? Vistune red or white?"

While Ellis was curious as to how a disembodied computer-voice might go about handing him a drink, he had more pressing concerns. "Actually, I could use a bathroom. I need to ah...urinate and would love a shower or a chance to brush my teeth."

"Urinate! But of course." A light went on inside a small archway he hadn't noticed before. *"Right this way, Ellis Rogers."*

Ellis pulled his pants on. They were clean, no stain of blood. He grabbed his pack and the rest of his clothing, and passed through the archway. Inside was a rain forest. Massive trees, covered in fragrant flowers and draped with vines, rose from lush vegetation where butterflies fluttered. He spotted a spring-fed basin formed from a sink-shaped rock jutting out from a cliff.

"Past the vines," he heard Alva say.

Passing through a curtain similar to what an explorer might machete through, he found a waterfall that cascaded into a beautiful lagoon.

"Sheesh," he blurted out.

"What was that, dear?"

"Nothing," Ellis said. "Just talking to myself."

"Why do that when I'm here?"

"Is this water always running?"

"Of course not. I turned it on for you. The waterfall is at forty degrees. Let me know if you'd like it hotter or colder."

Forty? Ellis touched the water, found it pleasantly hot, and shrugged.

There was no door to this wilderness space, and, feeling it best to get things taken care of before company arrived, Ellis used the artsy-looking toilet shaped like a tree stump. There was no water in its base, and he was shocked to discover that his urine vanished as it fell. He thought about his toothbrush and realized he'd forgotten one. With a sigh, he undressed and stepped into the lagoon.

"The water can come out at any speed, texture, or angle you like," Alva said, her voice slightly different in the lagoon, where the sounds of birds and the rush of water competed for his attention.

Ellis didn't reply and was pleased she hadn't felt the need to chat while he was using the toilet. He also had to wonder at the income level of an arbitrator. Maybe the profession was like a lawyer.

He waded into the pool and moved under the falling river. The water—hot and soothing—relaxed him. A hot shower always seemed so decadent, and there was something vaguely sexual about a bath. An atomized mist jetted out from the walls, turning the jungle steamy.

"Is there soap?" he asked.

Like a car wash, the water pouring out turned sudsy, but this flow smelled vaguely like lilacs. Ellis wondered what might happen if he asked for wax. That brought a smile, and he pushed his face into the stream. Ellis lingered in the water longer than he had planned. From the instant he'd discovered Warren's letters until this moment, Ellis had been overwhelmed. Too much had happened too quickly. Even lying in the bed, trying to mentally process everything, had been taxing. He hadn't allowed himself time to think, but bathing made him reflective.

Everything he knew was gone. He no longer had a house with its huge monthly mortgage. No cars needed inspections, oil changes, or new tires. He was free of everything—free of Warren and Peggy, his cheating wife and his bitter friend who had betrayed him. That life was over—buried by time, a lot of time.

In its place was something amazing. He'd achieved a version of his life's dream and survived the effort. He'd finally done something—something important. By the sound of things, Ellis was somehow the first person to travel through time. Everything had worked out perfectly, and yet while standing in the hot stream from the sudsy waterfall, Ellis began to cry.

He couldn't control himself, couldn't understand why he was sobbing. He should be happy, and it didn't make sense that after risking everything and winning, he should feel so miserable.

Although his marriage never reflected the kind of relationships idealized in movies, Peggy had been part of his life for thirty-five years, and he'd discarded her with less thought than he gave to a dubiously dated container of cottage cheese. He'd known Warren even longer. His old friend had always looked after and defended him, and he, too, went in the trash. Maybe they had an explanation...maybe if he'd just...but it was too late.

If it hadn't already been erased by time, Ellis would have torn down his garage. It was the symbolic sum of all his mistakes, from his son's death, to the erosion of his marriage, and finally the realization that running away was the height of selfishness. He hadn't even left a note, and Peggy would spend the rest of her life with too many questions and no answers.

He pushed his face into the spill and let it blend with his tears. He didn't know how long he stood there. He didn't care. He had no pressing appointments.

"How do I turn it off?" he finally asked.

An instant later the waterfall stopped, the pool drained, the mist faded, and hot, dry air began to blow. He was dry in just a minute or two, and put his clothes back on.

Passing back the way he had come, Ellis dropped his pack next to the bed before setting off to explore. The wonders of the bedroom and bath were nothing compared with the rest of Pax's home.

"This is the social room," Alva said with a note of pride as he entered a large chamber with a vaulted ceiling.

A cross between a Gothic palace and a Rainforest Cafe the large chamber combined the two motifs until the whole appeared as a beautiful ruin invaded by plants and giant trees. The walls were carved stone with intricate arches and ornamentation that framed more murals mimicking the Renaissance masters.

Ellis spotted a painter's easel, surrounded by color-stained rags and rustic clay pots filled with bouquets of filthy brushes. Beside them were splattered potter's wheels and carving tools. But what caught Ellis's attention the most was the far wall—or more precisely the lack of one. That whole side of the room was missing. No glass, just one vast opening to the outside, where a balcony extended as an oval pod.

The view was staggering. Pax's home was built into the side of a massive curved cliff that was shared by hundreds of other homes, each with its own balcony. The sheer walls of the canyon were dressed in flowers and creeping ivy. Massive trees grew up in the center and spread vast branches, creating a canopy that provided shade to the Central Park-sized common below. So mammoth was the space that people on their balconies across from Ellis were ant-sized, and everything across the way slightly bluer. Shafts of light filtered through the arena, and birds of all sizes and colors swooped and sang. Their songs echoed as if they were in a massive atrium.

Ellis descended the steps onto the balcony and was peering across at what he realized had to be a massive waterfall in the far distance when he heard Alva say, *"Welcome home. It was so nice of you to take that extra second necessary to let me know you were on your way, Pax. Oh wait—you didn't, did you?"*

"Don't start, Alva."

"What? A little courtesy is too much to ask?"

"Is Ellis Rogers in the bedroom?"

"Out on the balcony. Everyone loves the balcony."

"Were you nice?"

"I'm always nice, dear. Vin, do you think you could clean up your paints a little better next time? The breeze threw your rags on the floor and knocked over one of the pots."

"You control the breeze, Alva."

"But not your mess."

Ellis turned to see Pax enter the social room. Dressed the same as before, Pax smiled as their eyes met. "How are you feeling?"

"Have a headache."

"Cha said you would."

"Other than that, I'm a lot better. Even a little hungry."

"What do you like to eat?"

Ellis shrugged. "It's been two thousand years. I doubt you have burgers and fries anymore."

"Alva?"

"Derived from Hamburg, Germany, hamburger is low-grade ground meat from the dead bodies of domesticated animals known as cows or

cattle. A poor person's meal often treated in ammonia to eliminate common life-threatening contaminants. It was discontinued in 2162 due to health hazards."

"Seriously?" Pax made a face at Ellis. "So we don't have a pattern, I'm guessing?"

"Would you want one? We don't have a pattern for arsenic either."

Ellis chuckled. "I won't even ask about hot dogs."

Pax looked concerned. "You actually *ate dogs*?"

"No, dear," Alva said. *"But an explanation would hardly put you at ease. How about a nice minlatta with a tarragon oil sauce? It's a new pattern by Yal."*

"It's best to just agree," Pax said to him. "Alva will make it anyway."

"Sure."

"Vin, do you want a minlatta?" Alva's voice came from another room as Pax joined Ellis on the balcony. The voice of Vin was low, muffled, indiscernible.

"It's beautiful here," Ellis said. "I take it we aren't in Michigan anymore."

"Michigan?"

"That's where we met." He looked out at the sunlight. "Was it yesterday? Did I sleep that long?"

"You were out awhile."

"And we went through one of those portal things, right?"

"Yes."

"So where are we now? Africa? South America?" He had no idea. Ellis had never traveled much, but he'd seen pictures and movies, and places like this were always far away in Third World countries. Only what had been Third World two thousand years ago had moved up in the standings, he guessed.

"Hollow World," Pax replied.

Ellis looked puzzled.

"Eurasian Plate, Western Zone, Tringent Sector, La Bridee Quadrant."

"Wow," Ellis said. "That's a mouthful. And I'm sure a location was in there somewhere. I was expecting something like, I don't know—*Rio*. Any idea where this might have been about two thousand years ago?"

"Yes. Are you familiar with the city of Paris?"

"Paris, France?"

"Yes."

"This is Paris?"

"Sort of, except we're about five miles below where it used to be."

Ellis looked back out at the dramatic cliffs and the narrow opening in the canyon where he could clearly see the sky and distant mountains, at least as clear as his aging eyes would allow. He noted the trees and the birds as well, and finally replied with the eloquent response of "Huh?"

Footsteps interrupted them.

"Oh, Ellis Rogers, let me introduce Vin. We live together."

Ellis turned to see another DNA duplicate, this one dressed more dramatically than Pax in a double-breasted Dickensian tailcoat, ruffled shirt, and top hat. Ellis couldn't actually verify that this was another *exact* copy, as Vin was wearing a mask. It looked like porcelain but could have been a hard plastic. All white, it covered only the upper part of the face, leaving the mouth free and causing Ellis to think of Andrew Lloyd Webber's *The Phantom of the Opera*.

"Nice to meet you." Ellis held out his hand. As soon as he had, he realized he was making a huge assumption. Ellis was impressed that Vin took it—less impressed by the weak grip and shake.

"Vin is *an artist*," Pax said with enough drama that the title could have been swapped out with *the God Almighty*. "Most of the paintings and sculptures in our house are Vin's work."

"Don't forget your contributions." Vin removed the hat and set it upside down on the shelf near the archway to the bedroom. "You've done your fair share of pots. And they serve very well at holding my brushes."

Vin was also wearing a pair of breeches and high black boots like they'd just been out riding after foxes. The "artist" moved with a swagger and a sweep that made Ellis think of Shakespearean actors.

As Vin began to tug off the fingers of white gloves, Ellis looked back at Pax. "Did you say we were underground?"

This appeared to take Pax by surprise. "Hmm? Oh—yes. It might not be five miles, maybe only four. Obviously neither one of us is a geomancer."

"But I can see the sunlight."

"That's falselight." Vin spoke much louder than Pax—the actor projecting from a stage to a packed house—then paused to look out at the view, as if never noticing it before. Vin shrugged. "Adequate, I suppose."

"You think so?" Pax sounded surprised. "I've always found falselight to be amazing, especially after so much grass time. You can't tell it's not natural light."

"Perhaps *you* can't," Vin said.

"Oh—of course. I suppose to a more trained eye—"

"Exactly."

"Are you kidding?" Ellis said. "I don't care how trained your eyes are, that looks just like sun shining on a valley, and I've spent my whole life under the real thing. If that's fake, it's a miracle—and beautiful."

"I'm not certain you're qualified to judge beauty," Vin told him.

It sounded like an insult, but what did Ellis know. Maybe he was that Roman citizen getting hot because people were discussing the prospects of landing on Mars. He wasn't going to start anything over a misunderstanding. He was their guest, and who knew what passed for humor now. Instead, he went with humility. "My wife would agree with you. I could never see the attractiveness in the wallpaper she picked out, and was horrible at knowing which dress was better, but I think anyone can judge beauty—in the eye of the beholder and all that."

Vin smirked. "You've certainly dug up a Neanderthal, Pax. I'll grant you that. I was skeptical, but I think there can be no other explanation. It's like we'll be dining with a barbarian who might howl at the moon at any minute. You really should have asked permission. At the very least, we might have invited others to share the absurdity. We ought to get grams, as I can't imagine anyone believing it."

Ellis was certain *that* was an insult. Before he could reply, the Phantom of the Opera look-alike left them, disappearing through one of the archways.

Pax looked at Ellis with an awkward pout. "I think you might have unintentionally offended Vin a little."

"*I* offended *him*?—ah—Vin—whatever. Sort of a jerk, don't you think?"

Pax's eyes widened. "You have to understand, Vin is an *artist*."

"Yeah, I got that—paints all these pretty pictures, which is nice, but nothing compared with this view. That's like thinking your picture is better than the real thing. Talk about arrogant." Ellis pointed across the valley. "And the light moves with the passage of time. Incredible. Are you sure we're underground?"

Pax nodded.

"And you call it falselight?"

"When they made the first sub-farms, they had imitation sunlight for the plants, but not for the farmers. They lived in little cubicles. People need sunlight as much as plants do and workers became depressed. They kept returning to the grass whenever they could, driving down productivity. So they invented falselight. It became this whole industry and finally an art form—one of the first native to Hollow World, really." Pax gestured at the walls. "Vin did the paintings here, but those are just for fun. Vin's real work is out there." Pax pointed beyond the balcony. "Vin makes Hollow World."

"What do you mean, Vin *makes* it?"

"Like a sculptor chisels beauty out of a block of stone—that's what Vin does. Only Vin's stone is the whole of the earth—the entire lithosphere. We all live in Vin's creation of height, width, form, and function. Not just Vin, there are many renowned artists in all kinds of different schools. Like the ones who make the falselight or water artists—masters of reflection, drip, and splash." Pax recited this with a cadence and little dance step. "It's sort of their motto. All artists are highly revered for their talents. They're more respected than anyone, except the geomancers, of course."

"What's a geomancer?"

Pax looked at him and sighed. "Alva, what did you do all the time I was gone?"

"I showed Ellis Rogers where the shower was. Did you expect me to

explain the history of the world during a morning bath? And since I have your attention, dinner is served."

The dining room was like entering Dracula's castle. A long marble table set with crystal stemware and porcelain plates was illuminated by candelabras and surrounded by dark walls of carved paneling. At the far end was a massive pipe organ that dominated the room and began playing a dramatic fugue the moment they entered. It began deafeningly loud but, after a grimace from Pax, dropped to a whisper. None of the "outside" light reached this darkened chamber that, with its cathedral ceiling and vaulted supports, reminded Ellis of a church nave.

"Alva?" Pax said.

"Yes, honey?"

"Can we have something a little less morbid?"

"Vin always likes—"

"I know, but we have a guest. How about something from that Big Sky series you like?"

"Really? Okay!"

The paneling vanished, as did the pipe organ and ceiling. In their place, Ellis stood amid a field of spring flowers in a valley surrounded by distant mountains and capped with a vast sky. Gorgeous thunderhead clouds billowed up in the distance as the sun drifted toward the horizon. The grand table was replaced with a rustic picnic bench covered by a traditional red-and-white-checkered cloth and set with ceramic cups and a wicker basket. Ellis held still, disoriented and uncertain what had just happened.

Was he still in the dining room? He figured he was, imagined Pax had just adjusted the decorations like he might have dimmed the lights in his own house, but he wasn't just seeing it. Ellis could feel the breeze, smell the sunbaked grass, and hear the distant drone of a cicada.

"Are we still in your house?"

Pax looked amused. "Yes. It's just that Vin's taste tends to run a bit more heavy—more serious—than I prefer."

A shadow crossing the table startled Ellis, and he looked up to see a hawk. "Whoa. That's really cool."

Pax looked concerned. "Alva, turn down the breeze, please."

Ellis laughed. "Oh—no. I didn't mean...I meant it is very nice."

"Twentieth-century slang, Pax," Alva put in, and Ellis realized she sounded a lot like his aunt Virginia. *"*Cool *is a respected aesthetic, what we might refer to as* grilling *or* magnetic.*"*

"Really?" Pax said, looking dubious, then turned and began walking across the field. "Let me grab the meal and see where Vin got off to."

Ellis took a seat at the picnic table. When he looked back, Pax was gone, leaving him alone in the landscape.

In all directions the flat land extended out to a distant horizon. He was in a John Ford movie or a Windows screen saver and couldn't stop gawking. Ellis had spent the majority of his life in Michigan, mostly around Detroit, never able to get away from work. Aside from M.I.T., his one big trip was his honeymoon in Cancun. He'd always planned to go places, but never really had until he pressed the button on the time machine. Even then, he had remained in Detroit, but was now supposedly somewhere under Paris. None of that mattered. Perched on that picnic table, he knew he was a long way from home.

A blade of grass brushed Ellis's leg. He snapped it off and rolled the plant between his fingers, feeling the moisture in it. He held it to his nose and smelled the scent of summer lawn cuttings. *How is this possible?*

"Vin's not feeling well." Pax appeared again, walking back through the tall grass and holding a tray of food, the frock coat whipping with the breeze.

I bet. Ellis tried not to jump to conclusions, but he didn't like Vin. "Just us then?"

Pax nodded and set two steaming plates on the picnic table in front of them filled with pasta topped with a white sauce laden with minced vegetables. Ellis waited to see if Pax would be saying grace. Not everyone did, and it wasn't as big a deal as it had once been.

Pax began eating without a pause.

Ellis looked down at his plate and whispered, "Thanks." He wasn't really thanking God for the meal or even the miracle of surviving the time travel. He just appreciated that God had been there to listen when he needed Him the most. Maybe that was God's whole purpose—a hand to hold. Then again, just the day before he had expected to die of starvation, and if anything was likely to make him feel religious it was the miracles of the last two days. And there was something else—in this brave new world, God was the only one he knew.

"Whatever happened with the murder?" Ellis asked.

"Cha arranged for the disposal of the body," Pax said. "I spent the rest of the day and most of the night with those students who witnessed the scene to make sure they would have no lingering trauma. They were upset, obviously, but they'll be fine."

"Wow. Are people that fragile nowadays?"

"Murders might have been commonplace in your time, Ellis

Rogers, but we don't have them. And with the various safety features, even accidents are extremely rare. Death is alien to us."

"You mentioned that before. But how is that possible? What about old age and disease?"

Pax sucked in a noodle and reached for one of the red-checkered napkins. "The ISP eliminated diseases hundreds of years ago—aging took longer, of course. They only slowed it in the previous versions, but it was eradicated in this last pattern."

"Pattern?"

"Ah...are you familiar with genetics? DNA?"

"I know *of* them. They completed work on the Human Genome Project—mapping genes—a few years back, but were just starting work interpreting the data when I left."

"Right, okay. So, in a way the sequence of base pairs that make up DNA is like a recipe. Everyone—back in your day, I assume—was a little different, right?"

He nodded. "Like snowflakes."

"Well, the ISP tinkered with the sequencing, adjusting it mostly because of the epidemics that occurred back in the 2150s. All the drugs they had used stopped working, I guess, or the diseases got stronger—I don't know. Anyway, the ISP started altering DNA to make people more resistant to diseases, which caused all kinds of conflicts with people making drugs and other people who were against tinkering at all—well, it was a big deal. But anyway—after centuries of adjustments, the ISP unlocked the perfect pattern, which you see before you." Pax smiled and made a little seated flourish and bow. "Disease is just a horror of the distant past, and so is aging."

"You never get—how old are you?"

"Me? I'm only three hundred and sixty. I'm a baby. Part of the

Accident Generation." Pax took another swallow of food as Ellis tried to figure out what that meant.

Pax sighed and took a drink. "There's so much you don't know. I had hoped Alva would have taken some time to—"

A gust of wind blew Pax's bowler hat off. "Real mature, Alva."

Pax retrieved the hat and sat back down, keeping one hand on the brim.

"But if no one ever dies, isn't that a problem? With overpopulation, I mean," Ellis asked.

"There was a population crisis in the middle of the twenty-third century."

Ellis nodded, remembering Charlton Heston in *Soylent Green*.

"But not overpopulation—it was because of a depleting population. This was before the ISP wiped out death and disease, you understand. People were still dying, but fewer and fewer children were being born each year—a real emergency. Everyone was content and fulfilled and didn't feel the need. Most people had no children, and those who did had just one, which meant the world population was diminishing with each generation. So the ISP stepped in and filled the void."

"Manufacturing people?"

Pax looked surprised at the comment. "*Creating* new people from DNA patterns."

"And the religious community just let that happen?"

This appeared to catch Pax by surprise, resulting in an expression that was part confusion, part suspicion, as if Pax felt he was being intentionally obtuse. "There haven't been any religions for hundreds of years. I think the last church was in Mexico somewhere, but that was a *long* time ago."

"So no one believes in God anymore?"

"Of course not." The tone was flippant and condescending. Then Pax appeared mortified. "Oh—I'm sorry." Setting down the fork, Pax reached out and touched his hand. "I didn't mean to insult you like that. I didn't realize. I should have, but..." Pax looked sick.

"It's okay—really."

"But I should never have—"

"It's fine—trust me, you aren't the first atheist I've talked to. What were you saying about the population problem?"

Pax resumed work on the minlatta. "Oh—well, since the new patterns never grow old, it wasn't long before we reached the perfect population size. The only problem comes from accidents. People don't die from disease, but accidents still happen and create openings for new births. I was one of those—hence the Accident Generation. I, and everyone sharing this pattern, should live forever, which is why these killings are so horrible. Death is an awful tragedy to us."

"It was to us too," Ellis said. "So I'm guessing you don't have wars?"

Pax looked shocked and turned away as if Ellis had said an offensive word.

"Sorry. I didn't mean—"

"Part of the new pattern the ISP created was the removal of the Y chromosome and the aggression that came with it. It was the source of the vast majority of violence. Conflict of that sort hasn't existed in centuries." Pax grimaced and shivered for effect.

"The Y chromosome...you're talking about men—males. That's what people with the Y chromosome are."

"I've read about the sexes," Pax explained. "Seen some restored grams on the subject. It all seems so...complicated—and dangerous. And such an inadequate means of reproduction. Darwinism—

the haphazard selection of genes—produced such unpredictable results when everything was left to random chance. It would be like shuffling coords and jumping blindfolded through portals. It amazes me that it took so long to take control of our own existence. I can't imagine what people were thinking back then."

"You're aware that I'm male?"

Pax made an embarrassed face. "I suspected."

"Everyone is female then?"

"No. There aren't any sexes anymore. All that unnecessary equipment was removed just like the appendix. You used to have those, too, didn't you?"

Ellis nodded.

"The ISP pruned away all the leftover genetic branches because they were invitations to disease and malfunctions, not to mention just plain silly to carry around."

"Hair included?" Ellis ruffed his own.

Pax nodded, looking embarrassed again, and Ellis wondered if he was performing the equivalent of picking his nose.

"So, you don't have sex anymore? Sexual pleasure, I mean? Orgasms, we called them."

Pax looked at him, grinning.

"What?"

"I just realized you've never experienced delectation."

"What's that?"

His comment made Pax laugh. "Are you aware that pain and pleasure are generated in the brain? When you touch something, tactile information is sent to the brain, which interprets it and then provides you with a sensation. Delectation just skips the physical part. There's a whole art form where people devise new and incredible delectations. There's even a *classics line* that is supposed to re-create orgasms, inebriation, drug highs, and other sensations from the past. I've tried a few. I didn't like the inebriation one. It just made me dizzy, which really wasn't pleasant at all. The orgasm one was nice, but very short. Were they really only a few seconds long? If the reproductions are accurate, you're in for a treat."

Ellis had flashes from the Woody Allen movie *Sleeper* and decided to change the subject before Pax suggested trying out the orgasm machine or whatever it was. "So why were you at the crime scene? How did you find out about it?"

"I was called by the professor handling the tour. Twelve people saw the body. Some of them were bound to have emotional stress. Cha came with me, which is pretty routine. Then when you opened your eyes—well, who better than an arbitrator to handle first-contact?"

"Do you have any idea who the killer is?"

"We don't even know who the victim was." Pax offered a smile and touched his hand again—a gentle touch, soft hands. "Your assistance was amazing, by the way, and thank you again for that. The Grand Council feels the murders are the result of anger over the Hive Project. And I know there is a lot of emotion circulating—a lot of fear. I have my own concerns, as you can probably tell." Pax gestured at the material of the frock coat with a smirk, indicating something obvious that Ellis didn't understand. "I find it hard to believe that anyone upset over the Hive Project would resort to such extremes."

"What is the Hive Project?"

"Nothing, really. I mean, it's just research the ISP is working on. They've been at it for centuries and haven't gotten anywhere, which is why it doesn't make sense that someone would kill over it. We just aren't built that way anymore. Anger doesn't boil over into action—not like it did in your day. We fret, we yell, we scream, we cry, and we hug, mostly in that order, but we don't strike, and we never kill."

"Someone does."

Pax nodded thoughtfully.

Ellis had a dozen more questions. What was this Grand Council? How were people *made*? What did ISP stand for? Why were they underground? What was Hollow World? He thought of himself at that moment like some three year old about to drive an adult crazy with endless questions. Pax probably had questions too. Ellis realized that in his deluge of inquiries he had been an ungrateful lout.

"Say, I'd like to thank you for taking care of me," Ellis said as he wound up a forkful—two thousand years and still no better way to eat pasta. "I would have probably died if you hadn't."

Pax smiled, showing perfect white teeth that would have put any twenty-first-century model to shame. "It's the least I could do for the first-ever time traveler."

"Why do you suppose that is?" Ellis asked. "I mean, if I could do it, I would have thought there would be others. I kind of figured it would be commonplace these days."

Pax shrugged. "Alva?"

"Let me run a check, dear. One moment." A few minutes later she was back, although Ellis guessed she really hadn't *gone* anywhere. *"No, I'm sorry. There's nothing about time travel except fictional references in books and movies."*

"Weird," Ellis said. "It really wasn't that hard, all things considered."

"Perhaps you are just underestimating your abilities."

"Maybe."

"In any case, here we are, and since we don't have any experience with such things, it brings up a question," Pax said. "What do you want to do? Should I announce you to the world or would you rather I not?"

Ellis hadn't thought about it. He had just assumed sunglass-wearing men in black SUVs would be showing up to whisk him away to some debriefing or research lab. "I assumed you already had—that you were required to report me to your boss. You work for the government, right?"

Pax appeared to have trouble understanding, and while his host pondered this, Ellis took his first mouthful. It was marvelous. The complex flavors were hard to place. Tomatoes were in there somewhere, as were onions, but the rest was a mystery, and a wonderful one at that. "This is *really* good," he blurted out.

"Ha! See! I told you it was good," the vox said, her voice booming across the meadowland like God.

"You've made a friend of Alva," Pax noted.

"I can really taste the tomato, it's..." Ellis struggled to explain. "It actually tastes like a tomato—I mean the way they used to taste when I was a kid."

"They changed?" Pax asked.

"Oh—yeah. They mucked genetically with all sorts of foods. Made them larger, more rugged, resistant to disease, and uniform so they'd sell and transport better, but in the process they ruined the taste and texture. In my time, tomatoes had all the flavor of cardboard."

"With Makers, we don't have those problems. Food designers focus on taste. They are as much an artist as any other."

"Speaking of artists, I'm sorry I upset Vin." Ellis wasn't disturbed in the slightest and overjoyed to be eating alone with Pax, but Vin was Pax's...friend? Lover? "Are you two...um...?" He had no idea how to say it and settled for "Roommates?"

Pax was lifting a fork of food and halted, looking uncomfortable. "We both—live here together—yes." Pax lowered the fork and proceeded to rearrange the pasta on the plate.

"When you say *together*, what does that mean? Are you a *couple*?"

"Couple? I don't understand."

"Well, in my day most people who lived together were usually married. My wife's name is Peggy, and we've been married for thirty-five years. But there were those who lived together before getting married, and some people considered that immoral. There was an even bigger stigma when people of the same sex lived together for romantic reasons, so they sometimes would claim that they were no more than roommates. You see, the term *roommates* didn't suggest anything more than the sharing of living expenses. When I left, there was a big push for same-sex marriages, and, well...I was just wondering if you and Vin were married."

"No, Ellis Rogers. There's no such thing as marriage. My relationship with Vin is...unusual. People don't live together anymore. Everyone has their own home. Two people never share the same living space—well, they do, but not permanently, you understand."

"Why? Don't people like each other? Fall in love, that sort of thing?"

"Certainly, but people also need time to be alone to work, to reflect, to think, to rest. We can always be with someone simply by opening a portal. Hollow World is like one big house where everyone has a private study or office separated by a single doorway. The rest is the shared space. Didn't people in your day ever spend any time by themselves?"

Ellis thought about his garage. He'd spent more time in it than with Peggy. He also remembered some absurd statistic claiming that married couples actually spent no more than seventeen minutes a day with each other.

"People come together all the time. But with Vin and me, it's... well...it's complicated."

Ellis knew he was missing something. Pax meant more than was said, but he couldn't figure it out. Everything was hard to understand even when there was no pretense at diversion. Making guesses was almost useless. All he could do was draw on the past. There weren't men and women anymore, but that didn't mean relationships didn't have the same dynamics. Maybe Pax was like one of those impressionable young girls who moved in with a prominent older man whom they saw as worldly. The way Pax spoke in such awe of Vin's profession, maybe artists made the big bucks these days. Pax had certainly appeared subservient.

"Is this—" Ellis wanted to say *his place*, because Vin seemed like a man, and Ellis found it annoying to dance around the pronouns. "Is this Vin's home?"

"We share it."

"But it was originally Vin's place, right? Vin took you in? That's why you need permission to—"

"No—no, this is my home." Pax chuckled. "Vin would never tolerate a vox like Alva."

"Really? It's huge."

"There's never been any restriction on size in Hollow World. That's one of the benefits."

"Well, it's *very* nice."

"Thank you." Pax beamed. "Vin helped a lot, of course."

"Oh—so he paid for a lot of it? Or do arbitrators make a lot of money?"

"Money? What's *money*?"

"What's money?"

"Alva?" Pax called. "Can you explain *money*, please?"

"Money is an old English word that referred to anything used to represent a standardized object of agreed value that was traded for goods and services."

Pax looked stumped. "Could you simplify that?"

"You want something someone else has, so you trade something you have for what they have. You understand that, right?"

"Not really."

"This was before the Maker was invented. It made it easier for everyone to agree on relative values of things. Trading becomes a matter of math—so many of one thing equals so many of something else—understand? Historically shells, salt, metals, and paper promissory notes were used before digital currency was adopted in the twenty-first century. Of course, the whole monetary system was discontinued in the late twenty-third century with the advent of the Three Miracles, which is why you sound so dumb right now. Didn't they teach you anything at Bingham?"

"Oh wait." Pax thought a second. "Gold was once used, right? And silver? They made little round disks with them. I saw some at a museum once."

Ellis nodded. "Coins."

"Okay, yeah. Wow, being with you is making me wish I paid more attention to ancient history. Who could predict I would need to know all that stuff?" Pax's head shook. "No, we don't have money anymore."

"You don't have money?" A fly buzzed his pasta and Ellis waved it away, wondering if it, too, was part of the illusion, and if so, why it had been added. There was such a thing as taking realism too far. "How can you not have money? How do you get things you need?"

Ellis had hoped to pay for medicine, or surgery, or whatever he might end up needing with his grandmother's earrings, but he began to doubt that would be possible. He was getting ahead of himself, he knew. There was no guarantee they could help him. The future might have eliminated death for *them*—for the genetically altered—but could they do anything for the sick? Was it possible that medicine was just as obsolete as money?

"I don't—"

"Excuse me, Pax," Alva interrupted.

"Alva, Ellis Rogers was speaking. You shouldn't—"

"It's an emergency."

Pax looked worried. "Please tell me it's not another murder."

"It's not. It's a white code message."

"White?" Pax appeared stunned. "What the core is a geomancer contacting me for?"

"Do you want to hear it or argue?"

"Play it."

A new voice boomed over the open field that sounded just like Pax's except with a more confident, more formal tone. *"Pax. I directed my vox to contact you right away with this prerecorded message in the event that someone other than myself has stolen my identity and falsely entered my home. Please visit immediately and speak to my vox for more information. Abernathy will allow your portal. Two things you need to know: First, the thief who stole my identity is in my home at this very moment. Second, you should be careful, for this thief has already killed me. Geo-24."*

Timing Is Everything

Technically this was Ellis's second trip through a portal, but the first he was fully aware of. He asked to go with Pax, pretending it was because he was bored, and that he didn't want to be left alone in the house with Vin. He also told himself he was interested in seeing more of the world and was curious about the message. All of that might have contributed—did contribute—and those were the answers Ellis would have given if anyone asked. But the real reason was strange, unlike him, and hard to imagine, especially given the circumstances. The fact was the trip sounded dangerous, and Pax didn't strike him as a superhero. Ellis wasn't a hero, either, but he had a pistol and the Y chromosome to use it.

Pax hesitated only a moment before nodding and taking out a small device. Ellis thought it might be a pocket watch, because it was gold and linked to a chain. Pax fussed with it for a few seconds; then a shimmering hole appeared.

Alva said, "*Pax, be careful!*"

The trip was instantaneous, no different from passing through a normal door separating two rooms. Looking back the way they had come, Ellis could see the Big Sky country and the picnic table, empty except for their abandoned plates. The portal closed, winking out like televisions used to when they had vacuum tubes.

Ellis and Pax stood in the center of a Zen-garden living room. A perfect square, the room contained two equal-length white couches on a white carpet. A square white coffee table stood in the exact middle, and on it were three stones of different types cut to form a pyramid. A narrow strip along the baseboards and one near the ceiling illuminated the room, but most of the light entered through glass doors of square latticework, beyond which lay a real Oriental garden. Only the bonsai tree gracing the little table provided the room with color. The temperature was cooler than Pax's dining room, and Ellis felt a cough coming on.

"Excuse me! What are you doing barging into my home? Who are you, and how did you get in here?" The speaker entered from an archway at the far side of the room near the terrace doors. This one, like the first two he had seen, was naked except for a delicate necklace and looked identical to everyone else except for a scar on the left shoulder and two missing fingers on the right hand.

"I'm Pax-43246018, an arbitrator of the Tringent Sector. Who are you?"

Pax hadn't moved since they stepped through the portal, so neither did Ellis. There wasn't much space anyway. The living room was tiny compared to Pax's social room. Geomancers apparently didn't live as large as arbitrators and artists.

"Who am I? I'm Geo-24. Who else would I be? This is my home!"

"He's the killer," Ellis told Pax, staring at the missing fingers. "This is the one I saw in Greenfield Village." His chest tightened. Breathing was harder.

Pax looked worried.

"I don't know what you're talking about. Who—or what—is this with you?" Three-fingers asked Pax.

"This is Ellis Rogers," Pax said without looking away. "Who is helping me investigate a murder that took place yesterday on the North American Plate. Now please, once again, I know you are not Geo-24, so who are you really?"

"I *am* Geo-24! How dare you!"

"Look at the right hand," Ellis said, breathing slowly through his nose and trying to suppress the growing urge to cough. "This is the same three-fingered butcher who was cutting into the murder victim's shoulder when I arrived."

"Geo-24's vox, can you hear me?" Pax asked.

"I can indeed." The reply came from a decidedly male-sounding voice, a deep baritone with enough of a British accent to sound like Christopher Lee, and just as in Pax's home the sound came from everywhere.

"Can you identify this person in front of me?"

"No, which is why I contacted you. Geo-24 left instructions that I was to ignore the identification chip and ask three questions of my own choosing that only Geo-24 could answer. When this person arrived bearing Geo-24's identification, I asked the three questions. Incorrect answers were provided. Following the rest of my instructions, I forwarded the prerecorded message to you."

"This is ridiculous," the impostor said. "I have a malfunctioning vox. Have you declared me to be a fake to the whole of Hollow World, vox?"

"Please note, Pax-43246018, that Geo-24 had all the expected digits on both hands and that this impostor doesn't even know my name."

Off to the left, Ellis noticed another square table in the corner with something round on it. He might have ignored it in any other home, but this place was as spartan as a desert. A peanut on the floor would have screamed for attention. On the table was something much bigger and far more attention getting—a construction hard hat.

"I don't wish to call you by name. You've upset me," the three-fingered suspect defended. "Now answer my question."

"Given that you are not Geo-24, I need not comply with your demands, but, nevertheless, I have only informed Pax-43246018 as per previous instructions."

"I see," the impostor growled. "Well, that's something at least."

Holding a hand over his mouth, breathing through his fingers, Ellis took the three steps needed to pick up the hat. Inside he found safety glasses and gloves. "Pax," he managed to say. "Look at this." He held up the glasses.

Pax nodded and looked about to cry.

"You killed Geo-24?" Pax said just above a whisper; a wavering tone of disbelief filled the accusation with a haunting quality. Pax's expression was disturbingly familiar, as Ellis had lived with it for almost two decades. It was the look Peggy had worn each day after Isley's death. "Are you going to tell me who you really are?"

"I don't have—"

Pax lunged forward at that moment and tore the necklace from around the impostor's neck. "I can't let you leave just yet," Pax said, quickly stepping back.

With barely checked anger, the impostor stared for a long

moment, then, after a controlled breath, walked out of the room into the adjacent hall. Ellis took a step to pursue.

"Don't!" Pax almost gasped.

"Isn't there a door Three-fingers can escape out of or another one of those iPortal things in this house?"

The baseboard and ceiling illumination died. Only the falselight spilling through the glass wall allowed them to see.

"Pax? Pax? What's going on?"

"We're in trouble," Pax managed. "I don't think—"

The muffled sound of bare feet on carpeting grew louder as the killer returned, all three fingers wrapped around what looked to be a butcher knife.

At the same time, Ellis began to cough. The chest-ripping whoop felt as if it were scraping his insides from his stomach to his tongue. He bent over as one cough became a cascade of harsh body-shaking eruptions.

No one else in the room noticed.

"No—don't!" Pax cried as Three-fingers advanced. "Here! Here! Take it!" Pax took a step back and threw the little iPortal device so that it bounced off Three-fingers' chest.

"Too late for that," Three-fingers said.

Ellis was trying to grit his teeth, demanding that his body obey, even as it drove him to his knees as if a demon were trapped in his chest and determined to get out. He could only watch through blurry eyes as Three-fingers closed on Pax.

Their faces might have been created from the same sequence of genes, but looking at them, Ellis saw two distinctly different people. Three-fingers grinned with an eager malevolence, closing the distance between the two like a shark after a drowning swimmer.

No aggression my ass.

Like a caricature in a horror film trying to find the key to a car, Pax retreated around the table, struggling to pull out the pocket-watch-style portal device. Catching the edge of the table, Pax fell backward.

Three-fingers skirted the coffee table to where Pax lay.

The coughing fit reduced to a sputter. Ellis drew his pistol. "Stop!" he managed to croak. He had both hands holding the gun, his thumbs lining up like puzzle pieces, arms extended but not locked, just as he was taught. "Don't you fucking move!"

A portal appeared to Ellis's left. "Go, Ellis Rogers! Get away!"

Three-fingers only hesitated a second, quickly dismissing Ellis.

Guns. They don't understand guns!

Ellis didn't have time to explain. He held his breath just as they had told him at the gun range—he had to stop coughing—and squeezed the trigger gently.

Shit! The safety was on.

Pax screamed, warding off the attack with raised palms as the knife came down.

Ellis flicked the lever and pulled the trigger. At such a short distance it was impossible to miss.

The gun was a lot louder without the earmuffs. In the seconds afterward, he couldn't hear a thing. He smelled smoke and gunpowder, which made him cough again. His ears rang, hands vibrating from the aftershock. The barrel went up, shoving his arms with it. He hacked, eyes closed. Blood was in his mouth again, he could taste it, and when he opened his eyes he could see it.

The white wall and part of the glass door were splattered red.

Pax was on the floor, crying in a ball. Three-fingers had come within inches, but lay still. A dark puddle of blood grew, spreading out, seeping through the white carpeting that acted like a giant sponge. Three-fingers wasn't moving.

Ellis crawled to Pax. "Are you stabbed? Are you okay?"

Pax reverted to a series of hitching breaths, unable to speak. Pax's head shook. Ellis wasn't certain which question was being answered, then realized it was probably both. The gun was still in his hand. Another look at Three-fingers confirmed the threat was gone, but it took three tries for Ellis to put the pistol back into the holster. Once there, he remembered the safety was still off. Glancing at the wall, at the tracks of blood-tears, he pulled it out and gently engaged the safety before putting it away again.

"That's a gun, isn't it?" Pax asked, staring at his hip.

"A pistol—yes."

Pax didn't say anything else, just stared as if the metal at Ellis's hip was alive.

"You aren't hurt?" Ellis asked again.

Pax's cheeks were slick, hands shaking. "I almost died."

Pax looked over at the body and the spray of blood. There were splatters even on the ceiling. They dripped, leaving little dots on the white coffee table and the stone pyramid. The once perfect room of Zen-like serenity traded for the violent confusion of a Jackson Pollock painting.

With a gasp, Pax seized Ellis, hugging him tight. Fingers clutched him around his waist like talons, as Pax sobbed into his chest. Ellis reached out with his own arms, returning the squeeze, and the two shook together.

Ellis wasn't one for shows of emotion. He wasn't raised that way. They were good old-fashioned Protestants. By the age of nine, hugging his mother had already become awkward, and if they'd had fist-bumps back then, the two would have been early adopters. He hadn't shown much more affection toward his own wife, even early on, and later...It always felt more like work, when it should have come naturally.

But Ellis had never killed anyone before.

He told himself that if it hadn't been Pax, he would have hugged the couch. He just wanted to hang on to something. Pax was bawling into his shirt. He could feel the wetness and knew he wasn't too far away from a good cry himself. Hanging on helped. Feeling that he was taking care of Pax made it better. He just wasn't sure who was really helping whom.

Pax stopped crying and pulled away, still shaking a bit. "Sorry, I think I soaked your shirt."

"I'm surprised you didn't pass out from the smell," he offered, trying to sound tough and not sure why.

Getting up, Pax retreated from the room, and Ellis followed. They slipped around the corner into the corridor, which was just as empty of color as the living room. Pax stopped, flopped to the floor, and backed up against the wall.

"We need to call someone?" Ellis asked.

"In a minute," Pax said, struggling to speak clearly, blurting words out in a rush. "No hurry at this point...I'm still trying to... remember how to breathe right. I really am sorry...I suppose that wasn't very professional of me. *Homicide cops* in your day didn't run away from blood and cry like that, did they?"

"I don't know." Ellis sat beside Pax. "Maybe some did."

Pax's expression was dominated by a force of will illustrated by a gritted jaw. "*You* didn't."

Ellis offered a forced smile. "I watched a lot of westerns as a boy. John Wayne never cried."

Pax nodded as if understanding, but Ellis doubted it.

It took several minutes, but eventually Pax said, "I wonder who it was. That's the trouble with the master sequence pattern."

Out in the garden, the light was starting to fade. Ellis wondered if the falselight was synchronized with the light on the surface. Maybe they *were* on the surface; he really didn't know where they had ported to, and he had already determined he couldn't tell the difference between real and falselight.

"So we found the killer," Ellis said. "What do we do now? What's the procedure?"

Ellis found himself in a hurry to leave. He wasn't showing it, but he felt sick. Not like he had the day before—a different kind. He could smell the blood, or thought so, and the odor of gunpowder lingered large in the small home. He'd just killed someone. The idea—the recognition of his actions—had flashed across his mind several times like a random strobe light, but all the sitting had started settling it into his consciousness, coalescing into a real thought. He'd prevented Pax from being murdered, which was a good thing, but at the same time, Three-fingers looked just like Pax. The whole scene was surreal enough to be drug induced.

His hands were shaking. *Were they shaking when I pulled the trigger?* He didn't think so. He couldn't even remember the exact moment of the gunshot, couldn't recall what he had aimed at or if he'd aimed at all. Adrenaline—that's why he was shaking. Maybe that was why he wanted to leave. Fight or flight was kicking in, and he wanted to be gone, away from the blood, the body, and the reminder of what he'd done.

"I don't really know." Pax wiped the tears away. "You understand we're breaking new ground here. There's no procedure." Standing up, Pax adjusted the frock coat and vest, then paused. "Vox?"

No answer.

Pax walked down the hall, opened a door, and went inside.

Ellis stood up and was about to follow Pax when he heard a shuffle, then a click.

"Vox?" Pax called returning to Ellis in the hall.

The baseboard lighting flickered on once more, brighter now to compensate for the fading falselight.

"Vox?"

"Yes?"

"I'm sorry, what is your name?"

"Abernathy. I—Oh my! What happened?"

"You were switched off, then I was attacked. Ellis Rogers saved my life by...by killing Geo-24's murderer."

"Either of you injured?"

"No." Pax's head shook, and again Ellis wondered at the visual capability of voxes or if that was just habitual body language. "Abernathy, why were you required to ask questions when Geo-24 returned?"

"I was not informed."

"Did Geo-24 ask you to send that message to me—to me personally, or just to any arbitrator?"

"To you specifically."

"You and Geo-24 weren't friends?" Ellis asked Pax.

"Of course not." Pax looked stunned. "Despite your impression of me, I'm not fortunate enough to socialize with geomancers. Abernathy, do you know where Geo-24 went?"

"My records show Geo-24 went to the grass on the North American Plate."

"Had Geo-24 been doing anything odd recently?"

"Define odd."

"Different, unusual, inconsistent with normal activities?"

"Geo-24 suspended working on the garden, but that, of course, is not doing, rather than doing something odd. There was also the research on Pol-789."

"Research?"

"Geo-24 was scanning datagrams on Pol-789, which I define as unusual, because Geo-24's pursuits were always rocks and never people. Well, almost never. Geo-24 once conducted a similar investigation on you."

"Me? When?"

"About a year ago."

Pax paused, thinking.

"Who's Pol?" Ellis asked.

"Pol-789 is the present chief of the Grand Council."

"How important is that?" he asked, looking at Pax. Ellis wasn't certain how voxes worked, but they must be able to "see" somehow and able to read body language to some degree, because Abernathy was silent.

"In your day Pol would be like a prime minister or president," Pax explained. "Only government is nothing like what you're familiar with. It really only consists of fifty-two people."

"And they control everything?" Ellis asked, but it wasn't really a question. Dystopias in books and movies were always set up with a handful of men consolidating power through the control of technology.

"They make decisions on our behalf. People don't want to take the time to study every issue needed to make the right choices, so the Council serves as a dedicated group to do just that. It's a terrible imposition, which is why every two years there's a draft."

"A draft? To be in charge?"

Pax nodded with a miserable look. "Everyone has to submit their bio and fill out a questionnaire. Why the interest in Pol-789?" Pax looked up before asking the question, and Ellis realized this was always done when speaking to voxes, as if they inhabited the ceilings of homes.

"Pol-789 contacted Geo-24 a month ago, and the two have had several communications. I've actually gotten on quite well with Balmore, Pol-789's vox, as a result of arranging meetings."

"But you don't know what they spoke about?"

"No."

"All right. I guess that's it then." Pax took a breath and shrugged. "Abernathy, please contact the Dexworth office at the ISP. Tell them what happened. They'll send some people to remove the body. They should be getting pretty good at it by now."

"Will they clean the carpet?"

"You can ask."

Is there any way to get that much blood out of a white carpet? Ellis wondered. "Do you need to report this to your boss?"

"*Boss*? That's another one of your old-fashioned words, isn't it?"

"It means your supervisor," Ellis explained. "The person at your job who tells you what to do. The one in charge of hiring the employees."

Pax stared at him intently, head slowly shaking. "No one tells me what to do."

"How did you become an arbitrator?"

"I started speaking to people and realized I could help them, so I do—but okay, that's just me. Most people do take the aptitude test to help them."

"You don't work for a business or organization—the government?"

"I'm not sure what you mean by *work*, Ellis Rogers. Nowadays that term means to do something hard, or to do something you don't really like but have to."

"Yeah—that's pretty much it."

Pax looked puzzled. "But you talk as if it's something a person would do a lot of."

Ellis nodded. "Most people—most adults—worked eight or more hours a day—five, six, and sometimes even seven days a week. So yeah, you *work* a lot. Usually you have a boss who tells you what to do, and you get paid in return."

Pax had a sad look, as if just learning that Ellis had been the victim of some terrible crime. "No one here tells anyone else what to do. People do what they like for as long as it pleases them. When it doesn't, they do something else."

"You're not making sense. How do things get done—how do you get food to eat and furniture for the houses? Who makes the portal things?"

"Oh." Pax waved a hand at him. "The Maker takes care of everything."

The Maker? Ellis didn't like the sound of that. He imagined a world where everything was provided by some being who demanded human sacrifices. "Who is the Maker?"

Pax smiled, and Ellis thought there might have been a laugh if they were somewhere else at some other time. "The Maker isn't a person. It's a device, one of the Three Miracles. I'll show you when we get back home. I've got five of them, though technically three are Vin's."

"Dexworth has people coming," Abernathy announced.

Pax wandered back down the hallway and reentered the blood-stained room. The body lay faceup, eyes looking at the ceiling.

Only a small hole was visible in the chest. A larger exit wound must have been on the other side and the source of the blood spray, but Ellis couldn't see it and didn't care to.

Pax stooped and picked up the necklace that had been thrown. On it was a small device like an iPod shuffle. "It's Geo-24's. Why would anyone want to kill a geomancer of all people?"

"To impersonate him," Ellis offered.

"Him?" Pax smiled.

"Whatever." Ellis was flustered, standing in the room with the person he'd killed. Pax, who earlier had been far more upset, now appeared more at ease. "I'm just saying impersonation appears to have been the point of this."

Pax stared at the little portal device. "Okay, but why?"

"Well, what are geomancers? They don't appear to live very lavishly, but you talk as if they're rock stars."

"Rock stars?"

"Forget it—they're someone to be envied, right?"

"Geomancers are beloved and respected. Highly educated—they spend centuries studying, and they work selflessly in terrible conditions to protect Hollow World."

Ellis was working his way nearer to the garden window, away from the bloodstains. The last of the day's light was fading; night was on its way. "Protect it from what? What do they do?"

"In your day didn't you have something called meteorologists?"

"Weathermen, yeah."

Pax looked puzzled. "Only men could be meteorologists?"

"Huh? No—oh! Skip it, what's your point?"

Pax shrugged. "Just as I assume *weathermen* in your day were revered above all others, so are geomancers today."

"Weathermen weren't revered," Ellis said.

"I thought meteorologists were all that stood between survival and destruction back then."

"Destruction from what?"

"The weather. You lived during the Great Tempest, didn't you?"

"I've never heard of that."

Pax looked embarrassed. "Oh no—I suppose that didn't happen until the twenty-three hundreds, but wait..." Pax paused. "I thought the climate was changing as early as the twentieth century."

"There was some debate about global warming, if that's what you mean."

"So you were at the very beginning, then."

"Beginning of what?"

"The storms."

"What does this have to do with geomancers?"

"I guess you could consider them modern-day meteorologists, only instead of forecasting atmospheric weather, they forecast geologic storms. It doesn't rain or snow down here and we don't have tornadoes or hurricanes, but when the asthenosphere acts up, it can really ruin your life."

With a soft pop, a portal appeared in the living room between the bloody couch and the table with the hard hat. Five people stepped out, all twins of Pax except they wore matching white jumpsuits and gloves.

"Another one, Pax?" one of the five asked.

"I don't know who this is, other than Geo-24's murderer. That's who the last victim was, for what it's worth."

"A geomancer?" The tone was one of surprise.

"I know."

"Any idea who killed this one?"

"Ellis Rogers," Pax said, gesturing at him.

All five looked over.

"Am I going to be arrested?" Ellis asked.

"Arrested?" Pax looked at him, confused. "That's another of your old terms, isn't it?"

"Are they"—he nodded at the five—"going to take me and lock me in a room somewhere? Punish me for killing?"

"No, Ellis Rogers. No one is going to *punish* you." Pax said the word *punish* as if it, too, was unusual. "Things really were very different in your day, weren't they?"

Ellis was too relieved by the answer to question further, and he watched them move the furniture, clearing a path to haul the bag-wrapped body through the portal.

On the way out one turned to Pax and said, "So, this will be the last one, then?"

Pax nodded. "We can hope."

The dining room was a Gothic cathedral again by the time Pax and Ellis returned. The home was mostly dark except for the candles on the table and a dim mood lighting created by a faintly illuminated ceiling. Ellis noticed that the portal they returned through had opened to the exact place they had left, leading him to suspect that the placement of openings wasn't random. This got him wondering about what might happen if a portal appeared in the middle of a sofa. Perhaps it would appear and disappear without a trace, but what if it bisected a person? Pax had mentioned that accidents were few, so he had to assume something prevented such things from happening.

Loud music was playing, startling Ellis as the bass boomed through the walls and reverberated against his chest, thumping as if someone were patting him. The rhythm was strong and the melody catchy enough for a pop song, but the instant they stepped through, the sound died.

"You're safe!" Alva shouted, her voice booming as loud as the music had before.

Floor lighting appeared, and a new style of music played in the background. Ellis thought it might be something classical—it sounded like an orchestra.

"Is Vin gone?" Pax asked.

"Vin has a meeting, remember?"

"That's right." Pax turned to Ellis. "They hold a sector artists' meeting once a month. It's necessary to make sure they are all working in harmony.

"I think it's really just an excuse to brag, as that's all any of them did the times they held it here," Alva said with a tone of exasperation.

"Alva, you know you don't have to stop your music when I come home. Just turning it down is fine."

"Vin hates it."

"Well, I like it."

The classical changed back to the pop song.

Returning to the social room, Ellis was greeted by the breathtaking view again. This time he looked out on a night that was a beautiful image of lights. It might have been the New York skyline or the real Paris. He could see all the neighboring homes' windows as well as outdoor lights that strategically illuminated sections of the cliffs or the gardens below. Above, he saw stars and a half-moon rising. Looking out at the beautiful immensity, he understood the concept of Hollow World better. He was living in a work of art, every aspect taken into consideration for aesthetic appeal. Artificial. The word used to mean something inferior. Ellis wasn't certain that applied anymore.

Seeing the twinkling night, hearing the sounds of nature bleeding through, Ellis felt like James Bond on assignment in some exotic paradise.

"Can you go down there?" Ellis pointed toward the commons.

Pax chuckled, looking at him as if he were a precocious child. "Of course. That's the common garden. We hold tea parties every third morning, treasure hunts once a quarter, and you should see it on Miracles Day. Bag races, skib competitions, and the boat contest. Everyone gets the same materials, and we all have one month to create a boat that will win a race across the pond—no Makers allowed. It has to be completely built by hand. Some are just amazing. People can be so creative, and they long for a venue to express it."

Pax stood silent for a time, just looking out at the view. They both did.

"We aren't as fortunate as you," Pax then said.

"How so?"

Pax looked surprised. Hands came up, then fell in exasperated disbelief. Eventually Pax just laughed. "You're unique."

"I suppose," he said dismissively, not seeing any significance in being him.

"Don't you understand what a gift that is?"

"Not really."

Most people Ellis had known had gone to great efforts to be like everyone else. Blending in with the crowd was a survival skill just as important for humans as zebras. The odd man out was usually picked on. High schools were hotbeds of assimilation. That was where people were trained to disappear, to melt and conform so that they could continue doing so in the workplace. Only the nuts wanted to be noticed, the artists and madmen. The entire gist of the traditional father-son talk Ellis had with his dad had consisted of his father telling him the most important lesson he'd learned—never volunteer. His father had discovered that while serving under Patton in the Fourth Armored in France. The ones who volunteered never came home.

"Everyone here would love to be you. I suspect it's why Vin was so curt. Vin is a genius, but can also be very vain and jealous. I suppose we all are in our own way. We each struggle to establish a difference." Pax rubbed the material of the frock coat. "We all try to define ourselves by something to make us identifiable, to make us different, but..." Pax took off the bowler hat, revealing a bald head. "Underneath we're still the same."

Pax held the hat in both hands and leaned out over the rail, looking down at the lights below with a sad reflection, a sort of hopelessness that surprised Ellis.

"I wouldn't say that," Ellis replied. "*You're* very different."

Pax glared at him. The look was almost angry. "Why would you say such a thing?"

"Because it's true. I've only met a handful of people here, but you aren't like any of them. You're—I don't know—nicer, I guess. More empathetic—and *a lot* braver."

Pax continued to stare, and Ellis saw disbelief.

"When you first met me, Cha was terrified—everyone was—but you walked right up. You took me into your home. Didn't know who I was. Didn't know a thing about me—didn't even *ask permission,* apparently. And...and at Geo's place just now—you made that portal for *me* to escape, not for you." Ellis shook his head. "I don't think you're at all like anyone else. Not like anyone I've met here. Not anyone I knew before either. If anyone is unique, it's you."

Pax's lips were quivering. "Why are you saying all these wonderful things?"

Ellis shrugged. "I told you—they're true. Why would I lie?"

Pax blinked back tears.

"I like the hat too." Ellis smiled, trying to make light of the situation. He had no idea why Pax was crying. "Very dapper."

"Thanks. It's not original. I got a pattern from a museum—I'm not an artist like Vin. I can't invent new things." Pax spoke quickly, self-consciously, using words to fend off embarrassment. "This whole outfit is just a mishmash of stuff from the past. A few others wear these—they used to call them bowler hats or derbies. I wore a top hat for a while—that's another old hat—but I like this better. It stays on in high wind, and I've been logging a lot of grass time recently."

Pax turned back to the view and wiped the tears away—more promptly followed.

Ellis did the noble thing and looked away, pretending not to notice. Maybe if Pax were a woman he might have offered a hug or something, but Pax wasn't a woman. The best a man could do for another man was pretend not to see. Only Pax wasn't a man either.

Ellis was lost.

He liked Pax. For some reason he felt more comfortable, more relaxed, with this bald-headed arbitrator than he had with his wife, his mother, or even Warren.

They stood for a moment as Pax struggled to stop crying, using everything from the crux of an elbow to that derby hat to hide behind. Ellis reached out, placed a hand on Pax's shoulder, and squeezed gently. A minute later Pax slipped the hat back on.

"We have fireworks on Miracles Day too," Pax managed to get out with a struggle, then coughed and sniffled. "It's the best time short of a rain day."

"What's a rain day?"

Pax turned to reveal red eyes but a bright smile. "Oh...a rain day is great. When there's a nice solid cloudburst over one of the grass parks, I port up and...well, just stand in it. I start by standing, at least. Before long I'm dancing, spinning, jumping. Rain days are wonderful. We don't have weather down here. Sometimes as a treat the artists put on a weather show, but it's not the same as real rain."

"What about snow?"

"Snow is pretty, but it's not like rain. For one thing, as you've probably noticed, most people don't wear clothes—don't have them. The climate in Hollow World is constant, designed for—well, not for clothes. I'm almost always too hot, but it's my sacrifice for people being able to recognize me, as me."

"Like I said, I very much approve of your style," Ellis said. "Very classy."

Pax looked away again, lower lip trembling.

"I'm sorry. I don't mean to keep—"

Pax walked away, disappearing through a door at the far end of the room.

Ellis stood with his back against the balcony rail, feeling terrible.

"Ellis Rogers..." he heard Alva say, the vox's voice imitating a whisper. *"You, sir, are a wonderful human being. May I get you a drink? Would you like more food—you didn't get to finish eating. I have no clue, but I'll try and figure out how to make a hamburger if you really want one."*

"Is Pax okay? Did I say something wrong?"

"Pax has some serious problems, but you, my love, are most assuredly not *one of them. I just wish you'd visited us years ago. But honestly, I want to do something for you. Can I play you some music? Do you like music? I can play something you might know. How about this?"*

Ellis heard a quiet piano begin playing the first haunting chords to a most familiar song.

"This was popular in your day, wasn't it? Do you like it? It's one of my favorites."

A moment later Ellis heard John Lennon singing to him across the span of two thousand years. *"Imagine there's no heaven...it's easy if you try..."* Then it was Ellis's turn to cry.

After Pax failed to reemerge, Ellis went back to the room with the canopy bed. For the first time he noticed a little statuette on a shelf—a somewhat crudely sculpted but nevertheless beautiful depiction of one person lifting another up in the air, like a pair of dancers. Ellis touched it and heard a voice rich with emotion. *To Pax, thanks for all you've done for us. Honestly, I don't know how we could have survived without you—as far as I'm concerned you're the Fourth Miracle. Nal.*

Ellis realized that he'd seen other such statuettes around the house. He counted eight in just the bedroom, most up on high shelves, tucked away. Each was different. They showed a variety of artistic skills. One particular figurine, resting high on a shelf above the windows, drew his eye. More exquisite in its level of artistry and emotional impact than all the others, it illustrated a person lying in a bed of thorns, hanging on to the hand of another person who dangled from the edge of a cliff. He wanted to touch it, to hear what message it might contain, but it was set too high, and he wondered if that was intentional.

Still eager to please, Alva offered the best in modern entertainment. Televisions were gone, replaced by such things as grams, holos, and vections. Grams—the word was short for holograms—could be still or moving. They were the closest thing to movies or photos except they were true 3-D, in that the image extended into the room, and Ellis could walk around and view objects from different angles. Grams were spectator-only, but holos were interactive. Each was a complete environment that served as a total immersion computer game or educational landscape. He never got to discover what vections were, as Alva provided him with an educational gram titled simply: *Our Past*. This was a multi-part series similar to a Ken Burns documentary or something produced for the History Channel. Alva started him on episode eight: *Energy Wars*.

The presentation was emceed by a talking hourglass that danced and sang. It began with images of violent storms while the hourglass spoke about dwindling fossil fuels and global warming. By the mid-fifties—2050s—when Ellis would have been one hundred years old—the climate had become violent. There were numerous references to killer storms, and agriculture industries across the globe were fighting a losing battle to grow food in an increasingly hostile and unpredictable environment. Extensive greenhouse technology was used, but soon even these interior spaces were being destroyed by what the hourglass described as a *very angry Mother Nature*. The agro-companies began building underground farming facilities that were safe from the turbulent surface extremes and constructed housing for their workers. As the storms increased and the death toll rose, companies had a long list of applicants seeking jobs on the subterranean farms.

With a frown and a shudder that caused a little sandstorm in its head and stomach, the hourglass pointed out that the problems of a changing environment were among many challenges confronting humanity. Antibiotics had stopped being effective, and epidemics of super flus flourished, wiping out massive numbers of people. The outcry that resulted saw the establishment of the Institute for Species Preservation, which altered human DNA to combat the super viruses.

Of all the threats, the greatest problem of the mid- to late twenty-first century was still a lack of energy, which touched off a series of wars that only exacerbated problems. Apparently that still wasn't the worst of it, as near the end of the episode the hourglass alluded to even greater problems and something called the Great Tempest that struck in the twenty-third century and led directly to the Hollow Earth Movement and the Three Miracles.

The segment ended with a quote from someone born well after everyone Ellis had ever known was dead: *"Adaptation is the greatest ability of any living creature. Humanity's ability to adapt is proven, but our true talent is in our ability to make our environment adapt to us, and to be able to jump highest when the ground falls out from under our feet."*

Ellis fell asleep before the start of the second episode. This being just his second day in Hollow World his body still hadn't recovered from time-machine lag and dehydration, not to mention the unprecedented stress of having killed someone. That night he had a dream about a tornado that plucked him up from his garage in Detroit—which looked more like Kansas—and dropped him in a cave filled with giant super bugs. His little dog got in the way, and he accidentally shot it. Only it wasn't a dog—it was Pax, whose bowler hat was covered in blood. Peggy was crying, but Warren said, "I'd have done the same thing, you know. Any man would."

Sign of the Times

Ellis woke to the familiar wheezing congestion in his chest and this time found the rain-forest bathroom without Alva's help. Breakfast consisted of "something special" Alva whipped up. Eggs. The omelet not only tasted like eggs, but it looked and had the texture of eggs. The dish also had chunks of ham, green pepper, onions, cheese, and a little sprinkling of paprika on top. The only difference between it and a classic western omelet was that Ellis had never eaten eggs this good, which made him suspect he wasn't eating anything that had come out of a chicken—that and the fact it had emerged from a device that looked similar to a microwave.

Alva called it a Maker and had instructed Ellis to place a bag of rocks in it. The rocks came from a chute dispenser next to the machine that reminded Ellis of the bulk food dispensers they used to have at his Kroger supermarket. The chute was transparent, ran up through the ceiling, and was filled with coffee-bean-sized pebbles. He just needed to hold the bag to the mouth and rotate a lever to fill the bag. The rocks slid down and were replaced from wherever the chute originated, causing Ellis to think about the advances of hot and cold running gravel.

Alva instructed him to place the rocks, along with the bag, in the Maker. There looked to be a means to do a direct feed into the machine from the chute, but it wasn't connected. Then Alva told him not to touch anything and let her handle the "cooking." The machine hummed, and there was light. Then Ellis laughed as he heard the exact same *bing* that his own microwave made when it was done. Opening the door, he found the piping-hot omelet.

"It's an old pattern," Alva explained, *"but I thought you might like it."*

Ellis had been hesitant to eat rocks, no matter what magic trick had been done. After three bites he was a convert. "How can rock become food? Wouldn't you need organic material?"

"Everything in the universe is made of the same thing when you break the components down far enough," Alva explained. *"Then it's all in the way you rebuild and recombine aspects that make them organic, inorganic, liquid, and solid. Humans, after all, are made from the same material as stars."*

"Interesting. So if I put more rocks in, can I get coffee?"

"Sure! Classic, sweet, chocolate, vanilla, strawberry, guava, Tantuary, cinnamon-honey, maple, blackberry, latte, core-style, litho-roast—"

"Classic—black."

"Use one of the small bags."

He drew one out of the drop-down dispenser. Extremely thin, the bags were see-through and plastic-like. He placed the opening over the chute mouth and noticed the drink symbol on the lever. A quick tap and the bag filled with about a cup of the gravel, consisting of different types of uniformly distributed rocks. A bing later and he had his coffee, complete with a white ceramic mug.

The house was quiet, and Ellis took his meal to the social room. As Alva had predicted, he loved the balcony and continued to be mesmerized by the view. The quality of light was constantly changing, perpetually altering and revealing new, previously hidden surprises. That morning the sky was a pale pink, blending toward a yellow sun that had yet to show its face. The predawn light worked like a shadow play, creating silhouettes out of the trees and rock formations that were obviously designed to be seen as such. Ellis spotted a shadow-puppet tiger and across from it a bird. As the sun rose, the outlines changed so that the tiger crept forward, inching up on the unsuspecting prey.

Ellis pulled over one of the soft chairs and sipped his coffee as he watched this sliver of Hollow World waking. The coffee, unlike the omelet, did not thrill him. He liked his coffee strong, and this tasted like hot coffee-scented water. Maybe he should have gone with core-style or litho-roast.

Distant voices echoed from below, and he peered over the rail to see a group of early risers starting to play a game of some kind on the open lawn of the garden. A moment later Ellis heard music and thought it might be coming from one of the other homes, but then he discovered a quartet playing in a sheltered grove across from where the others were setting up their game. The music was soft, gentle—rising strings growing steadily stronger, plainly illustrating the rising of the sun.

Ellis saw others appear on the walking paths below, some alone and others in pairs. Two different walkers had dogs. They were the first pets he'd seen, and he was pleased to know man's best friend had survived the years. Across the open expanse, he saw others like himself on balconies with steaming cups, faces turned toward the light. Below, the music grew louder and louder, a beautiful melody. The game players paused to watch the rising sun, as if it were a flag raising and the little quartet was playing the national anthem.

As the yellow ball peeked above the horizon and spilled its first rays of golden light, the outline of the tiger leapt for the bird, but the bird had flown away. As the falselight sun rose and the atrium illuminated, Ellis saw that the bird and tiger were only fountains, tree branches, and the edge of the cliff. Illusions given life for those few seconds, a secret show provided by the artists for those knowing where and when to look. Ellis wondered how many other Easter eggs were hidden, and if they were different for balconies with other views.

"Beautiful, isn't it?"

Ellis turned to find Pax behind him, the glow of the morning sun bathing the familiar face. He had expected a robe or something, but like him Pax was dressed in the same set of clothes as the night before, only this suit failed to show a wrinkle, so Pax must have more than one.

"Gorgeous."

"Maybe you can understand now why we value our artists so much." Pax sat beside him. "And I see you've been introduced to the Maker."

"Alva showed me. The omelet was great. This coffee on the other hand..." He made a face.

"I drink Frizlana—it's a pattern of tea, but I know a great many people who like litho-roast."

Ellis could hear the faint shouts as the game began. Several of those on balconies leaned over to watch.

"Mezos are playing the Brills this morning," Pax said. "Each section of the community has its own team. I used to play on the Mezos about...sixty years ago, I guess. We were never very good. Lost almost every game. People still cheered for us." Pax sighed. "I'm sorry I abandoned you last night. I felt awful. Didn't get much sleep."

"I'm sorry I upset you."

Pax stared at him with that same bewildered expression. "You are just so..."

Ellis braced himself. He was expecting irritating or frustrating. Those were the words Peggy and his mother had used most often, and Warren had dubbed him an asshole most of the time and a prick on occasion.

"...just so amazing. I wish I could be like you."

Certain that Pax was joking, he laughed. Pax didn't laugh with him, and, realizing Warren had been right about him being an ass, he stopped. "I'm a miserable old man who's dying of an incurable sickness. You don't want to be me."

"Are you joking again? I can't always be sure, you know. Your humor is so...unusual. You must be, though, because...because, well look at you. You're unique—truly unique. You have hair—and it's *two* colors. Your skin sags, and has all those great creases, like a beloved knapsack that has been taken everywhere and shows evidence of every mile. No one else has that. And no one else has invented a time machine and ridden it two thousand years into the future or saved someone else's life by stopping a murderer. But...it's more than that. It's you. The way you act. The way you don't just look, but actually see—see things everyone else misses. The wear marks of glasses and...well...*me*. I feel special just being with you. It's a gift you have, this ability to hand out inspiration and kindness without any trace of motive. You're amazing."

Pax's eyes had that glassy, wide-eyed appearance again. "In Hollow World we all try to be different, try to stand out as original, but only you truly are."

No one had ever looked at him that way before. No one had ever accused him of being amazing, not even when he had opened his acceptance letter to M.I.T. There had been pats on the back and congratulations, but not even his own mother had showed such awe. Ellis didn't know what to do or say. He took a long sip from his coffee cup and discovered he had a little trouble swallowing.

"I realized last night I shouldn't be keeping you here," Pax went on. "I should make certain the GWC knows about the killings and about you. I'm sure they will have all sorts of questions, and they will take you to the ISP to fix your health."

"You think they could?"

"The ISP can do just about anything except bring you back from the dead, and you can be certain they're busy working on that. If it's only your lungs, they'll just outfit you with a new pair. That sort of thing is no big deal, just a port-in procedure."

"Seriously? Oh...ah...what about cost?" Ellis knew Pax said there wasn't money anymore, but that didn't mean there wouldn't be a cost.

"Cost?"

"What would I have to do or give to get these new lungs?"

"See—I can't really tell if that's a joke. You don't even smile when you say it."

"That's because I'm not joking. I want to know what will be demanded of me in return. I don't want to agree to anything without knowing what I'm getting into first."

Pax laughed. "Ellis Rogers, no one would ever demand compensation to *keep people alive*. You make us sound like monsters, as if people wouldn't help others unless they got something out of it."

Ellis thought to argue, to point out how competition kept a society strong, how altruism could lead to resentment. He felt he needed to defend the system he'd grown up in, only he couldn't figure out why. It also wasn't in his best interest, since all he had were a pair of diamond earrings and a few expensive rings he had forgotten to leave behind, none of which appeared to have any value in that world.

"I'll take you to Pol as soon as you're ready."

"What will happen then?"

"You'll be introduced to the Council, I assume. Lots of questions. Then I suspect you'll be introduced into society, and you'll no doubt become a very big celebrity. I can't imagine anyone in Hollow World not completely bleezing when they hear about you."

Ellis had no idea what that meant, but if it was related to being pleased, he didn't share the opinion. So far only Pax had shown any sort of pleasure at his existence. "I don't know what *bleezing* means, but I doubt Vin did it."

"Vin is..." Pax squinted in an effort to think.

"Used to being the unique one?"

"Exactly."

Ellis glanced out at the view again. The falselight sun was completely above the horizon, and the vast atrium was filled with what reminded Ellis of a bright, clear, autumn sort of light. He wondered if they had seasons. "Will I be coming back here afterward?"

"Pol will likely invite you to stay in Wegener."

"What's that?"

"I guess you could call it the chief city of Hollow World. It's on the Antarctic Plate in the Kerguelen micro continent. Each plate has its own center, and most are bigger, but each plate sends a representative to Wegener. Some of the best artists work there, so it's one of the most beautiful places in Hollow World."

"It's awfully beautiful right here," Ellis said, continuing to look out over the balcony.

The conversation held a tone of solemn finality. Maybe there was some truth to the idea that Ellis could see what others couldn't. The way Pax had come out that morning, so quiet and with such a soft tone of voice—apologetic, embarrassed even. The admission of admiration had borne all the openness of a deathbed farewell. Even if Pax refused to admit it, Ellis understood this was the last time they would be together. This conversation was goodbye.

Ellis felt a distinct sinking sensation, a general depression that settled over him, making it difficult to breathe, much the same way as the fibrosis. Pax and Alva were his only friends in this strange new world, and the idea of separating from them was just so painful—and ironic, he realized, as he'd just abandoned a whole existence, giving precious little thought to those he left behind. He had sacrificed Peggy and Warren, rolling the dice on a better trade. But that was before he knew what the future held, or so he told himself. So far everyone else he'd met hadn't been very welcoming. He and Pax had shared a life-and-death moment that left a mark and made him feel they were connected.

And then there was just plain old traditional paranoia. He worried about Pax's safety.

"You said you never met him, right?" Ellis asked.

"Pol? No. I'm an arbitrator, and I've never been a Council member or—"

"I meant Geo-24."

"Oh—no. Well, it's possible. I met a geomancer at a Miracles Day party once."

"When?"

"Maybe a year ago."

"What happened?"

"I don't remember. Like anyone, I was just excited to actually speak to a geomancer, you know? They so infrequently appear in public. I think the encounter only lasted a few minutes. Just some small talk. I probably asked a bunch of stupid questions, like anyone would. What it's like being a geomancer. Stuff like that."

"Don't you find it strange that Geo-24 was looking up your record *about a year ago*?" Ellis asked. "And don't you find it odd that he instructed his vox to contact you, and only you, in the event of his death?"

"I didn't say it wasn't strange, but it also doesn't make sense, and there's no point in pondering crazy things that can never be answered."

The quartet stopped their concert and began packing up as more people arrived with more balls and another group approached the big pond with toy boats.

"I'll be able to visit, right?" Ellis asked, looking back.

Pax reached out, took his hand, and gave it a squeeze. "I think...I think it would be better for everyone if maybe you didn't."

"Why?"

"It—it would just...it would just be better if you didn't."

"Is it Vin?"

Pax looked away.

"Were you up all night because you couldn't sleep or because you were talking about me?"

Pax let go of his hand. "We spoke about you."

"Doesn't like me much."

"That has nothing to do with it."

"So what is it then?"

"Vin thinks you're a bad influence."

"I bet."

Ellis was angry—too angry. Sure, he thought Vin was a pretentious prick, and he didn't like the idea of losing his only real friend because of such a tool. But Ellis actually wanted to punch Vin—hard. That was far too extreme an emotion for the situation. He wouldn't have felt that way if Warren had told him he couldn't hang out anymore because his girlfriend disapproved. He wouldn't have wanted to punch Marcia if she'd come between them, and he'd been friends with Warren for more than forty years. Granted, Marcia was a petite blonde with big blue eyes, and it would have been like beating up on a fawn. While Vin, on the other hand, was a pompous, melodramatic, diva, picking on the little ingénue who—

"We should go see Pol," Pax said. "I'll get your bag." Pax offered a courageous smile that Ellis knew was forced.

By the time Pax returned, Vin had stepped out of one of the doors into the social room and stopped abruptly. The mask had been left behind, and Vin was wearing just the eighteenth-century suit. Vin looked identical to Pax. Ellis's eyes shifted between them, his mind locking up like some computer asked to calculate the highest number or the absolute value of pi. If Vin put on a bowler hat...

"Why is Ellis Rogers still here?"

Pax crossed the room and pulled Ellis away.

Maybe Pax thought he might shoot Vin. The thought had

crossed his mind. They didn't seem to have any penalty for murder. He could offer the excuse that he was merely a product of his times. Pax pulled harder, shoved Ellis's backpack at him, then drew out the iPortal. Ellis heard the now familiar snap and hiss as an opening was made. Looking through it, Ellis saw a circular pool surrounded by trees, lawns, and stone walkways.

"Please," Pax begged him with a frightened face and motioned to the portal.

Ellis stared back, surprised at the emotion in Pax's voice. Maybe Ellis wasn't the only one to *see* things. He felt ashamed.

The portal shimmered, a perfect window into another reality that he just had to step through, but to Ellis it was another box of milk crates, another escape to a foreign place. He sighed and stepped through.

The first thing Ellis noticed was the gurgling sound of the fountain in the middle of the bowl-shaped pool that shot water up a good sixty feet. Tens of thousands of years had passed since humanity had escaped primeval forests, and there was still something about splashing water that had caused mankind to bring the babbling brook with them. Something soothing there, something embedded in the collective psyche—fountains were the clocks in puppies' beds, simulating the heartbeat of a missing mother.

The second thing he noticed was all the people. Ellis hadn't experienced a public space in Hollow World yet. He'd only looked down on the gardens below Pax's balcony. Some gathered in groups, some walked with purpose, but none noticed him—yet.

With childlike logic, he avoided looking at anyone, as if this would render him invisible. Besides, he didn't need to see their faces—they were all the same.

The third thing Ellis noticed was the city. He was in a small park surrounded by massive buildings. Each was unusual, few had sharp angles—not a single "box" in the bunch—and all were works of art. Shrunken down, they would be marvels on pedestals in any museum. But at dozens of stories tall, they were breathtaking. Most appeared carved from solid rock, free-flowing organic sculptures. The interplay of metals—copper, brass, gold, and silver—created designs inlaid as decorations on the buildings and in the plazas and walkways. Art deco met tribal expressionism; nature living in harmony with high-industry; the soft and the sharp, made and grown, all blending into something new. Above it all remained the blue sky, this one streaked by thin clouds.

The last thing Ellis noticed was that Pax had followed him through.

Turning, he revealed his wide-eyed surprise.

"How could you think I was going to abandon you?" Pax chastised him and displayed an irritated look so pointed that Ellis knew it was artificial. "Do you know where Pol's office is? Would you know how to find it?"

"In the past I just appeared where I was going."

Pax smirked. "You can't just port into the GWC. I'm sure you couldn't just port into the palace of the Prime Minister of the United States without announcing yourself first either. Not that Pol, or anyone else in the Grand World Council, has the power to execute people on a whim like people did in your day, but still—it's not polite."

Ellis couldn't help smiling. He was so happy Pax was with him that he overlooked the errors in history. Yet as they began crossing the park, Ellis remembered the history-grams and wondered if they really were errors. Two thousand years was a very long time. Perhaps at some point the United States did have a prime minister who ordered executions.

Pax led the way across the open plaza on which huge burnished metal shapes were embedded. Ellis guessed they must make some clever design that was indiscernible from the ground but would be lovely from the windows of the buildings. As they walked, Ellis saw a large river snaking in the distance and weaving between buildings. On the water were all sorts of boats, from traditional sailing ships to more exotic vessels which looked like they were powered by glass sails. No freighters, however, no barges hauling goods the way he'd seen on the Detroit River. Everything in this world was for enjoyment, as if every inhabitant was on permanent vacation. Where were the factories? Where were the men with jackhammers fixing the streets? For that matter, where were the streets?

Seconds after he appeared, people began noticing him. Heads turned. Individuals halted and just stared. Once they started walking, eyes grew wide, and those watching moved out of their way. Some mouths opened as if to speak, but Pax did not stop, and together they marched on. Ellis decided not to look back but heard mutterings and imagined a gathering there, swirls of people drawn close, eddying in their wake.

Finding the Grand World Council was easier than Pax had led him to believe, because it stood out dramatically like other capitols. In this case the building was center stage and topped by a giant sculpture of the earth made of gold and copper. The Hollow World globe didn't depict the continents on its shell, but rather the tectonic plates. Divisions of land and sea were lightly etched into the surface of the massive plate cutouts, appearing as ghostly afterthoughts, no more than spots on a dog. Europe and Asia shared a plate, but the Arabian Peninsula had its own. North America, South America, and Africa all had their own plates, but they were much larger than the continents themselves, because they included a portion of the ocean as well. Ellis noticed several others he couldn't place. Some were quite small, like one just off the coast of the American Northwest, and another near the Antarctic. Ellis wondered if that's where he was at that moment, on the tiny chip at the bottom of the world between the tip of what had once been Argentina and the Cape of Good Hope.

Inside, the building was bright and airy despite walls of glassy, black marble. Sculptures and mosaics filled the space. The largest spelled out HOLLOW WORLD in cleverly pieced-together shapes. Ellis thought the place looked more like an art museum than a government building—and a top-notch one at that. The temperature was the same inside as out, which spared him a coughing attack. Ellis reminded himself he wasn't entering from the outdoors, just moving between rooms.

Few people were in the lobby, and Ellis didn't see any desk or clerk. Pax walked directly to a blank wall and tapped on the polished marble. A touchscreen appeared, and Pax moved through a few menus until finding Pol-789. Underneath this was a list of names, and Ellis was surprised to see *Ellis Rogers* on it alongside *Pax-43246018*. Pax tapped their names, and a portal appeared beside them.

Stepping through, they entered a tiny office. Circular in shape, all the walls appeared to be glass, letting in the falselight and providing panoramic views of the city now far below. In the center was a beautiful round table etched with a detailed map that might have been a projected flat version of the Hollow World interior, while the table's centerpiece was a rotating replica of the giant globe Ellis had seen on the building.

"*Welcome,*" a very pleasant woman's voice—a vox—greeted. "*My name is Balmore. Chief Councilor Pol will be with you shortly. Please have a seat.*"

Ellis and Pax sat in two of the four chairs. Pax sat very straight, adjusting the frock coat and resetting the angle of the bowler hat, only to adjust it again a moment later.

"You don't come here often, do you?" Ellis asked, discovering he was feeling quite at ease by virtue of lacking any preconceived impressions. If this had been the Oval Office, or a palace, he might have been intimidated. Instead, this was just a room with a fancy table, and Ellis had seen more impressive principals' offices.

"I've only been to Wegener once, a long time ago, and I've never been inside the GWC, much less the Chief Councilor's office."

When the door opened, Pax jumped up, standing like a soldier at attention. Not familiar with protocol, Ellis followed suit.

The person who entered was another identical copy of Pax. That's how Ellis saw everyone, even though he understood that, at only a few hundred years old, Pax was far younger than everyone else. Full names, he guessed, were an indication. Like Delaware license plates, or online user names, the lower numbers must indicate age of creation and perhaps social status. Ellis considered the numbers might also just show the popularity of that name, but the fact that a geomancer was called Geo made him think otherwise. Geo-24 was probably very old—only twenty-three Geos had come before—while Pol-789 would be younger, and Pax-43246018 would be a baby in comparison.

"Wonderful—you're here," their host greeted them. "I'm Chief Councilor Pol. So nice to meet you. Please sit down."

Pol wore clothes, too, but had stolen fashions far older than Pax's or Vin's. The Chief Councilor was dressed in a bright-orange, Grecian-style toga, which was fastened at the shoulder by an ornate gold clasp in the shape of the tectonic world. Just as bald and dark skinned as the rest, Pol was the first to look normal to Ellis's eyes, appearing as any of the Tibetan monks that he had seen on television or the cover of *National Geographic* magazine. Pol greeted them formally, standing straight, with one hand in the fold of his robes like Napoleon.

"Thank you for seeing us," Pax said, sitting down. Ellis did the same, his eyes still taking in the views.

Pol was equally fascinated by Ellis, even bending to see what parts of him were hidden beneath the table. "Wonderful. Simply wonderful."

"Ellis Rogers is a real gift," Pax agreed. "The only one of his kind. As I explained in the memo, Ellis Rogers is here from the early twenty-first century, long before the ISP was formed, before the first excavations of Hollow World, and even before Monsanto started the first subterranean farms. His world still ran on fossil fuel, ate slaughtered animals, and lived every day on the grass at the mercy of the weather."

Ellis hadn't heard Pax speak like this before—so formal and filled with admiration. It surprised him.

"A true Darwin," Pol said, nodding. "And you traveled in a time machine like H. G. Wells—one of your own making?"

"I built it in my garage. It wasn't that hard. A guy named Hoffmann did all the real work. He figured out how to do it."

"Can you return to your time? Are you just visiting?"

"No. It's a one-way thing. I'm here permanently, although I won't be here long."

"No?"

"Well, you see—I have a medical condition that—"

Pol held up a palm. "Pax explained about that in the message sent to me along with an accounting of your role in helping to stop a murderer, who had killed one of our beloved geomancers. Trust me, all of Hollow World is in your debt, and we will see to it that any defect you have is corrected. You're a treasure to us, *and* a hero—not that you needed to be. Those at the ISP love this sort of challenge, and to work with a true Darwin, well..." Pol appeared at a loss for words.

Pol reached out and squeezed Ellis's hand. "We'll take great care of you." Pol then turned to Pax. "Thank you for bringing Ellis Rogers to us, and for your role in solving the murders as well. You've performed an invaluable service to Hollow World, Pax. I'll see to it that you're remembered for this."

Pol tapped the brooch at the shoulder of the tunic, and the portal reappeared behind their chairs. "And you can trust that I'll take very good care of Ellis Rogers."

A moment of silence hung. Pax stood slowly, eyes cast low.

"Thank you again, Pax," Pol said.

The time for saying goodbye was at hand again, and while Ellis was pleased to discover he'd earned a free medical procedure, he felt awful once more. What else could he do? What else did he expect? How long had he even known Pax? Ellis couldn't understand his own feelings. All he knew was that he enjoyed being around Pax, and the idea of never meeting again was so unpleasant he dropped into depression.

He put his game face on. Ellis was going to suck it up and be manly. He watched as Pax hesitated, then turned back to face Pol with serious, troubled eyes. "Who is Ren?"

Pol's smile vanished at the sound of the word. "I'm sorry, what did you say?"

Pax's expression shifted to sharp concern. "I asked who Ren is."

"I have no idea."

Pax continued to stare at the Chief Councilor, who looked increasingly nervous.

"What were you talking with Geo-24 about?"

Pol struggled to ignite that smile again. "I think it's time for you to leave us, Pax."

Ellis watched as Pax's expression shifted from concern to terror. "You're not Pol-789."

Pol replied with an artificial laugh that even Ellis didn't buy. "Of course I am. I wouldn't be able to enter this office unless I was."

"You could if you had Pol's chip." Pax stood up, and, reaching across the table, pulled the toga off the Chief Councilor's left shoulder. There, in the otherwise unblemished tawny skin, was a scar: well healed, but clearly visible, similar to the one Ellis had seen on Geo-24's impostor. The assault startled Pol, who reached out with both hands to cover up. As the Chief Councilor did, they both noticed Pol was missing a pinky and ring finger on one hand.

Pax gasped. "Who are you?"

All pretenses fell away. Pol tapped the brooch again, and some of the windows changed to what appeared to be a television screen. Only the show that was playing was the back of a person's head.

"Gar?" Pol said, and the person on the screen turned. "I need your help up here right away. We have a security problem."

Pax shoved the fancy table forward, striking Pol in the stomach and knocking the Chief Councilor's chair over.

The portal was still open behind them.

"Go!" Pax shouted.

Ellis never bothered to think. He dove through the opening and found himself back in the lobby. Behind him, through the portal, he could see Pol's mouth shouting a silent, *Stop!*

Before he'd had a chance to reorient himself, Pax had hold of his hand and was pulling him toward the exit doors. "We have to get outside so I can open a portal," Pax said, already digging the device out of the frock coat.

"What's going on? Why are they after you?"

"They don't care about me—it's you they want."

The snap and hiss of multiple portals popped in the lobby, and others stepped out and spotted them. "Hey! Stop!"

Pax and Ellis pushed out the front doors back into the false-light sunshine that gave no feeling of warmth. Ellis saw Pax pause and fiddle with the device, then a new portal appeared directly in front of them. With Pax still holding tight to his hand, they jumped in together.

Ellis was standing inside a massive stadium. Tiers of seats rose up before him numbering in the tens of thousands, most filled by spectators looking down at a green field where a game was being played. The crowd roared, several jumped to their feet, clapping. None noticed Pax and Ellis.

Pax, still holding his hand, pulled Ellis up a set of steps and around a pillar that was marked SEC-B 200-300 in bold white numbers.

"Where are we? What's going on?" Ellis asked, having to shout over the cheers of the fans.

"We're at Tuzo Stadium," Pax replied, struggling feverishly with the portal device. "I was here last week. Had the location pre-programmed and I didn't have time to pick anywhere else."

Ellis peered around the pillar. On the field athletes were battling with three separate balls. Instead of uniforms, the players were painted different colors. Ellis guessed there were three different teams: one blue, one orange, and one yellow.

"What's going on? What happened in Pol's office? What was all that about Ren?"

Pax was busy with the portal device again, but darting furtive glances down the steps. "I need to pick a place outside, somewhere on the grass where you'll be safe."

"Safe from whom?"

"I don't know, but that wasn't Pol-789. Whoever we just met was involved in Geo-24's murder, and I think also might have killed Pol-789."

"How do you know—"

"Got it," Pax declared as another portal appeared.

Ellis could hardly see anything inside the opening. The far side was dark.

Pax took hold of his hand once more. "Let's go before they catch us."

The moment Ellis stepped through the new portal, he was hit by a bath of hot, humid air and knew he was no longer in Hollow World. The light that spilled in from the stadium illuminated a scene of thick vegetation. Large, broad-leafed plants and massive-trunked trees hugged them. The ground felt moist beneath his feet, the air thick with the scent of dirt and plants, and everywhere were the whoops, chatter, shrieks, and cries of living things.

An instant later the portal snapped shut, leaving them in darkness.

"Where are we now?" Ellis whispered, terrified to move, but Pax pulled him along, rushing blindly into the slap of leaves.

"On the grass—South American Plate, Amazonian Biome, Basin Quadrant."

"We're in the Amazon jungle?"

Pax halted. "I—I thought—" The words were frightened, panicked. "I didn't know it would be dark here. I can't see what I'm doing!"

"Hang on—relax." Ellis stopped. Pulling off his pack, he fished out the flashlight.

"Shine the light on my Port-a-Call," Pax said, holding up the device.

The little controller had a tiny screen and a touch pad, and Pax was doing something that caused new numbers and words to appear. "You said you left your time machine not far from the Ford Museum, right?"

"Yeah."

"And you have more food and water at that machine?"

"Sure."

"Okay, then I'm going to open a portal for you near the museum. They'll never be able to find you once you step through."

"Wait—what about you? You sound like you aren't coming."

"I can't. I have a chip like everyone else. They can track the PICA in my shoulder as I pass through any portal. They knew we were in Tuzo Stadium. They'll know we're in this jungle too. They'll trace the exact spot we ported to, but because we're outside Hollow World, because we moved from the port-in, they can't know exactly where. Once we split up, they won't be able to find you at all."

"Who's they?"

"The murderers. Whoever that was in Pol's office, I guess. I thought we'd stopped the killing. We didn't. It's obvious this isn't just random. People are being murdered and replaced. We need to find out why. We're probably the only two who know."

"I bet Geo-24 knew—or suspected," Ellis said. "That's why he was investigating Pol. That might be why he was killed."

"Maybe," Pax said. "But Abernathy mentioned that it was Pol who contacted Geo-24 first. So what did Pol want from Geo-24?"

"Something suspicious enough to make Geo-24 ask questions that might have gotten him killed."

"At this point it could be anything. All I know is that they're after you." A portal appeared in the dark. This one also led to a leafy darkness, just not as thick. "There! Go!"

Ellis hesitated. "What about you?"

"Don't worry about me, run!"

"But I do worry about you. If I disappear, they'll come after you."

"I won't tell them where you went. I swear."

Ellis sighed. The electric filament that outlined the open portal painted Pax's face and the surrounding giant leaves with a ghostly light. "I know you won't. You'd die before telling them."

"Yes..." Pax nodded, eyes grave, face desperate. "Yes, I would."

"Which is why I'm not going through that portal. Not without you."

"But I can't go. I have a chip, and they'll be here soon."

Ellis let his hand settle on the pistol at his hip.

"No," Pax said, lips trembling. "Please don't."

"I won't leave you."

"No more killing, please. Just go."

The pain on Pax's face was horrible to witness. This was the only living friend Ellis had. He would kill anyone who tried to harm Pax, and yet just then he was the one causing the pain. There had to be another way.

"What if we got rid of the chip?" Ellis asked.

Pax stared at him for a moment. "Do you have your knife in that bag?"

Ellis nodded.

"Okay, okay..." The portal snapped out of existence. "But let's get farther away from the port-in. It will give us more time."

Using his flashlight, Ellis led the way, pressing through thick ferns. They splashed through water and trudged over a tangle of roots and plants until they found higher ground at the base of a vine-wrapped trunk that afforded a small open patch. The ground was spongy, a buildup of organic material—dirt in the making. By the time they stopped, Ellis was soaked. Maybe it was the air condensing on him, the spill of water from leaves, or just plain old-fashioned sweat, but his clothes were plastered to his body, dragging on him like weights. His breath was also coming in gasps, that same harsh crackle. It hadn't bothered him nearly so much in Hollow World. Now it was back. The shift in temperature and humidity wanted to remind him his life was on a timer.

Pax had already stripped away the frock coat and was unbuttoning the white shirt. There was something awful about watching Pax undress, like seeing a superhero forced to strip off a mask. Underneath, Pax was like all the others.

Ellis dropped his pack and drew out the hunting knife. Ellis had purchased the blade off Amazon's website, which, at that moment—in his growing anxiety—struck him as ironic. "We should sterilize this somehow."

"Why?"

"Prevent an infection."

"There isn't a germ on this planet that's interested in my cells." Pax sat against the tree. "Just make sure you don't nick yourself."

"Right."

Ellis knelt beside Pax. Holding the flashlight with one hand and the knife in the other, he wiped his dripping forehead with his sleeve, but he only exchanged one wetness for another. "Do they put these things in deep?"

"I don't know."

"I think this is going to hurt."

"Yeah, and you'd better hurry. They will eventually come here, and I'm not sure I..."

"What?"

"I'm not sure I won't scream—I think I will, actually."

Ellis tilted the light up and saw the glassy look of Pax's frightened eyes. The light also shone off the big blade he held as if he were about to have a knife fight in some old western. What he needed was a scalpel, a razor, or an X-ACTO blade. Doing surgery with a six-inch Bowie knife was insane.

"Are you sure you want me to do this?"

"Yes."

"I mean, I know this was my idea, but I don't want you to think you have to—"

"Do it. Just hurry." Pax was trying to sound brave, and actually did a fine job—braver than Ellis felt, holding that knife handle slick with sweat. He'd never cut anyone before. The closest thing was digging a splinter out of Peggy's finger with a needle. That ordeal had lasted almost fifteen minutes, with him pinching and probing and her jerking and crying. The stress of that tiny splinter had exhausted Ellis—this scared the hell out of him.

He struggled to take a breath as he held the big stainless-steel blade up against Pax's perfect skin. It looked huge, as if he planned to use a barbecue fork to fish out crabmeat. He remembered the online product description: *perfect for gutting a deer in the wilderness.* Knowing he'd need his other hand, he gripped the butt of the light with his teeth, then firmly grasped Pax's shoulder. If he was going to do it, he couldn't pussyfoot. He had to cut deep and fast. Anything less would just add to Pax's misery. Recalling where he'd seen the other scars, he made a best guess.

"Brace yourself," he mumbled around the flashlight. Ellis took another breath and pushed the blade into Pax's shoulder.

Pax cried out and jerked sharply, forcing Ellis to squeeze hard to hold Pax still. He shoved deeper. Pax cried louder. The sound was almost surprised—a consternated "Oh!" that lingered as if Pax were starting to sing "Oklahoma." It only took a second to make a slice big enough that Ellis could have inserted a quarter in. Blood dripped out, but not as much as he had expected. Ellis had imagined a spray of some kind, like Pax was a balloon filled with blood. With the cut made, he had to find the chip, and there was only one way he could do that.

Ellis pressed his index finger into the opening and began to probe. Pax shifted, thighs drumming as if the ground were on fire. More blood was coming out. Several streaks teared down the full length of Pax's arm, spilling on the back of Pax's hand that spread out on the jungle floor like the roots of a tiny tree. Pax's fingers dug into the mulch, ripping it, squeezing it. He could feel Pax's body quiver, hear a shuddering breath. Ellis was uncertain which of them it belonged to.

Somewhere in the night the relative quiet of the jungle exploded into squawks and shrieks.

"They're here," Pax managed to whisper with a stolen intake of air.

Ellis ignored the sounds. A python could have slithered up his pant leg and he wouldn't have cared. He had his finger buried up to the second knuckle in Pax's flesh, worming its way around tendons and...he was pretty sure—yes, that was a bone. Just when he was starting to despair at not finding anything, Ellis's fingertip touched something oddly solid. Wafer-thin, it might have been a tiddlywink. He inserted the blade again, excavating toward it. He forced himself to tune out the grunts and gasps, jerks and jolts. The best way to save Pax pain now was to just focus and get the job done.

He was close, and if he'd had a pair of needle-nose pliers he could have yanked the damn thing out, but instead he had to use the blade again. He cut in a second incision, creating more of an X opening, giving him room to put both fingers inside. Pax's head was back, bouncing against the tree and popping the brim of the bowler hat up, eyes squeezed tight, lips pinched, shaking hard. Then Ellis caught the thing. A slick disk he pinched tight between two fingers and pulled. It came free with a sucking sound that coincided with a cry from Pax.

"Got it!" Ellis gasped in triumph.

He set the disk aside and pulled the first-aid kit out. He tore the wrapper off a sterile pad, held it to the wound, and began wrapping a gauze bandage around Pax's shoulder. When he was done, he repeated the process with the medical tape.

Somewhere in the darkness he could hear snapping branches.

Pax's face was slick with moisture. "They heard me. We need to go."

"Wait," Ellis said. "If we send this chip through a portal, they'll think it was you, right?"

Pax nodded.

"Then dial up someplace crazy."

Ellis used his big, bloody knife to strip a chunk of bark off the tree, then taped the chip to it. As he did, Pax worked the Port-a-Call with one hand. The portal opened. Through it, all Ellis could see was a star field. He wound up and pitched the chunk of bark as hard as he could through the opening. Pax closed the portal and began dialing up the next as Ellis stuffed everything back in his knapsack, including Pax's shirt and coat.

Somewhere to their left, Ellis heard people hacking through the undergrowth, and he saw a light splash across the underside of the canopy. The shrill voices of an excited jungle cut the night.

Pax popped another portal next to them, showing the same nighttime forest as earlier. Ellis threw his pack over one arm and scooped Pax up with the other, and together they staggered through the opening.

Another Time, Another Place

Pax was still asleep when the sun came up.

Ellis sat on the hill, marveling at the notion that he was very close to the same place he had been on his first morning after time traveling. He was back in Dearborn, Michigan, and somewhere down the slope to the south was Greenfield Village. The only difference between the sunrise that morning and the falselight dawn he'd witnessed at Pax's home was the heat he felt and the realization that the genuine article was somehow less beautiful. The real sunrise was now a bit plain, like going back to vanilla after tasting peanut butter chocolate fudge crunch.

Ellis remembered how sad he'd felt the last time he sat there. He'd just lost everything, and believed he would die alone. He had the whole world, and yet no one to share it with. Ellis looked down at Pax nestled against the pillow of his knapsack, covered in the blanket of the frock coat. He lifted the corner to check the wound. He'd changed the pad once already—the old one had been a bloody mess. He threw it as far away as he could. Blood attracted animals to campsites. All they needed was a bear.

The current pad was still white.

The night before, after replacing the bandage, Pax had unexpectedly fallen asleep propped up in Ellis's arms. He had panicked, thinking that blood loss had caused Pax to pass out. He woke Pax, who assured him nothing was wrong. "I'm just exhausted, and this"—Pax squeezed his arm—"is nice. Lying here feels good, and I haven't felt good in a very long time."

Pax fell asleep again and left Ellis replaying those words over in his head. Did anyone feel good for long? Ellis couldn't remember the last time he felt that wonderful brand of no-worries-no-regrets good. Such moments were lost to the mists of youth, but most likely they never existed at all. If he really thought about it, being a child had been a nightmare of fears and a frustration of restrictions. Like photographs that yellowed, memories got rosier with age, and no memories were older than childhood.

Wallowing through the sludge of unremarkable routine, dodging bouts with disaster, humanity still survived off fleeting gasps of happiness. Ellis wondered if he'd ever feel truly good again, or if even that mundane dream had slipped past him. In the still night, on a silent world with Pax sleeping safe beside him, Ellis realized this was his moment to breathe.

As the sun rose, he was still thinking about what Pax had said and wondering what the words meant.

"Morning," Ellis said, noticing Pax's eyes flutter open.

Pax shivered.

"Hungry? Care for breakfast?"

"You have a Maker?" Pax yawned while struggling to button the shirt.

"No—good old-fashioned canned goods." Ellis pulled a Dinty Moore stew out and held it up to the sun. The label was scraped and torn from rubbing something inside his pack, but the image of a steaming bowl of hearty meat chunks and vegetables was still visible. "Two-thousand-year-old beef stew. Yum."

Pax fixed the can with a skeptical stare. "Am I going to like this?"

"Depends on how hungry you are. How do you feel?"

Pax grimaced. "Like someone stuck a sword in my shoulder last night. Where did you get such a mammoth knife?"

"The Internet."

Pax sat up, glanced at the bandage, then began getting dressed. "The Internet—I read about that. Information Age invention, like the steam engine or electricity—started a revolution, right? Lots of people mention the Internet during arguments about the Hive Project. Everyone saying it's like that, and how well that worked out. But then people are always comparing extremes to make a point. The Hive Project is either as good as the Internet or as bad as the Great Tempest."

He handed the can to Pax, who began studying it, as Ellis rummaged around for the can opener. He hoped he hadn't left it back at the time machine or, worse yet, in his garage. "So, exactly what is this Hive Project I keep hearing about?"

Pax was smoothing out the torn section of the label and studying the can with a skeptical expression. "It's an initiative the ISP is pushing for—the next step in evolution, they call it." Pax paused and thought a moment. "The Internet globally linked everyone through machines and wires, right?"

"Some would say tubes." Ellis grinned, but Pax only appeared confused. "Never mind—old joke."

"Well, the ISP wants to do the same thing, only they want to put the machines in our brains."

"Make you like cyborgs or something?"

"No, that's just a metaphor—sorry. There's nothing mechanical involved. They want to alter our biology to make it possible for humans to link telepathically."

"Is that possible?"

"They think it is." Pax rotated the can to look at the picture on the label. "The way the ISP presents it, the Hive Project would solve all of our problems."

"Hollow World has problems?"

Pax smiled. "Yes—many."

"No war, no discrimination, no disease, no pollution, no violence, no class warfare..."

"I didn't say we had the *same* problems. Well—I suppose you could say we still suffer from one remaining issue that manifests itself in several problems."

"Like?"

"Communication. Misunderstanding. Isolation. You see, with the Hive Project we'd all be joined as one mind and know each other's thoughts and feelings—all part of a giant whole. Misunderstandings would be a thing of the past. Everyone would know what everyone else knows, so it would eliminate the need to relearn knowledge in schools. Like the Internet—like global communications—the Hive would make it possible for humanity to leap forward creatively as never before."

Pax tapped the can and then shook it. The dubious look remained. "They also say the Hive would solve the identity-maintenance problem." Pax touched the bandage. "We wouldn't need chips to tell who we are—we'd just know—or maybe we'd all be one, so it wouldn't matter. It would be impossible to lie or cheat. We could also abolish government altogether. All decisions would be made as a whole—no more suspicion or deception—no need for laws, really. It's believed that compassion will overflow and the whole human race will unite in perfect harmony."

"Sounds a little too perfect." Ellis found the bag of peanut M&M'S and set it aside. "Why the debate if it's all going to be so grand?"

"That's the ISP's formal prediction. Not everyone agrees, of course, and there's the problem of eliminating individualism. You might have noticed how a lot of us try to stand out in a world of so much homogeneity—tattoos, brands, and piercings are ways people take great pains to be different. You probably find those things strange, huh?"

"Tattoos and piercings? No, we had those in my day too," Ellis said, and smiled as he finally found the opener. "Fairly popular when I left, in fact."

"Really?"

Ellis took the can back from Pax and, setting it in the grass, began to open it. "Oh, yeah. Some people spent thousands of dollars getting their whole bodies inked. You aren't the first to seek to be different."

"But all of you were Darwins, already unique. How can anyone be *more unique*?"

"Believe me—people tried."

Pax looked baffled, then shrugged. "Anyway, there's a huge fear over losing identity. We already look the same, sound the same, smell the same, and now they want us to think the same—to dissolve our identities into a molten soup of conformity. No one will ever be special again, no one will be able to have any privacy, the whole world will always be there, in our heads, listening to every stray thought, every impulse, every desire."

Ellis shivered. "Sounds like hell."

"What's hell?"

"Pretty much what you're describing—a bad place for bad people."

"A lot of citizens of Hollow World would agree with you." Pax watched him rotate the metal wheel around the can lid. "This is fascinating. It's like a histogram or one of those historical reenactments they do at museums. Only those people are just acting, guessing. You've actually done this before."

"Open a can? Oh yeah—and for the record, you're easily impressed."

He slowed down. "The trick is not to let the lid fall in. Near the end, the torque will tilt the lid up enough to get your finger underneath so you can bend it back. There, see?" He lifted the lid up. "But be careful of the jagged edges. They can be sharp."

"Incredible. It's like camping with a caveman."

"Oh yeah, Neanderthals loved Dinty Moore."

Pax scowled. "I'm young, not an idiot."

"No, you're not." Ellis looked for the spoon. "How about you? What do you think about this Hive thing?"

Pax hesitated, then said, "I'm scared of it. I like my hat and coat. I like that people recognize me at a glance, see me as different. Opinions don't matter, though, which is why I find all the protests more than a little silly. Doesn't make sense to scream about something you have no control over."

"I don't understand."

"If the ISP had the means to go ahead with the Hive, they would."

"But I assume you could pass laws to stop them."

Pax's head shook. "Doesn't work that way anymore. Like I mentioned before, no one tells anyone else what to do—or not do."

"What about—" Ellis almost said murder. "What about theft? You don't tolerate stealing, do you? You must have laws restricting that."

Pax smiled at him. "What can you steal from me that you can't make for yourself? Or that I can't reproduce in an instant? I wear a new suit every day. We don't have a problem with theft."

"But you must have conflicts that need to be resolved."

"Of course. That's what I do as an arbitrator. I solve those problems. Almost all of them are the result of a misunderstanding, misplaced anger, or irrational fear. You can't make laws to govern accidents or emotions—no two are ever alike. They have to be worked through, solved like a puzzle." Pax looked out at the hillside. "Thing is, none of it matters anyway. The ISP can't do it. They don't know how. Been working on the project for centuries and never found the combination to that lock. I don't think they ever will. They also wanted to make it so people could fly—they never did that either. Still, the very idea scares a lot of people. Those in favor are often ostracized, and now there are these murders. Some have said they're linked—a violent reaction to the ISP's continued work."

Ellis found the spoon and offered it and the can to Pax, who sniffed the contents.

"And you eat this?"

"It's not considered a delicacy—and it's supposed to be heated."

Pax took a taste and made a face but nodded anyway. "It's not revolting—I guess."

"That's only because you're hungry. Just about anything tastes better when you're outdoors and starved."

They shared the can and spoon, passing them back and forth as they reclined on the hill and watched the sunrise bathing the hillside in warmth. Birds sang. Cicadas droned. A light breeze swayed the trees and blew the white of dandelions away.

When the stew was gone, Ellis tore open the M&M'S. "Here," he said, "give me your hand." He poured half the bag.

Pax looked at the little round balls with curiosity. "Very... colorful."

Ellis chuckled. "You eat them." He popped a red candy in his mouth.

Pax looked skeptical for a moment, then mimicked him. A moment later a big smile appeared. "These are wonderful. What do you call them?"

"Candy—M&M'S." He thought to add that they were invented by Forrest Mars after he saw soldiers eating chocolate in the summer sun during the Spanish Civil War, but figured that wasn't such a good idea. "Melts in your mouth, not in your hand."

Pax picked up and studied the little yellow bag, turning it over and back. "I'll have to see if Alva can find a pattern for this. If not, we should save some and find a designer to create one. The world should not be denied."

Ellis laughed. "Well, at least the twenty-first century has one point in its favor."

He felt good, which was amazing considering that the night before he had suffered his worst coughing fit ever. It was just after they had arrived back in what had been Michigan and Ellis felt like he was going to hack up half a lung. His chest still felt raw, but aside from that, everything else was hitting that perfect balance of being just right. The wind ruffled his hair, drawing Pax's attention and creating a smile. He was neither too cold nor too hot. His lungs weren't burning. He wasn't tired or hungry. If he thought about it—if he looked back or forward—he would describe that moment as the tranquil eye of a hurricane. Panic or depression should have been appropriate. Instead, he was smiling, eating M&M'S, and even the can of two-thousand-year-old stew was enjoyable. As unlikely as he could imagine, it was a perfect moment.

"I wish it would rain," Pax said. "They can't even make that happen in an ARC."

"What's that?"

"Alternate Reality Chamber. Artists program illusions in a fixed space that simulate reality—sort of like what you see with falselight, only in an ARC they control everything—except the user, of course—and as such they can really suspend your sense of reality." Pax ate another candy. "We've had problems with ARCs, though. People get addicted to them. Years ago, a lot of people died. They entered and never came out. Died of dehydration and malnutrition. You see, they only *thought* they were eating and drinking. The Council required safety time-out features after over thirty people were found dead."

Pax settled close to him again, leaning on his shoulder and looking out at the view. "But they can't simulate rain."

"I'd think that would be pretty easy," Ellis said. "Just put sprinklers on the ceiling. You know—spray water."

Pax smiled. "But that's not rain. That's just water falling."

"Isn't that what rain is?"

"No. Rain is a gift—it's life, salvation, ecstasy—it's the whole world, every plant, insect, and animal rejoicing together as one.

There's just something that makes you feel so alive in a rainstorm, especially if there's lightning and thunder. Then it's as if the whole universe is joining in."

Ellis remembered watching thunderstorms from his front porch with his dad. Those times had been nice—one of the few memories he had of just sitting quietly with his father. Thinking back, it was similar to watching a fireworks display on the Fourth of July, but nothing like what Pax described.

"What's it like to have a family?"

Ellis was surprised by the question. "What do you mean?"

"I imagine it was wonderful, like teams in sports, everyone working together, loving each other without reservation."

Ellis laughed. "In theory. In reality—not so much."

"Really? I just think living back in your time would have been wonderful. I was a member of an anachronism group. We'd get together and dress up in wigs and shirts and blue jeans—complete with real belts and wallets. Some even had replica plastic cards in them. Oh, and shoes! We wear timepieces, pretend to text each other on phones, and watch really old restored grams. I liked the ones without color the best. The ones where people wore hats all the time."

"And vests and long coats?"

Pax smiled and nodded, tapping the bowler and making a little hollow sound. "Some of us would pretend to be male and others female, and we'd dance. I remember that once someone actually had a book—a real one. A collector had brought it. A literary classic. We had to wear special white gloves to touch it. And the book's owner could actually read. I remember sitting and listening. It was amazing. Just incredible."

"Do you remember the name of the book?"

"I'll never forget it, *Second Chance,* by Danielle Steel. The mastery of language in your day was just so magnificent. I picture that time as so romantic and adventurous."

Ellis bit back a slew of comments, wondering if Pax's view of the past came from watching Fred Astaire movies. *Probably wonders why I don't begin crooning and doing a little dance step.*

Pax rubbed the bandage.

"Don't play with it," Ellis said. "Let it heal."

"I feel strange knowing the chip is gone. I have no way of proving who I am now."

"They put those things in at birth?" *Is* birth *even the right word?*

Pax nodded. "In a way, it was more me than I am."

"I doubt that. Where did I throw your identity chip, anyway?"

"Into space, somewhere near Neptune's moon Triton—assuming the orbit was right, and it should be—I used the coords for the planetarium there. The Port-a-Call updates those things."

"There's a planetarium on Triton? Wait—space? You can open portals into the vacuum of space? Why didn't it suck us out?"

"Here, let me show you." Pax sat up and took the portal maker out again. Dialing it, Pax created an opening before them. All Ellis could see through it was water. The entire opening was filled with a solid aquamarine color, and in that slice of water, Ellis saw fish swimming by. "That's the ocean—right near the equator, about forty feet below sea level, and as you can see, the water doesn't spill out, because a portal isn't a hole in the sense we think of one." Pax poked a finger into the cross section of ocean and drew it out dripping. "That's how we get rid of waste, you know. Not that there's a lot. Most can be reused in the Makers, but what can't is ported into the core. That wouldn't be possible if there was any bleed-through. Open a portal to the core and you'd incinerate yourself from the heat, right? We used to port trash into space, but the HEM objected."

"HEM?"

"Hollow Earth Movement. One of the oldest organizations we have. They started everything."

The portal must have been near a coral reef or something. Ellis watched a small school of striped angelfish flash by. The whole thing was like one giant aquarium.

"The planet was in bad shape—look who I'm telling—you know, right? But it got worse. Pollution, climate change, the storms that resulted as the natural system began to clean house. They used to say we made the earth sick, and she vomited. The surface up here was scarred, ripped up from overuse. Roads were everywhere—concrete was everywhere. That's where the phrase *to concrete* comes from—it means 'to ruin.' The HEM was a group of people interested in restoring the surface by getting everyone to live underground. No one listened at first, but then they found major allies in the old corporations looking for subterranean farm workers."

Self-conscious, Ellis picked up the empty can and slipped it in his pack.

"That's what started everything. But the HEM has gotten a little nutty—or maybe they always were. Now they're against anything aboveground being touched. Some are against people even visiting the grass. And it's like, what's the point? I can understand the prohibition against ruining the surface with building homes and such—I mean, why would you? If you want to be outside, you go to the surface. If you want to be inside, well, that's Hollow World. But to go to all this trouble to restore the surface but be prevented from ever enjoying it? It's crazy.

And people love visiting the grass. Luckily they don't make the decisions anymore."

Pax ate another candy just as a shark passed in front of the portal opening. Finding the Port-a-Call, Pax closed the door.

"Could that have come through?" Ellis asked.

Pax nodded sheepishly.

"What are we going to do now?" Ellis asked.

"I don't know. I'd almost like to just stay here. Core the HEM, it might be nice to live on the grass as in days of yore. If we could get a Maker and a Dynamo to power it, the two of us could disappear into the forests and live a life of frontier people and have wild adventures."

"Pretty sure Daniel Boone didn't have a Maker, and you might think different when winter comes. What about Vin?"

"Vin? Vin would be relieved to be off the hook. Finally rid of me."

Ellis found this admission a surprise, and more than a little familiar. He never expected to meet someone in the future he could relate to so readily. Certainly not someone like Pax.

"But you're right, we can't stay. We need to find out what's going on, only I don't know how. Everyone who knew anything is dead."

"Not everyone." Ellis thought a moment. "I have an idea."

The atmosphere in the home was that of a face covered by a white sheet, the haunting silence of an all-too-recent ghost story. Ellis and Pax entered Geo-24's residence exactly where they had the first time, only as expected the place was empty. A sheer curtain had been drawn, muting the morning falselight and blurring the image of the Zen garden outside. No police tape marked where the body had lain; nor were there boundaries marked off by ribbons of yellow plastic. After his conversations with Pax, Ellis was not shocked at the lack of official presence; he was, however, surprised by how clean the place was. The carpet and walls were spotless—not even a stain. Ellis wondered if an old-school forensic scientist could find evidence or if the whole room had been spaced through a portal and a new one constructed.

"Who's there?" the vox said in the same British baritone as before.

"Abernathy, it's us, Pax-43246018 and Ellis Rogers."

"I'm not detecting your PICA, Pax-43246018, nor that of Ellis Rogers."

"Ellis Rogers never had one, and I cut mine out."

"How curious."

"We are being hunted by the same people who murdered Geo-24, and I'm attempting to move about invisibly, so I hope you haven't notified anyone of our arrival."

"Whom would I notify? And may I inquire who Geo-24 is?"

Pax glanced at Ellis with a concerned look and whispered, "I think they might have cleaned up more than just the blood."

Ellis listened to the snap and hiss of the hole back to Michigan, which Pax had left open. Ellis couldn't help but think of it as "the getaway portal." He had counted on the idea that voxes might be like servants back in the nineteenth century—thought of as little more than furniture and overlooked when cleaning up. So far he was disappointed.

"If you're not Geo-24's sexton, whose sexton are you?" Pax asked.

Neither had taken a step farther into the room. They stood right before the coffee table. Ellis noticed that even the little drop of blood that had marred the stone pyramid centerpiece was gone.

"I have no client at this time."

"And you don't recall who your client was previously?"

"I'm not aware that I've ever had a client."

"It might still work," Ellis told Pax, but the vox overheard.

"What might?"

Pax nodded. "We'd like you to contact another vox on our behalf, a vox that you used to be on friendly terms with."

"I don't recall being on friendly or unfriendly terms with anyone."

"That's because you've had your memory erased, but that doesn't matter, because the other vox will remember you."

"I don't understand."

"It's not important that you understand. You merely need to set up communications between myself and another vox. That shouldn't be a problem, right? It's not like your client has forbidden you to assist strangers?"

"As I mentioned, I don't have a client."

"Wonderful. Then there's nothing prohibiting you from helping us."

"Whom do you wish me to contact, and what do you wish me to inquire about?"

"I want you to contact Pol-789's vox. Inform the vox that you are Abernathy and that I am Geo-24 and that I would like to speak with it."

"I thought you said your name was Pax-43246018?"

Pax glanced at Ellis and shrugged. "I misspoke."

"Seriously?"

"Yes—I do that. It's a quirk I have."

"I'm a sexton without a client, not a vox without a properly calibrated telencephalon."

Pax frowned. "Can you determine if I am Pax-43246018 or Geo-24?"

"No."

"Then what difference does it make?"

"Would you like me to make contact now?"

"Yes—audio only, please."

"This is Vox Abernathy contacting you on behalf of Geo-24."

"Oh—Abernathy! How nice." It was the pleasant-sounding lady's voice Ellis had heard when they had entered Pol's office. His heart, which was already beating faster than normal, began to trot as he felt a rush of success that made him grin.

They were in.

Ellis wondered if this was how hackers back in his day felt when they had broken into government computers. *"Do you wish to speak to Pol-789?"*

Pax and Ellis both shook their heads.

"No, that will not be necessary. Geo-24 would like to speak directly to you. Is that acceptable?"

"Of course, of course!"

"This is Geo-24," Pax said.

"How wonderful of you to call. Pol will be so thrilled you did. Let me—"

"No—wait! It's not that important—actually, it is a little embarrassing. You see, Pol provided me with some information, and I have misplaced it. I was hoping you could just send it to Abernathy. Would that be possible? I'd like to take care of this without involving Pol. You understand, I hope. As a geomancer,

I'd prefer not to let it get out that I made a mistake and lost something important."

Pax stared nervously at Ellis, who crossed his fingers.

"What information?" Pol's vox asked. No suspicion, no tone at all, which concerned Ellis. The friendliness had faded, but this was a machine, and Ellis didn't know if that was even something to look out for.

"Everything you have on Ren."

Ellis looked at Pax, surprised. The plan had called for investigating what Pol had originally contacted Geo-24 about. There had been no mention of a Ren.

"Ren? Is there a number designation?"

"No, I don't think so...just Ren."

"No, I—oh, wait—yes, here. I actually only have a port location associated with that name."

"And where would that be?"

"North American Plate, Temperate Biome, Huronian Quadrant."

Pax mouthed to Ellis, *That's where we just were.* "Could...ah..." Pax began pulling the Port-a-Call out. "Could you provide exact coords?"

The vox responded with a series of numbers and letters that meant nothing to Ellis, but which Pax feverishly entered into the tiny device.

"Thank you. Say goodbye, Abernathy."

"Thank you so much for your time," Abernathy said.

The link was severed, and Pax slumped into one of the white couches, staring at the portal device. "Okay, so we have a location, and it's right back where everything started—back at the Ford Museum."

"I don't understand," Ellis said. "Who is this Ren? You mentioned the name before in Pol's office—why?"

"I get the impression this Ren is behind everything. The fake Pol and even the fake Geo-24 take their direction from Ren—no-number Ren—*Ren Zero*." Pax picked up one of the little white throw pillows from the couch and hugged it. "I've never met a zero or an original anything...well, except for you. And I've never heard of a Ren before, and this one is on the grass."

"But how do you know about Ren?"

"Fake Pol said it."

"No." Ellis shook his head. "Fake Pol never mentioned Ren. You were the first one to say that name."

"I must have heard it someplace else then."

"Where?"

Pax sighed. "Ellis Rogers, do you trust me?"

"Yes."

"Then can you just believe me when I tell you that I have it on good authority that someone named Ren is behind the murders and not question me further on how I know?"

Ellis didn't have to think. He trusted Pax. He trusted Pax more than he'd ever trusted anyone. Pax was the first person he'd known who—more than once—had proved themselves capable of thinking of Ellis first. His mother had always taken more than she gave, feeling that granting him life had been more than enough for her part. Peggy had given all her love to Isley, holding back nothing for him. Pax had asked for little, given much, and demonstrated a willingness to die for him—and they had just met. Still, he couldn't help feeling hurt at the discovery of a wall between them. Pax was keeping a secret.

"I suppose," Ellis replied. "But don't you trust *me*? I sort of thought we—I mean, I thought we were becoming close, you know? After all, you let me cut you open with a deer-gutting knife." He smiled.

Pax was looking at the pillow and breathing heavily. "Isn't there any secret you'd prefer not to share with me? At least not yet?"

The image of Isley hanging from the garage rafters flashed through his mind, and he nodded. "Fair enough."

"If it helps," Pax said gently, "I've never spoken to anyone of it before. But if I were ever to tell anyone, it would be you, Ellis Rogers. I don't think you would judge me like others might. So maybe one day you can tell me your secret, and I'll tell you mine."

Ellis nodded but didn't think he could ever tell Pax about Isley. There was simply no way Pax could begin to understand. "So, are we going to find this Ren?"

"I am," Pax said firmly, almost defiantly.

"What's that supposed to mean?"

"It means it's my responsibility. The point of being an arbitrator is to keep the peace. I can't let murderers continue killing."

"What about me?"

"You're the one they want. It would be pretty stupid to take you with me." Pax put down the pillow and stood up. "This is dangerous, Ellis Rogers. It's not your place. Are you an arbitrator?"

"I'm an engineer, but let me ask you this...do you have a gun?"

"Of course not." Pax glanced at his hip, that familiar expression of horror darting across Pax's face.

"Do you think anyone besides me has one?"

"No."

Ellis smiled. "Then in this society that practically makes me Superman."

"Superman?"

"A fictitious hero with supernatural powers—pretty much invincible."

"Pretty much?"

"Never mind. I'm too old and sick to be on the run."

Pax's eyes softened. "I don't want you to get hurt."

"Superman, remember?" He thumped his chest.

Pax didn't look pleased. Maybe the humor wasn't translating.

"Let's go together. Like it or not, we're a team now. Good cop, bad cop."

Pax nodded. "You're very strange, Ellis Rogers." Pax smiled and then added, "I like that. Let me contact Cha. Someone else ought to know about a conspiracy that's reached into the office of the Chief Councilor just in case we disappear into the grass."

"Are you sure you can trust Cha?"

Pax smiled. "I'm an arbitrator. Believe me...I'm a very good judge of people."

Entering Greenfield Village for the second time in a week, Ellis possessed an entirely new outlook. What he had seen as the forgotten remnants of humanity, he now viewed as a museum within a museum. The Henry Ford Museum used to house artifacts from America's first two hundred years, but as he and Pax walked through the quaint gravel lanes, Ellis understood that the site itself had become an artifact worth preserving. The garbage bins that dotted Main Street, complete with plastic bag liners, were no longer trash receptacles but roped-off antiques. So were the ticket booth, ATM, public phone, and restrooms with their archaic symbols for men and women. What was a preservation of the past became part of the exhibit as museums themselves became the history.

Around noon they ported to the front gate and walked the sidewalk-lined streets with drooping bluebell lamps and Civil War-era architecture. No one stopped or greeted them. No one was there at all.

"Volunteers help maintain the museum," Pax mentioned as they walked through empty streets. "And I've heard a few have actually begun living here full-time, history students, professors, and such, but this place was never all that popular."

"I imagine the murder won't help attendance."

"No—I doubt it would."

Ellis thought of Hollywood backlots—it was too well kept to be a ghost town. All the lawns were trimmed, the gravel smooth. Occasionally they would pass a buggy or a buckboard parked on the side of the road. After several days in Hollow World, being in Greenfield Village brought a flood of familiarity. Ellis fit among the curbs, pavement, shutters, and fences. He understood the windows and the sewers. A plastic garbage bag fluttered in the wind where it was held in place by a large rubber band—an old friend waving. Even the way his shoes slapped the pavement spoke of home, of cars, plastic bottles, and cellphones. Ellis was time traveling again, the sensation of tripping through eras becoming disorienting. He felt as if he'd woken up in the cozy comfort of his own epoch, the sights and sounds so much easier to accept than the idea of interdimensional doors spilling into the lithosphere where disembodied voices made convenience-store-quality coffee from gravel. After only a few minutes he might have begun to question whether any of it was true if not for the person walking beside him with cocked bowler, pin-striped pants, and silver vest.

Pax had explained that the coordinates supplied by fake-Pol's vox indicated the Firestone Farm in the northwest portion of the village. They both had felt it best to approach cautiously, so instead of using the Port-a-Call, they walked through the tree-shaded memory of the Industrial Age. He saw Pax focus on the old buildings, then glance at him with a curious look. Ellis could hear the unasked question, *How did people ever live like this?* He had felt the same way when watching the History Channel when it showed the ruins of Pompeii or ancient Egypt.

They walked past the Wright Brothers' cycle shop and Edison's Menlo Park complex. Cutting through Liberty Craftworks, they went by the glass and pottery shops, the gristmill, and the printing office before reaching Firestone Lane. At the end of the dirt road stood a two-story red-brick building with a green-shingled roof, a welcoming porch, two chimneys, and a perfect white picket fence. It was an honest house, a solid place of early virtues and Yankee determination. The mid-nineteenth century boyhood home of tire magnate Harvey Firestone had originally been in Ohio, but Ford had it moved to his village in Dearborn. Painstakingly restored to its 1885 likeness, the Firestone estate wasn't just a museum piece. It was a working farm and had been even when Ellis visited for his school trip well over two millennia prior. As they approached, they could see sheep, cows, and horses in the pastures that lined the road. They also saw people.

Ellis spotted five. One off to their right was tossing hay with a pitchfork into the horses' corral. Two more shooed cows from one pen to another, calling out "Mon boss! Mon boss!" A fourth opened the door to the house, focused on them, then retreated inside. The last sat on the porch at the end of the road. Creaking the boards beneath an old-fashioned rocker, the stocky man watched their approach. He was wearing an Amish-style straw hat and button shirt left open to the waist, revealing white chest hairs against deeply tanned skin. Black trousers were held up by suspenders. His bare feet thrust out toward them as he sipped on a glass of tea.

"Well, if it ain't Mr. Rogers. Wonderful day in the neighborhood to ya, old man."

Ellis stopped, staring in disbelief. The man's hair was long and white, and he had a chest-length beard that made him look a bit like a cynical Santa Claus. But there was no doubt—the man kicking back on the porch was his old friend, Warren Eckard. Despite the *I've-seen-the-face-of-God hair*, and a few more wrinkles around the eyes, Warren looked great. The layer of fat that he had built up after high school was gone. The luxury package of a pregnant stomach, love handles, and pale-skinned man breasts had been replaced with the sportier look of defined muscles and a Caribbean-fisherman's tan.

"Warren?" was all Ellis could say.

Pax halted beside Ellis, looking understandably confused.

"Didn't expect to see me again, did ya?" He laughed with a bemused smile. "Figured I'd be dust, right along with the rest of them, right? Almost, pal, almost. You're the surprise. I expected you years ago. You just arrived, didn't you?"

"Yeah."

Warren shook his head with the same disappointment he used to exhibit when seeing a woman past her prime wearing an outfit meant for a teenager. "Don't make no sense, does it? I've been here three years."

"Who are you?" Pax asked.

"Sorry," Ellis replied. "Pax, this is Warren Eckard, an old friend. We grew up together."

"Met in high school. You know what that is—Pax, is it?"

"An institution of education?"

"Close—it's a place where they kill dreams."

"Warren, how did you get here?"

"You, buddy—you and your time-machine notes. Remember Brady's? Ought to. It was only a few days ago for you, right? I kept your time-machine blueprints—stuffed them in the glove box of my Buick that night. When you went missing, the cops had dogs and forensic types all over your place. Peggy couldn't figure out if you had killed yourself or just took a powder. Your disappearance was a big deal. No one figured out what happened—no one but me. I knew it the minute I poked my head in your garage and saw all those cables and that poster—the old Mercury Seven. The one you had in your bedroom when we were in high school. I figured you either made it or died in the attempt, but either way you were gone and none of them was ever going to find you."

The door to the farmhouse opened again, and Ellis saw a face shadowed by the screen peeking out.

"Hey, Yal," Warren called over his shoulder. "Bring these nice folks some tea." Warren drew in his feet to grant them passage. "C'mon up, have a seat out of the sun. Gets hot this time of day."

Ellis slipped off his backpack, climbed the weathered steps, and pulled over a wicker-backed rocker, feeling as if he'd just entered into an old-school western. *Bring these nice folks some tea?* It was as if Warren had become Gary Cooper. Ellis didn't think Warren had ever tasted tea. For half a century he'd been a black-coffee-and-domestic-beer man, with the occasional shot of Jack or Jim when he could afford it.

"Careful." Warren pointed at Ellis's chair. "That one doesn't have a backstop on the runners. If you rock too far, you'll go ass over shoulders—I know—I've done it."

Pax moved in under the shade of the porch, but didn't sit. Instead, Pax stood rigidly to Ellis's right.

"Got something against sitting?" Warren asked.

"No," Pax replied.

"Nice getup." Warren gestured to Pax with his glass of tea. "You fit in perfect here. Well, not so much here as Main Street. That's where the hoity-toity class of folk with your sort of finery would have strolled with walking sticks and umbrellas. Out here on the farming frontier, we just let the rain fall on us."

Ellis expected some comment about loving the rain, but Pax remained oddly silent.

Yal stepped out, carrying two glasses of coppery tea with a pair of mint leaves in each.

"No ice," Warren apologized. "Lack of refrigeration is the biggest disappointment, but you get used to it. I tried cutting ice off the pond with an ax and packing it, but it don't last. Dex says we need volume. In the old days they had icehouses, big places packed in straw and sawdust. Takes a long time to melt that way."

"I still don't understand," Ellis said. "What are you doing here?"

Warren sipped his tea and rocked back in a casual rhythm as if this was normal—a typical Sunday afternoon with the neighbors. He pointed to his stomach, tapping it. "I got pancreatic cancer just like my old man—runs in the family. Seven years after you left, I started feeling sick and got the bad news. I figured if I followed you into the future there might be a cure."

Ellis failed a suppressed laugh.

"Glad the news of my impending death amuses you, old pal."

"It's not that. It's just that on the day I told you about the time machine, I left out that I had idiopathic pulmonary fibrosis."

"Idio what?"

"My lungs are shot. It's fatal and incurable except by a transplant, and I didn't want to take a pair of lungs that some kid could put to better use. I thought your dad had a heart attack, like mine."

Warren shook his head. "No. My dad lingered. Slow torture. He used to make train noises in the bedroom while we were having dinner. For years I thought he had gone nuts, you know? Later my mother told me he was in so much pain near the end that he needed to scream but didn't want to scare us kids. So my old man made these *choo-choos* and *woo-woos,* like he was three and playing with a Playskool set of wooden train cars. I wasn't going to wind up like that."

"Treatments have come a long way since your dad died."

"Yeah, they wanted me to do that chemo-shit. But that wasn't for me." He shook his head with a frown, his eyes looking down the length of Firestone Lane. "I wasn't going out that way. I figured going forward was worth a shot. Even if it ended up frying my ass, that was better than sucking a bullet out of the barrel of my .38, which I seriously considered.

"I still had your blueprints. Kept them out of sentimentality, I guess. I couldn't understand any of that crap, but I knew this fella—college kid, electrical engineer at Ford—who used to inspect the line. His uncle had been laid-off from NASA. I took the kid out for beers and got him laid. I became his best friend after that. He and his uncle helped. They thought I was loony, and were convinced it wouldn't work. But as long as I paid for the gear, and the beer, they humored me. 'You can't create a contained gravity well using milk crates, batteries, and an iPad,' they had said. Course, I knew better...because you'd already done it."

Warren focused on the two moving the cattle. He stood up. "Goddammit, Hig! Just kick her in the ass! Where the hell is that stick I gave you?"

"I...ah..." Hig, who was wearing a wide-brimmed black hat, looked lost.

"You need to teach Dolly who's boss." Warren shook his head. "All these bald bastards ain't got no gumption."

"*Gumption?* Since when did you become a regular on *Hee Haw*?"

"Comes with the territory, my friend."

Warren resumed his seat, and Ellis marveled. Four days earlier, Warren couldn't belly-up to the bar and rest his elbows at the same time. As he sat back down, Ellis could once again see the old fullback.

"So how was it you arrived ahead of me if you left seven years later?"

"Not a clue," Warren replied. "Flunked science, remember?"

"What have you been doing?"

Warren grinned, first at Ellis, then at Pax. "Working my ass off, is what. You can tell, can't you?"

"Yeah—you look good for Santa Claus."

"Funny guy." He hooked a thumb at Ellis while looking at Pax. "Been a laugh a minute, hasn't he?"

Again Pax didn't reply, but only stood holding the tall glass of untasted tea.

"I popped in up north in the woods. I'm guessing you did too. Only you were probably smart enough to follow the river, right? I didn't. I just thought the world was fucked, you know? Everything gone. So I dug in, built a lean-to and eventually a cabin."

"You built a cabin?"

"We ain't talking the kind on the maple syrup bottle. The place was a hovel, mostly made of fallen trees, thick branches, and shit, with a sod roof that leaked. Bugs everywhere too. That first winter was hell, but it kept me alive."

"How'd you eat?"

"I brought my Browning Lightweight Stalker with the scope. It's just like hunting up north, except the forests around here are packed with game. I'd kill one deer and be set with food for a week. Wasted a lot until I discovered how to cure it. Puked on bad meat a few times, working out the kinks. And this"—he slapped his stomach where his belly used to be—"is what a nearly all-protein diet and constant exercise does for you. Shows you what clean living can do for a man, eh?"

"So how'd you end up here? You eventually find the river?"

"Nope. I never had reason to go south. Most of the best hunting was north of my cabin. Wasn't until the baldies found me that I realized I wasn't the last person on the planet. They stumbled on my cabin like yuppie tourists discovering a UFO. Freaked them the hell out when they saw me. Granted, I looked like a bear—not much need to shave—but they were the ones buck naked. Little Ken dolls—all of them."

Ellis smiled.

"You thought so too, didn't you?"

He nodded.

"They were skittish as hell. Anywho...they stared for a long time, kinda like your friend here." He winked at Pax, who was watching every move Warren made. "Eventually I asked what they were staring at, and they freaked again. Guess they didn't think I could speak or something. We started talking then, and the more I learned the more I was sickened to discover what became of mankind. No more women—you know about that?"

Ellis nodded.

"Everyone masturbates now. Everyone lives underground in one big video game or something. I started setting a few of them straight, telling them how it used to be, how people were supposed to live—like I was doing in my cabin. I talked about taking responsibility for themselves and not relying on others for anything. Talked about individualism, and it turns out these folks are starved for it. That's why they get these weird tattoos and dress up. They're all identical, so they have to do something to tell each other apart. So I straightened them out, you know? They saw me as this mystic wise man, like that guru the Beatles hung with."

"Did they believe you about traveling through time?"

"Never told them about that. They were already spooked. Thought I was a Darwin—which I guess is like a Bigfoot to us. They asked if they could come and visit again. I said sure, but only if they didn't tell anyone else. I didn't want a bunch of these hairless clones turning me into a sideshow attraction. They kept their word, 'cause only the same ones ever returned. They'd ask to invite a couple of others, and I said that was okay. I kinda liked the company, you know. Nice having people listen when I talked about society's problems and the right way to fix them, not to mention finally getting some respect, you know? Some really became convinced I was right, and they decided to move to the purity of rustic life. Soon I had a compound of five cabins. Then Dex had the bright idea of moving down here. They had a fucking farm—a whole town—no one told me. Dex arranged for us to be the caretakers at Firestone. I guess there's always been people that took turns living here and keeping the place up—mostly college types doing some kind of research or community service or just back-to-earth nuts. We've been here about a year and keep to ourselves."

"You've only been out here then? Didn't you ever go to Hollow World?"

Warren made a melodramatic shudder. "No interest in that. They tell me about it. Popping through portals, device orgies, designer pets, fake sun, everybody always naked and not a pair of tits to be seen. They can keep that crap." He spread out his arms. "I have all this to myself. A whole world of God's beauty."

Right then Pax dropped the glass of tea. It shattered in a burst of bronze liquid.

They both looked at Pax, who remained focused on Warren. "You ordered the murder of Pol-789."

"I what?" Warren started to laugh, but stopped and stared, puzzled. "What did you say?"

"You're Ren. You ordered the killing and replacement of Pol. You wanted a spy on the inside."

"I hope there's a joke in there somewhere," Warren said. "Not neighborly for a guest to come on a body's porch and accuse them of murder."

"You're the one hunting us—the one that sent the search party—you wanted Ellis Rogers to be brought to you."

Warren nodded. "Asked is more like it. Once I discovered there was a Hollow World, I asked about Ellis. And I told everyone that if they ever found another guy like me—going by the name of Ellis—to have him visit. Isn't that how you got here? How else did you know how to find me?"

"You're a liar as well as a murderer," Pax declared.

Warren's face darkened as he stood up.

"Excuse us a second, Warren." Ellis took hold of Pax's arm and pulled. They climbed down the porch, moving away. "What's wrong with you?"

"Ren is a murderer. He killed Pol-789 and very likely Geo-24. Maybe others."

"That's ridiculous. I witnessed the murder. I saw who killed Geo-24, remember? And that person is dead now. Why would you think Warren had anything to do with that?"

Pax hesitated. "I can't—I can't tell you."

Ellis's brows rose. "You're accusing a friend of mine of murder, but you can't tell me why?"

"I'm sorry. You just have to trust me."

Ellis sighed. He looked around at the few others working the farm, then back at Pax. Whatever threat they expected hadn't materialized. He'd anticipated—he didn't know what, actually—maybe a modern mafia or perhaps shadowy troglodytes. Instead, they had found Warren, his oldest friend, pretending to be Pa from *Little House on the Prairie*. For the first time, Ellis questioned if there had ever been a threat. After they caught the killer of Geo-24, everything had been fine until Pax became convinced Pol was an impostor. And why was that? There had never been any evidence of danger.

"Why did you think Pol was an impostor?"

"I...I just did."

"Pax—I need a little more than that."

"I know. I just can't give it to you." A miserable frown formed on Pax's lips.

"Why not?"

"Because—because you won't believe me, and if you do...you could hate me. I don't want you to hate me."

"What in the world could make me—"

"I can't tell you!" Pax shouted.

"Okay, okay." Ellis held up his hands. Then a thought crossed his mind. "Why do you live with Vin?"

"What?" Pax asked incredulously.

"When I first arrived, Alva insisted you were not crazy. Why would she say that?"

Pax took a step back and could no longer look him in the face. "Alva said that?"

"One of the first things I was told. Why would Alva feel it necessary to assure me you weren't crazy?"

Pax looked at the ground, at the gravel beneath their feet, crushed stone and dirt. "I've had some trouble."

"Trouble? What kind of trouble?"

"I don't want to talk about it."

"Is Vin there to watch you? That's why you need permission to invite guests into your own home, isn't it?"

Pax took a deep shuddering breath while still studying the fine surface of Firestone Lane. "Vin has been very kind to me."

"Why is Vin there, Pax? What's wrong with you?"

"You just have to trust me. Ren is a killer."

"Do you think he's going to kill me?"

"I don't know. I don't know what he's planning, but he's planning something, and it's not good." Pax looked up, eyes pleading. "We should leave. Warn Hollow World."

"Warn them of what?"

"I don't know!" Pax screamed, fists tight. A pair of nearby birds took flight at the outburst.

Ellis reached out and Pax folded into his arms. Pax was shaking. "I'm so scared. I don't know what to do."

"Do you trust me?" Ellis asked.

He felt Pax nod against his chest. "Yes."

"Then this is what I think you need to do. You said it was Warren who was after us. Who wanted me to come here. That means no one is chasing us now. So I think you should go home."

"What? No, I—"

"I'll stay and talk to Warren and find out what's going on—if anything."

"You can't." Pax pulled back.

"You've had a stressful couple of days. You were almost killed, then suffered a brutal operation, and topped it off with a can of Dinty Moore stew. Anyone would be upset."

"I'm not leaving you. You don't even have a portal."

"You can come back tomorrow, okay?"

"I can't leave you alone with a killer!"

"Look, I've known Warren since I was fifteen! He's not a killer."

"He is, and he's lying."

"You need to trust me this time. Warren's not going to hurt me." He put his hand on Pax's shoulder. "You go home. Take a nice waterfall shower. Have Cha look at that shoulder. Eat a solid meal, and have a good night's sleep. Tomorrow at this time, port back here. By then I'll know a lot more and we can discuss what to do next, okay?"

"Why can't we both go home, do all that stuff, and then both come back?"

"Because I need to talk to Warren, and...some of what I have to say is private."

Pax stared. Ellis could see tears brewing. "I'm scared."

"I'll be all right."

"I'm scared for both of us."

"Go home and rest. Maybe talk to Vin."

A tear slipped. "Be very careful."

"I will."

Pax reached up for the Port-a-Call. "Alva's right."

"What do you mean?"

"I'm not crazy."

All in Good Time

"Your friend seems a little upset," Warren said as Ellis sat back on the rocker beside him.

Pax was gone. Ellis had seen the familiar Gothic dining room through the portal and felt a desire to go along. Pax's place was already more of a home to him than anywhere he'd known since his childhood, but he did feel better now that Pax wasn't here. He could speak more freely, and he had some issues to address with his old friend.

"Pax has been under some stress—been investigating some murders."

"Didn't think they had those in Hollow World. The hairless been telling me they got rid of murder, death, warfare—both the regular kind and class—death, racism, sexism, poverty, all that shit."

"Well, someone made an exception."

"So what's the bug up his butt?"

"His?"

Warren smirked. "His, her, its—whatever. Didn't seem like stress.

Acted sorta jealous of me. You two trying out some new-age sex toys? I hear they have this thing called a—"

"It's not like that," Ellis said, louder than he'd planned.

"Good. I thought maybe you were going native, walking on the other side of the road, so to speak."

"I said it's not like that."

"Just saying, it seemed that way. And you never know. You hear about guys that go to prison and figure they got no choice, you know?"

"Like I said, Pax has just been under a lot of stress. We've been through a lot these last few days."

"Yeah, well, we all have our crosses to bear. But damn, it's good to see you. I've been wondering if you'd ever show up. Thought you might have gotten something wrong and fried your ass."

The day was winding down. The lazy light of late afternoon reminded Ellis of after-school time, even to that day. Warren was right; it was hot out. He could see the heat waves rising, making the fields blurry, and hear the cicadas whining as loudly as the traffic used to be on old Michigan Avenue. Ellis, who still hadn't seen a calendar, reasserted his belief that it was mid- to late summer. He could smell the grass and the scent of manure coming from the barn, and hear a horse snorting. There was corn in one of the fields, and it had to be elephant-eye high.

"Like your piece," Warren said.

"My what?"

"Your gun." Warren pointed at the holster. Ellis had almost forgotten it was there. It appeared invisible to everyone else. "Lemme see it."

He only had a fraction of hesitation before pulling it out and handing it over. After all, this was Warren.

The two had met in the tenth grade—when Warren had also been known by just *Ren,* because two syllables were one too many for high schoolers to deal with, and in 1971 *War* was as unpopular as Nixon. They had shared a locker that Warren kept crammed with excess football gear that he had refused to leave in the gym. Old number forty-eight—the jersey was always there. In those three years, Ellis didn't think his friend had ever washed the thing, and he'd had to hold his breath whenever he went for his books. Ellis didn't care for the moose he had been forced to share space with until Ricky "the Dick" Downs targeted him.

Ellis was struggling to get his physics book past the set of shoulder pads when Ricky showed up and thought it might be fun to bounce him like a basketball. Ellis got in one good punch, but back then he'd only weighed one twenty, and the feeble blow just made Ricky mad. The Dick howled and punched Ellis in the stomach. Blowing his wind out wasn't going to be enough to sate Ricky after having been hit. That boy had a mean streak. While he liked to pretend he got his nickname from the size of his prick, everyone knew Ricky the Dick was the sort to kick dogs for laughs.

"Now I'm gonna learn ya why fighting back is a bad idea." The Dick had told him. "There's a pecking order to the world, and God put you at the bottom."

Ellis expected he'd be waking up in an ambulance, but that's when Warren showed up. Like a game of *Stratego*, where a sergeant took a scout but a marshal took everything, the scenario played out; Ellis was the geek; Ricky was a basketball player with big sweaty hands, jabbing elbows, and a love of intimidation, but Warren was an offensive fullback on the football team. The "Eckard Express" they had called him on the field, and Ellis caught just a glimpse of Ricky in his Led Zeppelin T-shirt flying across the hall. He had left a dent in locker 243 before collapsing to the tile with a grunt followed by tears.

The principal had wanted to suspend Warren and Ricky both. He wasn't interested in the excuses of two thugs, but Ellis was a straight-A student with no record of trouble. When he spoke on Warren's behalf, Ricky the Dick received suspension for a month, and Warren only got a talking-to.

After that, Warren and he became best friends, his only friend for forty-three years. Ellis never was good at making new ones, and those he found had bigger dreams than Detroit could support. Warren, on the other hand, was steadfast, and the two settled together like sediment at the bottom of a lake. They were like Vietnam vets who could only fully relate to other combat vets—Warren understood him.

"Browning, right? Nice little weapon." He turned the pistol side-to-side and peered one-eyed along the barrel, aiming down the length of Firestone Lane. "Funny, isn't it? I told you I didn't want to see the future, that I'd rather go to the past, but I wasn't thinking back far enough. The Old West—that, my friend, was the *real* sweet spot. When every man had a pistol on his hip, and every crime ended in a hanging. You just went out, built a house, and lived your life, and if anyone tried to stop you. *Bam!* What happens in Tombstone...stays in Tombstone. Now here we are in the future but toting guns, living on a farm, and all on a planet with few people and no rules—except those we make."

Ellis could hear Pax's voice in his head, screaming, *You gave him your gun! The man is a murderer!*

He watched Warren play with the pistol, his two missing fingers making it more of a challenge to hold properly.

Two missing fingers. Same hand, same fingers; *coincidence* didn't cover that adequately. There had to be a connection, but this was Warren Eckard in front of him. He'd known the man all his life. He grew up with him, had his first beer with him. They saw the first *Star Wars* movie at the Americana Theater together. Warren was like his brother—a close, protective older brother who'd always watched out for Ellis.

Only...he was different too.

Not just the white hair and beard or the weight loss—there was something in the way he talked. Warren had never been a happy man. He'd spent his entire adult life complaining about how he had gotten screwed. First there had been his mother and teachers who insisted he do better in school, forcing him to quit the football team when his grades had failed to meet expectations, and ruining what he *knew* was a promising career. Later it had been his bosses, his wives—who had become ex-wives—who never understood his worth. Then there was the government, incompetent and corrupt that destroyed everything. He'd spent years preaching from the pulpit of a bar stool. Many people heard; no one listened. Not even Ellis. He found it hard to heed a voice that dripped of so much self-pity, but all that was gone now. The unfocused grumblings were replaced with a strange optimism that made Ellis wonder if he really knew his old friend anymore.

But it's still Warren, isn't it?

Ellis watched him holding the gun and had to repress a desire to ask for it back.

"I was right too. This is the life." Warren looked over with a sage expression that was another new part of his attire. "It's hard. Don't get me wrong. I thought I might die that first winter. Actually ate bugs. Nearly died trying out different berries, until I could tell the good from the bad. That's the trick of it, learning the good from the bad. Knowing which things you can trust to help keep you alive and those that will sicken and kill you. But My Lord, Ellis, that spring—it was like what all those Bible thumpers used to talk about—a come-to-meeting with God. I felt born again. I crawled out of that grave of dirt and sticks into a new life, a new dawn for old Warren Eckard."

Warren checked the pistol's magazine, slapped it back in, slipped off the safety, and cocked it.

Ellis felt his heart quicken.

"I realized there was nothing holding me back anymore. I was free. I could do anything I wanted. No one around to stop me anymore. No laws at all, you know?" He gave Ellis a wicked old-man grin and a wink that shortened Ellis's breath.

What kind of laws we talking here, Warren?

"If I fucked up, it'd be my own fault. I didn't think anyone else existed, so I felt like Adam. Just me and God walking in Eden, before that bitch, Eve, showed up and ruined everything." He chuckled and looked at Ellis. "Why you so quiet?"

"Can I have my gun back?"

He laughed. "Am I making you nervous?"

"Well, you don't have a good track record after taking the safety guard off mechanical devices. Just concerned you might make a matched set of missing digits by shooting yourself in the foot."

Warren offered the sort of smile that Ellis couldn't read: amused, polite, condescending? Then he slipped the safety back on, lowered the hammer, and handed the pistol back before taking another sip of his tea.

"I'm actually surprised you're enjoying this so much." Ellis felt his heart coast as he checked the pistol, assuring himself that the safety was indeed on. "No beer, no ice, no football, no women. Not like you."

"I was a man of no account in a world of wealth. Now I'm a king in a land of absence. Everything is before me. You see, it's like I was a leftover part in a completed picture, but now the world is a blank canvas."

"When did you become a philosopher? Four days ago the most eloquent thing coming out of your mouth was the jingle of a beer commercial."

"That's part of it. No TV, no radio, no Internet, and precious few books—with no diversions, a man thinks...a lot. I've done a lot of soul-searching, and I realized that I was a poor man, who also didn't have any money," he said with an amused look, watching to see if Ellis caught the twist of words.

He gave a slight smile.

Warren returned it with a wink. "The world has been erased. We can build whatever we want. We can be the founding fathers of a new civilization. Do it right this time."

"There's already a civilization. Millions of people might disagree with your vision of the future. From what I've heard, they consider the surface kinda sacred."

"You've spent time with them. You know what they're like. A bunch of children. They won't fight. We're like that Spanish guy that landed in Mexico..."

"Cortés?"

"Yeah—him. He whipped the whole country of Mexico with just a handful of men."

"He defeated the Aztec Empire with five hundred men, advanced technology, and smallpox."

"Yeah, whatever. We're like him. We're the only two *real* men left in the world. The rest are—I don't know, really, but they synthesized aggression out of them. They remind me of my second wife. They'll scream and pout, but the worst they'll ever do is call you names and occasionally throw something. We could rule this world with nothing more than our fists and a hunting knife, and yet we both have guns. That practically makes us gods."

Or devils.

He smirked at the look on Ellis's face. "Relax. I'm not applying to be the next Hitler, just saying the baldies are content living underground, so there's no reason we can't make a town for ourselves right here. Why should they care?"

"They might."

Warren seemed to ponder this, sipping his tea thoughtfully. Inside, there was a banging of pots and pans and the clap of a cupboard.

Ellis looked down at his gun. Funny that he hadn't put it away. He always had in the past. He set the pistol in his lap, slid his backpack between his feet, and pulled out his coat.

"You cold?" Warren asked.

"No." The single word sounded ominous, but maybe only to Ellis, because he alone knew what was coming next.

Ellis pulled the letters out of his coat pocket, where they'd been since 2014. He had considered not mentioning them. What good could come from bringing them up now? Peggy was dead, that whole world gone. For Ellis, however, the hurt was only a few days old, and there was no going forward until he dealt with that wound. His mother had taught him the best way to avoid infection was to pour a solid dose of hydrogen peroxide on deep cuts. It would hurt like hell, but it had to be done before any kind of bandage could be put on—before any healing could take place.

Ellis didn't say a word. He just handed over the letters. Warren looked at them, puzzled, shuffling through the small stack. "Oh," he finally said, understanding filling his eyes. "Damn, these are really old. Peggy kept these, huh?"

Ellis only glared.

"What?" Warren asked. Not a trace of guilt, not a hint of remorse.

"You were fucking my wife."

"Yeah, I was."

"Right after my son died, you were screwing Peggy."

Warren was nodding like one of those stupid bobbleheads on a car dashboard.

"Have you got anything to say?"

Warren shrugged. "What do you want me to say, Ellis? That was over two thousand years ago."

"Not for me. I just found out."

Warren nodded with a *fair-enough* expression. "So, you want me to say I'm sorry. Is that it?" Warren looked over at the pistol, still in Ellis's lap. "Or are you planning on killing me?"

Is this how these things happen? The subconscious just takes control? Is that the real reason he sent Pax away? Was he ashamed of what he might do? Pax thought so well of him; he didn't want to ruin that. Wasn't it always the same thing in the aftermath of a shooting?

He was a peaceful man, Officer. Never had a bad word to say about anyone. Don't know how he could have done it. It just wasn't like him.

He looked back at Warren. "I don't want you to say you're sorry—I want you to actually *be* sorry."

"Okay."

Okay?

"Goddammit, Warren! You were my friend. My only *real* friend. You had all kinds of women. I had one."

But you weren't doing anything with her no more, were you, buddy? You and Peggy hadn't shared so much as a real kiss in months. And I was getting fat and not the looker I once was. So we did it. I had her in your bed on that nice lavender comforter. Used to sneak up there three times a week to rock that headboard against the wall. Glad you didn't come home from work early. As they say, if the bed's a-rockin', don't come up the stairs. Peggy even kept her high heels on.

Ellis realized his finger was inside the trigger guard of the gun.

"You really want the truth?" Warren's eyes glanced at the gun in Ellis's lap. "She was mad at you. Hated you. Blamed you for Isley's death—but you already know that." Warren rubbed his thumb thoughtfully along the side of his near-empty glass. "I was with her that day. I had stopped by to borrow your ladder just as she was coming home. We went to the garage, and we found Isley together. She screamed, and I held her while she cried.

"Then a month or two later, when she started writing me letters, I figured it was because we shared this moment, you know? But I think she was just trying to hurt you. It wasn't like she wanted me. She wanted to get back at you. I didn't know that beforehand. It was only the one time—but you already know that from the letters." Warren handed them back to Ellis.

"We were in the back of her car parked in the corner of a Denny's parking lot where we went after the bar had closed. Both of us were drunk. Wasn't my finest hour by a long shot. I guess I thought I was helping her—and I was, just not the way I thought. I figured I was lending comfort to a woman cut off from her husband. Instead, I was providing her with the means to punish you. Course it didn't turn out that way, because you never found out—until now. Like one of those World War II mines that blows off a kid's foot fifty years later. She could have told you—don't know why she didn't. She'd also said she was going to get a divorce. Didn't do that either. If you want to know what I think, I honestly believe that even though she wanted to, she just couldn't stop loving you."

Warren swallowed the last of his tea—Ellis just swallowed.

"Her revenge backfired in the end. After you did your vanishing act, Peggy became convinced you killed yourself because of those letters. I tried to tell her about the time machine, but you can imagine her reaction. When I insisted that's what happened, she stopped taking my calls. Never got any response to my emails. She moved to Florida about a year later—but I doubt it was just to get away from me. Never remarried."

Ellis's gaze had drifted away from Warren to the fields, but snapped back at the sound of those last two words.

"How'd she die?"

Warren raised an eyebrow. "How should I know?"

"You said she never remarried. If she was still alive when you left, you would have said you don't know if she ever remarried."

"Mr. M.I.T."

"So how did she die?"

Warren sighed. "Car accident."

"Anyone else hurt?"

"She was alone. Hit a cement freeway viaduct."

Ellis narrowed his eyes. "Bad weather?"

"Drunk, I was told." Warren held his stare for half a minute. "At the funeral, her sister, what's-her-name—the one in Omaha—Sandy! Sandy mentioned Peggy had begun drinking after you left. They tried to get her help. Tried to get her to AA or something.

Didn't work, I guess." Warren watched him a second. He must have looked upset, because Warren felt it was necessary to add, "She, ah—she finally forgave you—for Isley and such."

"How would you know?"

"That photo, the one she took of you and Isley at Cedar Point—the one she folded you out of? Sandy said she found it among her things. The fold was bent back, and Peggy had written the words *I'm sorry* across it with a black Sharpie."

Ellis began to sob.

The kitchen of the Firestone Farm smelled wonderful. Moist air, born of baking bread, bubbling pots on a cast-iron stove, and meat cooking in the oven made Ellis think of childhood Thanksgivings, Christmases, and Easters. Shadowy figures worked in the streams of light entering the windows and screen door. That, too, reminded Ellis of holidays—of years ago when he was very young, and they used to visit his grandmother. Her house was old enough to have a coal chute, and in the basement she had an icebox and a concrete basin with an angled side where a washboard would attach. His grandmother's place had been wired for electricity but wasn't native to it, and many of the rooms were left dark.

The Firestone Farm lacked sound as well as light. The silence was surprising and far more noticeable than Ellis would have expected. For nearly sixty years he'd known the sounds of the inside: air-conditioning fans, the rattle and hum of refrigerators, the buzz of fluorescents, the squawk of television, and the music of radios and stereos. The farm had only the scuffle of bare feet, and the slow tick of a wall clock, which dominated the audio landscape as a metronome setting the room's tempo. Unlike the coziness of smells and light, the lack of sound was disturbing—the dead atmosphere of a power outage.

They had all paused when he entered, turning while holding clay pots of steaming vegetables. They stared with the same looks Ellis had seen on the students at the crime scene. Maybe they had heard him crying. He'd sobbed for some time while Warren politely took his pistol for a walk to the barn, granting him some privacy. By the time he had returned, Ellis had stopped crying and was feeling empty and achy, as if he'd thrown up. They sat for a long while in silence before someone called them in for dinner.

"Quit your gawking, and get the food on the table," Warren snapped, coming in behind Ellis. "Have to excuse them. To the baldies, we're like Marilyn Monroe, a unicorn, or maybe even Jesus. Been two years, and I still catch them looking up my skirt. Isn't that right, Yal?"

Yal was the one with the apron. Despite each of them wearing the same Amish-style black pants and white button shirt, Ellis could tell them apart because each had their names stitched on their right breasts like old-fashioned gas station attendants. Yal had been the one peeking out the door, who now turned away sheepishly to resume stirring a big blackened kettle.

"Have a seat," Warren said, dragging a chair. Then he walked to the butcher's block and began sharpening a big knife on a strap that hung from the wall. "I slaughtered the fatted lamb for you." He grinned. "Except that *ole cotton ball* was ancient, and I butchered her early this morning before I even knew you were coming—but hey, let's not squabble with details, right?"

The table was already set with several homemade bowls filled with thick-cut carrots, potatoes, sausage and sauerkraut, and a basket of big fresh rolls. On a plate was a clump of butter, and it took Ellis a moment to recognize it, not having seen butter that didn't come in a plastic tub or wax wrap. The fist-size glob had finger prints.

"You're in for a treat, Ellis," Warren declared. He covered his hand in a towel and threw open the oven's door. "This is how a man was meant to eat. Everything's fresh from the garden, the barn, or the woods." He hauled out a big pan, holding what looked like a quarter of a lamb, the flesh golden brown. As he set the roast at the head of the table, the others took their seats. Besides himself and Warren, there were five—each with Pax's face but not quite—too somber, too blank.

When they were all seated, Warren folded his hands, and the others imitated him.

"Dear Lord, thank you for this food, and for not frying Ellis's ass like we'd thought you'd done," Warren said briskly, followed by, "Amen."

"Amen," the others replied in chorus.

In all the meals Ellis had eaten with Warren, his friend had never said grace before. To his knowledge, while the man had always proudly declared himself a Christian, he'd never been to church—not even on Christmas. Thinking about it, Ellis wasn't sure what denomination Warren was, and he wondered if even Warren knew.

"May I get you more tea?" one of the others asked from across the table.

"We also have milk and wine," another said with eager-to-please eyes.

They all stared in anticipation of his next word.

Ellis didn't care. "Ah—tea's fine."

The one who suggested it failed to suppress a smile and jumped up as if having received a great honor.

Standing at the head of the table, carving the meat, Warren smirked and shook his head. The scene reminded Ellis of a Norman Rockwell painting, if the artist had grown up in a community of identical Mennonite gas-station attendants.

"I didn't think religion existed anymore," Ellis said as Yal passed a bowl of carrots into his hands.

"One of the things I'm working at fixing," Warren said. "Never thought I'd be a missionary called to spread the word of God among heathens. I guess that comes with that whole being-born-again experience. Got Dex to dig me up a copy of the Bible, and I have them all reading it. Oh—right. Guess I should introduce you." Warren pointed with the carving knife that was dripping grease. "Dex, Hig, Ved One and Ved Two, and Yal. Dex is our resident surgeon and my third in command. He popped a new heart in my chest not long after we first met. Took care of the cancer and inoculated me against the new viruses too."

"I was a member of the ISP team before coming here," the one with the DEX stencil said.

"Was part of the problem, now part of the solution." Warren slid out mutton chops to a parade of plates. "Hig was a tree hugger or something."

"A bio-doc," Hig said. "I was a member of HEM."

"That's the tree-hugger movement," Warren added.

"The Hollow Earth Movement," Hig said softly, passing Ellis the potatoes.

"Whatever. Hig is now our best fieldhand—great with the crops and the animals. Ved One plays a fiddle."

"I was a composer of holo symphonies," Ved One said. "But yes, I also play a violin."

"Ved Two—no relation." Warren laughed. No one else did, but Warren didn't appear to notice. "Was a tattoo artist."

"I interpreted internal personal expressions into outward identities."

"And last there's Yal—our newest convert. Yal is our cook. So if you don't like the food, blame Yal."

Ellis looked at Yal and waited, but no correction or clarification was forthcoming. Yal sat at the foot of the table struggling to eat left-handed and not doing a good job. Yal's other hand remained hidden under the table. Ellis noticed for the first time that the order of food passing was consistent. Warren dished out the meat to Ellis first, then to Dex, then Hig, the two Veds, and finally to Yal.

The meal had all the wholesome purity that an unevenly heated stove could provide. The gravy had lumps, the bottoms of the rolls were burned, and the potatoes undercooked. The carrots were tasty, the sheep tough but savory, and the sausage and sauerkraut was wonderful, and Ellis didn't think he liked sauerkraut. Imperfection bore its own virtue. Just as a concert album littered with technical errors was filled with more life than a perfectly tweaked studio production, the meal possessed more simple honesty than Ellis had experienced in years. This was what all those characters in movies had spoken of when they yearned for a home-cooked meal, back before the McDonald's revolution, before the quintessential American meal came in a box.

"Had four new lambs arrive this year," Warren was saying. "Funny as hell to watch Hig and the Veds experience the miracle of birth."

"Doesn't seem natural," Ved One said. "More like a sickness."

"See what I have to deal with?" Warren sighed. "Oh—and a great job burning the rolls, Yal."

"I'm sorry. I've only worked with a Maker. I'm not used to a stove."

"We don't want excuses here. Get your shit together. It's a stove, not a rocket ship, and your days of relying on a Maker are over."

"I will do better next time, Ren Zero."

"The name is Ren!" Warren raised his voice. "Just plain Ren. We aren't numbers here—we're people, dammit."

Several shifted their eyes to the Veds.

Warren looked annoyed. "I've been meaning to change your names, might as well start now so poor Ellis doesn't get confused. From now on Ved One will be called...Bob, and Ved Two..." Warren twisted his lips, thinking. "Ved Two will be Rob." He nodded, agreeing with himself. "Restitch your shirts right after dinner, understand?"

The two nodded in perfect unison, which appeared to irritate Warren.

Conversation dried up for a few minutes, the vacuum filled by the ticking of the clock and forks scraping plates clean. Warren glared around the table while the others stared at their food.

"Just the six of you maintain this whole farm?" Ellis asked. He didn't really care, just wanted the silence to disappear. He needed noise, the flow of words to knock out the thoughts crowding their way into his head, thoughts about Peggy and a photograph with the word *sorry* written on it. Warren said it was written in a Sharpie marker, but Ellis imagined it was scrawled in blood. He should have left a note. He should have said goodbye.

"Just the six of us live here," Warren said. "We add new converts by *invitation only*, of course."

"Mib will be moving in soon," Hig said. Ellis noticed that this Firestone fieldhand had a slightly darker tan than anyone else at the table except Warren.

"Which is good, because we could use someone who can run the glass shop," Warren said.

Dex pointed at Yal. "We've lost several glasses lately."

"Yes, it will be wonderful when Mib arrives." Yal stood up then, and with a restrained look began to clear the table of empty bowls.

"Yal's tired of being the new kid," Bob said—or was it Rob?

"Six live here?" Ellis asked.

"Technically there are seven, but Pol doesn't live here anymore. Used to, but got picked for the underworld High Council. I gave him permission to serve. Thought it would be in everyone's best interest to have a"—he formed air quotes with his fingers—"*man* on the inside, as it were. Pol was one of the original three who found me. You'll meet Pol tonight. Great organizer. If I died tomorrow, Pol would take over."

"Take over what?"

Warren just grinned.

Yal came by and picked up the bowl of potatoes, and Ellis noticed the bloody bandages on the stumps of the last two fingers on Yal's right hand.

~

As night arrived, Warren lit the hurricane lamp near the door and escorted them into the living room, leaving Yal to handle the cleanup. "It takes a long time to break them of the bad habits they pick up living in the underworld. They think everything is easy. They get here and find they're wrong," Warren explained with his new wise man's voice—the Detroit Dalai Lama.

The living room's décor was right out of the Civil War, with a couch and two matching black upholstered Queen Anne chairs that looked like something Lincoln might have been shot in. Pea-green-painted walls and dark mahogany only added to the formal funereal atmosphere. Everything had the smell of old books, old wood, and old people that might have been some form of rot. The place was hot too. The sun had baked the house, and the heat lingered in the wood, stone, and plaster. Dex and Hig shoved the windows open, hoping for a breeze, but got only the loud racket of crickets. This had been the life of pre-air-conditioned homes and why so many houses had porches.

Ellis, who felt his shirt sticking to him, was about to suggest moving to the porch when Warren took a seat in the big chair near the dormant fireplace. He put his bare feet up on a stool and said, "Don't you love this room? I can't walk in here and not think of Washington and Jefferson and all the others that created our great country."

"I don't think the United States exists anymore."

Warren's eyes lit up. "That's just it—it does. This room—this farm is like one of those seed banks they created to allow us to rebuild the world after a global disaster. This village is the seed—the cutting—that will help us regrow America. We've got everything: a producing farm, blacksmith, glass, and pottery shops. Hell, we even have Edison's lab here. This is the heart and soul of America."

Hig sat on the couch. Ellis sat beside him.

"As we repopulate, we can expand outward from here. We can clear the land, build more farms, and then send some men to start looking for old mines. Maybe we can get a refinery working again."

"Hard to repopulate without women."

"Dex has that covered, right, Dex?"

"The ISP kept all the patterns going back to the first ones. They won't be exactly originals, *not like the two of you*," Dex said with reverence, as if speaking to twin popes. "They were altered for disease resistance, and aesthetic appearance, but natural selection should erode these initial genes back to a random state."

"Still, a pretty small gene pool, right?" Ellis said. His mind filled with thoughts of royal families and jokes about rural West Virginia.

"Hey, the whole world started with just Adam and Eve, and we did fine with that," Warren said. "So the plan is for Dex to grow us a little harem of women. We'll be like two old pride lions, like the biblical patriarchs of old begetting a whole new nation of Americans. Go forth and multiply, you know? Think about that. We'll literally be the founding fathers of the new United States."

"And what if these women don't have any interest in being human incubators? You ever consider that?"

"Outdated thinking, my friend. That's the product of a feminist movement that doesn't exist anymore. We'll teach them it's a sacred duty and great honor. They'll be thrilled to contribute in such a vital way."

"Even so, you're in your sixties now, right? By the time these women are of age, you'll be in your eighties."

"Not a problem. Dex says he can extend my life for another hundred years at least."

"Yeah, well, maybe you...you got your new heart and clean pancreas. I don't think I'm gonna be around much longer."

"Jesus, didn't they fix you already?" Warren asked.

Ellis felt the crackle in his chest—wind across a field of steel wool. "No."

Warren turned to Dex and hooked a thumb at Ellis. "Needs a new set of lungs."

Dex nodded. "Absolutely. Not a problem."

Are all major surgeries dispensed out of vending machines now? Ellis was thinking to ask when he noticed a flash outside. No one moved—no reaction at all. Just as Ellis was thinking they didn't see it, he heard a creak followed by the slap of the screen door.

"Pol is here," Yal called.

Pol-789—or fake Pol—Ellis didn't know anymore—entered the living room. As youthful in appearance as all of them, and still dressed in the flamboyant orange robes of state, Ellis thought the Chief Councilor looked a bit like a college freshman attending a Halloween toga party.

"Aha!" Pol said the moment he saw Ellis, and added with a big smile, "Wonderful. You made it. I've been looking everywhere."

"You've met?" Warren asked.

"Yes," Pol said, smiling. "Briefly, at least. Ellis Rogers was in my office yesterday with Pax-43246018."

Ellis was impressed the Chief Councilor remembered Pax's full name. Ellis had never been good with names, particularly foreign ones with odd-sounding vowels and double consonants. Memorizing a series of numbers after a single telling was hopeless. He imagined Pol was the sort that could have recited his license number—if only they still had them.

"We'd just been introduced, and I was making plans to come here to reunite old friends, when events transpired beyond my control." Pol stared at Ellis, marveling, studying him until Ellis felt uncomfortable.

"What kind of events?" Warren asked, indicating Pol should take a seat.

Pol turned back to the kitchen. “Yal? Can I get a glass of wine?”

“Of course, right away.”

Pol smiled at all of them before sitting in the other Queen Anne chair, which Dex had promptly vacated. Hig got up from the couch to let Dex sit there. Then Rob, or Bob, got up in turn to shift position. Ellis felt he was watching a silent version of musical chairs.

“We have a seating order,” Warren explained. “In the down-under they’ve forgotten all about authority, hierarchy, and structure. People just do whatever they want. I’m getting them familiar with discipline and the pecking order. Pol is number one, then Dex, then Hig, then—” Warren squinted at Ved One. “Are you Rob or Bob?”

“Bob, you said.”

“Okay, then—Bob, then Rob.”

“Do *I* have a place in this order?” Ellis asked. “And does it require me cutting off my fingers?”

Warren looked uncomfortable, but only for an instant. Then the serene face of an old master returned. “The fingers...well, the finger cutting is necessary for a few reasons. Identification, for one. My way of making certain I can tell the good ones from the bad. These underworlders change their shirts and you can’t tell one from another. Tattoos are easily put on and taken off. Fingers are a different matter. Plus, sacrificing them shows a commitment to the cause. I don’t want anyone here who isn’t in one hundred percent, and these people don’t understand *real commitment* anymore. They do something for a while, then change their minds and try something else. They don’t have marriage, don’t have countries. How can they understand the concept of loyalty? People won’t sacrifice two fingers without giving things a lot of thought. It's the dues they pay to join me—to be special."

"And me?" Ellis held up his right hand, wiggling his fingers.

Warren shook his head. "You're a Darwin like me."

"What's that mean?"

"Means you're not one of them. You're above the law." Warren raised his voice a bit. "And in case there's any doubt, Ellis stands equal with me, and you will show him the same respect and recognize his authority just as you do mine."

They all nodded. Ellis was sitting in a huddle of dogs that idolized a wolf.

Warren turned back to Pol. "So tell me who this Pax is and what happened in your office."

Pol sighed. "Pax is an unusual case. Works as an arbitrator to some effect, but...well, there have been complaints of strange behavior."

Strange behavior? Ellis wondered what normal was in a world where people walked around au naturel, danced in the rain, no one worked, and their world leader dressed like Julius Caesar.

"Then a few years ago, Pax tried to—"

Yal entered and handed Pol a glass of blood-red wine.

"Tried to what?" Ellis asked.

Pol took a dainty sip. "Pax opened a portal to the vacuum of space and tried to walk through it."

No one said anything for a heartbeat. Each pair of eyes tried to process the sentence as if it were a riddle, one of those logic problems where a hunter who lives in a house with four windows all facing south shoots a bear, and people try to figure out the color of the dead animal.

"What?" Ellis felt the empty sensation rock him again. He was beginning to feel a little punch-drunk, an emotionally battered fighter unable to put his arms up to defend himself.

"I thought that wasn't possible," Warren said. "Thought those things—well, you said they had safety features blocking people from doing stupid shit like that."

Dex, who was nodding, spoke. "They do. Living tissue is blocked from passing into hostile environments."

"They do *now*," Pol corrected. "The original CTWs had fixed destinations, so no one thought anything about it, but the first few generations of portals—they could go anywhere. After a few accidents, safety features were added."

"But that was centuries ago," Dex said.

"Pax, it turns out, is an antique collector of sorts," Pol explained. "If it hadn't been for the residence's vox blocking the field, Pax would have committed suicide."

Ellis felt guilty. He hadn't had anything to do with the portal incident—didn't even know how long ago it had happened—but he had just sent Pax away, crying. *What is Pax doing right this moment?*

"Are you saying this Pax person is insane?" Warren asked.

"Mentally ill," Pol said. "Unstable. It's why Pax lives with Vin-3667, a renowned artist. Vin volunteered to watch over Pax. I talked to Vin two days ago. Vin felt the excitement of being with Ellis Rogers has caused Pax to slip, and suggested Pax bring Ellis to me. Felt that Ellis Rogers was an upsetting influence."

"So what happened?"

"The two arrived on schedule, but then Pax began venting, going sonic."

"Leave out your underworld slang, Pol," Warren said with a growl. "We speak proper American here."

"Forgive me. Traveling between cultures is—"

"Get on with it." Warren shuffled his feet, recrossing them on the stool in a manner as decisive as a judge banging a gavel.

"Pax became very upset," Pol went on. "Acting threatened and frightened of me. Completely irrational. Before I could act, Pax had hauled Ellis Rogers through a portal, and the two disappeared. Thinking Ellis Rogers had just been abducted, I gathered people to help with a rescue. We chased them to Tuzo Stadium and into the jungles of the surface. Then we registered Pax stepping out into space."

"Again?" Warren asked.

"To be honest, I thought the worst, for both of you." Pol looked back at Ellis with a smile. "But here you are, safe."

"Pax is fine too," Ellis replied, although he wasn't at all convinced that the Chief Councilor's concern was sincere. Seeing the confusion on Warren's face, he added, "We ejected Pax's chip through a portal into space to avoid being followed."

"Well, that's unfortunate," Pol said. "Now we have no idea where to look. Pax really should be found and helped. Do you know where Pax might be?"

Ellis shook his head. Maybe it was his long bias against politicians, but he didn't trust the wine-sipping Buddhist monk.

I've looked after Pax for centuries, wonderful, wonderful person, and not at all crazy, you understand.

He remembered the tear running down Pax's cheek.

I'm not crazy.

Was he being blind just because Pax was the first friend he'd made?

He focused on the statesman monk. "How did Pax know about Ren? In your office, Pax asked if you knew who Ren was, and you said you didn't know. Why is that?"

Pol shrugged. "I have no idea how Pax knew. To be honest,

I had no idea who Pax meant. The question was so completely without context. Like you said, how could Pax know? I've never spoken to anyone about Ren."

"None of us is allowed to," Hig said.

"Shut it while your better is speaking," Dex snapped, and Hig cowered into the upholstery, looking at the floor.

Pol ignored them both. "I suppose if the question had been about a Darwin named Ren living at Greenfield Village, I would have given a different answer, but I was caught off guard and downright confused."

"And what were you talking to Geo-24 about? Pax asked about that too. I didn't catch your answer."

Pol glanced at Warren briefly as he sipped from his wine again. "How much do you know about Hollow World?"

"A little. Spent about two days there."

"Do you know about the geomancers?"

"They're like weather forecasters, only they predict seismic storms, right?"

"Wonderful, but that's only part of what they do. Geomancers are the descendants of the old energy corporations. Dyna Corp founded the Geomancy Institute in the years just before the Freedom Act." Pol looked concerned. "How much of Hollow World history are you familiar with?"

"Very little," Ellis said. "I watched a show where a dancing hourglass told me about how everyone moved underground. Didn't get all the way to the Great Tempest, though. I fell asleep."

Pol looked at Warren.

"Go ahead and fill him in. It will save me the trouble." Warren got up, heading for the kitchen. "Hey, Yal, why don't you bake cookies or something? Make your lazy ass useful."

No one moved to take Warren's seat, and Ellis wondered what would happen if he did.

"The thing you have to understand is that the Three Miracles changed everything: the Dynamo, the CTW, and the Maker."

"CTW?"

"Controlled Terrestrial Wormholes. Most call them portals."

"Oh—yeah, I know about those."

"The Dynamo was invented first, and initially the technology was tightly controlled by Dyna Corp, which supplied the world with limitless energy."

"Wait a second, what do you mean limitless energy?"

"A Dynamo is a..." Pol looked at Ellis, searching for the right words. "Well, it's like what you might know as a battery, only it never runs out of power. Well, not never. Never is a very long time, after all. The Dynamo is *mostly* self-sustaining, although it does lose a small percentage of power each cycle, given that even a tiny Dynamo generates enough power to operate a whole quad of Hollow World for years, it's as if they are eternal. Similar principle as the sun. It has a finite lifespan, but since that is so long, we never really think about it running out."

"Fascinating."

"Ellis used to work on batteries and solar power back in the day." Warren mentioned, returning with a ceramic cup of something.

"Lithium-ion cells mostly," Ellis clarified. "At least until everything was moved to LG Chem in South Korea."

"How interesting all this must be for you then," Pol said, and smiled. "But getting back to your question—along with the agro businesses, Dyna Corp built most of early Hollow World. They were the first to put their headquarters underground. People were out of the weather, but now had to be concerned about seismic shifts, and that's when they established the Geomancy Institute. It is devoted to the study of not only seismic activity but also prevention of dangerous shifts."

"How do they do that?"

Pol started to speak, hesitated, then held up a finger. "I'll get back to that. We have two more miracles to get through." Pol took a sip of wine. "The Dynamo was created as a result of the Energy Wars of 2185."

"You can always count on a war to move along innovation," Warren said, retaking his seat.

"Another group had been working on solving the transportation problem. Traffic on the surface had become unmanageable, and elevators into Hollow World were jammed, dangerous, and cut into the workday. But it wasn't until Dyna Corp bought the CTW technology and applied the unlimited power of their Dynamo that the portal was made practical. This threw construction in Hollow World into a frenzy, because portals allowed for easy transportation of heavy equipment and the easy disposal of dirt and rock. All strictly controlled by Dyna Corp, which built portal booths everywhere, allowing people to pay to travel. This also coincided with the Great Tempest, a worldwide nonstop storm that killed millions of people left on the surface. There's a wonderful holo that was made recently about the heroic evacuations called *Ariel's Escape*."

The others all nodded enthusiastically.

"I loved the part where Nguyen opens the portal as he's falling," Hig said.

"Great holo," Dex agreed with a big grin. "Completely unrealistic, but a great holo."

Warren yawned.

"Anyway," Pol went on. "The Great Tempest caused the invention of the Port-a-Call that we know today, but it wasn't sold except to a very few. Now, the Great Tempest was followed by the Famine. The storms had wiped the surface of usable soil, and there just wasn't enough food in Hollow World to feed all the refugees. And that's when the Maker was invented. Created by Network Azo—known to the world as Net. She was an employee of Dyna Corp. Almost overnight Maker booths popped up alongside the portal booths. They had a touchscreen menu—think they only had about a hundred patterns at the time, and after a retinal scan that deducted money from a digital bank account, you could use the Maker to create anything from a chicken dinner to a new shirt. Only problem was that few people had any money. Most had evacuated the surface with nothing. They were starving in the old tunnels while an unlimited supply of food was right at hand. All that dirt and stone could have been turned into vegetables and loaves of bread. Net was appalled, but the patent was owned by Dyna Corp, and when she protested they fired her."

Warren started to scowl as he shifted uneasily in his seat, sipping from his cup. The others, in contrast, were leaning forward, listening intently. They all must have known the story, but Ellis assumed that in a rural farmhouse that lacked even an old radio, story time was grand entertainment, even if it was a rerun.

"That's when she did it," Pol said. "Net wrote a pattern for her own invention and made it public—a free download. People could walk into any Maker booth and create their own Maker. Net was arrested, but the dam had burst. From her cell, she called on everyone to revolt against the tyranny of a system that artificially forced restrictions that led to the deaths of thousands. It wasn't long before a Dynamo and a portal pattern were stolen and released to the public. After that, everyone could go anywhere and make anything and all for free. Dyna Corp and the agro companies—well, just about every business collapsed. Net became a hero, the mother of Hollow World, and the first Chief Councilor."

"And the destroyer of humanity as we knew it," Warren said.

Pol nodded solemnly. "But the Geomancy Institute remained untouched. The last vestige of the Dyna Corporation, they continue to indulge in secrecy, divulging their knowledge and techniques only to fellow geomancers and only after they pass the long and grueling initiate process. They are followers of the Faith of Astheno, and no one who isn't a geomancer really knows for certain what they do down there. It's suspected that they track the currents in the asthenosphere, determine where pressure is building up, and—using portal technology—relieve the pressure before it causes a damaging shift in plates. Which means they are all that stands between Hollow World and certain destruction."

"So what do you think happened to Geo-24?"

Pol looked toward Warren, who nodded.

"That was an unfortunate incident. You see, one of our associates was speaking to Geo-24 about our plans to settle the surface—just general questions concerning long-term climate and such. We weren't sure if Firestone was the best place in the world to start such a project. Geo-24 was less than encouraging, and there was concern that the geomancer might urge the HEM to interfere with our plans. Since geomancers have considerable influence, this was a real danger. We hoped this would not be a problem, but one of us wasn't satisfied with just hoping for the best. This *ex-member* was—well, there's no other way to say it—a zealot. The idea that the geomancers were plotting to stop us became an obsession.

We don't know all the details, but it seems that the unthinkable happened...but you saw that for yourself, didn't you?"

"And you were okay with this?" Ellis looked at Warren.

"Hell no, and that psychopath knew better than to come back here." Warren said.

Pol looked at Ellis. "I believe this person tried to become Geo-24, but you and Pax saw past the disguise."

"Why do you think Pax accused you of being an impostor?"

"Pax has been called in to help arbitrate a number of deaths. I can't express enough how unusual and stressful that can be. I suspect Pax is suffering from paranoia and sees conspiracies around every corner. As we've already established, Pax is not of sound mind."

"And the scar on your shoulder?" Ellis asked.

"This?" Pol exposed the mark. "Hig actually gave me this almost a year ago with a scythe." Pol pointed at Hig, who displayed a guilty look.

"I remember that," Warren said. "Lucky Pol didn't lose the whole arm. Hig was still learning the ways of the farmer. But it's proof that what doesn't kill us makes us stronger."

"Survival of the fittest," Pol said, smiling.

"Now to the real point of this meeting," Warren said.

This is a meeting? Ellis had thought the point was to digest the food they'd just eaten.

Warren stood up and, setting down his cup on the green tablecloth covering the little oval table, hooked his thumbs under his suspenders like some old-timey preacher. "I'd all but given up hope of finding Ellis, but God has guided him to us, and I feel more certain than ever that the Almighty has sent both of us. It's just like when he sent John the Baptist and Jesus to set mankind—

who had gone astray—back on the path of righteousness. It's an abomination what mankind has done to itself. Ellis and I are here to help guide you in ridding yourselves of your sins. Abandoning Him, and His teachings has led to a self-made hell, but we'll create paradise." He turned to face Ellis. "I've already begun to tell my friend of our plans to reintroduce women. How is that going, Dex?"

Dex's face scrunched up miserably. Bad news was coming. "I tried again, but the ISP refuses to grant me access to the patterns and development labs."

"Pol?" Warren said. "As Chief Councilor, can't you do something to fix that?"

"Not really. Hollow World doesn't—well, you know—work like Firestone Farm. I have more authority here than there. I can guide and suggest, but I can't compel anyone to do anything. Policy decisions like that are made by a general vote. Even then, the ISP can ignore it if they want to. People just don't take orders in Hollow World—because they don't have to. But that's where Ellis Rogers can help us."

"Me?"

"Yes," Pol said, looking over at Warren, who picked up his drink and motioned for Pol to continue. "You might not know it, but you're a celebrity."

"Huh?" A mosquito had entered one of the windows and was buzzing around Ellis's head near his left ear. The pest, the faint flickering light, and the heat were all aggravating. *How did people ever live like this?*

"Your appearance in Wegener caused a riot—not literally, of course, but people have been sonic—ah, excited—since they spotted you. Grams have circulated everywhere. There's all sorts of inquiries going on. People want to know about the Darwin sighting. Most think you're a hoax, a joke of some kind, maybe some sort of street theater or an interactive art exhibit. Everyone is waiting for the next sighting."

"Why are they so shocked?"

"No one has ever proved a Darwin exists."

Ellis pointed at Warren. Pol smiled. "We keep Ren a secret, at his request."

"Meaning I'd kill the bastard who betrayed me." Warren took a second to eye each of them with a cold stare.

"I can see now the wisdom of his decision," Pol said. "You, on the other hand, have already been exposed. If I take you back, if I show you off as real, all of Hollow World will be at your feet. A genuine Darwin—a unique man—the people will worship you."

"And you plan to use my celebrity status to do what exactly?"

"You go public with your story of time travel and how lonely you are for a mate, and the doors of the ISP will be flung wide to accommodate you. To do otherwise would be a cruelty, and Hollow World is never cruel. You and I will go on a tour of Hollow World. We'll see all the sights, meet the people on all the plates. It will be simply wonderful. You'll be loved by all—and then I'd like to see anyone try to deny you a woman. The people really would riot then."

"What do you say, Ellis?" Warren asked. "Care to be the first ambassador of the New United States of America?"

Ellis didn't know what to say.

Everyone at Firestone Farm was out of bed at first light except Yal, who rose long before. The *new recruit* already had the stove stoked, had gathered the eggs, and was mixing muffins by the time Dex led Ellis out the kitchen door, showing him the way to the outhouse. The morning air embraced with chilly, damp arms—a world silent and gray. Dew-laden grass gave off a pungent, wholesome scent of summer; the odor of the outhouse was stronger still.

Simple. That was the way he saw the world that morning, now that he had put a little time between himself and the death of Peggy. A man couldn't get much simpler than sitting bare-assed on a hole cut in the top of a wooden box in a rickety shed. Ellis had sore muscles from the lumpy bed, and the damp chill was bracing—even though it was summer. How would it be when snow covered the path, and he couldn't sit because the seat was too cold? But peering out the gaps between the wall boards, Ellis felt good. The night before everything had an ominous, oppressive tone, but much of that was likely due to the news about Peggy and having to send Pax home. Emotions were peculiar that way. Nights affected attitudes too; mornings were always the happy optimists. And in the light of day, he had to admit there was virtue in a simple, uncomplicated, unfettered life.

On his way back, Ellis paused, just standing in the yard to witness the morning. Birds sang, frogs peeped, and a light breeze brushed the blades of grass. The brilliance of the sun pierced leaves, casting shafts of gold that splashed against the weathered boards of the barn. Ellis felt as if caught in a coffee commercial. A lovely middle-aged blonde wrapped in a homey cardigan sweater should appear behind him with a steaming cup and a life-loving smile. The breeze blew, and Ellis, dressed only in his T-shirt and pants, shivered. This was the difference between reality and replication. Hollow World presented a beautiful picture, a movie of sight and sound; the real world addressed all the senses, delivering the bad with the good.

Behind him the screen door slapped. The sound, hardly noticeable the night before, cracked offensively.

"Come with me, Ellis Rogers," Bob said. The former Ved must have worked by candlelight the night before, because Ellis saw the new name stitched where the old one used to be. Bob carried four bright steel buckets, swaying them as they walked to the barn. "Ren teaches us that nothing is free. That everything is reached through hard work and self-reliance. The Maker is a cheat and a sin. It makes life too easy, and a pain-free life is not the way God intended His children to live."

"You believe in God? You're a Christian?"

"I'm working on it. I want to please Ren, but..." Bob looked troubled. "I've lived five hundred and twenty-eight years now, and it's hard to believe in something that's supposed to be so vital, and yet I've never heard of it before. Plus, a lot of the teachings center around an afterlife, but everyone in Hollow World lives forever. I'm still trying to make sense of it all and it's hard with everything based on the word of just one person."

"And a book."

"Yes, the book. Have you read it?"

"Parts."

"Ren reads to us in the evenings. He won't let us use the holos. He's read several books, and, honestly, so far I prefer the ones by Agatha Christie." Bob looked up at the sky. "I still have problems believing in something I can't see."

"No one heard about germs before either," Ellis said. "And most had to take their existence on faith. Scientists are sort of like priests that way."

Bob nodded. "I see your point, but germs don't demand our belief in them in order to save ourselves from eternal suffering, do they?"

"They do if you're visiting a leper colony."

"A what?"

"Never mind."

"Besides, the ISP has made everyone in Hollow World immune to germs. And people don't die anymore, so this whole idea of a better afterlife is just...well...silly." Bob frowned.

"So why are you here?"

"To be special—to be like you and Ren. You're just so—I want you to know how much I admire you. We all do. Ren explains that to be like you, we need to build character. Can't be an individual without character. He says it's through pain and struggle that we grow as people and become unique. We need to be rocks like the two of you instead of what we are, dandelion puffs blown in the wind."

"Ren called you that?"

Bob smiled. "No—my own thought. Nice, don't you think?"

"Very poetic."

Bob threw the latch on the barn and pulled the big doors open. Inside was a dark, manure-scented cave defined only by white slices of light cutting between vertical boards. "Everyone needs to be responsible for themselves. No free rides. If you can't cut it, you don't deserve to live. It's that simple."

Ellis grinned, hearing Warren's words spilling out of Bob's mouth. In his head, Ellis imagined a giant clown getting out of a tiny car.

"Survival of the fittest," Bob said. "That's the Darwins' creed, isn't it?"

"That was Charles Darwin's theory of natural selection—which traditionally hasn't coexisted all that comfortably with Christianity."

Standing before the row of cows, Bob paused, looking at Ellis with a puzzled expression. "I don't know about such things, but"—Bob held out the buckets— "Ren said you'd want to contribute for your breakfast."

"Oh, right, of course. No free lunch." Ellis smiled and took the pails. "You'll need to show me."

Ellis expected milking a cow would be a complicated thing. It always was in movies, but, then again, according to Hollywood grown men, who could build highways and clean out putrid city-sewer tunnels, couldn't manage to change a baby's diaper without rubber gloves and a gas mask. The process was remarkably easy once he formed a rhythm and was assured he wasn't hurting the cow by tugging. The hardest part was avoiding the swish of the manure-coated tail while sitting on the little stool and holding the bucket between his knees.

Bob watched until satisfied that Ellis was doing okay, then went about feeding and watering the barn's other residents.

"How long have you been here—at this farm?" Ellis asked over the jet of milk hitting the side of the pail.

"Little less than half a year."

Ellis couldn't see Bob, who was on the other side of the cow that had been introduced as Olivia. "And you like it better than Hollow World?"

"Oh—much!" Ellis heard the scrape of a shovel. "I didn't think I would, and I didn't at first. Life in the forest must have been hard.

Only Ren could appreciate *that* challenge. Too advanced for the rest of us. But here it's much—well, it's a lot easier."

"Don't you find it boring? Even a little stupid—I mean, struggling when you don't have to?"

"That's the point. It's unpleasant living here—especially when you don't feel well and you have to go out in a cold rain. I'll stand at the door sometimes just looking out and wonder what the bleez I'm doing. Then I force myself, and a funny thing happens. I get the work done, hating all of it, but afterward I feel great. I mean, I'm exhausted and filthy, but I know I did something. We call it Ren's magic. It's like a delectation that you can get all by yourself. You don't need a device to feel pleasure, and the good feeling lasts for days. I never really felt that back in Hollow World. Nothing anyone does really seems to matter there. That's another part of character building—a sense of pride."

By the time Ellis finished filling the four buckets, he had sore hands, and, as inclined as he was to ridicule Warren's patchwork of philosophies, he had to admit it did feel good to do something worth doing. Everyone in the house would appreciate the milk, and the cows appeared to appreciate being relieved of their bloat. In all his years of ten- and twelve-hour days filled with thousands of hours of meetings, he had never felt that sort of pride or accomplishment. Somewhere along the way people had traded the virtues of work for a steady paycheck.

"It makes the food taste better when you've a hand in making it," Bob explained, picking up two of the pails and leading the way back to the house, each of them sloshing buckets of steaming milk.

Breakfast was better than dinner, consisting of unburned blueberry muffins and omelets. After the meal, Warren abandoned him and disappeared upstairs with Pol and Dex. Ellis didn't mind; he didn't know exactly when Pax would return and preferred they meet alone. He helped Yal with dishes, then walked out the front door and down Firestone Lane, figuring Pax would port in about where they had separated the day before.

What am I going to say?

Hig was out cutting hay, and Ellis marveled at the ingenuity of the mowing machine. Circling the field in a clockwise manner, the two big horses—Noah and Webster—pulled the device, which appeared to be little more than two big wagon wheels and a seat. A crankshaft and connecting rod transformed the rotary power of the axle into the reciprocating motion of the saw blade that sliced back and forth between triangle ledger plates as they combed through the grass. The whole thing was just a larger version of hair clippers, but what Ellis found fascinating was how it was powered by the rotating wheels. It shouldn't have come as such a surprise; he'd seen the same concept in a push lawn mower. This just worked so much better cutting a wide swath with each pass as Hig drove the horses from the seat between the wheels.

The smell of cut grass filled the air. Ellis sighed.

What am I going to say?

He didn't really know.

Warren had invited him to be part of his little village. Life at Firestone might be harder than he was used to, and for Dex, Yal, Hig, and Bob, this might be a pretend life, like dude ranching used to be, some sort of rugged vacation or spiritual retreat. But for Warren and himself, who didn't have a natural place in Hollow World, this could be home. He was a bit too old to be hauling bales of hay, but it was familiar and felt real, and he liked the idea of building something. Having faced death with nothing to show for it, he had discovered such things mattered.

But then there was Pax.

Ellis found he was anxious for Pax's return, and surprised to find he was trembling as he waited at the fence. He couldn't help thinking how great it would be if Pax would join them at Firestone. They could share a house, farm the land, create their own food, and read around the stove in winter. Living with Pax would be different from how it had been with Peggy. What had attracted him to her was sex. When it dried up, and it had all too quickly, all they shared was their child. At Isley's passing, all that had remained was convenience. It would be different with Pax. He felt—

I thought maybe you were going native, walking on the other side of the road, so to speak.

Warren was nuts. He liked Pax—that was all. Who wouldn't like Pax? The two of them just sort of clicked, like old friends who'd just met. Friends-at-first-sight, if there was such a thing. Pax made him feel better about himself, made him feel like he was someone important. Pax had a strange way of making him feel happy. That's what good friends were supposed to do, right? Maybe he just never had a really good friend before. Maybe that was why...Ellis watched Hig orbit the field, wondering if it was possible to fall in love with someone—just someone—not a woman, not a man—just a person. *What is love anyway?*

Ellis shook his head, trying to clear his thoughts. *What the hell am I thinking?*

He was starting to feel a little light-headed. His hands felt a bit numb as well.

"Ellis Rogers."

There hadn't been a flash or pop, but when he turned he saw the familiar bowler hat and silver vest. Pax's face was rich with joy—beaming with a wide smile.

Pax ran the distance between them and without warning hugged Ellis tight. "I was worried. I'm so glad you're all right."

"I missed you too," he said, noticing how Pax smelled like cinnamon, like the room he'd first awakened in.

Pax drew back and shot a quick glance over Ellis's shoulder at the house and another at Hig and his horse team. "Can we go? Alva misses you too."

"What about Vin?"

"Vin can kiss my hairless butt."

Ellis couldn't help laughing, which made Pax laugh, and he was surprised how much he enjoyed that sound and seeing Pax happy.

"C'mon." Pax formed a portal just behind them, and once more Ellis could see the dining room. "Alva has a hot-chocolate pattern for you to try."

"Hot chocolate, eh?"

"With something called marshmallows—although Alva won't tell me what they are. Every time I ask about food from your time she says, 'You don't want to know.'"

Ellis hesitated. He wanted to go. But...

You hear about guys that go to prison and figure they got no choice, you know?

"Pax," Ellis began, "I don't think I can."

"What do you mean?"

The dining room looked so inviting, and yet...

You two trying out some new-age sex toys?

"I think I'm going to stay here."

"What?" The word was spoken in a barely audible whisper that killed the smile.

Ellis felt horrible. "I don't really belong in Hollow World, but I was thinking that maybe you might consider staying here, too—with me."

"What are you talking about? Everyone belongs in Hollow World. That's *the* world. People aren't meant to *live* on the surface."

"But what would I do there?"

"Live, like everyone else."

"But I'm not like everyone else."

"I know. Don't you think I know that? But..." Pax looked again toward the house. "This place, these people, that *Ren*—they're... bad. They're...evil."

"Warren is like my brother." Ellis sighed, realizing how useless it was to describe that kind of bond to someone who had never been part of a family. "He and I are very close. We've been through a lot together. He's always been there when I needed him—always."

"You have to listen to me, Ellis Rogers. We didn't solve all the mysteries concerning the murder of Geo-24. Something else is going on. Geo-24 was killed for a reason. The real Pol-789 was killed for a reason, and Ren is behind all of it. Ren said they came to this farm a year ago. Well, a year ago was when the first murder took place, and it was then that protests against the Hive Project became more organized and vocal. Protests against something that isn't even possible. They're up to something, something horrible, and if you stay here..."

"What? I'll become evil too?"

Pax looked down at his pistol, still strapped to his hip. Wearing it had become a habit.

"Of course not—you could never be. That's why they'll have to kill you. They will kill you, take your gun, and then kill others. Come back with me, please."

"But you still can't tell me why—why you think any of this?"

Pax looked away. "Can't you just trust me?"

"Pol told me about your past—some of it, at least. Why Vin lives with you."

Pax sucked in a breath and quivered. Tears formed. One slipped down, leaving a glistening trail. "That was personal, confidential. The real Pol would never tell anyone."

"Pol was just trying to help."

"Help Ren, you mean. Ren's not your friend. They want you for something. Something they need. Something they can't get on their own. I wish you could just believe me. I've never lied to you."

Ellis felt horrible. He hated the look on Pax's face, knowing he had put it there. Pax had been so happy, and now... "I don't think it's a matter of lying. Maybe it's just that you don't know the difference."

Again Pax stared at him, injured. "Because—because I'm crazy?"

"No—I didn't say that."

"But you think there's something wrong with me."

"This isn't about you. It's about taking responsibility for one's self. It's about doing something worthwhile. And...think about it for a second. I've known you for what? Three days? I've known Warren since I was fourteen. We share a history, a life, a world. I understand him. He understands me, but I barely know you."

"I understand you, Ellis Rogers, whether you believe it or not. I also know that if you stay here, they'll use you. They'll take your gun and—"

"Here." Ellis unbuckled the holster and pressed it into Pax's hands. "Space it if it makes you feel better. Do like we did to your chip. Destroy it. I don't care. I'm going to stay here. Warren traveled two thousand years to find me. I can't just abandon him to go drink hot chocolate. He needs me—more than he knows, because he's got some really stupid ideas that I'm going to have to straighten out. We're going to try and build a future, a real future in a real world with real people."

"*Real* people?"

"I—I didn't mean it that way."

"How did you mean it?"

"I meant..."

"You meant people like you—Darwins."

"Well—yeah. Warren thinks we can get the ISP to provide access to some female patterns, then we can restart a natural population here."

Pax didn't say anything.

"Pax, I'm going to stay. You might not understand it, but I belong here, I think. I was actually hoping that maybe you could join us."

"Join you? You aren't hearing me, Ellis Rogers. These people are murderers. They killed Geo-24. They killed Pol-789, and they're planning on doing something much, much worse. They—"

"I know you are afraid of them, and you were right about Geo-24, but they didn't have anything to do with that killing. Well, one of them did, but it wasn't sanctioned. They didn't know what that person was up to. That's why the killer assumed Geo-24's identity; they weren't allowed to come back here. Warren wouldn't forgive a murderer. Believe me, Warren has always been pro death penalty. And Pol isn't an impostor. You're just seeing things. You're letting your imagination get away from you. You're just being—" Ellis stopped himself.

Pax stood rigid, staring, shivering as if it were midwinter.

"Paranoid? That's what you were going to say, isn't it? And that's just another way of saying I'm crazy."

The door to the house slapped. Ellis could hear the crack echo behind him.

"Please," was all Pax said, the word spoken in a whisper, another tear falling.

Ellis looked over his shoulder. Warren, Pol, and Dex were on the porch, looking their way. "Maybe you should go."

The look on Pax's face broke Ellis's heart.

As Pax walked through the portal, as the opening to that homey space in Hollow World closed, he felt oddly drunk, dizzy even. Ellis reached out to steady himself with the fence but couldn't feel the wood. His whole arm was numb. Then the pain exploded in his chest. No warning. A truck just hit him. Ellis collapsed, bouncing off the fence and landing on his back.

The last sight he saw was the blue sky. His last thoughts weren't of Peggy or Isley, but of Pax, a woodstove, and maybe a dog. Yes, they definitely should have had a dog.

Time Heals All Wounds

When Ellis woke, the blue sky was gone, replaced by a white luminescence. He was on his back. A bed. Thin mattress, thin pillow, thin blanket, with what looked like white porcelain safety rails. He was naked but warm. Maybe the mattress was heated. Maybe he didn't need heat anymore. From somewhere came the sound of an ocean's surf. Not loud, not harsh, but soft, gentle, relaxing.

"Welcome, Ellis Rogers," a feminine voice said. No one around. The voice came from everywhere. *"How are you feeling?"*

"Feeling? I'm not feeling anything."

"Wonderful," said the soothing voice.

Stillness—total stillness, and white light, and the undulating roll of waves.

"Did I die?"

"Yes."

While not completely unexpected, the answer still surprised him.

So this is death? Not so bad. Could have been a lot worse. Death is a lot like a spa.

He was still breathing. Maybe he only thought he was. Residual memory or something. Maybe dying had a decompression process, a PTSD cooldown. If this was death, life was certainly cause for all kinds of stress disorders. He had to be dead. He could breathe perfectly. He took in deep breaths the likes of which he hadn't experienced in years.

"Are you God?" he finally asked, already thinking that the feminists and goddess worshipers had it right all along.

"I'm Maude."

"Maude?"

"Yes."

Ellis wasn't sure what to make of that. All he could think of was the 1970s television show staring Bea Arthur. The thought of Bea Arthur as God was a bit disturbing, and yet he could see it in a weird way. Only the soft voice wasn't that of the Maude from the television show. This voice was serene, gentle. More like a voice from a meditation CD. Still, Ellis had a bigger question he needed answered. He hadn't smelled any brimstone, but he might not have reached the penthouse either. "Where am I exactly?"

"Recovery Room 234-A, Level 17, Replacements Central Wing, Institute for Species Preservation, Wegener, Kerguelen micro continent, Antarctic Plate, Hollow World, Earth."

"Hollow World?"

"Yes."

"Maude?"

"Yes?"

"Are you a vox?"

"Yes."

"I'm not dead then, am I?"

"No, not dead. You only died."

A portal opened and someone entered the room. Ellis had no idea who. The individual was naked, with no distinguishing marks. All Ellis knew was that it wasn't Pax, Pol, or anyone else from the farm. This person had all their fingers. That narrowed the possibilities to only several million. Ellis actually had no idea about the population of Hollow World but imagined it to be significantly less than the billions that had roamed the continents back in the days of China and India.

Ellis's visitor looked around, frowning. "Maude, Ellis Rogers is awake. Can we have something a bit nicer than sterile nothingness?"

The white walls and glowing ceiling disappeared, and Ellis found himself on a beach. Overhead was a cobalt sky, and at his feet was an aquamarine ocean. Sensuously curved palm trees reached into view, and billowing white clouds drifted like cotton balls. He'd had a screen saver that looked just like it called *Hawaiian Dreams.*

"Hello, Ellis Rogers, I'm Wat-45, your attending physician."

"I heard I died."

"You did—you did indeed." Wat tapped the air, producing a wall and an input screen. He continued to tap through a series of images, while overhead a seagull cried. "But we fixed that."

"Really? How do you fix death?"

"That's what we do here at the ISP. We treat it like a disease—which it is." Wat turned. "In your case, your body had shut down—massive heart failure. Your brain functions would have died, too, but they were frozen by the quick action of Dex-92876—a one-time associate here. I believe you know each other?"

Wat paused. Ellis nodded, pleased to discover he could still do that.

"Once your brain was locked up safe and secure, it was merely a matter of growing you a new heart and lungs. We actually gave you a deluxe package, a complete new set of organs, as most of your old ones were badly worn. Not surprising after two thousand years, eh?"

Wat offered him a smile, then resumed tapping on the wall. Ellis could see transparent images of organs flashing by.

"You've got some nice ones now. Top of the line. We augmented them to provide stronger heart walls and expanded lung capacity. You'll be able to run a marathon twice over and hardly notice. We also inserted a molecular-level decay resistor, which won't do much for your preexisting cells, but will ensure these new organs never need replacing."

Ellis couldn't help thinking about how each time he bought a new car the salesmen always mentioned the rustproofing and how important it was in Detroit. *All that salt eats away at the body. With our undercoating, you get a guarantee of a long life.*

"Wow—" Wat paused on an image that to Ellis looked like a Rorschach test. "Your old lungs were a disaster. You can take them home if you like, but if you prefer not to, we'd love to keep them."

"That's fine." *Seriously, did people keep them?*

"Great." Wat swept a hand across the wall; the images scrolled by, stopping when Wat tapped. "Ah, yes—we grafted new sections of arteries where we saw signs of impending collapse. Where the tubing was clogged, we dredged out the mess." Wat turned again with a shocked look. "None of us could believe what we saw in there. It's like you were pumping sludge through your circulatory system instead of blood."

Wat focused on the wall images again, which were superimposed on a sailboat that had appeared on the horizon and was coasting through Ellis's organs. "Your liver was weakening, so you got a new one, as well as a new spleen, pancreas, kidneys, bladder, gallbladder, stomach, and a full set of intestines—large and small. The old ones were torn up and clogging as if you'd been eating glass and gravel for the last few years. You weren't, I hope." Wat offered another happy smile. Too happy. The doctor reminded Ellis of a puppy greeting a new visitor.

"And..." Wat punched a few more screens. "Oh, you have new eyes. Old lenses were getting thicker, less transparent, and less elastic, the pupils shrinking."

Ellis was shocked and found himself involuntarily blinking.

"Ciliary ligaments and muscles were weakening too. Your ears were fine, though, as far as we could tell, and we didn't bother with the skin either—didn't think you'd like to wake up looking like me." Wat laughed high and giddy, like a schoolgirl at a teen-idol concert.

"And...oh! You were inoculated for disease. Turns out you died of *extemdiousness*, or double-D disease, as it was once called. One of the old designer viruses that still lingers. Looks like it was racing your fibrosis to see which could collapse your ventricle walls first. Not much of a race, really. The pulmonary fibrosis didn't stand a chance against a virus built to kill people. The extemdiousness is what took you down. Nasty bug. Highly contagious and aggressive, it incubates for a few days then attacks multiple systems at once, killing quickly. You *drop dead* without warning—hence the name. Hard to believe there was ever a time when people created these things on purpose." Wat closed the screen, leaving them once again in the unblemished serenity of the island beach. "And that's it."

Wat turned around with a pleased look. "You should feel a *whole* lot better. I would take it slow to begin with, just as a precaution. You want to get accustomed to the new organs. Let them ramp up to speed. So, don't actually try running that marathon I talked about...for at least a few weeks. Also, you're going to experience a day or two of fatigue. Despite the boosters, your body has gone through a really big shock, and it will take a while to adjust. You'll be normal in a week. Just get plenty of rest, and..." Wat stepped closer, staring for a long moment. "I just want to say what an honor it has been to work on you. I heard—we all heard—the rumors, and saw the grams, but when Pol-789 brought you in, everyone's chin just hit the floor. It was just..." Wat choked up, took a deep breath, and blinked repeatedly. "I'm sorry. I told myself I wouldn't cry, but—" Wat took a second and then said, "I swear, you're the fourth miracle. You really are."

"How long will I be here?"

"As long as you want."

"I mean, how long before I can leave?"

"Oh—" That nervous laugh again. "You can leave whenever you like. But I hope you aren't in a hurry. A lot of people would love to meet you. Well, we've all *sort of* met you, but it wasn't you, was it? Not really. You were mostly dead at the time."

Ellis turned on his side and pushed up. He felt fine. He took a deep breath—better than fine. He took another, a deeper one. The air just flowed in—no resistance at all, no coughing fit. As the blanket fell away, he looked for scars. Nothing. Still the same old chest with salt-and-pepper hair and skin that was losing its elasticity.

"The Chief Councilor, Pol-789, is waiting to see you."

"Do I still have clothes?"

"Oh yes—of course. Maude, tell Mak to bring Ellis Rogers's things in here."

An instant later a portal popped and another naked citizen of Hollow World entered with Ellis's backpack and a bundle. Through the portal opening, Ellis spotted a small crowd peering through. Mak looked more starstruck than Wat had been and froze upon entering. Wat had to pull the backpack and clothes away and place them on the bed. His shirt and pants had been cleaned and folded.

"I—" Mak began, then simply stepped back through the portal.

"What can we say?" Wat grinned. "You're a sensation."

Like a hospital or an airport, the ISP was a massive world unto itself, but designed with the aesthetic of an investment-rich start-up wanting to foster a creative environment. Rex, who looked just like Wat, but was introduced to Ellis as one of the administrators of the ISP, took him on a tour of vast atriums, courtyards, and playrooms filled with everything from normal-looking chessboards to holo-chambers with green and red lights indicating if they were in use. He wondered if any of them understood the origin of those colors. They walked past labs and through corridors, which Ellis thought had been built either before the portal was invented or were used in an emergency in case Port-a-Call units failed. He also saw his first portal booths, hulking leftovers from days before Net Azo's bloodless rebellion. Several people still used them.

"Their destinations are locked in place now," Rex explained. "If you're going back and forth, it's easier to just walk through rather than having to dial, especially if your hands are full. A lot of us don't even use our POCs here."

The central feature of the institute was what they called the Grand Cathedral, rather ironic for a world that no longer practiced religion. A domed space bigger than a football stadium, it was the central campus, the gathering place of ISP associates. White columns rose to a ceiling that did not impersonate the sky, but rather displayed an art show of light and color that slowly changed in pattern and design. The floor was divided into sections raised to different elevations, with the lowest filled with a decorative set of shallow, circular pools that spilled in a series of waterfalls. The edges of the pools were seating areas bordered by brilliant, tropical flowers.

"I think it would be cruel to deny Ellis Rogers such a small thing," Pol was saying as they moved through the Grand Cathedral. Ellis was being treated like a superstar, and Pol was just one in his entourage. Rex had introduced him to no fewer than a hundred people since he'd woken up. He couldn't hope to remember who they all were, especially since the ISP dress code appeared to demand unmarked nudity, and everyone was officially defined as an ISP associate, even Rex. They all orbited around Ellis, a constant swarm of identical grinning faces.

"It's not a small thing. Creating a human being is never a small thing," Rex insisted. "There are many issues—policies—such as the population cap."

"There have been two recent deaths that aren't yet accounted for."

"But females from the old pattern..." Rex looked sheepishly at Ellis. "Ah—I don't want to sound...well, we don't like going backward, and this would open the door for random conceptions. You're speaking of introducing a whole new subset of people."

"We understand that, but Ellis Rogers's intention is to live on the surface."

"HEM won't like that."

"But they also won't protest too much," Pol said. "After all, this is Ellis Rogers we are talking about."

Pol had been there when Ellis woke up. According to Wat, Pol had never left. The Chief Councilor, Dex, and another unidentified member of Hollow World had carried Ellis into the ISP, and while the others had come and gone, Pol had remained steadfast. The Chief Councilor was the first person Ellis saw that he knew, and since his recovery Pol had never left his side.

"I plan to introduce the proposal under the allowance for re-introducing an indigenous species." Pol walked slightly ahead of everyone else, sweeping around the glassy pools, the orange toga slapping Pol's calves.

"You're not serious? They're humans," Rex said.

"Most certainly an indigenous species to the surface of the planet, don't you think?"

"But you'll be opening the door to a two-class system. This runs contrary to everything we've tried to achieve. History is filled with examples of humanity killing and enslaving others because of their differences. We've nearly eliminated all that, which has reduced divisions between people to a fraction of what they used to be. Now you want to undo everything?"

"But think of Ellis Rogers, here," Pol insisted. "Think how lonely he is. We aren't asking for a nation, only a single woman that he can find happiness with."

Ellis felt like Frankenstein's monster, with Igor pleading with the doctor for a wife.

"But the potential for children..."

"She can be sterilized," Dex said. The Firestone resident surgeon looked odd without the Amish duds, and could have blended in with the rest if not for the lack of fingers. "I can handle the procedure myself. We don't even need to involve the ISP if that's an issue. I only need the pattern."

Rex looked uncomfortable. "I'll consider it, but I can't make such a decision alone, obviously."

"Which means you won't do it?"

"There has to be a consensus."

Pol looked disappointed, and turned to Ellis. "Have they been treating you poorly?"

"Poorly!" Rex said. "Of course not."

"Perhaps we should let Ellis Rogers answer that."

"Ah—well," Ellis began. Rex and some of the others looked ashen. "Everything is wonderful and all. I'm just concerned—well, I just realized I don't know how long I've been here."

Pol began to nod. "You've been time traveling again, Ellis Rogers. I brought you here just about a month ago."

"A month?" Ellis was stunned. "But—I thought—someone told me a transplant was a walk-in procedure."

"It is," Rex assured him. "The month was the time it took to grow the organs. For most people, we have what they need banked, or if they're unusual—though very few are—we just look up their pattern and build the tissue needed before they come in. Then it's just an hour or two procedure. But you're unique. We had to sample your DNA and build from scratch. To avoid the unpleasantness and stress of waiting a month with your body hooked up to support, we kept your brain locked in stasis."

"A month," Ellis repeated. *What about Pax? Does Pax know where I've been? Or does Pax think I no longer care? A month!*

"Now that you are better, Ellis Rogers, I wanted to let you know that I am setting up a world tour. The rumors that ignited when you first visited me have exploded during your stay here. Everyone wants to see you and hear you speak."

"Why?" Ellis asked.

No one answered. They all looked at each other, dumbfounded.

"Why?" Rex asked. "Ellis Rogers, as I just mentioned, you're unique."

Ellis shrugged.

"In Hollow World"—Pol took over—"that makes you extraordinary. A symbol of hope to some." Pol looked at Rex and a few others gathered beside them. "And concern to others."

Ellis saw Rex frown. "The Hive Project will not steal individualism. Its purpose is to eliminate misunderstandings similar to the one we are experiencing at this very minute."

"Clearly, as I didn't mean to suggest anything other than that some people might see Ellis Rogers as a rallying point for an anti-Hive agenda."

"The Hive Mind will be the greatest leap forward for our species since the opposable thumb. The single advantage humans possess above all other creatures is our minds." Rex's voice heated up, growing more passionate. "Every major advancement has been a direct result of amplifying the contributions of that organ. Language allowed the transfer of ideas, writing boosted that transfer, the printing press scaled it, and the Internet took it global, unfettered by restrictions. Each of these inventions has coincided with a boom in species advancement—and all those will pale in comparison with the limitless possibilities of our whole species functioning together for the first time as one harmonious entity."

This was obviously a sore spot in an ongoing debate, and the concise, speech-like argument impressed Ellis as having the familiarity of something often repeated if not actually rehearsed.

Rex went on as Pol listened with a polite but unmoved expression. "Standardized language was a major advancement, but any language is limited by its inability to precisely convey thoughts. Misunderstandings and even intentional deceit have always introduced conflict. We've managed to eliminate most of the violence associated with these, but we've only been treating the symptom—not the disease. The Hive will finally cure us."

"One might argue," Pol said as if he were on the floor of the Roman Senate, "and many have, that death also cures many illnesses. You can eliminate poor eyesight by merely plucking out a person's eyes. And there's the question of whether a salmon would be cured of its need to swim upstream if it were turned into a bird. Or would the salmon simply become extinct?"

"Has a caterpillar ever complained about turning into a butterfly?" Rex asked.

"If only we could ask."

"Ah." Rex looked smug. "Once more the limitations of language!"

Pol smiled. It was not a friendly expression.

"But I was told the Hive Project was a failure," Ellis said. "That you've been working on it for centuries and haven't got anywhere. Isn't that right?"

Rex frowned and nodded. "Just too many possibilities, so many combinations, and we're working blind. In the past, random mutations offered examples to work from. We're convinced it's possible, because the history of our species is littered with stories of humans with extrasensory capacities, but we've never managed to map the DNA of an authentic telepath, because we've eliminated natural selection. The random event can't happen anymore. We don't even know what we're looking for. There's a few sequences of genes we've never fully understood, and we've tried randomizing these in recent patterns, but you're right. The Hive Project is little more than a dream at this point."

"We all have our problems to deal with," Pol said with an inflection that was less than sympathetic. Then, turning to Ellis, he added, "As I was saying, I have been scheduling a tour of the world and with your permission would like to kick it off tomorrow, if you are feeling up to it."

"So soon?" Rex complained.

"Unless there's reason to suspect Ellis Rogers is not fully recovered, that something went wrong with the—"

"Of course nothing went wrong!" Rex said. "We just hoped to have a bit more time."

"You've had Ellis Rogers for a month. The rest of the world wants to see him, and I'm certain Ellis Rogers would like to see the rest of Hollow World. But all that will begin tomorrow. Now you have a speech to give."

"A what?" Ellis asked.

They were approaching the center of the Grand Cathedral where a small stage had been erected. Portals began popping like flash-bulbs; in minutes the great hall was flooded with a sea of faces. All looked at him.

"We were hoping you'd say a few words to the associates here," Rex said, the eager look of a child in the administrator's eyes.

Ellis watched as more and more portals popped. This had been arranged, timed. Some sort of notice or memo sent. He wished they had asked him. As the audience assembled, murmuring like some giant boiling pot, he felt obligated. He couldn't say no.

Ellis had never spoken to a crowd before, except the two times at Warren's weddings where he gave the best man's toast. All he did then was make fun of his friend, which Warren made easy. This was a whole new world. "What do you want me to say?"

"Whatever you like," Rex told him.

"But I don't—"

"It doesn't matter. Everyone will be thrilled just to hear your voice."

"Remember, Ellis Rogers"—Pol gave him a wink—"the administrator of the ISP just said it doesn't matter what you say."

Ellis was trying to figure out what Pol meant as Rex escorted him up a set of steps. As soon as he ascended the stage and faced the crowd, the chamber fell silent. Not even a cough. Did these people ever get colds anymore?

"Ah—hello," Ellis said. He was startled as his voice boomed, amplified somehow. He looked around, bewildered.

At the sound of his voice, the audience roared. Ellis shifted his weight, feeling awkward. He didn't know what to say, how to stand, what to do with his hands, or where to look. He tried to remember what his English teacher once told him about speaking in front of a crowd. *Just imagine your audience is naked.* He nearly laughed, but managed to restrain himself to a big smile. The crowd saw it and cheered again.

When at last they quieted, he said, "I guess I'd like to thank everyone for saving my life. I feel great, by the way. You did a good job."

Again the crowd cheered, and Ellis waited for them to calm down.

"I, ah—I really don't know what else to say."

"What do you think of Hollow World?" someone shouted.

"It's very nice. Very *clean.*"

"What's your favorite holo?"

Ellis shrugged. "I've never tried one. Still getting used to the showers and voxes."

This brought a round of laughter and more applause.

"Are those your real clothes?"

"Yes. I probably should get some new ones. I've been wearing these for over two thousand years now."

More laughter. More applause.

Ellis looked down and saw Pol with Dex alongside, looking up at him with anticipation, but he wasn't sure why.

"Do you have a home here yet?"

"Actually, I think I will be living on the surface. It's more familiar. That is, if that's allowed."

Shouts of encouragement rang.

"Do you think you'll be lonely without a woman?" It was Pol. He was staring pointedly and gesturing with his five-fingered hand for him to say something, as if the two shared a secret, only Ellis had no idea what that secret was.

Ellis hesitated, and the pause gave the crowd a chance to quiet down. "Ah..." Ellis thought about the question. He thought about Peggy. He thought about Pax. "Yes," he said. "I hadn't counted on that when I traveled through time. Almost everything I knew is gone. To you maybe I'm special because I'm one of a kind, but I'm also the last of my kind. And one is the loneliest number, isn't it?"

He didn't expect anyone to remember the Harry Nilsson/Three Dog Night song, but that was one of the perks of being ancient. He could plagiarize with impunity. Everything old was new again. Feeling awkward and just wanting to get away, he came off the stage to an ovation and the crowd reaching out to touch his ankles as he climbed down the steps.

"Beautifully done," Pol shouted in his ear. "I'll do wonders with that. Our tour will begin tomorrow, so you need to get some sleep. Dex and I will be back in the morning. Now unless you need anything—" Pol pulled out a Port-a-Call.

"Pol?" Ellis said. "Have you seen Pax?"

"No. Should I have?"

"I don't know." Ellis took a step closer, lowering his voice. "Have you heard anything?"

"About Pax? No, and as you're aware, Pax isn't an easy person to keep tabs on anymore."

He nodded. "Could you contact Vin at least? I'd like to let them know what happened to me, okay?"

"Right away. See you tomorrow."

Pol formed a portal and stepped through. Ellis couldn't see if it was to the Council office or Firestone Farm.

Perhaps he should go to Pax's home. If he had his own Port-a-Call he would. He considered asking Rex, but Wat had been right. He was feeling run-down and tired, like he was fighting a cold. Maybe in the morning before they left, he could get Pol to swing by Pax's place. It wasn't like it was out of their way.

"Rex?" He turned to the ISP administrator. "Has anyone tried to see me since news got out that I was here?"

"Everyone," Rex said. "Absolutely everyone."

Quality Time

Ellis had tried several times to contact Pax but failed. By all accounts Pax had disappeared. As part of his agreement to go on tour, Ellis insisted Pol do everything possible to locate Pax, including daily messages to Pax's home, where even Vin had no clue where the arbitrator had gone. Ellis was struck by the irony that by cutting out Pax's chip, he was the architect of his own misery. This sense of guilt plagued him as Ellis finally submitted to the grand tour.

Pol had been relentless with the schedule. Each day Ellis traveled to some new corner of the world or another planet altogether. There weren't nearly as many inhabitants in Hollow World as Ellis had expected. Just over 123 million, the majority of mankind having died during the Great Tempest. They all resided inside a honeycombed earth, scattered across the fifty-two tectonic plates, but with portals they could travel anywhere in an instant.

Mars looked nothing like Ellis had expected. After spending

most of his youth dreaming of being the first person to walk on its surface, the ease of the trip removed that mystique. For the most part it was no different from Hollow World except for the ubiquitous Mars logo placed everywhere. This was because the vast majority of the Martian resort destination was below the surface. The little bit of the planet he was able to see from the viewing domes looked like Nevada under a hazy pink sky.

He did get to see the Mars rovers. They were still out there, preserved as part of Odyssey Historic Park. The rovers were the Red Planet's second-biggest tourist attraction after Olympus Mons, the largest Martian volcano and the tallest mountain on any planet in the solar system. The one highlight of Mars was that Ellis got to see robots. He'd wondered where they were. *Buck Rogers* and *The Jetsons* had promised flying cars, jet packs, and robot maids. Once again Ellis was disappointed. Previously used to safely explore the landscape of the planet, they'd become a novelty for tourists. Robots were remote-controlled machines sent out to transmit 3-D visuals and fetch rocks as souvenirs. Mars had become like Niagara Falls, a cheesy tourist trap. And like vacationers to a Mexican resort, where tourists preferred the sand-free hotel pools to the ocean, most Mars visitors preferred walking around the virtual holo than suiting up to experience the real thing. Ellis did indeed don the suit and join the mechanical delivery bots, but after a lifetime of waiting, the experience was anticlimactic.

New planets had been discovered, like Trinity, which was outside the galaxy, but no colonies had been established. The East Indian Tea Company didn't exist anymore. Everyone had plenty of room, and nothing beyond novelty remained to drive humanity to the frontier.

While travel everywhere was instantaneous, the outings were taxing. He felt good. He was, in fact, incredibly fit for a fifty-eight-year-old man who'd just died and had his organs replaced. His energy wasn't perfect, but he figured that was more a result of thirty years of reduced exercise than the surgery. What drained him were the crowds. Everywhere they went, hundreds of people waited. As far as the public was concerned, Ellis was bigger than Olympus Mons. Unlike the gathering in the ISP's Grand Cathedral, these were filled with people wearing clothes and sporting tattoos. By the time they were visiting Challenger Deep, the lowest point on Planet Earth, Ellis began to see his first imitators.

"Pattern designers are working 'round the clock to create Ellis Rogers wear," Pol explained, seeing Ellis staring back at a gawker who wore an identical flannel shirt and jeans.

Pol had enormous amounts of energy, finding time to report to Warren each night even after a long day of appearances. Apparently it was important to keep the technology-deficient farm informed on Ellis's global impact.

That day, he and Pol had stood under the illuminated dome of Challenger Deep, and looked up at a dead, dark world of empty water. They were too deep for fish. Ellis had preferred the city of Atlantis, an artificial coral reef surrounding a thousand-story-tall see-through city, also known as *The Aquarium*. The Deep was just scary. The knowledge of all that water above left Ellis haunted by the thought of a crack in the glass.

"It's wonderful. The whole world is going Ellis Rogers crazy," Pol said. "People are sharing your speeches. Ellis Rogers masks are big, and a hyper-realistic interactive holo featuring an interview with you is the most popular in the world for the second straight day."

"I'm surprised people aren't having plastic surgery done," Ellis said.

"Plastic surgery?" Pol asked.

Ellis gestured at his face. "You know, it's where doctors alter your features surgically. With all this desire for individuality, I'd think more people would have done it."

"There are limits to self-expression," Pol said. "People want to be individuals—not different."

"How's that?" Ellis spotted another Ellis Rogers wannabe entering the sea-dome, this one with the same JanSport pack slung over one shoulder.

"Putting on clothes, even applying a tattoo, just adds a layer of identity. It doesn't fundamentally change a person. People don't want to *be* something different—they aren't dogs longing to be cats or even horses wanting to be zebras, although they might paint on stripes to *look* different. You're fascinating to all of us. Not only because of your divergence from the norm, but your complete acceptance of it. You honestly don't mind being separate, being alone in your singularity. This courage is what so many of us admire when we see you. We'd like to think we'd be just as comfortable standing out, being a real individual, but actually doing it—that's a bravery beyond most of us."

The backpacker offered Ellis a shy smile. He smiled back, embarrassed for staring. Ellis casually looked up at the dome where the illuminated ocean was filled with vents and motes. While what he saw was real, it looked more artificial than anything he'd seen in Hollow World.

"You see, there's a comfort in belonging to a whole. Humans are social animals," Pol explained. "But people don't live together in groups like in your day. Once it became possible to survive separately, those traditional groups like families and tribes dissolved. In Hollow World they maintain a sense of community by being the same—exactly the same. They live any way they like, keep what hours they choose, follow such pursuits as they find interesting, while believing they're always part of a greater whole. They don't really want to be different so much as noticed—recognized." Pol held up his maimed hand. "Those of us at the farm are different. Permanent alteration will be part of our future. And you're a big part of that future."

"What sort of future is that exactly?"

"I suppose that will be up to us, now, won't it?"

Ellis's growing popularity was putting pressure on the ISP, and Pol had him make speeches at most of the places they visited. He got better at speaking, although most of what he said at each stop was identical. He talked about how different the world was now, thanked the ISP for saving his life, and expressed his appreciation to all of Hollow World for their warm welcome. Pol had him follow this with a plea for help in convincing the ISP to release the original female pattern so he didn't have to be so isolated. Pol insisted he repeat the *one is the loneliest number* line from the first speech. When Ellis admitted it came from a song, Pol dug it out of the Wegener Archives and blared the recording before and after each speech, making it the Ellis Rogers theme. Occasionally he heard people singing it, usually the ones in the flannel shirts. At his speeches, the crowd, hundreds of identical voices, would sing the song together.

In addition to tourist attractions, Pol took him to a sporting event and an art exhibit, but Ellis found the historic sites and museums to be the most interesting. He was delighted by the chance to visit Egypt's pyramids—which looked a little worse for wear but were still hanging in there. He also had the chance to walk through the South African Museum of Prejudice and Segregation, the ruins of New York, and the Forbidden City of China. The most interesting by far, however, were the famed Museum of War and Museum of Religion, both located in the historic city of Jerusalem.

Pol arranged for Ellis to have special access to the vaults in the Museum of War, where he got to see the stockpiles of weapons—those items they didn't have room for on the official floor display—weapons still considered dangerous. They had preserved everything from Greek bronze-era swords, to British ship cannons, to American thermonuclear bombs. What shocked Ellis the most was that the themes of the two neighboring museums were similar: *the tragic mistakes of humanity*. While Ellis believed in God, he recognized the contributions in terror and bloodshed such beliefs had generated over the long history of mankind. One exhibit redefined the Four Horsemen of the Apocalypse as greed, pride, fear, and religion—the leading causes of war.

While riding on a moving walkway through a tunnel, various scenes from history were played out on either side by lifelike, but fully digital, constructs. A narrator said, "The errors in judgment were unfortunate but necessary roads taken on the long journey from the barbarity of the past to the enlightened peace of today."

Behind him, Ellis heard someone explain how at one time roads were physical things rather than mere metaphors.

The crowds were significantly smaller in Jerusalem—the museums were less popular than the Mars simulators or see-through Atlantis—but Ellis was captivated as he walked the timeline of humanity's religious history from prehistoric burial mounds containing personal items that suggested a belief in an afterlife, to the last active church in El Grullo, Mexico—eventually destroyed by the Great Tempest. Ellis entered holos where he could stand in churches, temples, and mosques and listen to sermons about the growing apathy toward God or experience virtual battlefields so realistic that he jumped out to avoid being sick. The Three Miracles and the ISP were responsible for the final eradication of war, but religion had disappeared much sooner, and the cause was far less definitive. Organized belief wasn't outlawed. There had been no discovery refuting the faithful's claims, no great atheistic crusade. Religion, it seemed, had just been forgotten.

Each night Ellis returned to Wegener with Pol, to a room as spartan as the home of Geo-24. Ellis didn't care; he just wanted a place to be alone. The grueling schedule kept him joined with Pol like a newlywed couple on their honeymoon, and Ellis was growing weary of both Pol and the tour. He'd recovered from his surgery, but told Pol he was still suffering from fatigue just to get a break.

He spilled the contents of his backpack on the bed and sat like a kid on Halloween night, looking through his haul. The flashlight, his compass, water purifier, first-aid kit, matches, rain gear—still in the bag with the Target store label. This was all he had left. Spotting a bag of peanut M&M'S, he tore it open and popped a red one in his mouth, savoring the taste of the twenty-first century like never before.

In the last few days, Ellis had seen marvels. He'd traveled to the depths of the ocean and outside the solar system such that he could spit in the eye of the meager accomplishments of the Mercury Seven. He'd gained what he'd come for—a cure, a new lease on life. Looking at the cheap assortment of sporting-goods-store junk, Ellis could only think about what he'd lost. He longed for a good cheeseburger, a normal toilet, and the sound of traffic or his computer booting. Even the things he used to hate he missed: endless commercials, driving in traffic, the sound of his cellphone, even the vicious fighting between Republicans and Democrats. What movies had he missed? What achievements? What disasters?

He popped another candy in his mouth, closed his eyes, and saw himself helping Isley with his math homework. Then he was shopping with Peggy for a television, then just raking leaves on a Sunday afternoon. Memories—perfection in an airtight glass—frozen in untarnished beauty.

He spotted the glint of gold under the raincoat—Peggy's rings. He reached into his pocket. Ellis still carried his wallet and phone, though he didn't know why. He just couldn't bring himself to discard anything. He flipped past his license to the photos of Peggy and Isley. Fuzzy, pocket-scarred—he should have brought more pictures. Why didn't he bring pictures?

He missed Peggy.

He pressed the power button on his phone. Lights came on. He checked his messages. Peggy's call was still in his voicemail. He pressed play.

"El? Oh goddammit, El, pick up! Please pick up." Her voice still quivered, still frightened. *"I need to talk to you. I need to know what you're thinking...I'm sorry, okay? Seriously, I am, and that was years ago. I don't even know why I kept the letters. Just stupid is what it was. I'd honestly forgotten about them.*

"I know I should have told you. Jesus, I wish you'd just pick up. Listen, are you still at Brady's? I'm driving over. I'll be there in twenty minutes. We can talk then, okay? Please don't be mad. It wasn't Warren's fault. It wasn't anyone's fault, really. It just happened, and I know we should have told you, but...well...If you get this before I get there, don't go anywhere or do anything crazy, okay?"

Ellis was crying when he pressed the return call button.

He listened.

Silence.

&

Her name was Sol.

She wasn't really a female, but Ellis thought she was close enough. The voice and mannerisms were there, even though Sol had been born years after the sexes were being phased out. Sol was a first-generation standard pattern and had no number designation after her name because Sol was the oldest living human in existence—or had been until Ellis challenged her for the title.

Pol had obviously thought their meeting would make for a good promotional stunt, and was probably right, but Pol hadn't stuck around to see the performance through. The Chief Councilor had other matters that day and, after introducing them, left Ellis and Sol alone. Although the visit was advertised, the crowds stayed away. Ellis wasn't certain if Pol had anything to do with that, or if Sol herself commanded the sort of respect that meant unwanted guests would refrain from intruding on her privacy.

They were in Sol's home, a strange and cluttered collection of memorabilia from her long life, and Ellis felt it was the most normal home he'd visited so far. For one thing, there were books—actual paper books—and an old tablet computer. She had hats, and sunglasses, and pens. A dresser, a closet, a clock, and a coatrack with coats. Sol's most beloved possession was mounted on the wall above a faux fireplace and was a photo of a real woman. Asian eyes wreathed in short black hair looked out from the silver frame.

"That's Network Azo," Sol told him. "Savior of the world. People were always waiting on God back then. My mother was very religious and told me not to put stock in Azo, that she was just another person and would eventually break my heart. People always felt that way then. No faith at all in people, just in old stories and books."

A whistle erupted from the kitchen, and Sol held up a finger. "Tea!" she shouted and rushed off.

Ellis watched her scurry out of the room in her flower-print dress, thinking how much like an old woman she acted and yet she still looked like she was twenty-five. Sol was in fact beautiful. Different from the others, with facial features not quite to the final stage, the real difference was that Sol had hair—hair she kept short and black.

"How do you like your tea?" Sol called.

"Really more of a coffee guy."

"Cream and honey it is then."

She returned with an old-fashioned silver tray and dainty porcelain cups that steamed. "Don't you just love authentic tea? I mean steeped, not *made*. I shouldn't say that in front of her, though." Sol pointed at the portrait above the fireplace. "But I think even Azo would still appreciate the effort it takes to run hot water through leaves. She believed in hard work."

Sol took a sip and smacked her lips in a most undignified manner. "Ah...that's the stuff."

She waited until Ellis tried his. The color of caramel, it tasted almost like a mocha latte.

"Good, right?"

He smiled.

Sol looked back up at the picture. "She never did, you know.

Net Azo never did disappoint me. My mother was wrong. My mother was always trying to find fault with others. Everyone used to do that. They hated the idea of heroes for some reason. Used to say they wanted them, but always sought to destroy any who tried. They hated the future too—which is what accounted for everyone being so disappointed, I think. When you expect tomorrow to be concrete, even if it isn't, you feel it is because that's somehow better than being wrong. But I never did. I knew Azo was a true hero. She was perfect. Abraham Lincoln freed the American slaves, but Network Azo freed everyone."

"You had a mother?" Ellis asked.

He was looking down at the little beige cocker spaniel sleeping on the floor, its big ears splayed out like Dumbo. The animal showed gray around its muzzle and hadn't moved during the entire visit. It only opened its eyes briefly when they had arrived. Perhaps Sol had the oldest dog too.

"Uh-huh. Back when I was born we still had surrogate parents. The ISP provided the DNA pattern, but I was raised by Arvice Chen in the affluent Predat Sector. She wanted a daughter, but got me instead."

"No father?"

Sol shook her head. "Marriage was an oddity by that time. People were all moving underground. It was a whole new world."

She took another sip, then set the cup back on the saucer, where it made a petite click. "Lots of changes were happening at the time. No one who has it good ever appreciates change, you know. Like my mother—she hated change. Hated having to leave the sky and *go to an early grave*, as she called it. I honestly don't know why she volunteered to raise me. She certainly wasn't a forward-thinking woman. Maybe she thought she could influence the future through me. She imagined the future would be worse than the past, some awful disaster. Most people did. And just to be fair—it did look that way. The Great Tempest had come, and millions of people were swept away. The Apocalypse, my mother had called it—ever heard of that?"

Ellis nodded. "People said the same things in my day."

Sol smiled. "I like you, Mr. Rogers. You like my tea?"

"Yes."

"You've got good taste too." She winked. "So, what's it like traveling through time?"

"Disorienting."

"I can believe that." Sol bobbed her head.

"The whole trip was really just a blur for me. Kinda felt sick afterward. I wouldn't suggest it."

Sol smiled at him. No wrinkles at all, but Ellis thought she had old eyes. After his visit to the ISP he imagined they weren't original, but maybe there was truth to the adage about eyes being windows to the soul.

"Is the future everything you'd hoped for?"

Ellis laughed, and she laughed with him. "No," he said. "I can honestly say I never expected this."

All the windows of Sol's home were covered by sheer curtains. That might have added to the homey feel. Ellis's mother had done the same thing. What caught his eye was how they moved. The curtains rippled and billowed as if in an intermittent breeze wafting past an open sash. Occasionally they split apart, and Ellis could see flowers in a window box: violets, azalea, and chrysanthemums—old-fashioned flowers.

"I'll bet you didn't. I heard about your campaign to get a woman, and it sounds like you're getting your wish granted."

"Really?"

"That's the rumor. I'd advise against it, but I suppose you know more about women than I do. Were you married?"

"Yeah. Almost thirty-five years."

"Not very long. Did something happen?"

Ellis was surprised, until he remembered whom he was talking to. "How old are you?"

"See, if you were to ask a woman that, legend has it you'd get slapped." Sol remained silent, showing a little coy smile. Just when he was certain she wouldn't answer, she asked, "When were you born?"

"May 5th, 1956."

"Let's put it this way..." Sol tapped her lower lip. "You're four hundred and four years older than me."

Ellis started working it out. Sol was 1,718 years old—nearly two thousand years herself—only she hadn't skipped any of it. She was a Mel Brooks and Carl Reiner comedy routine come to life.

"You look shocked. You come in here with this crazy story of flying through time on a set of plastic boxes, and you're looking at me funny because I can still remember when people had sex? How you making out with that, anyway? I'm guessing you might be experiencing some withdrawal." Sol gestured at the books. "I read, you know. So few do these days. I like the old paper books, as you can tell. Hard to get. Most of the things I have were antiques when I was born. The books I created from patterns I put together myself and based on the few genuine relics. So little survived the Great Tempest. Everyone relies on holos and grams. That's the one thing my mother gave me that I appreciate. She taught me to read. Sex is in almost all the books. Men especially have a need for it—a failing sometimes. A lot of the books call it a natural drive. I don't know if I buy that. Can it be a natural drive if you can choose not to? Eating is a natural drive, but I can't abstain from it."

Sol scanned her bookshelves, and so did Ellis. She had a fine collection. Plenty of history books, which must be like photo albums for her. One was titled *The Age of Storms*, another *The Empty Holo*. Most of the titles and authors he didn't know and guessed the books had been written in the intervening millennia, but he did spot Dickens, Poe, Dante, Cervantes, Austen, Hemingway, and Kafka. Ellis smiled when he saw Orwell, Jules Verne, and Heinlein's *Stranger in a Strange Land*. He also noted King, Patterson, Steel, Roberts, and was particularly pleased to see Michael Connelly—a title he'd never seen before. And there were at least twelve books with the name of *Sol* as the author. These appeared to be a variety of fiction, memoirs, and history texts. "In books it seems as though men *need* a woman, physically. Is that true? Are you *dying*?"

Ellis smiled. "We've already determined that I was married for over thirty years. I'm used to it."

He didn't think she'd get the jest, but Sol burst out laughing so hard she nearly spilled her tea.

"Oh, I do like you, Mr. Rogers."

"I like you too, Sol. Sol..." He repeated the name thoughtfully.

"It's another word for *sun*," she said.

"And a Martian day," he added.

"And an abbreviation for *solution*."

"And an acronym for *shit outta luck*."

This made Sol laugh. "I never heard that one. It's nice to talk to someone more my age."

"People in Hollow World pick their names, don't they?"

"Yes. Everyone takes the Gaunt Winslow Evaluation Nascence, a sort of aptitude test developed by Wacine Gaunt and Albert

Winslow that seeks to predict which endeavors will provide a person maximum happiness. Many people denounce the GWEN as ineffective, but everyone takes it, even if only out of curiosity. At that age most people pick a direction and choose a name that reflects their decision. In the early days, the test produced a printout that provided the answers in a series of three letters, and people adopted these abbreviations as their names. The tradition stuck. Silly, I suppose—as most traditions tend to be—but no different from when people were called Carpenter, Miller, Taylor, Potter, or Smith—and it helps skip the obligatory: *So what do you do?*"

"Thought so. I noticed a few. Pol seems short for politician, and Geo is obvious, but a few, like Cha, are baffling."

"Physician, right?"

"Yes."

"Usually it's Hip, Par, Doc, or Wat, but some pick Cha, which is short for *Charaka*, a famous Indian physician born around 300 BC and referred to as the Father of Medicine."

"And Sol?"

She smiled. "I'll leave that for you to decide, but I can tell you this...they retired the name. I'm the only Sol."

He smiled back. "Okay, I'll give you that one." He sipped his tea, and a question popped into his head, a question that had circled him the night before as he fell asleep amid the M&M'S and camping gear. "What's the point?"

"The point?" Sol gazed at him, not so much confused as intrigued. She didn't look any older than a college coed, but he wondered if Sol's age isolated her just the same. Did her *way of thinking,* her interest in books and old things, make others shun her? Think of her as cute but out of touch? Did she appreciate company as much as a homebound grandmother?

Ellis nodded. "What's the point to life? I never really thought of it too much before I traveled through time. I did it not only to look for a cure to a terminal illness, but also to escape my life, which as it turned out, didn't work. But now that I'm here I think about it. Do you know what a parallax is? It's an astronomy term. You can't tell much about something looking at it from one point. You have no depth, no reference. If you move and look at it from a different angle, you can determine distance and such. Traveling through time is like that. I saw how things were, and, after shifting ahead, I see how they are and...I don't know. I thought I'd be able to understand more about the *why* part of life, but I don't. You've lived through it all, had a lot more time to reflect."

Sol looked empathetic, soft eyes blinking at him. "I think that's one of those questions everyone has to find the answer to for themselves."

"Had a feeling you were going to say that. Everyone always does."

"But..."

"There's a but?"

She nodded and looked down at her cup. "I can tell you what I found for myself. When you've lived through as much as I have, you understand that the old Buddhists were right in a way. Everything comes and goes. Nothing is forever. Not even God. My mother called Him eternal, but Jesus and His dad turned out to be a fad like all the others. At least that's how I saw it when I was just a girl of one thousand—my rebellious stage." She winked at him. "God was just a superstitious holdover from when we thought fire was magic. But it's been centuries, and still people seek something. I can see it in their eyes, hear it when they talk. They don't call it

God anymore, but I think it's the same thing. A natural drive like wanting food, water, and sex." She smiled.

"Even after all the tinkering, the ISP got rid of sex, but we still have a natural longing to feel a connection with others. We've outgrown the concepts of magic and demons, but there remains a longing for something. The problem is, we can't define it because the word *God* has become meaningless. It has the wrong definition. It means some all-powerful man who knows all and judges everyone, and I don't think that God ever really was that, any more than lightning and thunder was Thor. We can still sense it, still feel it acting in our lives, and we yearn for it, knowing that somehow it has the answers we've always sought."

"So what is God then?"

"I don't know."

"Really? All that and you are going to leave me hanging? C'mon. You don't strike me as the type to have lived this long and not have a theory, at least."

Sol smiled. "I do have a theory."

"Can you tell me?"

Sol shifted in her seat, straightening up, smoothing out the wrinkles in her skirt. "It's not a currently popular idea."

"Why do I get the impression that isn't a problem for you?"

Sol grinned. "Did I mention I like you, Mr. Rogers?" She drained the last of her tea. "It isn't a problem. That's the benefit of being this old. You get very lonely, and are bored a lot, but you also really don't give a sonic bleez what anyone else thinks about you."

"So, tell me. What is God?"

"The future."

Ellis gave a puzzled face.

"Humans have longed for many things, and when we put our

heads together we have usually found them. Weak as mice we tamed a planet and traveled to others. We satisfied our needs for food and shelter easily enough. Then we fulfilled our dream for peace and defeated death. But one aspiration remains. We've never satisfied one of our most primal desires: our lust for God, our need for a spiritual side. We've never really gotten close. But what if that's because it hasn't been possible—until now? What if we were caterpillars having precognitive dreams of flying? What if we were seeing our own future—and that desperate longing manifested itself in this ethereal hunger, this unfathomable lust for more out of life? My mother always said that we each had a little bit of God inside. It's the part that guides us and tells us to treat others well. I think that's true. I think we are all protective containers keeping precious treasures inside, but we are also holding them prisoner, isolating them from each other." Sol leaned forward over her teacup. "What if God is simply humanity joined?"

"You're talking about the Hive Project."

Sol didn't reply; she only smiled and ran a finger around the lip of her empty cup.

"My mother believed that heaven wasn't really a place. It was merely the act of being one with God, and if you were, then you would know everything and never be frightened or angry or frustrated. You would experience eternal love. Everyone has an innate desire to be part of something greater than themselves, Mr. Rogers, and that's what I think God is."

"Good news," Pol said after stealing him from Sol's home.

Pol had popped into the middle of Sol's living room. From the way Sol nearly dropped her cup, and the vicious look on her face, Ellis guessed forming unannounced portals in other people's homes was considered impolite at best. Without so much as a hello to either of them, Pol waved him over, saying it was time to go.

Normally Ellis was happy for the go sign from Pol. Despite the low-gravity floors in the art shows and museums, he was always exhausted by the end of a visit. Part of it was physical—the standing for hours felt more taxing than swinging a pickax—but what really took a toll was the need to be "up." The feeling that he had to entertain the mobs that followed him was grueling. When Pol entered this time, though, it was different. Ellis was genuinely enjoying his visit with Sol. The tea was good, he liked the homeyness of the room, and he liked Sol. Each time she answered a question, five flooded in to replace it. More than that, she was comfortable—like Pax.

"Dex and I were just at the ISP." Pol spoke quickly once they were both back in Ellis's room in Wegener. "Dex has the pattern and the processing equipment. Everything we need. Isn't that wonderful?"

Pol was all grins, and Ellis wanted to join in, to be a part of the celebration, but his heart wasn't there. Part of him was still back with Sol, still thinking about God. His deflated backpack was on the floor, empty. He'd never refilled it. Pol blathered on about the details of how he finagled the deal. While Pol talked, Ellis noticed one of the cans of Dinty Moore stew. The battered container sat upside down on the illuminated table next to the bed. He must have put it there the night before. He'd brought four, but had only put two in his pack when he'd left the time machine. Didn't think he'd need more. Looking back, Ellis had only expected to be gone a few hours, but that can had been in his pack for more than five weeks. It looked just like its sister can and probably tasted the same.

"I want to go see Pax," Ellis said.

Pol looked annoyed at having such a wonderful victory monologue interrupted. "We don't know where Pax is."

"I want to go to Pax's home. If Pax isn't there, I'll speak with Alva or Vin."

"Fine, but we still have one more appointment to make."

"Why?" Ellis found himself annoyed. "I've spent the last week blindly going wherever you wanted because Warren needed the pattern, but you have that now. I think I've earned a vacation."

"And you can start it tomorrow," Pol said. "But right now we have an invitation to tour Subduction Zone 540 as the honored guests of the Geomancy Institute."

"But we have the pattern, right? So why—"

"I worked very hard to get this invitation. GI is notorious for its secrecy. No one who isn't an initiate is ever granted access to the low zones. They keep the coords a secret. It's easier to explore space than penetrate the low zones where the geomancers do their magic. It would be a terrible insult to turn them down and horribly embarrassing to me as Chief Councilor."

Ellis looked longingly at the can of stew.

"Listen, we won't stay long. I'm sure the geomancers don't want us around anyway. We'll pop in, look around, and then say our goodbyes. After that, I'll help you look for Pax—okay?"

"Right afterward?"

"Absolutely."

Ellis frowned but nodded.

"Wonderful." Pol drew out the Port-a-Call. "This should be most interesting. I've never been to the low zones—like I mentioned, no one outside the Faith of Astheno really has—and Sub Zone 540 I'm told is the center of everything. I'm also told it's warm. Ready?"

The Geomancy Institute looked nothing like the rest of Hollow World. In one week Ellis had seen Olympus Mons, stood on the surface of Mars, looked up from the greatest depths of the ocean, visited the oldest remaining ruins of humanity, and traveled to a planet in another galaxy. All of it paled when compared with Subduction Zone 540. The best way Ellis could describe it was like walking into a Wagnerian epic vision of Nidavelir—the steel mill of the gods—beautiful in its hellish horror of spraying molten stone whose spiderweb entrails formed erratic patterns. These infant rock entanglements became the girders and smokestack-silhouettes of an organic industry built on the bank of a volcanic River Styx. Lava falls spilled into glowing seas from which gas blew bubbles and choked Ellis's new lungs, making him nauseous. The hair on his arms recoiled from the bristling heat as if he'd just stepped into a preheated oven. His ears were attacked by chest-thumping booms of what could only be a giant hammer beating on the anvil of the world.

Strong hands hauled him inside an illuminated walkway.

The pounding became muffled, but more important Ellis could breathe, although his eyes continued to tear too badly to see much except blurry lights.

"Welcome to the Geomancy Institute," someone shouted over

the pounding. "I'm Geo-12, your tour guide. You'll have to bear with me. I've never done this before. We've never had visitors."

Ellis felt a gloved hand take his and shake—the first firm grip he'd felt.

"You must be Ellis Rogers, then—honored to meet you."

"Why did you give me such exposed coords?" He heard Pol ask, his tone angry.

"Everyone ports in on the rail their first time here. Initiates are required to use the rail port for their first year, and to find their way to the tunnels on their own. It fosters respect, and serves as a reminder of the very real dangers of working the sublevels. Up in the litho you use terms like *core* or *astheno* as if they are mythical things, like dragons or Hades, but down here they're our noisy neighbors."

Ellis wiped his eyes for the fourth time and was starting to see again, although he still winced as if he were cutting a bushel of onions. Almost everything was a smear of brilliant and fluid yellow light.

"Follow me," Geo-12 told them.

"Can't see too well," Ellis said.

"Don't need to. Just walk forward. I'll let you know if you're about to fall into a pool of liquid peridotite. Almost never happens anymore."

"Almost?"

He heard a chuckle.

Ellis moved forward, his feet landing on a smooth glassy surface. As they walked, the pounding grew softer and the air fresher.

"The real danger down here is the gas—as you already noticed. Using portal-technology, we can create worm-tunnels to move around. Really the only way to do it. Nothing can stop the heat down here. But being in the tunnel you aren't really *here* anymore. You're in an alternate *here,* looking through the opening at the churning, beating heart of the world."

Ellis opened his eyes and froze.

They were standing within a hellscape on a transom of light. All around them was lava.

"Better than coffee, huh?" Geo-12 grinned at him. "Been working down here for centuries, and this walk through the Sea of Gehenna is always an eye opener. Don't worry. We haven't had a tunnel failure yet. Everything down at this level runs off the Big D, and nothing's going to interrupt her."

"Her?" Ellis asked, surprised at hearing a gender-based pronoun.

"The big lady herself." Geo-12 gestured around them. "The planet—Mother Earth. She's one mammoth, naturally occurring Dynamo generating forty-four terawatts of heat every second. These tunnels, which are just a series of elongated portals, are permanently dedicated. Haven't been shut off in more than a thousand years." Geo-12 stopped to face them, giving Ellis a good look at the geomancer.

Geo-12 wasn't like everyone else. The lines were subtle, but there was a variation. Just as Sol had appeared more feminine, Geo-12 appeared a tad more masculine. Ellis wondered if it was the result of twelve being an earlier model, or if they made different patterns for geomancers, suggesting they were bred for this. Their guide wore a long gray coat of a thick material that might have been leather or even rubber. What looked to be safety glasses rested idly on Geo-12's head.

"This is the infrastructure of Hollow World. It's what keeps all those people above us alive. Old Gaia, she's a living thing, you know—not a tame lion, if you get my meaning. And she don't much care about us at all. She does her own thing: percolating, blowing bubbles, rolling over. She's moody—has her quiet moments and gets irritable, like anyone. We're all the little pixies that whisper in her ear and try to calm the old lady down when she gets riled."

"And how do you manage that?" Pol asked.

"The earth is a giant pressure cooker that needs to release her heat. We aim to predict where the pressure will build and then relieve it before it goes pop. Another way of thinking about it is, we help the old lady fart so she doesn't have a bowel movement that erases Hollow World or at least rearranges it beyond recognition."

"That can happen?" Ellis was shocked.

"It can—but it hasn't. Been well over a thousand years since the last recorded mishap. I think we're doing a pretty good job. Was worse for you, right?" Geo-12 looked at Ellis. "Back in the days of weather? All of us study ancient meteorology—lots of corollaries there. Every year you had multiple hurricanes, numerous tornadoes, thunderstorms, blizzards, fires. We have the same sort of things down here—much more manageable and preventable, but with a greater potential for catastrophic disaster. So we don't like making mistakes."

They continued down the self-illuminated tunnel to a central hub, like the spokes of a wagon wheel except the tunnels branched out in all directions. There they found a large room filled with wall and ceiling screens displaying images in various colors. Filling the chamber, a hundred other geomancers, dressed in similar mad-scientist garb, watched the changing colors on the screens.

"This is the brain—the center of our system," Geo-12 explained, leading them to a balcony railing so they could look down at the activity. "From here we monitor the core, asthenosphere, and lithosphere, the convection and conduction. Most can be handled remotely, but often teams need to go out off the standard lines. That's when it's dangerous. Gas can build up. Any breach in a tunnel can cause instant incineration."

"Why would they—why do *you* do this?" Pol asked, stunned.

Ellis could tell that Pol didn't understand why anyone would live down here. He imagined the conditions were similar to coal mines and steel mills around 1900, but those workers didn't have a choice. They needed the money to feed their families.

"It needs to be done," Geo-12 said with a taciturn quality that reminded Ellis of Gary Cooper. "Really the only thing that still does."

That was the answer. Why didn't Superman live on a Caribbean island playing Xbox games? Why did firemen run into buildings everyone else was running out of? Why did people risk their lives by volunteering for combat duty, and why did that guy in *Lost* keep pressing that stupid button? In a world where little else seemed to—this mattered.

Pol paused and looked out through the transparency at the frothing world of liquid rock that swirled and spouted around them. "You stop earthquakes here?"

"And cause them," Geo-12 replied. "Earthquakes, volcanic eruptions—there are 540 volcanoes in the world. We use most of them as vents. Small regulated spews avoid the big nasty explosions."

"And what would happen if this facility failed?"

Geo-12's eyes widened, then displayed a sour look. "A temporary malfunction or shutdown wouldn't cause much—"

"What about a prolonged failure?" Pol asked.

Geo-12 shifted uneasily, as Ellis imagined the geomancer was envisioning it.

"Well, plates would snap. We've been regulating things so long, a sudden halt would be catastrophic. What happened to the surface of the planet during the Great Tempest would be nothing compared to the destruction in Hollow World."

"What about on the surface?"

Geo-12 shrugged. "Be some earthquakes there, too, and a few major volcanic eruptions until the pressure bled off, but nothing too devastating—there's nothing up there to be damaged, really. Plus there's open sky above, unlike in Hollow World where there's a ceiling, which would crash. And there are some areas of Hollow World where natural lava chutes have been blocked or diverted that would be free to flow again. It'd be a world-altering event. Luckily, that can't happen. Almost everything is automated now. We have our own vox, if you will, that functions as a safety net and even double-checks our actions. If everyone disappeared tomorrow, the institute would still monitor and clear most of the issues. There might be a shock here and an unscheduled eruption there, but nothing too horrible. For the unthinkable to happen, this whole facility would have to disappear, along with all the people who run it."

Then Ellis gave his usual speech. By then he'd polished it to a disappointing monotone. The geomancers didn't appear to notice and asked questions mostly about weather and the forecasters of the past. One of them actually knew the name Willard Scott, who was thought to be something of a hero. They were disappointed to discover he had not experienced the Great Tempest. Ellis was not at all disappointed at having skipped that portion of history, particularly when one geomancer asked, "Is it true that people resorted to cannibalism even before the sun disappeared?"

&

"Welcome back, Ellis Rogers!" Alva sounded like a schoolgirl with a crush.

Ellis stood in the same familiar dining room, but everything felt different. The Gothic décor was darker, heavier, and some classical fugue played oppressively through the same unseen speakers that Alva spoke through. If he hadn't been there before, Ellis could have concluded that Pol had dropped him off in Dracula's castle. The one thing he could be certain of—Vin was there.

Ellis turned back and saw Pol, still standing in the Councilor's office. Pol waved goodbye and closed the portal. Since leaving the Geomancy Institute, Pol had seemed anxious, the promise to help find Pax forgotten. Ellis was annoyed at the breaking of the bargain, but also happy to be free of Pol. They'd just spent too much time together. Pol pretended, and might have even believed it, but their shared company hadn't been *wonderful.*

Ellis called out, "Anyone home?"

"I just told Pol that Vin is here, didn't I?" Alva replied.

"I suppose, but—"

"But that's not what you want to know." The words were spoken with a hint of sadness, and Ellis realized that Alva would have easily passed the AI Turing Test—the ability to fool humans into thinking they were communicating not with a machine but with another thinking, feeling person. Even though Alva had admitted to being some sort of computer, his mind refused to accept that. He imagined her as a curmudgeonly, but lovable, woman in her fifties always speaking to him from the next room. Alva was Pax's mother.

"Is Pax here?"

"No. I'm afraid—"

"So you've returned," Vin said, entering the dining room still in his Phantom of the Opera costume, which was augmented this time with a cape. Vin didn't look happy to see him—or that might have just been Vin's normal frown. Ellis had yet to see another expression to judge by. "Back to cause more mischief, I presume? Hate to disappoint you, but Pax isn't here."

"Do you know where—"

"How could I know that? How could anyone after you ripped the PICA from Pax's shoulder? Nice bit of butchering, by the way."

Definitely not happy to see me. "Are you saying that Pax never came back?"

"Briefly. In tears. With your murderous weapon in hand." Vin stood before Ellis, arms folded, glaring out from behind that porcelain half-mask. "I tried talking. I tried to...but you had Pax wound tight, didn't you? Couldn't hear me anymore. Instead, all I saw was despair—that's what you created. And that gun. After driving the poor thing to the brink, you put such a tool in Pax's hands—like handing a red-label illusion to a fantasy-deprived holoholic. Isn't that right?"

"What are you saying?" Ellis felt his stomach tighten. "You're not—did Pax do something? Are you saying Pax—that Pax did something with my gun?"

Ellis's heart began to pound, his hands shaking. *That's not it—please, God, don't let that be it!*

Vin walked away, three hard steps, fists clenched as if holding back a desire to kill. "Were all people in your day so stupid? That's why you had wars, isn't it? Wars, murders, rapes, and torture. All of you self-centered and as sensitive as the concrete you choked the planet with. A pack of cave-dwelling Neanderthals killing for food and recreation." Vin's voice was growing shrill, sounding more feminine, nearing hysteria. "Since you hadn't noticed, let me explain—Pax isn't a strong person. That's why I live here. That's why I put up with all this misery."

The lights flickered.

"Don't mess with me now, Alva!" Vin shouted, and took a step toward Ellis. The *Phantom* still held clenched fists.

Vin wants to hit me. You want to see insensitive? You want to see Neanderthal? Go ahead and take a swing.

"Pax has a history—a history of being weak." Vin looked down at the dining table, opened a hand, and brushed fingertips across the surface. "Wonderful person. You don't know—Pax would *never* mention it—but Pax has helped thousands of people, people beyond desperate, people who'd given up. We don't have the violence that you did, but people still get angry. We keep it locked up, sealed inside, only it's a poison that the mind needs to expel to save itself. With no way to purge ourselves of the hate, frustration, and anger, the result is depression and self-loathing. The ISP has been ineffectual at addressing the problem. Emotions are tricky, they say—like nerves. If nicked, a person can lose all sensation, and you could kill the desire to live altogether or create a psychopath. No one could help the really bad cases. Some of the arbitrators even came to think the condition might be contagious. Emotional diseases can be. They took to calling severe depression the New Black Plague."

Vin looked back up into Ellis's eyes. "Can you imagine? Living in an immortal body, faced with an eternity of pain and misery? This was the great fear of all of us. Spiraling depression on a grand and infinite scale. At least with the medieval plague there was release."

Vin placed a second hand on the table, making small, invisible designs on glossy wood. "There was an artist. The plague was known to afflict the creative minds to a disproportionate degree, and this artist—a genius, everyone said—suffered horribly for years—suffered in secret. The problem only became known after the creative genius couldn't take it anymore. Used a spoon to gouge out the eyes." Vin's hands stopped moving. "Didn't deserve to see beauty, you see. Wasn't worthy of the gifts bestowed. Went through six sets of eyes—the ISP just kept putting in new ones. Didn't matter. The loss of sight didn't alleviate the pain. Nothing did. Nothing could, because no one could ever understand the misery or the source. The isolation, the helplessness, it all fed upon itself, the well always growing deeper and darker.

"People felt sorry for the artist—pitied and avoided the poor wretch. The situation was simply hopeless, you understand. Then there was Pax—incredible, amazing Pax. When no one else could understand, could see, Pax did. Pax could enter the darkness, stand there alongside, feel it, and face it. Pax clawed out patches of light. No one else could ever understand, truly understand, but Pax did. And just knowing someone else understood—not being alone anymore—made all the difference. It took time, but that artist recovered, and Pax has done that for so many."

Vin took a deep breath and, reaching up, lifted the mask briefly to wipe away tears. Ellis noticed small white scars.

"But such profound empathy comes at a price. Pax feels more deeply and powerfully than the rest of us. This gift is also a curse, I think. Maybe some of the plague Pax draws from people lingers. I don't know. But Pax is so very fragile—and so sensitive—has to be—like your fingertips." Vin lifted a hand and stared at it, fingers flexing. "If they weren't sensitive, they couldn't do their job, but being sensitive they're more susceptible to pain. Pax is like that."

Vin turned away, moved to the nearest chair, sat, and looked toward the pipe organ, eyes unfocused.

"What happened?" Ellis asked. "Why did Pax—why did you have to start living here?"

"I don't know. Pax has never told me. I learned about it through mutual friends. Pax was in an emergency room under observation. No one knew what to do. What Pax needed was Pax—someone who could look inside and understand the demons. But there is only one Pax. Still, I couldn't let...I volunteered to move in, to watch and protect Pax. I'd do anything, you understand—anything, only I'm not Pax. I can't do the magic, and I watched the depression creep in. And then you came." Vin looked up, that same frown returning. "I knew you were trouble. I could see hope in Pax and knew that was like raising an egg over hard ground. The fall would come, and all the king's horses and all the king's men wouldn't help. Pax is a treasure of untold worth...and you destroyed that."

"Are you saying Pax is dead?" Ellis felt sick, his brand-new heart on the verge of breaking. *Not again. I can't have done it again.*

"Probably."

"*Probably?* What the hell is that supposed to mean?"

"Pax was in quite a state after seeing you last, and pistols don't have safety features. They don't have auto-locks that prevent damage to living tissue when placed against a person's head, do they? And there aren't any voxes on the surface to call for help. Thanks to you, the only means of locating Pax is floating somewhere near Neptune." Vin's lips quivered. "I haven't seen or heard from Pax in over five weeks."

"Listen, I just came here to see if Pax was back, to see if Pax was okay. I wanted to talk—wanted to say I was sorry. I would have come sooner, but I died. I just woke up a week ago. Pol said Pax wasn't here and had me doing—" Ellis let his shoulders slump as a crushing weight settled. "It doesn't matter. Have people searched for Pax?"

"Of course." Vin was visibly crying. Tears slipped down from under the mask, leaving tracks that glistened in the light. No sound, though, just a quivering lip. "I mobilized every close friend Pax has—and that's a big army. If Pax ever wanted to seize control of the planet, it wouldn't be hard. But no—we've been looking for weeks and still nothing. I'm all but convinced Pax is lying in some out-of-the-way place on the surface with that gun of yours in a cold hand."

"There's no way at all to find Pax?"

"It's a big planet. I just hope wherever Pax is, it's raining. Pax loved the rain, you know?"

The Time Is Now

Ellis had every intention of setting off on a quest to find Pax, but it took all of five minutes to realize that wasn't practical. He had no idea where to begin looking. If Vin and Pol couldn't find Pax after more than a month, what chance did he have? Ellis didn't even own a Port-a-Call.

Leaves were just starting to turn yellow and the air was cooler than when Ellis had left, but little else at the farm had changed. All the shifting through time was disorienting, as if he were skimming through the book of his life. Ellis returned to the farm less out of desire and more out of a lack of anywhere else to go. Vin had been more than willing to open a portal to Greenfield Village, wanting Ellis to be gone just as much as Ellis wanted to leave. While Warren and the others would take him in, and had saved his life, Ellis wasn't sold on the New America idea. He wasn't convinced that Hollow World was so awful. He'd seen the beauty for himself, and his conversation with Sol had only deepened his appreciation. A world without constraints, fear, or pain—wasn't that how most imagined heaven? And yet it did feel empty. Not because of its lack of challenge or individuality—he would still have plenty of that—but something else entirely. Both Warren's New America and Hollow World remained bleak and meaningless to him for one simple and unexpected reason—they both lacked Pax.

Alva has a hot-chocolate pattern for you to try.

He remembered looking at the portal, seeing the dining room.

I could have gone. I could have walked through. How hard would that have been? Why didn't I? I would have if I had known what it meant to Pax.

He remembered Pax's face and the single desperate word... *Please.*

One more bad decision; one more death on his conscience.

Ellis paused at the end of Firestone Lane and stared down its length at the old farmhouse. For good or ill, this would be his home. Where else could he go?

The only one in the farmhouse was Yal, who, as always, was cooking.

Ellis didn't have a watch—no way to tell the time except by the sun. Late afternoon, he guessed. Maybe five o'clock. Being autumn now, the days would be shorter, so maybe four o'clock? What was it, September? October? The stalks of corn in the field were brown. When did that happen in Michigan? Had the climate changed? He was annoyed with how his points of reference continually shifted. Just as he was settling in, he had skipped ahead again.

"Master Ellis Rogers." Yal nodded, almost bowed, when Ellis entered to the scent of something baking—smelled like bread.

Pots boiled and chopped carrots and onions cascaded on the cutting board like splayed decks of cards. Yal was wearing an apron stained with handprints and held a towel in one hand, a butcher's knife in the other.

"Master?" Ellis didn't like the sound of the word, especially on an old-fashioned farm.

Yal nodded again. "Master Ren has decreed that the two of you should have a formal address as per your status in the community."

"Our status? What's our status?"

"As leaders, mentors, superiors." Yal scooped up the carrots with the blade of the knife and slopped them into one of the bubbling pots.

"Masters? What's wrong with elder, teacher, sir, or even sensei?"

"I think Master Ren felt *master* was more appropriate."

"Yal!" Rob stomped along the porch, entering the kitchen covered in dirt and sweat, a wooden switch in hand. Rob raised the stick threateningly. "You lazy turd! Get your ass—" The former Ved Two halted, spotting Ellis. "Oh—" Rob quickly lowered the switch. "I didn't know you were back, master."

The honorific combined with the stick in Rob's hand set off alarm bells.

"I was just coming by to whip some sense into Yal. Need to do that on occasion."

What kind of place is Warren making?

"Why?" Ellis asked. "You can see Yal is working." He pointed at the peeled potatoes, the chopped onions and carrots.

"That doesn't matter." Rob began to clap the stick into his palm. "It's the pecking order. Ved One—ah, Bob—beats me, so I get to beat Yal."

"And I'll get to beat Mib, right?" Yal asked.

"Of course."

Ellis couldn't take his eyes off the stick as it slapped in Rob's three-fingered hand. About as thick as his thumb, there was still bark on it, green and white patches where the branches had been trimmed off. *There's a pecking order to the world,* Ricky the Dick had reminded him, *and God put you at the bottom.*

"But Yal isn't doing anything wrong," Ellis protested. "It doesn't make sense."

"Spare the rod and spoil the child," Rob said. "This is survival of the fittest. We don't want weak people here. Members of the Firestone Family need to be hard as rocks to stand the brutal days ahead. Yal is still the new recruit. Master Ren wants to toughen the young one up. Indoctrinate Yal to the way things are done here."

"Are you kidding me?" Ellis asked.

"Ah—no, master." Rob looked puzzled. "That's right from Master Ren's own mouth. He wants us all to be tough as he is. Fact is, I'm trying to help Yal here. Master Ren has decided that we'll be divided into *hes*, *shes*, and *its* based on how we behave. Now that we'll be living among real humans—once the women arrive—he wants to get us ready. Yal is on the list right now as a *she*."

"What's wrong with that?"

Again that puzzled look. "Master Ren says women are inferior to men. Yal won't want to be a woman, but will be unless I can shape his ass up."

"Shape his *ass up?"*

"Yeah, Master Ren thinks Yal might be a little too light in the loafers."

"Yal doesn't even wear shoes."

"It's a figure of speech. It means—"

"I *know* what it means. It's something Warren taught you, but apparently he skipped the lesson on sarcasm."

Rob continued to stare at him, bewildered.

Ellis was angry. He was mad at Rob for blindly following orders, mad at Yal for gleefully accepting a beating with the promise that the cook could do the same to the next recruit. He was angry with Warren for creating such a vicious system. Mostly he was mad at himself. For that he had plenty of reasons.

"Where is old *Master Ren,* anyway?"

"In the village—Menlo Park, inside Edison's workshop."

"I think maybe I ought to have a talk with him."

Ellis aimed for the door, but stopped short, reached out, and pulled the switch away from Rob. "Don't go hitting anyone anymore."

"But Master Ren—"

"Yeah, I know. Master Ren likes hitting a little too much, and if I'm going to live here, that's going to have to change."

Ellis marched the length of Firestone Lane. Thinking back, he realized he'd made a lot of excuses for Warren over the years. Warren had lost control many times, and he had pulled his friend out of more than a few bar fights, usually because of something stupid that Warren had said. Then there was the time Ellis visited the Eckard household. Warren's second wife, Kelly, had answered the door wearing her husband's big mirrored aviators. The sunglasses, long-sleeved shirt, and makeup couldn't hide the split lip.

"Fell down the stairs," she had told him with Warren looking on.

"Maybe you should consider moving to a house that doesn't have steps," he had replied, never knowing if she understood his meaning. Kelly wasn't any better at catching innuendo than Rob. That was the closest he had ever come to defying Warren.

It only took two thousand years to sink in, but Ellis Rogers could be taught. Maybe it was time Warren learned about the second half of the Bible.

ஃ

The Edison laboratory was on the other side of the village, closer to where Ellis had found Geo-24's body—where he had first met Pax. He had run by it that day, taking no notice of the long peak-roofed building that looked like an old train station with its white clapboard siding, decorative porch posts that gave the impression of archways, and round attic window bisected by muntins to look like crosshairs on a rifle scope. This wasn't the real Edison lab. By the time Ford thought to relocate the facilities in the 1920s, there was nothing left to move. The buildings had been removed or collapsed. Ford had his workers reconstruct this replica based on photographs and using scavenged materials, but Ellis imagined there wasn't much difference between the Dearborn version and the New Jersey original.

Ellis reached the start of the Menlo Park complex, passing the green-tarnished, bronze statue of Edison, sitting grandfatherly on a rock as if about to impart some word of genius. As he walked up Port Street, he saw someone. Although too far away to read a name tag, the Amish outfit suggested that either the person was a member of the Firestone Farm family, or the Mennonites of Pennsylvania had not only survived unobserved but were taking a vacation at the Henry Ford Museum. Whoever it was, they had been leaning on the picket fence surrounding the Menlo Park complex and rushed inside the lab the moment Ellis appeared. By the time Ellis turned onto Christie Street, Warren was on the front porch of the lab waiting for him.

"Well, well, if it ain't Mr. Rogers. The prodigal son returns." Warren stood, his shirt buttoned to the neck, sleeves rolled up to the elbows, with what looked to be grease staining his hands. "How you feeling?"

"I thought it was Master Rogers?" Ellis said. "Isn't that what you ordered them to call us?"

"It is indeed. Figured it was important to establish these things early."

"What things? The pecking order?"

"Yeah." Warren glanced behind him at the lab, and, putting an arm around Ellis's shoulders, led him down the steps and out into the yard, where the afternoon sun was casting shadows. In a lower voice he added, "These baldies are nice enough folks, but let's face it. They really aren't human—not like you and me, and not like our children will be. Thing is, they aren't going to die. We'll be stuck with them forever. I just want to make sure they understand their place in the new world order."

Their place? New order? Ellis wasn't sure if he was in the Old South or Nazi Germany, but wherever it was, the year had to be around 1936. "And what place is that?"

Warren squinted at him. "What's with you?"

"I was just at the farm, where Rob was about to beat Yal with a stick because it was Rob's turn to be the bully. Told me it was your idea?"

"Ellis, these underworlders have no concept of authority. I'm working at establishing that. We'll need discipline once we get going. Folks are going to have to learn to obey orders."

"See, that's the problem right there. Why do they have to learn that? I can see wanting to have women and children and families again, and I can understand the sense of accomplishment in providing real work with real benefits, but that doesn't mean we have to form a fascist state. Why not be a society of equals?"

Warren looked at him as if he was having trouble hearing. He used to do that a lot at the bar, mostly when anyone complained about football or suggested his views on women were outdated.

"Because we aren't," Warren said. "That's socialist talk."

"*We hold these truths to be self-evident, that all* men *are created equal*—second paragraph of the Declaration of Independence, remember that?" Ellis said, his voice rising.

Warren frowned. "Yeah, right—all *men*. That's you and me, buddy."

"I think Jefferson meant all *humans*."

"Jefferson was a pretty smart guy," Warren said with a smug smile and a condescending wink. "I think if that's what he meant, then that's what he'd have written. Ole Tommy had quite a few slaves running 'round Monticello, you know. Didn't have any problem differentiating between men and those who served them. Fact is, people aren't the same. You're smarter than I am. I'm stronger than you are. These are facts. People want everyone to be the same, but we just aren't. No one is—well, except the baldies. That's the problem, and they know it. That's why they're here. You and I know how to live in a real society. We understand initiative and thrive on competition. Real men don't back down from a fight. We know how to take care of ourselves. And when the shit flies, we'll be the ones who know how to survive. That makes us more valuable, more important. It's not an insult to them, just a fact of nature. Sure, we'll all be equal, just some of us will be more equal than others."

"That's what the pigs said."

"Huh?" Warren looked at him with squinting eyes.

"That's what the pigs said in George Orwell's *Animal Farm*."

"Never read it."

"You'd have liked it. Short, easy to read. About corrupt leaders of revolutions—basically an attack on communism."

Warren smirked. "Don't be stupid. Do I look like Stalin? We're going to build this new society, you and I, not some greedy politicians, rich fat cats, or intellectual elitists—just us, two regular Joes, and we won't make the mistakes everyone else did."

"I'm pretty sure everyone else said the same thing."

"Quit being a prick, will you? Listen. We both remember what it was like when we were kids. Life in the fifties was perfect. Women raised the children. Men provided the money. Children were safe and happy, and the government didn't interfere. Everyone knew their place, and America roared like a well-tuned GTO. I'm just trying to get us back on track."

Ellis wondered if Warren remembered the last conversation they'd had in the bar. It would have been nearly a decade for him, so he doubted it. His friend never had the best memory, even as a kid, but that shouldn't matter. They had talked about "the good old days" enough that the topic was permanently burned into Warren's brain. Nostalgia was a popular bar-stool topic, and they had reminisced often.

"How would you know what life was like then? How could either of us? We were three years old in 1959. You've invented a world in your head that never really existed—false memories injected into your brain by television shows that you remember as documentaries. The fifties had their own set of problems." Ellis was talking to himself just as much as Warren. He was thinking out loud, honestly looking for an intelligent answer.

Warren rolled his eyes.

"No—really," Ellis said. "Think a second. I've recently gotten a longer view of the past. We both have. Looking back—I think the brain has a way of erasing the bad stuff. When I remember Peggy, I hardly recall the arguments or the frustrations. I only remember the good times. People are always saying how their high school years were the best in their lives, but I bet if any of them really went back, if they had to deal with parents and teachers and restrictions and peer pressure to do stupid things, they wouldn't think so. And when we were kids, what did we really know about the world? We both believed in Santa, too, right? Kids are isolated from the real problems, so, of course, it seemed better."

"Yeah, yeah, and the fifties sucked for women, blacks, and the gays, right? Big fucking deal. Look around, Ellis. They don't exist anymore, and they aren't going to, because you and I will be the fathers of the new human race."

"Do you really think women are going to be satisfied with the June Cleaver existence you've mapped out for them? Of course, they won't really be June Cleavers, will they? The Beave's mom could vote, and smoke, and discovered there was more to life than the scent of Pine-Sol. They divorced their Wards so they could have careers. You don't want that, so instead you've ordered a set of female slaves that won't ever talk back. But father knows best, right? So that's okay. Or don't you care just so long as your version of the past is created?"

Warren looked at him and shook his head as if he were nuts. "We have the tools to make paradise on earth. I just plan on using them."

Ellis stared at his friend while overhead a chevron of geese honked its way south. "What is paradise, Warren?"

"What do you mean, what's paradise?"

Ellis had a sinking suspicion Warren's idea of paradise was a world the way *he* wanted it to be. The idea that others might not agree—and not be wrong—never revealed itself as so much as a flicker in the dark quiet of a certain mind.

"I always thought—well, at Thanksgiving everyone would always ask for the same things, right?" Ellis said. "Beauty queens always gave the same answer when asked what they wished for. World peace was always at the top of everyone's list. After that, everybody added an end to world hunger, then the elimination of disease, discrimination, and the absence of want. Isn't that supposed to be paradise? But that's Hollow World, Warren. They've already done all that. Isn't Hollow World already paradise? Maybe we're just not seeing it because it's so alien to us. It's like—you know—really winning the lottery. Everybody dreams about it, but if it were to happen, we wouldn't be happy because it wouldn't really be exactly like we envisioned. It wouldn't be the end of all problems. Nothing ever is. Maybe we can't see that Hollow World is paradise, because it's perfect but we're not."

"Bullshit." Warren waved a calloused hand at him.

"How is that bullshit?"

"Because it's all wrong. Paradise isn't a lack of want. That's hell, brother." Warren glanced back at the lab again, then, clapping Ellis on the back, encouraged him to take a few more steps away. "This is the mistake everyone makes. Life is all about conflict. The *pursuit* of happiness—that's life, not the achievement. It's all about the journey, my friend. Everyone always used to ask how God could let terrible things happen. They didn't understand. I didn't, either, until I was alone under a pile of snow in a shack I built with my own hands, surviving on worms. I was teetering on the brink, Ellis—I really was. Thought I was going to die, and I can honestly say, I've never lived so fully and deeply before. Every minute, every decision I made could decide if I would survive or die. When spring came and I felt the warmth of the sun and ate that wonderful bushy-tailed squirrel—man—I knew I was alive. I was part of nature like every other animal that made it through the long dark. I never felt like that before, but that's how we're supposed to be. Life is intended to be a battle, a struggle. God designed it that way. Think about it. Everything is always in constant conflict. Heat versus cold, light versus dark, gravity versus...whatever. Every living thing in existence has to fight and kill to survive. Even plants are in competition with each other for light and water. The whole ecosystem is based on conflict. Who do you think did that? It's God, Ellis. God made the world like a cage match. You go in and you fight to win or die trying."

"Survival of the fittest," Ellis said, putting that piece in place. In one season in a branch hut, Warren had managed to succeed where centuries of scholars had failed—reconciling science and religion.

"Exactly." Warren nodded. "You see, everyone thought Darwin was anti-religion, but they had it wrong. They just refused to see the real God."

"A sadist God?"

Warren smirked. "You only say that because you think conflict is bad. It isn't. It's like competition in capitalism. It drives the system and makes it work. Just think for a second. How much fun would it be to play a game like *Monopoly* if you started out owning everything and having all the money? The fun of playing the game is trying to win. Once you've won, what's the point of playing?"

"So you think God made it so no one can win?"

Warren clapped his hands together, then tapped his nose with his index finger. "Look at history. Every time we solved a problem, it caused two more. Solve world hunger and what happens—over-population, right? Discover penicillin and you get super bugs. The world is a problem-creator so we humans never run out of things to combat, because that's what we love to do. But the baldies, they don't understand this. They're trying to wipe out problems, engineer away conflict, and it's driving them insane. They spend their time painting pictures and singing songs. That's not living. That's what people do in prison."

"So how's this going to work?" Ellis indicated the lab. "Repopulating the world? We don't have the pattern to make males, right? So what? Are we going to screw our daughters or just have our sons sleep with their sisters?"

"Like I said, it was good enough for Adam and Eve, but we don't have to do that. Your sons will marry my daughters and vice versa. It's all very simple, really. I don't know why you're kicking up such a stink."

Ellis sighed. "I don't like this idea of a pecking order. It's—it's just bullying for the sake of bullying. These people were designed to resist violence—which is a good thing—and here you are training them to fight."

"They need to be toughened up. They need to know how to fight."

"Why? Who is there to fight? Did that squirrel you ate put up that much of a battle?"

Warren took a deep breath and shook his head slowly. "Do you think the moles underground are gonna be fine if we build a prosperous society here on the surface? What did I just tell you about conflict?"

"You're expecting to fight Hollow World?"

"Of course." Warren raised his arms, then slapped his thighs.

"They're nonviolent. They don't even have a police force, much less an army. They don't understand weapons. There's no way they'll attack us."

"You've heard of this Hive Mind thing they're working on, right? How long before they insist we get chips planted in our brains so they can control us?"

"The Hive Mind has nothing to do with control—"

"Of course it does. That's all anything is ever about. Once they implement it, they'll be unstoppable, like a colony of single-minded ants. They'll be the Borg, rushing from their holes to wipe us out if we refuse to be assimilated. Well, I'm not going to let that happen."

"Warren, the Hive Project doesn't even work. They can't do it. You're scared of nothing."

Warren glanced back at the lab again. How many times was that?

"What's going on in the lab?"

"Huh?"

Ellis pointed. "Is Dex starting the female Chia Pet farm in Edison's lab?" Ellis had to admit that was surprisingly apropos. Thomas would have been pleased.

"Oh—uh—yeah. Dex is working on all kinds of things. They've already got the first batch of eggs growing in some sort of incubator that he and Pol brought back."

"All kinds? Other than making baby girls, what's Dex up to?"

"Probably best if you don't know," Warren said so thoughtfully, so seriously, that Ellis focused on the lab. He tried to see through the windows, but they were covered.

"Why is that?"

"You know I love you like a brother, Ellis, but you've always lacked the conviction of your beliefs."

Ellis shifted his attention off the lab and back squarely on Warren. "What the hell is that supposed to mean?"

Warren had his straight-shooter face on. The tough-love train was heading Ellis's way and looking to pick up a passenger. "If you really wanted to be an astronaut, you could have, but you settled for a mid-level white-bread job. And when Peggy got pregnant, you should have told her *Hasta la vista,* bitch. But you've always been weak. Let's face it, Ellis, if you were a lifeboat captain with too many passengers, they'd all die because you couldn't make the tough decisions. It's nothing to be ashamed of. It's just the way you are. A lot of people are that way."

Ellis felt like Warren was telling him he shouldn't be ashamed to come out of the closet. *Not that there's anything wrong with being compassionate.*

"What's going on in the lab, Warren?"

"The future."

"Haven't we both had more than our fair share off that plate?"

"You can't understand—not yet. But you would if you had spent that winter with me. You see, when I crawled out, I knew I had been spared for a reason. Course, I didn't know what that was at the time, but Moses didn't know why he survived being exiled to the desert either. God had a purpose for me."

"What's in the lab, Warren?"

"It wasn't until I met Pol, Dex, and Hig that I began to understand I had been saved from cancer and a killing winter for a reason. So I could fix the world—so I could be the new Savior—kind of a second coming of Warren Eckard. We really are like Jesus and John the Baptist. I'm doing the heavy lifting at first to pave the way—to prepare the people—for you to use that brain of yours and guide them. I can't do that as well as you. You got all the education. My gut tells me what's right, but I can't explain the hows and whys like you can."

"How are you preparing the people?" Ellis began walking back toward the lab.

"It took a year, Ellis, and the hard work of everyone here, mostly Pol and Dex, but especially Hal."

"I never met Hal. Who's that?"

"Oh, you met him," Warren told Ellis as he stepped on the porch. "You killed him."

Inside, the white walls were lined with black shelves filled with bottles of various sizes and colors—wooden floor, wooden tables, wooden chairs, everything battered and beaten, but sturdy as a carpenter's shop. Big windows would have let plenty of light in if not for the heavy curtains. As it was, oil lamps illuminated the long tables that were crowded with contraptions of brass, glass, and wire. At the far end stood a church-style organ with a sailfish fin of pipes and ivory keys. In front of it, three people were gathered, working on the contents of a large white-plastic crate that rode on its own set of wheels. Ellis had no idea who they were, not just because they had their backs to him, but because they were dressed up like astronauts—no, not astronauts. They weren't wearing helmets—more like hoods.

"I wouldn't go any closer," Warren warned. "Already too close,

I would imagine. Dex says the radiation level could be toxic. The baldies are more resistant than we are."

"Radiation?" Trying to solve the puzzle, Ellis turned his head back and forth between Warren and the crate.

"You have no idea how hard it was to find enriched plutonium in this day and age," Warren lamented with the same tone he used to complain about the traffic on the Southfield Freeway. "They don't have a pattern for that, you know."

When Ellis's sight finally settled on the white-polymer crate with its convenience wheels and old-fashioned, black-and-yellow radiation symbol, a single thought repeated in his head: *That can't be what I think it is.* Ellis had little trouble comprehending interdimensional portals that let people step from one planet to another, Makers that created cups of coffee from gravel, and imitation sunlight miles underground, but his mind refused to accept what he knew was right in front of him.

"What's going on, Warren?" Ellis asked, his voice pleading for his friend to explain it all away. Hoping he would say, *It's just a joke, buddy—a gag. You should see the look on your face. That big plastic case over there with the reinforced clamps and the US military stamp—that's just a giant espresso maker. We're all gonna have lattes!*

"I don't plan to make the same mistake President Truman did," Warren said. "You know, Patton told everyone we should have rolled our tanks right on into Russia at the end of World War II. He was right. Same with China. Instead, we waited—and what happened? The Ruskies got the bomb, and China ended up buying our asses."

"What's in the goddamn box, Warren?"

"It's a present—a little housewarming gift for Hollow World." Warren laughed. "Literally. Shame Hal won't see the bang. Hal was the physicist—or whatever they call it now. Hal's plan, really. The trick was to place the bombs in the right places."

Ellis noticed the lids for two other plastic crates on the floor under the table. Both had the same bumblebee-colored warnings, but their associated crates were missing.

"Three H-bombs aren't going to erase that honeycomb they got down there, but if put in the right spots..."

"Subduction Zone 540," Ellis said to himself. Words were spilling out on their own accord as his brain locked up, freezing like a deer in headlights.

That can't be what I think it is.

"Exactly. Subduction Zone 540. Then the whole place will collapse like an old lady stripped of her walker."

"You used me?" Ellis glared at him. "This whole publicity tour to gain sympathy was just a way of—" Ellis looked back at the plastic crate. "Did you take that from the museum in Jerusalem?"

"The war museum—yeah. Pol said your name would open all the doors, and it did. Everyone was falling over themselves to give you anything, even a backstage tour of the weapons of mass destruction. We thought news traveled fast in our day. A week of promotion and you're the David Cassidy of the forty-third century. All Pol needed was the coords, and all he needed to get those was to be there."

"Then, what? You just went back and ported them out? Ported them here?"

"Yep. Slick, huh?" Warren chuckled. "No security at all. The place is a joke. Considered taking a tank, but the thing wouldn't start, and the portals are too small."

"I opened the door for you." Ellis found even his new lungs didn't work so well when he was drowning in stupidity and humiliation.

"Might have been able to get in there without you, just would have taken longer. The Geomancy Institute was the ball-buster. Those bastards take their work seriously. And they're smart too. We tried getting inside by talking to one, but that geomancer noticed something—got all antsy. Luckily the poor slob just blurted out his suspicions. Hal was the one who knew the most about geology and stuff. The only one who could hope to pass for a real geomancer, and I had conditioned Hal, like I did the rest of them—like I have Rob reeducating Yal. I call it desensitivity training. They're never gonna be real men. Don't have the killing mentality—the advantage of the Y chromosome, as Dex puts it. Hal took care of Geo-24, but by the sound of things, our bald Einstein did a pretty piss-poor job of killing you and Pax—not that I wanted him to." Warren held up a hand, warding off a rebuttal. "Hal was acting on his own with that."

Ellis was fitting the puzzle pieces in place, and a picture was finally taking shape. Warren in a bar beating up strangers; Warren's wife being so clumsy she fell down flights of stairs; Warren's desire to play quarterback—to be in charge—when his real talent was as a fullback.

The trio in hazard suits at the far side of the room had ignored them, but then one turned. It could have been anyone's eyes peering out of that shielded hood, even Pax.

"Two are already set—just got this last one. Having trouble with the timer or something, I guess. Not really needed, but I like to be thorough. Operation New Dawn is about to commence." Warren looked at the clock on the wall. "About three hours, I figure—Dex has the bombs set to blow precisely at 14:54 Hollow World core time, which translates to sunset here. So in the morning, this village will be all that's left of humanity. Just think of that, Ellis, the whole world cleaned, reset, and ready to sprout anew from our two seeds. And after I dropped out of high school, my mother never thought I'd amount to anything."

"This is insane!" Ellis's voice rose in volume and pitch more than he expected. He sounded a little hysterical, a man on the brink, but maybe that's what Warren needed to hear. Ellis had to convince his friend just how bad an idea this was, and calm conversation just wasn't going to cut it. "You know that, right, Warren? I'm talking totally off-the-fucking-hook nuts!"

Warren shook his head with that same condescending you-just-don't-understand smile. "Ellis, why do you think you and I are the only two people to travel through time? If we could do it, don't you think everyone else could have too?"

"No—not really. Hoffmann's equations were wrong. His idea wouldn't have worked at all if I hadn't figured out the mistake, and I didn't tell anyone. You were only able to do it because you had my notes."

"Oh, so you're the only one in two thousand years who could have figured out that error? We're the only ones here. You don't find that a bit strange?"

"Perhaps, but...well, maybe there's a minimum jump threshold, and that's why we traveled two thousand years instead of two hundred. More people might have tried but haven't showed up yet. Not to mention it's not the kind of thing you try without a really good reason. The high probability of death is a pretty big deterrent. Heck, even the most devout people who are convinced they'll wind up in heaven aren't taking the leap of faith to the afterlife. Even after Jesus came back and said the water's fine, people are still terrified, and in the case of time travel, no one can go back to assuage their fears. It's no coincidence that both of us had terminal illnesses. Neither of us would have tried otherwise."

Warren smirked. "You know what I think? I think no one else has done it because it isn't possible."

"Huh?"

"C'mon, Ellis, milk crates and batteries? Seriously? Do you think that would actually work?"

"But it did."

Warren shook his head. "Divine intervention, buddy. The Almighty picked us both up and chucked us into the future to be a pair of Noahs. And when the sun sets, *we will be*." He looked out the window again and chuckled. "It's Friday—did you know that? Gives a whole new meaning to TGIF, don't you think?"

"I can't let you do this. If this isn't some joke—if you're serious"—Ellis looked at the crate and the three people in hazard suits working over the table—"and it looks like you are...Shit, Warren, there's no way I'm gonna let you kill millions of people."

"Well, that's the thing, isn't it, buddy? They aren't really people, now, are they? I'm doing this for us, and the world. You can't tell me you like the idea of humanity living like Ken doll moles. Mankind got off course, slipped the rails, and skidded right over a cliff. We have the chance, right now, to put the old Lionel back on the metal. We can fix everything, and maybe this time God will approve and usher in the end of days."

Ellis was shaking his head in broad swings. "Sorry, Warren. This isn't going to happen."

Warren looked at him sadly. "Already has, pal."

"I'm going to put a stop to it."

"Really?" Warren chuckled, a sound that made Ellis cringe. "How? Bombs are already in place. We're just running out the clock. Besides, you seem to have misplaced your pistol. Or do you plan on fighting me and the rest of the Firestone Farm?"

Warren put up his fists like he was John L. Sullivan and laughed.

Ellis glanced at the three working at the table.

Warren noticed the look. "Trust me, everyone here—everyone on the farm—is in this one hundred percent. You're not going to change their minds. They'll do anything to stop being the five hundredth or ten thousandth of someone. After the bombs go off, they'll each be one of just a handful, and after some plastic surgery, they'll each be unique. They'll each be *special*."

Pax was right. Warren was planning on doing something much, much worse.

Ellis took a step toward the door and stopped.

"Where you gonna go? You don't have a portal. Weather is getting colder, and not as many baldies are coming up here this time of year. There's nothing but wilderness beyond this village. Trust me, I know that well."

Ellis hesitated.

"I'll tell you what," Warren said in his old, barfly-friendly voice and clapped him on the back. "I've been working with Yal to build a still. We've made a few quarts of this awful moonshine from corn—you know it's not just for fructose syrup anymore." He winked. "Tastes like gasoline, but does the trick. What do you say the two of us go get loaded like that time when we snuck the Kool-Aid rum punch into the Bob Seger concert at Pine Knob. They don't need me here. We can take a few bottles and hike up to the old Rouge River. I know a spot, a hill that looks down so that you can actually see old Detroit. The city ain't there no more, but you can see where it used to be. You can see the Detroit River and a smidge of Canada where the Ambassador Bridge once was. We'll get hammered on corn juice and remember the old days when we used to be rusted gears bound for the trash bin. C'mon, Dex has a book around here of pattern variations. It has pictures. We can pick out what we want our future brides to look like."

Ellis felt boxed in. Warren was right—what could he do?

Fact is, people aren't the same. You're smarter than I am. I'm stronger than you are. These are facts.

Ellis couldn't argue with facts. Warren had aged about a decade beyond Ellis, but he'd had work done too. Maybe a lot of work. With his broad chest, thick arms, and a neck the size of Ellis's thigh, Warren looked like the football star he'd once been. And even if he could subdue him, Warren was right, Ellis was outnumbered. If they all joined forces, and there was no reason to think otherwise, they would overwhelm him easily.

You're smarter than I am. These are facts.

"What do you say, Ellis?"

"If you don't mind, I think I'd prefer to drink alone," he replied, feigning frustration and not having to act too hard. "You say Yal knows where this battery acid is?"

"Yep. Strong stuff. Don't kill yourself. We just got done putting you back together."

The distance between the Menlo Park complex and the Firestone Farm hadn't changed, but the trip back took forever. Ellis jogged a lot of it and discovered Wat hadn't been joking. He was hardly winded. He might actually be able to do a marathon if his leg muscles weren't still fifty-eight years old.

Warren had him trapped. Maybe at one time there had been a dedicated portal booth back to Hollow World from the village, but just as cellphones had turned public phones into ugly, broken-down eyesores, the Port-a-Calls had made portal booths obsolete. Without a portal maker he couldn't get back to Hollow World, and if he couldn't get back, he couldn't warn anyone.

There had to be a way to communicate, but Ellis hadn't ever seen a Hollow World cellphone. Still, when he had first woke up on Pax's bed, Alva had said she had *contacted* Pax, and that Pax had *replied.* So, communication was possible. Maybe the Port-a-Call was multifunctional like a smartphone. Any way he looked at it, Ellis had to get his hands on one.

Yal was still busy cooking, shoving new splits of wood into the burner through the top of the big iron stove. No one else in the kitchen—hopefully no one else in the house.

"Master Ellis." Yal grinned at him.

Yal was wearing the standard nineteenth-century white-shirt, black-pants ensemble that everyone at the farm favored. Yal kept the top two buttons open, revealing a V of skin. Nothing else was visible, causing Ellis's hopes to sink.

Peggy—who hated carrying a purse—always used to complain how women's clothes never had any pockets. She constantly misplaced her keys and wallet. For a time she kept her license and credit cards in a little plastic pouch that she wore around her neck like a security badge. It worked until she lost that too. But in a world where clothes were optional, Ellis imagined Peggy's onetime solution would be commonplace. Hal had worn Geo-24's Port-a-Call that way...maybe a lot of them did.

"How's dinner coming?" Ellis asked, clapping Yal on the back and leaving his hand on the cook's shoulder near the neck. He pretended to give Yal a friendly rub while using his thumb to feel through the shirt for the bump of a chain or strap.

Nothing.

Pax always kept the Port-a-Call in a vest pocket. Maybe Yal did too.

How much does Yal know? Will he fight me or obey his master?

Ellis spotted the cast-iron fry pan sitting idle on the sideboard. One solid hit with that and Ellis wouldn't need to worry about winning Yal's cooperation. How ironic that just a few minutes ago he was fuming about Rob beating Yal with a little stick.

Let's call that plan B.

"Yal?"

"Yes, master?" Yal halted fueling the stove in order to give undivided attention.

Yal...the name finally triggered a memory from his first meal in Hollow World. "Yal...you're a cook," Ellis said stupidly.

"Yes, master." Not surprisingly, Yal looked confused.

"No, no. I mean you were a *real* cook, before coming here, weren't you? I ate...something called a minlatta—I think?"

"Minlatta with tarragon oil sauce," Yal said. "That was one of the last patterns I designed."

"It was wonderful—really wonderful."

Yal tried but couldn't suppress a smile. Ellis imagined Yal didn't get much praise around the farm. "Thank you. That's very kind. Cooking is a lot harder without a Maker."

"I don't know about that," Ellis said. "I can boil potatoes, but I wouldn't have a clue how to boil water with a Maker."

Yal shrugged, but the smile was still there, and Ellis saw his chance. "Yal? Do you have a Port-a-Call?"

"Me? No. Master Ren collected them from all of us during the initiation ceremony." Yal glanced down at the white bandages still on the stumps of his missing fingers. "It's part of our commitment to the farm."

"How do you leave then?"

"We don't."

"I've seen Pol and Dex leave."

"Well, if Master Ren wants us to go do something, he provides us with a POC, but we have to give it back afterward. No one leaves without Master Ren's permission. I think Pol is the only person who has one all the time. That's because Pol is always jumping back and forth."

"Where does Master Ren keep the devices he takes from everyone?"

Yal shrugged. "In his room maybe?"

Ellis abandoned Yal to his boiling pots and went up the farmhouse stairs. He found it easy to locate Warren's room—it was the only one locked. He tried kicking the door like in the movies, but either modern-day doors weren't built very well or they were all props because all Ellis got out of his kick was a sore foot. He might have broken a toe, but the pain wasn't that bad.

He had to get through the door, find a Port-a-Call, figure out how to use it, and get back to Hollow World in time to find someone to ring the alarm and send in the cavalry. Somewhere in the shadowy corners of his mind were questions: What cavalry? What alarm? And who exactly could he get to ring it? One of the things Ellis liked about Hollow World was its lack of central authority—its lack of any authority at all. *No one tells anyone else what to do,* he remembered Pax saying, as if the very idea of giving or accepting orders was inconceivable. Now, however, that was a problem, but it was the *next* problem. *Small steps*, he reminded himself. He also remembered to slow his breathing to avoid hyperventilating.

He ran back down the steps, drawing a look from Yal, and spotted the fireplace poker. He picked it up and with a reassuring smile at Yal, he raced back up the stairs. Once again he thanked the ISP for his new and improved set of lungs, even though his leg muscles and injured toe were not so pleased.

He shoved the point of the poker into the doorjamb and pried back the wood, splintering it. He jabbed it in again, splintered more. On the third try, he caught the metal faceplate of the lock and bowed the metal pole as he threw his full weight on it and prayed Archimedes was right about levers and worlds. The latch popped, the door swung open, and Ellis raced in.

Like the rest of the house, the bedroom was vintage Old West. Floral wallpaper competed with a just-as-busy diamond-patterned rug. White-lace-covered windows looked like three square ghosts standing vigil around the simple wooden bed. A mirrored dresser, complete with washbowl and pitcher, a wooden trunk, and two nightstands filled out the bedroom. Ellis laid into the locked trunk with his trusty poker. He didn't so much open it as bash and rip it apart. Inside he found an old familiar high-school yearbook, an empty bottle of Jack Daniel's, Warren's football jersey—old number forty-eight—and what looked like a watch battery and a microwave. No bag of Port-a-Calls. No guns.

He searched the rest of the room and found nothing useful. There was a Bible on the nightstand that looked new. Thinking how books sometimes were hollowed out to hide things, he flipped through it. Ellis found nothing except that the bookmark ribbon lay somewhere in Leviticus.

Warren had anticipated the others looking for the POCs and had hidden them.

He looked under the bed and through the drawers of the dresser.

Nothing.

Disappointed, Ellis returned to the footlocker and pulled out the little appliance. Thinking there might be POCs inside, he shook it.

"That's a Maker."

Ellis's heart skipped as he looked up to see one of them standing in the doorway, the name tag covered by a black wool coat that went perfectly with the wide-brimmed hat. Ellis froze, guilty as sin, caught with his hand in the cookie jar.

"For such a back-to-basics fellow, it's interesting that Ren has a Maker and a Dynamo hidden away, isn't it?"

Ellis was worried the sound of his heart pounding was audible. What would Warren do when he found out? Lock him up, probably. Chain him in the chicken coop or something. He set the Maker down, and looked for the poker.

The coat-wearing intruder took a step toward him, and Ellis was just about to reach for the poker—which he'd left on the floor—when his visitor stopped, turned, and carefully closed the door, providing them with privacy.

Something in the person's movements and expression was familiar. There was a gentleness around the eyes, concern in the line of the jaw, and the mouth was on the verge of a smile.

"Pax?" Ellis said the name as a wish with equal parts hope and disbelief.

The smile exploded into a giant grin. "You recognized me!"

Ellis physically wavered. He hadn't expected the response. As much as he might have hoped, as much as he prayed for it to be true, it wasn't really possible...was it? "Is it really—"

Pax rushed forward, wrapping him in a tight embrace. "I've been waiting for you. Thought you'd never get back."

"Oh my God!" Ellis whispered, smelling the scent of cinnamon. "It's you—Pax, you're alive!"

"Of course, I'm—"

Ellis returned the hug, squeezing as hard as he could, and then, without thinking or caring to think, he kissed Pax—a long, hard kiss on the lips. A tear slid down Ellis's cheek, and he said, "Oh Jesus, Pax, I thought—I thought that you'd killed yourself. I thought I had—God, you're still alive!"

"Yes, Ellis Rogers, I'm fine—a lot better, now that...that..."

"What?"

Pax looked at him grinning, showing off those perfect teeth. "I can't believe that you recognized me."

"Listen, Pax, we need to leave. We need to go right now."

"Together this time, right?" Pax smiled at him hopefully.

"Absolutely."

Still holding on, Ellis felt Pax's body stiffen. The arbitrator pulled away and stared intently into Ellis's eyes. The bright smile was snuffed out and replaced by horror. "Oh no—oh..." Ellis felt Pax begin to shake. "They're going to concrete Hollow World."

Ellis nodded. "Three nuclear bombs. I think they've already placed the first two. They'll go off in less than three hours—at precisely 14:54 Hollow World core time."

"What are we going to do?"

"We still have a chance," Ellis said. "If we can find the bombs, we can use your Port-a-Call and shove the warheads through to give your PICA company."

"But how will we find them?" Pax pulled the POC from a vest pocket.

"They'll be at the Geomancy Institute."

"I think that might be a big place, and they'll have hidden them, won't they?"

"Probably, but that's okay. I know a way to find them. We just need to make a stop on the way."

END OF TIMES

The forest was not as Ellis had remembered. He recalled his journey as frightening—a trip through the unknown. It had been night and the woods were intimidating. This time the soaring trees seemed majestic. Angled shafts of sunlight pierced the high canopy with angelic elegance, dappling the cascading river of moss-covered stones.

He and Pax scrambled up the rocks, following the river. The two had ported out of Firestone Farm back to the hill where they'd shared the stew. From there Ellis took out his compass and notepad, and made general guesses that Pax worked into the Port-a-Call. They performed a series of upriver jumps until Ellis felt certain they were close. Approaching from the opposite direction was more confusing than he expected, and he couldn't find the marks he had carved in the trees.

That boulder looks familiar. Did I stumble on that?

They were running out of time.

"Yes, any Geo. Ask Vin. This is an emergency. Listen, just let me talk to Vin, okay?"

Behind him, Pax was speaking to Alva, although it looked as if Pax were talking to the sky.

"How are you doing that?" Ellis asked. "How are you communicating? Is it through the Port-a-Call?"

"No. Just a con...what? No, I wasn't speaking to you, Alva. I was talking to Ellis Rogers...What? We're sort of busy at the moment...Okay, all right!" Ellis heard Pax huff. "Alva says hello."

"What's a con?"

"Huh? Oh, it's a microscopic receiver-transmitter implant. Just about everyone has them."

"So, what? You just think about who you want to talk to and then talk?"

"Sort of, yeah...Vin? Yeah, I'm with Ellis Rogers, and we have a very serious problem...Of course, I'm alive. Listen, I need your help...Thanks, I knew I could count on you. I need permission and coords to the Geomancy Institute, and I need them right now... Yes, I'm serious...No! Don't talk to Pol-789! Don't talk to anyone on the Council. Go right to the institute...Yes...Yes...Tell them it's for me, and that I'm bringing Ellis Rogers. Tell them—tell them *the sky is falling*...Yes, that's what I said. The sky is falling. Tell them that...You don't need to understand, and I don't have time to explain. Just do it, Vin."

"The sky is falling?" Ellis asked as he trudged up the riverbank.

"It's a code phrase geomancers use. It indicates the most dire of circumstances. It means drop whatever you're doing and get on this, because if you don't, the world will end."

"Code red," Ellis said. "That's what we used to say." He saw it then, the bright pale scar cut into the bark of the giant tree—a crude arrow pointing to the right. "There!"

He pointed up the slope. "Up here, I think."

They climbed, and Ellis was becoming desperate. Just as he thought they wouldn't be able to find it, he caught a glimpse of bright red and blue.

"There it is!" he shouted as they ran to the pile of plastic milk crates surrounding his old van seat.

"*This* is your time machine?" Pax asked, stunned.

"I told you it wasn't much to look at."

Ellis ran to the cooler.

His sweater was still where he'd left it. Throwing it over his shoulder he popped the top off the cooler. More cans of food, bottles of drinking water, and the Internet-purchased Geiger counter were still with the rest of his gear. He had no rational reason to expect it wouldn't be—just the general nightmarish fear that the worst would always happen when he could least afford it.

"This is it." He picked up the little handheld and showed it to Pax. The Mazur PRM-9000 was the size of a thick iPhone and looked a bit like a garage door opener except that it had a green digital display and a red LED warning light in the design of a radiation symbol.

"And that can find the bombs?" Pax asked.

"It should. Warren wouldn't even let me get near the one they had at the lab because it was leaking radiation. The website I bought this from said it had excellent sensitivity for detecting even low levels of radiation in food, which was why I paid six hundred dollars for it. So it ought to be able to pick up a plutonium-leaking nuclear warhead."

Ellis slipped the Geiger counter into his back pocket. "Have we gotten coordinates yet?"

"Not yet. I have Vin and Alva working on it. They're calling in favors on my behalf from a few people I've helped in the past."

Ellis pulled his sweater on and plucked leaves off it. Now that the weather had cooled, he found he was happy to have it again. "So you just, what? Think Alva or Vin and they can hear you?"

"They hear a faint tone or the name of the person who is trying to talk to them. The person being called can either accept or reject."

"Wow."

"Alva was being a real pain, though. Without my chip, the con can't verify who I am. And they can't call me, either, because they don't have a designation to transmit to. Alva refused to accept my call until I answered all these questions. I actually guessed at one. I suppose it's good that Alva is so careful, but—" Pax promptly turned away looking up at the trees. "Uh-huh...Really? That's fantastic! Oh, thanks so much. Yeah, hold on. Let me get the POC out." Pax grabbed the Port-a-Call. "Okay, go ahead."

Pax dialed up the coordinates to the Geomancy Institute. A portal appeared, through which Ellis could see the control room in Subduction Zone 540. "We're all set. Thanks, Vin."

Looking through the opening, Ellis said, "I know you don't like it, but I wish I had my gun right now."

Reaching around, Pax drew the pistol out from where the coat had been hiding the weapon. "If there was ever a time for Superman, this is it, don't you think?"

Ellis took the gun. He felt less confident holding it this time. He'd seen what it could do to a person, and the metal felt heavier than before. He checked the chamber to make sure it was loaded. "C'mon, let's go."

❧

The moment they entered, dozens of people turned to face them. Expressions of irritation, annoyance, and suspicion were the big winners. As before, the geomancers were all wearing long coats and dark-blue safety glasses, some of which were propped on their heads or hanging around their necks. Above them giant screens displayed thermal weather maps of the planet that changed in real time.

"Ellis Rogers, I hope you aren't planning on making a habit of taking tours here," one of the many said, approaching them. "I thought I had impressed upon you the seriousness of the work we do here."

"Geo-12?"

"Yes, and I—"

"Shut up and listen." If anyone wasn't looking, this got their attention. Everyone in Hollow World regarded geomancers highly, and a show of disrespect was shocking. Even Pax looked stunned.

"In about two hours, three nuclear bombs will explode and destroy this facility." Ellis didn't feel the need to explain the ramifications to people who knew them far better than he did. "The warheads have been ported in and placed somewhere nearby. We need to find and eject them into space."

"How do you know this?" It wasn't Geo-12 but one of the others who stepped forward.

"A group of people living on the surface wants to destroy Hollow World," Pax said. "They have been responsible for several deaths over the last few months. One was Geo-24, who the killer had been impersonating."

"Who are you?"

"I'm Pax-43246018, arbitrator."

"I've heard about you. I'm Geo-3."

"Pol-789 was with you on the tour here," Geo-12 told Ellis.

"Except that wasn't the real Pol." Ellis took out his Geiger counter and pressed the power button.

The device beeped once, the LED flashed, and an alarm sounded. The backlit LCD read 55.8 μSv/hr.

Ellis had no idea what all this meant. He'd never used a Geiger counter before, and he unfolded the accompanying directions. He scanned for a way to interpret the readings, but while it explained the use of the four buttons and spoke of recalibrating, the paper had no indication of what was a good number and what was bad. Ellis made the assumption that the flashing light and alarm wasn't a positive sign.

Geo-3 stepped forward, took the device, and stared at it a moment. "An antique? Cute. Radiation levels here are naturally higher. It's one of the reasons we don't allow visitors, and when we do, it's only for short periods. Initiates are altered to withstand these conditions. Still..." Geo-3 looked concerned. "846, run a standard on ground zero and put it on the main."

Ellis had no idea who was being spoken to. There had to be close to a hundred individuals manning stations. The place looked like NASA ground control staffed by a welders' guild. Those who didn't wear the long coats and glasses worked naked at their illuminated virtual 3-D stations, each of which could have been nothing more than an incredible video game. Some even had snacks and drinks beside them. No tattoos, scarves, or masks. Ellis imagined geomancers didn't care as much about standing out.

"What is it?" Pax asked.

"We only do a general condition survey once a month for known areas, but if this antique detector of yours can be trusted, it's indicating we're over the mark on radiation."

A moment later the big center screen changed to a stylized image of a sun—a circle with numerous rays shooting out from the center. It took a moment for Ellis to realize it was actually an overhead view of the control base he was standing in. Over this were laid the ghostly colors that Ellis had seen in spy movies when they used thermal imaging. Numbers ran across the bottom like a news crawler.

"Look—at—that." Geo-3 walked toward the screen, causing nearly everyone in the room to look up.

"What?" Ellis asked.

"The radiation *is* too high. But why? 47, get a lock on the rad source."

Everyone watched the main screen as colors were isolated and filtered out until just yellow and purple remained. Then the image moved and zoomed, closing in on the center of the purple cloud.

"Give them coats and glasses," Geo-3 said, pointing at Pax and Ellis.

Geo-12 ran to a wall and retrieved the protective gear from a shelf and some pegs.

"Come with me." Geo-3 took a step and then stopped, turned, and shouted to the room, "Wake up Geo-1 and Geo-2. Tell them *the sky is falling*."

~

The glasses made it possible to see in the bright portways. They passed through the viscous molten stone, but didn't go far out the door—just a few steps.

"There," Geo-3 said. Looking through the walls of the portway tunnel, Ellis spotted a dull metal object set in the natural black rock about a football field away. "That could be an old-fashioned bomb."

"I can barely see it."

"On the side of the glasses," Geo-3 said. "Two sensors. Top zooms in, bottom zooms out."

Ellis ran his fingers along the rims of the frame, as he fingered something smooth his sight changed, pulling the image of the bomb closer until he could see the familiar radiation symbol on the dull-metal casing. "That's one." He turned to Pax. "Can you use your Port-a-Call to create a portal underneath it? Let it just fall out into space somewhere?"

Pax's head was shaking. "Port-a-Call portals are limited to vertical formations for safety reasons, and besides that's too far. The maximum distance a POC can open a portal is twenty-five feet, right?"

Geo-3 nodded.

"So someone has to go out there?" Ellis asked.

"It's not as bad as it looks," Geo-3 said, leading them all back inside. "And don't worry about it we'll take care of that one. But you said there were two others, right?"

"Yeah...but they were working on one of them so they may have only placed two."

"And we have two hours?"

"Less than that, I think. The bombs go off at 14:54 Hollow World core time."

They reentered the command center, and Geo-3 pulled off the safety glasses. "I want an immediate extraction on the P-grid. Send Alpha team to deliver the package into the void where it won't bother anyone. 1004 through 1020, supply search teams with scanners set for a danger threshold above the envelope at a range of five hundred."

"I don't think we have enough scanners," someone said from the upper deck.

Geo-3 looked annoyed but took a breath. "You have a Maker. Use it, and be quick or we're all gonna die—so no pressure." Geo-3 turned to Ellis and Pax. "I honestly don't know how 1028 passed the entrance exam, much less survived the initiate program. His father must know someone."

"Father?" Ellis was shocked.

Pax touched his back. "It's a joke."

Geo-3 smiled at them. "The two of you need to relax. Stress is not your friend."

"We've only got minutes before we die in a nuclear explosion, and that's if I got the time right," Ellis said.

Geo-3 laughed. "So?"

"Well, if that isn't a time to stress, I don't know what is."

A portal popped in the center of the command, and a geomancer in a hard hat walked out. "Status, Three?"

"Just another day, One."

"That bad?"

The two exchanged grins that looked genuinely pleased. They could have been Top Gun fighter pilots, climbing into cockpits on the way to a dogfight.

"'Fraid so. We got three antique nuclear explosives hidden around the sublevel set to explode in less than one hundred and twenty-three minutes. Found one conveniently located right outside. I'm sending Alpha to eject it."

Geo-1 looked incredulous. "Nuclear explosives? What the bleez?"

"Honestly, I haven't taken the time to ask. Figure we can do that later over antique cocktails."

"Good enough," Geo-1 said. "Prometheus! Wake up, old lady!"

"You know I don't sleep," a powerful voice boomed, and Ellis was certain that if the planet itself could speak, this was how it would sound.

"Prometheus, we have a problem here."

Ellis couldn't help thinking he was watching a live-action remake of *Apollo 13*. All around, people rushed with purpose, grabbing hazard suits and pulling them on. No panic, no fear visible. He and Pax could have been in a firehouse watching the men suit up and slide down the pole.

"I have been monitoring the situation," Prometheus's powerful voice boomed.

"If you would be so kind, please punch us to Full-Core. It's time to make sure everyone is awake."

"Announcing Full Core," Prometheus said, and an alarm echoed. The sound inside the control room was muffled. But Ellis also felt a rumble as something large was moved, although he couldn't see what.

"We've got at least one and possibly two more explosives to locate," Geo-1 shouted. "Everyone not crucial, hit the portways. The rest I want remote-tracking. Keep your cons open for information about locations. Report the moment you find something."

"What can we do?" Pax asked Geo-3.

"Stay out of the way and let us do our job."

"Is this really just another typical day for you?" Ellis asked.

Geo-3 grinned. "Oh, the stories I could tell."

❧

Ellis and Pax had climbed up one tier of stairs to the second-floor stations and stood near the rail, which kept them out of traffic. The elevation made it easier to watch the Jumbotron, as they didn't need to crane their necks so far. They stood holding on to the balcony rail, watching the big monitor as the purple cloud dwindled and disappeared.

A cheer filled the command center, but it was brief, as there were still two more to eject.

"I never knew it was like this down here," Pax said. "It's so scary—exciting, but scary. The rest of Hollow World has no idea. We show geomancers respect and all—revere them, observe Geomancer Day—but I don't think anyone above us has a clue why. Until you actually come here and see it—you can't really know."

"That's one gone," Geo-1 told them, climbing up the stairs. "And a team near Amethyst Ring says they have a lock on the second. They're moving to eject it now. But there's been no sign of the third. Are you sure there were three?"

"They were working on the third when I left," Ellis said. "Having trouble with the timer. It's possible they couldn't get it to work at all. The bombs are pretty old."

"About as old as you."

Ellis was wondering why Geo-1 never asked who or what he

was. Most Hollow World residents gawked. The geomancers didn't seem to notice.

"You know me?"

"Can't go anywhere without hearing about Ellis Rogers. You're as popular as the last tank of air at the bottom of the sea. So I'm old—real old, and these bombs are older than I am. Where'd they come from?"

"Museum of War in Jerusalem."

"Makes sense, but those warheads wouldn't be live. The radioactive materials would have been removed."

"They obviously managed to rearm them."

Geo-1 nodded. "So there might not be a third to deal with?"

"I don't know."

"I hope not." Geo-1 looked up at the screens. "Cause we can't find it. And that disturbs me."

Ellis imagined it took an awful lot to disturb Geo-1.

"How long do we have?" Ellis asked.

"Thirty minutes, and I—"

Geo-1 stopped, eyes darting about the way people do when listening to a sports broadcast on earphones. "Fantastic! I don't need to remind you we're in a race here, right?" There was a pause. "Good work!" Geo-1 looked up and grinned. "We got it. Right outside in the Sea of Gehenna portway—just appeared on the readout. Delta team is on it."

"Did you say it just appeared?" Ellis asked.

"Yep. Must have just ported it in." Geo-1 fixed Ellis with a crushing stare. The face was that of a twenty-something, but the eyes were old, and hard as those of a salt-leached sailor. "And you're positive there were only three?"

"That's what I was told and what I saw."

"Okay then, looks like we have this."

Ellis wanted to check the time, but the battery of his cellphone had finally died. He wished he still wore a watch.

"Could I use one of your Makers?" Pax asked.

Geo-1 pointed. "Third floor."

"Does it have a standard menu?"

"It's custom—but it has the basics too."

"Thanks." Pax took Ellis by the hand and led him up to the third floor, where they found a small bank of industrial-designed Makers in various sizes, each connected to an auto-feed gravel chute. One was the size of a walk-in freezer with huge double doors that would have been roomy enough to summon a Buick. A hand wave from Pax made one of the smaller countertop models light up.

"Antique watches," Pax said.

A panel came to life and displayed a series of 3-D timepieces that rotated in midair. They were projected images but looked solid, as if he could pluck one up. Ellis saw complicated diver's watches, digital ones, diamond-encrusted bracelet pieces, multicolored plastic ones, pocket watches, even an original Ingersoll Mickey Mouse with a leather band.

"Have a preference?" Pax asked.

"A digital." Ellis pointed when Pax didn't understand.

Pax selected the watch pattern. A flash occurred and a *bing*. Pax opened the door and handed Ellis the watch from the image. It felt warm and blinked 12:00. He played with the buttons, discovering the watch had a timer before he worked out how to set it, which he did according to the displayed Hollow World core time. If what Warren told him was accurate, they had seventeen minutes. Ellis set a countdown running. Then they returned to their perch.

"Pax," Ellis said, "how did you know I wanted a watch?"

Pax shrugged. "You just looked like you did."

"Seriously? You thought I *looked* like I wanted a watch."

"Well you must have, right?"

"And how did you *know* I didn't kill Geo-24 when we first met? Did I just *look* innocent?"

"I've told you...I'm an arbitrator and a good judge of character."

"But you also knew the Geomancer's phrase about *the sky is falling*."

Pax smiled uncomfortably.

"You learned that from your first meeting with Geo-24, didn't you? During that conversation on Miracles Day, right? Only I'll bet Geo-24 never told you."

"I don't know what—"

"You probably said something that Geo-24 picked up on. You made a mistake because you were flustered and starstruck. You slipped and Geo-24, being trained to detect even tiny anomalies, noticed. That's why Geo-24 was researching you. I bet your record was extraordinary. All those people you helped, like Vin. No one else could do anything. Even the ISP was helpless when Vin continued to scoop out pair after pair of eyes with a spoon. But you were able to save them all, weren't you? Able to understand, to feel their pain."

"Understanding and helping people is what arbitrators do."

"But your skill goes beyond understanding, doesn't it? You found out the code phrase from Geo-24, just like you found out about Ren from Pol. You tried to warn me about them. You knew what they were going to do."

"No. No." Pax's head shook. "I didn't know about all this. If I had—"

"You're right. You didn't know...until you found me at Firestone

Farm. I was telling you how we had to leave, and then you brought up how they were going to *concrete* Hollow World."

Pax looked frightened, drawing away from him. "Ellis Rogers, please, don't—"

Below them the command room erupted in surprise as someone dressed in a full hazard suit entered, dragging another behind. The moment they cleared the tunnel Ellis could see the streak of blood the limp body trailed across the floor.

"People are with the bomb!" the member of Delta team who was standing said as others rushed to help the bleeder. "There was this series of loud pops, and 884 fell. I felt a pain in my...in my..." The team member collapsed. As he did, Ellis saw a small hole through the suit near the shoulder.

"Warren," Ellis told Pax. "He's guarding the bomb."

"Send Beta and Alpha teams in to—" Geo-1 started to say.

"Don't send anyone else!" Ellis shouted from above as he and Pax scrambled down the stairs to the cluster surrounding the wounded geomancers. "He'll kill anyone who comes close."

"Who's *he*?" Geo-1 asked.

"Warren Eckard."

"Another Darwin?"

"Yes. He has a gun and will shoot anyone coming near. He must have discovered we're spacing the other bombs and intends to make certain this one goes off. He'll probably wait until the last second and then port out."

"Can you—can Prometheus create a portway to the bomb?" Pax asked. "Isolate it?"

Geo-1 nodded. "But it won't help. Portways are tunnels with open ends. When the explosion goes off, half the force will blow back through here, ripping GI apart."

"Like the barrel of a gun," Ellis said. He glanced at his new watch: *00:14:53.* "I'm going to need a Port-a-Call."

"I've got one," Pax said firmly. "And yes, I know what you're thinking—and no, that's not going to happen unless you shoot me dead. And yes, you're right, we don't have time to argue. So let's go."

"Promise to admit to me how you do that, and you can come."

"I'll tell you anything you want to know if we live through this."

"Deal."

"You might want to have everyone evacuate," Pax said.

"Yeah." Ellis nodded.

Geo-1 turned to Geo-3. "Call it. Purge Hollow World—everyone to the surface."

"I hope they still remember the drill," Geo-3 said.

"In fifteen minutes, if we're all still here, you'll know if we were successful. If not..."

"What are you going to do?" Geo-1 asked.

Ellis drew out the pistol. It felt cold. "Stop him."

Time's Up

Ellis refused to wear a suit. It would take time, but more importantly it would hide who he was. Warren thought nothing of shooting "the baldies," but he might think twice about shooting him.

For all his bravado, Ellis really didn't expect to kill Warren. It wouldn't come to that. If he absolutely had to, Ellis would just wing him, shoot him in the arm or leg and kick his gun away like they did in the westerns he and Warren had grown up watching. He remembered how the digital watch had blinked 12:00 just before he set the time—high noon—the traditional time for a showdown gunfight.

Warren wouldn't really shoot me, would he?

The Warren Eckard he knew in 2014 wouldn't, but this was Master Ren. Something fundamental had happened to him in that cabin in the woods. That experience had changed his friend, profoundly. For one, it got him to read the Bible, and Ellis hadn't imagined anything would ever do that. Somewhere in those pages he had found permission to beat and kill. Warren had developed calluses on more than just his hands.

With the clock reading *00:12:53*, Ellis and Pax stepped out into the portway tunnel that crossed the molten Sea of Gehenna. An eerie silence—just a faint hum that came from the stream of portals. Sound didn't pass through the barrier any more than water, heat, or the vacuum of space. This was good, because they were walking through a bubbling ocean of rock, and he was pretty sure at this distance both of them would have already evaporated.

"Stay behind me," he told Pax.

The tunnel ran in a straight line, and even in the brilliance of the Sea of Gehenna, Ellis thought he could see two wavering objects in the distance, like cars on the horizon of a sunbaked highway. This was the apocalyptic hellscape he'd been expecting, but he had never thought that he and Warren would be the two road warriors facing off.

Maybe it wasn't Warren at all. Maybe Pol was there, or Dex, or Hig, but Ellis couldn't imagine Warren giving his gun to anyone. Still, they might have all left by now. Maybe Delta team had caught Warren just as they were wheeling the bomb through, and, after shooting, they had jumped back through the portal to Firestone Farm. The bomb might just be sitting there ticking. *And maybe Santa Claus, the Tooth Fairy, and the Easter Bunny shared a condo in Tampa—and maybe Isley didn't kill himself, and Peggy didn't become an alcoholic because I'm a selfish ass. Maybe* was just a convenient shield to hide behind when *reality* proved to be a bitch.

Reality's bitchiness didn't let Ellis down. As they got closer, he could see the white plastic crate; beside it stood Warren. He was alone, dressed in a radiation suit, but the hood and gloves were off and lying on the ground in front of him. He was busy fumbling with something and didn't notice their approach.

"Goddammit!" Warren cursed at the thing in his hands. "Fucking piece of shit."

Ellis kept the gun in front of him, cupped for firing just as he'd been taught, but he aimed the barrel at the ground. In his mind, he imagined he looked like one of those dashing detectives rushing up a New York City stairwell. In reality, he felt sick and was sweating so hard he wondered if the heat really was leaking through the tunnel.

"Warren," Ellis said, his voice a little shaky.

Warren's head jerked up. As it did, Ellis saw the Port-a-Call in his hands.

Fear flashed on Warren's face, then confusion, and finally a nod. "Well, if it isn't Mr. Rogers."

"I told you I wasn't going to let you do it. And I found my gun. Move away from the bomb." Ellis looked for Warren's rifle, but didn't see it. "We've neutralized the other bombs you placed. All five of them."

Warren narrowed his eyes, then laughed. "Nice try, but you're lying. We only ever had the three."

"Thanks for confirming that," Ellis said, and watched as it took a second for Warren to scowl. Then Ellis raised the barrel of the gun a bit. "Now back up. I don't want to shoot you, but I will if I have to."

"You'd shoot me? You'd fucking shoot me? I'm your best friend, Ellis. I protected you in school. I got you your first real job. I loaned you the money for your first car. I was the best man at your goddamn wedding! And you're gonna shoot me? No fucking way."

"To save millions of people—you're damn right."

"They aren't people. You and I are the last real humans, Ellis. All these others"—he pointed at Pax—"are an abomination—test-tube sideshow freaks. This is our one chance to fix it. Don't you see? That's why we were sent here. That's why God chucked us through time. He needed our help in putting His world back together. God needs us to kill off these abominations so that His real children can fulfill the scriptures. You have to be able to see that."

Ellis shook his head, taking slow steps forward. He wanted to close the distance in case he did have to shoot. He wasn't a good shot. He'd only fired the gun a few times. He'd managed to hit Hal because he was at point-blank range. Warren probably wouldn't let him get that close. "I have a problem anytime anyone uses *kill* and *God* in the same sentence."

"That's because you haven't read the Bible. God—*the real God*, not the liberal-bullshit-hippie God—is like a Mafia boss. The God of the Bible ordered killings all the time. Ordered his number one follower—Abraham—to kill his own son. Talk about some messed-up shit. Then He had Moses slaughter all those Egyptians and the others who were on the wrong side when he came down the mountain—they changed that scene for the movie *The Ten Commandments*, but it happened. And God ordered Joshua to take out Jericho—killed a whole city, every man, woman, and child slaughtered. Why? To make room for His chosen people. And that's what I'm doing. That's what God wants *us* to do."

"Not today." Ellis took a step forward. "Now back up—I mean it, Warren."

"Shoot him," Pax said.

Ellis was shocked. Pax's tone was dead serious. More than serious—earnest. Remembering how Pax had reacted to the last shooting, he couldn't understand. "*What?*"

"He has a pistol," Pax spoke quickly. "Tucked in the belt of his pants behind his back. It's his little Sig P245, the one he never told you about because he bought it when he decided to rob Olson's Liquor over on Fenkle. Ford was on strike, and Kelly was whining about money. He hid the gun for years. Only now he's going to pull it out and shoot you with it."

"Warren?" Ellis stared across the length of the golden tunnel at his friend.

"He thinks you can't be trusted anymore," Pax went on. "He thinks you've been brainwashed by us—by me especially. He's thinking I'm controlling you right now like a puppet master. Maybe we did something to you when we operated on your heart and lungs—put something in your brain, a chip perhaps. Yeah—that has to be it. The fuckers put a goddamn chip in Ellis's brain, and now they control the poor bastard. He's a zombie for them now. Holy fuck! How is that freak—that fucker is reading my goddamn mind! Saying out loud everything I'm thinking as I fucking think it! Oh shit! Oh shit! Sorry, Ellis—Jesus, man! I really hate to do this, but if there is any of you left in there, you know I have to. Goodbye, buddy."

Warren twisted, reaching around behind him.

"Shoot him! Shoot him now!" Pax yelled.

Ellis flipped off the safety. He could do this. He took aim at Warren's left thigh and pulled the trigger. He was rushed, frightened, and the instant he pulled that trigger, he knew he'd missed.

Squeeze the trigger. Don't pull it!

That's what the instructor had said at the gun range; that's what the instruction manual had indicated too. Take a deep breath, let a little out, hold it, and very slowly, gently, *squeeze* the trigger.

Maybe that worked on a gun range where they had nice earmuffs and nonthreatening targets with concentric circles. Things were a tad different when you were standing near a ticking H-bomb in a transparent corridor over a lake of lava, and your best friend was about to blow your head off because he thought you were a zombie.

The gun shoved Ellis back, his arms popping up like they had last time. He needed to bring the gun down, take better aim, and shoot again before—

Ellis hadn't missed. He could tell because Warren jerked.

There was a hole in the center of Warren's radiation suit. Not in his thigh, but in his chest. If Warren had been one of those silhouette targets at the range, Ellis would have scored a perfect bull's eye. His oldest friend glared at him, shocked. He tried to speak, the mumbled gasp drowned mostly by the echo of the gunshot. Knees buckled, and Warren crumpled face-forward to the floor of the tunnel.

Ellis didn't understand.

What just happened?

He stood frozen, looking at Warren, confused.

I didn't kill him. I couldn't have killed *him.*

Ellis expected Warren to get up even though he knew he wasn't going to.

Warren can't be dead. I aimed for his leg! I aimed for his leg!

Pax had the Port-a-Call out and jogged forward.

A portal leading to a star field of open space appeared inside the corridor. The conflicting energy of the portal in a portal created a rainbow of colors that sparked like a Tesla coil. From the wide eyes of Pax, Ellis could tell the light show was unexpected. Still, Pax had the presence of mind to shout back at Ellis, "Hurry! We need to roll this through."

He looked at his watch. The glowing blue numbers read: *00:3:48.*

Ellis ran forward and helped Pax push. The portal was only three feet away and right in front of the warhead, but even on wheels the bomb was hard to move. The thing felt like it weighed the same as a Volkswagen, and the portway gave little traction. Ellis's feet were slipping and sliding. Then the case began to move, rolling slowly at first but then picking up speed.

"Don't follow it through," Pax warned, grabbing him. "Let it roll."

The bomb continued to coast without their help, but when it reached the portal, it slammed to a stop.

"Storm it all!" Pax shouted.

It was obvious what had happened. The opening Pax made was an inch too high, and the wheels caught the lip. Objects needed to fully pass into a portal. Another safety feature, Ellis guessed, to stop people or things from being sheared off. Unless they could lift it and heave it through, the portal would need to be lowered.

Ellis looked at his watch: *00:2:38.*

Pax pulled out the Port-a-Call again, and a second later the light show ended as the portal to space disappeared.

Ellis glanced down at Warren. There was a hole in the back of the suit. A much bigger one. Blood bubbled up like a tiny artesian well and drained down his sides onto the floor of the portway, where it made a growing puddle, spilling out bright red that was being illuminated from below by the lava. Warren wasn't moving—wasn't breathing.

"Stupid, stupid!" Pax was shouting even while manipulating the tiny control. Another portal appeared, this one at the same level, but a foot to the left. "Wrong bleezing coords, Pax!"

"Two-minute warning," Ellis said.

The portal winked out.

Pax glared at the Port-a-Call with a fierce intensity that reminded Ellis of Isley playing with his Game Boy. *Epic boss mob, Dad!* he had shouted when Ellis had told him to empty the kitchen's garbage. *I'm down to my last life!*

Another portal appeared, kicking out a new lightning-storm light show that caused it to flicker. This portal dipped down below the surface of the tunnel about a foot, and at the intersection the two wormholes fought each other. The whole portway flickered briefly, threatening to cut out.

Don't worry. We haven't had a tunnel failure yet. Everything down at this level runs off the Big D, and nothing's going to interrupt her. Ellis hoped Geo-12 was right.

The new portal was also three feet back. Pax wisely realized they would need a runway to get the bomb rolling again.

Without a word, the two began pushing, only to find that Warren's blood had spread out across the floor of the tunnel and partly around the bomb. It was like trying to push a car on ice.

Ellis pulled off his sweater and threw it on the ground, giving them something to get traction on.

00:01:31.

Leaning in, they threw their weight into it. Ellis was feeling the sweater about to give, when the bomb began to roll. The whole case inched forward at a snail's pace, and once it was beyond the sweater, they couldn't help it anymore, even though Pax continued to try until slipping and falling in the thin sheen of blood.

00:01:15.

Ellis raised his wrist so he could watch the clock and the warhead at the same time. The bomb inched forward at an agonizingly slow pace.

"One minute," Ellis called just as the bomb reached the portal and then—

Pop!

The sparking hit a high note, and Pax's portal lost its battle with the portway and vanished.

"No!" they both cried as the bomb rolled a few more feet and then stopped.

Pax took up the Port-a-Call again. "It's not working! It's not *working!*" That last word came out as a scream.

"Warren's—get Warren's!"

Together they rolled Warren over.

He's dead. The thought was there knocking to get in, but Ellis didn't have the time. He found the little device with its touch-sensitive screen, but the whole thing was covered in blood.

"I can't get it to work," Pax cried, wiping the screen on the thigh of the Amish pants. "It's not the blood—it just won't work! It's broken like the other one."

Ellis looked at his watch. *00:00:34.*

He stepped forward, reached out, and took Pax in his arms. "My God, how I wish you were a woman."

Pax settled against his chest and squeezed. "What difference does it make? I'm me."

"Yes, you are." He'd spent almost thirty-five years married to Peggy, but he'd never felt this close to her—to anyone. *What happens if your soul mate is in the wrong body?*

He felt Pax smile.

"And you're telepathic."

"Uh-huh." Ellis felt Pax's head rub up and down against him. "I hear the thoughts of those near me—feel their emotions as if they're mine."

00:00:20.

"Why couldn't you tell me?"

"I couldn't tell anyone. If anyone had known—if the ISP had discovered—they could have used me to make the Hive Project a reality. I like my bowler hat. I didn't want everyone's uniqueness taken away—I couldn't stand for it to all be my fault."

"That's why you tried to kill yourself. To deny them the secret."

Again he felt Pax nod.

00:00:10.

"I wanted to explain, but I was afraid people would reject me, hate me. Still I knew if anyone would be able to understand, be able to forgive me—it would be you."

"Even though you know what I did to my son, Isley?"

"Yes."

"He told me he was in love." Ellis felt tears fill his eyes. "Only it was with another man. I told him he had to get over it. That what he was feeling wasn't love. It couldn't be, because love like that was only between men and women. I told him he had to choose between his family and this queer of his, because *my son* wasn't gay."

"I know," Pax said. Ellis looked down and saw that Pax was crying too. "And I know, afterward, you would have done anything to take it back."

"I don't even know why I said it." Ellis was sobbing. They both were, as they stood hugging each other over the dead body of Warren Eckard in the molten Sea of Gehenna and waiting for...

Pax was the first to say it. "Shouldn't we be dead by now?"

Ellis wiped his eyes and looked at his watch.

It blinked *00:00:00.*

"The timer." Ellis looked at the bomb sitting in its little chariot, a black silhouette against the blast furnace. "Warren said they were having trouble with the timer."

Pax looked at the bomb too. "Does that mean it won't go off at all, or do we just have more time?"

"Does it matter?" Ellis took the Port-a-Call from Pax and began scrubbing it with his shirttail. "Spit on your hands, wash them clean."

"It won't work. I told you, it's not the blood."

When Ellis had cleaned the device, he carefully handed it back. "Try it again anyway."

Pax struggled. "No. It still won't work. It's frozen. I think the interaction with the other tunnel broke both of—oh, wait." Pax looked puzzled. "The lock is on this one. No one puts the lock on." Pax slid a finger across the surface of the device. "There."

Another portal appeared. The warhead was out of the blood pool, and the two shoved again until the bomb was rolling forward at a good pace. They watched as if it were a caisson carrying a casket.

"Go! Go! Go!" they both began to yell as it neared the opening to space.

They watched it pass through the field and continue drifting at the same snail's pace, but now through a field of stars. With a popping *crack!* the portal, just like its predecessor, collapsed.

Ellis looked over at Pax. "We're alive."

Time Will Tell

Ellis and Pax arrived at Firestone Farm with a full force of twenty geomancers, including Geo-1 and Geo-12. It was believed that despite their indenture to Warren Eckard, the *Cult of Ren*, as Pax had dubbed it, would still be cowed by the awe-inspiring presence of an army of geomancers. Ellis imagined geomancers as some kind of cross between Tibetan monks and the firefighters of 9/11.

Once his eyes adjusted from the incandescent radiance that was the Geomancy Institute to the moonlight of the rural Midwest, Ellis saw that the farm was dark except for a single light that burned in the kitchen of the farmhouse. He also noticed, with some concern, that even the crickets had stopped their noise. In all the time he had been there, the crickets and frogs had been an overwhelming soundtrack. As they all stepped onto the surface of the world, they were greeted by only wind, rustling leaves. Ellis got the impression that the geomancers didn't get out much. They stared at their surroundings like Iowans in Manhattan. A bunch of mad-scientists dressed in lab coats and safety glasses, they gathered before the open portal until it winked out, leaving them in darkness.

The farm felt different. The house, the road, the barn, even the fields had always been a virtual postcard from home. Ellis followed the line of the wooden fence, getting his bearings. As he did, he noted the dark loft-eyes of the barn and the field of corn. It all reminded him of a Stephen King novel. Something bad had happened there.

They were all still looking around when Ellis heard Pax suck in a breath. He followed the line of sight and saw the body on the side of the porch. Four steps later, Ellis could read the name ROB on the blood-soaked shirt.

"Another," Geo-1 said, pointing down the lane to where another body lay.

Holding his gun in both hands again, and keeping an eye to the fields, Ellis walked down and turned the body over. It was Bob. Clutched in his hand was a pair of bloodstained sheep shears.

They all waited before the porch. No one wanted to go inside. Geomancers fought a daily, high-stakes battle with the primordial powers of a thermal dynamic planet, but two dead bodies in front of a farmhouse had left them helpless. Ellis wasn't a cop, and had never served in the military, but he was from Detroit. This was his landscape, his jurisdiction, and that made it his job to look inside.

He advanced, holding his arms bent, the barrel pointing up the same way Jaclyn Smith used to in *Charlie's Angels.* Why he didn't think of *Mannix*, *Adam-12,* or *Hill Street Blues,* he didn't understand. The door was open, and Ellis rotated in with extended arms, sweeping the room. He looked down the sights of the gun, still drawing from his vast repertoire of television, movies, and crime novels.

At first he thought the kitchen was empty. A wheezing sound told him otherwise.

His view was hindered the moment he stepped in front of the hurricane lamp mounted next to the door frame. The room became a frightening shadow play of his own silhouette. Scaring himself, but also knowing anyone waiting would realize where he was, Ellis felt his palms sweating again as he moved around the table, searching for the source of the wheezing. Three slow sidesteps later he found Yal seated against the lower cabinets, head slumped, chin to chest. Blood dribbled out of Yal's mouth, soaking the white Amish shirt.

Movement behind him galloped his heart. Ellis turned, only to see Pax leading the geomancers in.

"It's Yal," Ellis said, and without knowing why, except that he felt more was needed, added, "Yal was a cook—the one who designed the minlatta we ate."

With a face filled with dread and concern, Pax knelt down. "Still alive." Pax touched Yal's cheek, and the cook's eyes slowly opened.

"We should get Yal to the ISP," Geo-1 said. A portal popped open between the table and the iron stove. One of the geomancers went through. Soon after, three ISP associates rushed back out, carrying a stretcher device. Pax stayed with Yal until they sent the cook through the portal.

Ellis had other responsibilities, and searched the rooms. The Civil War funeral parlor was empty. The table and Warren's chair were overturned. The main floor was clear, leaving him with the stairs. They creaked with Ellis's weight. *Great*, he thought, *nothing like announcing myself to the crazy at the top of the stairs with Warren's hunting rifle.*

He climbed with his back sliding up the wall, his arms out, aiming up the steps. His new heart was pumping hard, his stomach climbing its own set of steps up his throat. At the top of the stairs he found Hig, stabbed to death.

He entered Warren's old bedroom and was carefully peering under the bed when Pax entered. "Pol and Dex are gone."

"How do—"

"Yal," Pax replied to the question he was about to ask. "Couldn't talk, but I was able to see what happened."

Pax sat on the bed, looking sick. Ellis put his pistol down and sat alongside, close enough that their shoulders touched.

"What did happen?" Ellis asked.

"Yal thinks Dex started it. Sabotaged Ren's Port-a-Call, locking it—that's why I had such trouble. I've been using POCs for centuries, and I had trouble figuring it out. Ren didn't have a chance. If everything went according to plan, Ren would have died along with the rest of us. That would have left just those here on the farm—perfectly positioned to survive a holocaust—and whatever few survivors that might have escaped. Ren and Pol had both expected there would be some, but assumed they wouldn't survive without the infrastructure of Hollow World. They had planned to hunt down and kill those who did, tracking them by their chips."

"So Dex double-crossed Warren?"

"Hard to say. Yal doesn't understand it, really. Maybe Dex and Pol were working together to take control, or they might have both been out for themselves, looking to double-cross the other. All Yal knows is that once it was revealed that Warren was dead, that his POC had been sabotaged, everyone started fighting."

"Survival of the fittest," Ellis said thoughtfully. "Warren got his wish. He wanted to *toughen* them up, teach them the value of conflict, the value of reaching for the top. They learned well. So, where are Pol and Dex?"

Pax's head shook. "Yal doesn't know—just saw portals open. Yal expected to die—would have, too, if we hadn't come along."

"Will Yal be all right?"

"Physically, but Yal's having trouble understanding their deception. People from Hollow World aren't used to such behavior—Yal never saw it coming."

Ellis sighed. "You can never tell what a person is thinking."

Pax looked at him with a sad face. "I can."

By the time they returned downstairs, more ISP associates were on the scene and most of the geomancers were gone.

"So, will this be the end of it?" one of the ISP associates asked.

"Cha!" Pax greeted the physician with a warm hug. "You got here fast."

"Went to the ISP after the evac was canceled. Figured there might be injuries. People being careless with their POCs because of the alarm. So I was there when the accident alert was triggered."

"I've missed you."

"A lot of people have missed *you*," Cha said. "Rumor had it... Well, I'm glad to see the rumors were wrong." Cha turned to Ellis. "I hear you got a complete organ rework. Staying out of the sun now, I hope."

"Nice to see you again, Cha," Ellis said. "I never got a chance to thank you."

Cha shrugged his tattooed shoulders. "It's what I do. Speaking of which, if you'll excuse me."

Cha left them to speak to others on the stairs.

Ellis and Pax walked down and out of the house, where more people had gathered and lights had been set up. Several people recognized Ellis and headed their way. Pax grabbed Ellis's hand, and the two slipped into the shadows of the cornfield, then out into the village.

They came out on Main Street and walked along the old-fashioned lane in silence. Too many emotions. Too many ideas and memories. Ellis found it hard to think. He would need a month just to sort through everything himself and decompress. Peggy was dead; Warren was dead. He didn't feel as much as he should, just a certain dullness, which meant the wave was likely on hold. The same had happened with Isley. He didn't react right away. Some people do. For Ellis, shocks took a while to settle in. This was the calm before the storm.

He didn't know what to do about Pax. He'd spent almost four decades with a woman, and the only thing he had in common with Peggy was sex. Could the opposite work? Were his feelings even real? Maybe he just thought he loved Pax because of all they had been through together. Plus, Pax could read his mind and tell him exactly what he *wanted* to hear. Couldn't that be a huge part of why he felt so comfortable?

Ellis glanced over, realizing that Pax was likely eavesdropping on him at that very moment. He stopped Pax in front of Wrights' cycle shop and shivered with the autumn wind.

"Is it awful?" he asked.

"Awful?"

"Hearing other people's thoughts. Knowing what they really think about you, about each other, about all the little stupid things. You were just *listening* to me a moment ago, weren't you?"

"A little."

"I'm sorry if I—"

"Don't be sorry. You shouldn't be sorry about your thoughts. They're who you are."

"But it's got to be awful, right? In all the science fiction books and movies, telepaths are usually driven insane because they can't block out the constant thoughts of everyone around them."

Pax looked at him dubiously. "Really?"

They were under the green-and-white-striped awning that shaded the picture window with the old-fashioned bicycle. Pax took a step and leaned against the lamppost near the curb before saying, "When you're in public, you hear conversations, right? You can't close your ears. You can't *not* hear them. Does that mean you're insane?"

"No, but I'm also not hearing *everything*," Ellis countered. "Or is it like background noise? My wife used to have the TV on all the time for that very reason." He looked at Pax, who looked so young. "Do you even know what a television is?"

"Of course I do. You had a big Sony projection screen that took up a lot of room. You used to flip-flop between getting a brand-new flat-panel model and a desire to just get rid of it altogether. Sometimes you felt that Peggy loved the television more than she loved you."

Ellis raised his brows. "So you know—that's good."

"I also know it bothers you," Pax said.

"That you hear every stray thought I have?"

Pax offered a nervous smile.

"Not in the slightest," Ellis replied.

"Liar."

"And I hate you, by the way," he added.

"Liar."

"Listen," Ellis said, "if we're going to continue...well, whatever this is...that's something you'll have to accept about me. I'm a habitual liar."

"Liar."

"Okay, now whose point are you proving?"

Pax started to speak and then stopped, looking puzzled.

"Ha!" Ellis clapped his hands together.

Pax smirked and then, reaching out, hugged him tight. "I love you."

"Why?" Ellis really wanted to know. He didn't have the gift to read minds, and he honestly couldn't understand why a young, gifted person like Pax would care for a lonely, miserable old man.

"You aren't miserable," Pax said. "And you've seen my home—I love old things. And as for being lonely...well, everyone is. That's something I hope to change. I want you *not* to be lonely. I spent my entire life trying to fix things, but I never wanted to fix anything more than to take away your sense of loneliness. To make you see that you deserve to be loved. That love really is possible, and not just something trivialized in books and on television. And you're not alone; so many people feel the same way."

"Is that it? Is that what I am? A broken watch you want to fix?"

"No." Pax took a breath. "I love you because of everything I see in you. It's because of how you took a chance, came to a new world, and risked your own life to save it, me, and all the people you didn't even know. You're so much better than you think you are. I can see you—who you *really* are—without the cloud of your self-doubt and the weight of your regrets. My gift is more than just the ability to hear thoughts, a lot more. It's like I *am* you, in a way. I don't just know what goes on in your head, I understand it too. As twisted as Ren was, I understood him—even sympathized, because part of me was Ren. So I can see you very clearly, and believe me, you're beautiful. But also I love you because...well... because you recognized me."

"Huh?"

"When I showed up at the farm, dressed like this—like all the others—you knew it was me."

"I don't see why that's such a big deal."

"It is. Trust me. It is."

The bodies had all been gathered up and spirited out. Ellis wondered what they did with them. If death was such a rarity, the earth sacred, and God nonexistent did they bother with burials anymore? The ceremonial burying of the dead was one of the first civilized things humanity ever did, the first thing that indicated empathy and a belief in an afterlife. What did it mean if such a fundamental milestone had been rescinded? What did it say about the human race going forward?

The thought disturbed him as he walked alone through the empty streets of Greenfield Village. Morning had come and gone as did all the people from Hollow World. Ellis moved down Main Street past the J. R. Jones General Store. The two-story clapboard front with big picture windows draped with red, white, and blue bunting looked like every general store Ellis had ever seen in a period movie. Maybe that was the reason the store—the whole village—felt more familiar, more precious than his own neighborhood. Ellis didn't miss his suburban cookie-cutter home, but he did feel a loss for the general stores and the village greens that had once been the heart of communities. They were more than just places. They were icons of an era—of an epoch. Ellis could already see the untended grass growing high. Now that the members of the Cult of Ren had turned Greenfield Village into the crime scene of not just one, but multiple murders, would people stay away? Would the village be left to decay and disappear?

Ellis took a seat on one of the benches. The seat was cold. Autumn was coming to old Michigan and with it that strange phenomenon of being hot where the sun shone and chilled in the shadows. Night was coming earlier now. In two thousand years the seasons remained, and as always the turning of leaves and the shortening days depressed Ellis—just more dirt on a grave that was smothering him.

Despite what Warren thought, Ellis had read the Bible—or most of it, at least. He'd skimmed through parts where he felt God could have really used an editor. This probably made him the last living believer—God's remaining faithful. Not that Ellis was all that faithful. He'd always felt it would be a toss-up which way he'd go after he died. He never felt he'd intentionally caused anyone suffering, but he hadn't spent his life healing the sick of Calcutta or even volunteering at the local soup kitchen. Then there were the two killings. He hoped he'd get credit for saving millions of innocent lives, but who knew how the score was kept? Did the end justify the means? Would Jesus have condoned the killing of Hitler? Warren might have even been right. God routinely condoned mass murder. Or was Sol right? Was God something more, something that transcended the Bible? Was God not known—not knowable—because God didn't exist yet, except in the form of a promise? Was heaven that point where humanity finally joined together as one? Would that act of uniting be the birth of God?

As a favor, Pax had gone to supply answers to the people of Hollow World. Pax knew Ellis didn't want to face crowds yet, and there would be massive ones waiting. After the global evacuation, everyone knew about the bombs. Everyone would know the part he played. Not only was he unique, but now he would also be seen as the man that saved Hollow World. Ellis needed time alone to sort things out. He had a lot to sort.

He'd lost his son, his wife, his lifelong friend. He'd lost everyone he had known, and his entire way of life. In the New Testament, Jesus was quoted as saying: *For what shall it profit a man, if he shall gain the whole world, and lose his own soul?* Nowhere did it say anything about losing the whole world. But since he had, did that mean he could get his soul back? He'd felt an emptiness since Isley died. What he had done must be a mortal sin, and if he couldn't forgive himself, how could he expect God to.

So now what?

Ellis looked at a row of sparrows perched along the peak of the general store. Each silhouetted against the clear late-autumn sky. Wind blew the grass. There were no voices, no sounds of traffic. The world felt dead. At least his world was, and lingering in a make-believe graveyard wouldn't help.

Ellis had been kept busy since his leap forward. The few moments he had a chance to think had been moments he'd stopped treading water. He sank, only to be saved each time by currents driving him forward. But the currents had played themselves out, and Ellis had hours of isolated silence to ponder, to evaluate, to drown.

He tried to consider the possibility of a future, but before he could he had to face one inescapable truth. He couldn't be with Pax. He knew Pax loved him, and he...How could he return those feelings? As he had told Isley, that sort of love doesn't exist except between a man and a woman. And how could he be around Pax—who knew his every thought and that the feeling wasn't mutual.

Ellis watched the sparrows all take flight, flying south as one flock.

&

Ellis walked down the lonely lane between the wooden fences.

November in Detroit had to be the definition for dreary. Once, long ago, it had conjured visions of gray slush, cars splattered with the chalk of salt, naked trees, yellow grass, and unforgiving skies. That day the snow was delayed, there were no more cars or roads to salt, but the grass had still yellowed and the skies remained just as vindictive. A handful of grocery-bag-colored leaves clung stubbornly to trees, their families and friends lost, blowing across the fields. Ellis was cold and shivered.

Pax found him there, alone on the road.

"My hero," Pax said.

"Don't say that. I—" Ellis's voice choked. He couldn't see and closed his eyes, forcing the tears out. "Pax…I can't…I can't love you."

Ellis felt a thumb on his cheek, wiping the tears. "But you do love me."

"No, I don't."

"Of course you do, Ellis Rogers. I can feel what you feel. You do love me—you just don't know what love is."

Hands cupped his face, lifting it gently. "All your life, you never learned, because no one showed you. Not your mother, who didn't know how to express affection. Not your wife, who blamed you for the death of your son. Certainly not Warren. Not even your son, who didn't trust that you would come around. None of you understood what love really is. It's not lust, or dependence, or infatuation, or familiarity. Love isn't a fondness or butterflies in your stomach."

"Then what is it?" Ellis managed to ask.

"Love is the degree to which you are willing to sacrifice your own interests for those of another. It doesn't matter what sex you are. It doesn't matter who you are, or were. It only matters that you care more for someone else than you do for yourself. It's when you eat minlatta with tarragon oil even when you hate pasta because someone with you enjoys it. It's when you value being alone more than anything but agree to move in with someone because they need you. And believe this, Ellis Rogers, for I am quite certain that love is most certainly when you push away the one person in all the world you want to be with because you think your thoughts would cause them pain."

Ellis couldn't move. Couldn't think.

"Give it some time. You've had a rough month."

Ellis nodded. "I died right after you left, after I told you I was going to stay on the farm, did you know that?"

Pax nodded. "I sort of died then too. I hope you aren't planning on killing me again."

Ellis struggled to look at Pax—at that sympathetic face with those perfect eyes, stormy eyes, loving eyes. Ellis's nose was running, and he wished he had a tissue—a good old-fashioned Kleenex or even a paper towel. Pax handed him the decorative handkerchief from a coat pocket. He blew, wiped.

"Does Alva still have that pattern for hot chocolate?"

Time Well Spent

"*Welcome back!*" Ellis heard Alva exclaim the moment he and Pax returned. *"Will you be staying? Is the temperature in here too cold? Too hot? Can I brew you some tea, Pax? Some coffee, Ellis Rogers?"*

"We're fine, Alva," Pax replied.

"Soup then?"

"We don't need anything. Really."

"Okay—I'll make soup."

They walked to the balcony. Ellis wished he still had a pair of the geomancer glasses. Someone was waving to him from across the park, and he couldn't tell who it was. He consoled himself with the realization that even with the glasses, he wouldn't know. He was back in Hollow World, and no one wore name tags.

And everyone knew him.

He'd already achieved pop-icon status before the story about the Cult of Ren had spread. When news circulated that Ellis had helped save the world, he finally had become the modern Charles

Lindbergh as Pax had predicted, only with a good dash of Marilyn Monroe thrown in. Three different producers had asked him to consult on holo productions of the events. Five others asked to do his biography, in full interactive immersion, and another—a scholar with the University of Wegener—wanted him to consult on a series of historical holograms where users could explore twenty-first century America. They would build it; all he had to do was walk around and tell them what was inaccurate. Ellis was actually considering that last one.

"Is Vin here?" Ellis asked.

"No, Vin has moved back home. I don't suspect I'll need Vin watching over me anymore."

Ellis felt depressed. He didn't know why. The feeling wasn't anything solid, nothing he could get a grasp on. He just didn't understand it. Everything had concluded for the best, he supposed. But looking out at the beautiful view, standing beside Pax in that wonderful home, he had an overwhelming sense of... guilt. Survivor's guilt perhaps. Everyone he had known was dead and gone—Warren too. Even though he hadn't meant to, and even though Warren had to be stopped, he could not get past the fact that he had killed his best friend. And for that, he was being called a hero.

Pax took his hand and squeezed. "Give it time," Pax assured him.

Ellis nodded.

Pax looked over the balcony. "They're playing again."

"Mezos versus the Meerkats," Alva said.

"Who's winning?"

"Mezos are up by one."

"Ah." Pax smiled. "That's good. I hope they win this time."

A wonderful, multicolored bird fluttered up and landed on the railing, where it sat, watching both of them with a cocked head. Fall was coming to Detroit, but on the balcony in Hollow World it looked like spring.

"Pax," Alva said.

"Yes?"

"This might not be important to you right now, but you did insist that I tell you."

"Tell me what?"

"Quad seven grass—it's about to start."

A smile grew across Pax's lips. "Thanks, Alva."

Pax released Ellis's hand and took out the portal device.

"What's going on?"

"We're going to the grass, to my favorite place in the world—Quad seven."

"What's in Quad seven?"

With a single touch, Pax called up the portal, proving the location was preset.

"Pax? What's in Quad seven?"

Pax continued to smile. "Follow me."

The two walked through the portal into an open field of lush, knee-high grass and beautiful purple flowers. Soaring high above, and to either side, were dramatic cliffs—sheer faces of chiseled granite thrusting up out of a tranquil meadow. Slender white lines of waterfalls plummeted to a valley floor that was ringed in tall pines. The place was oddly familiar. He had looked at this scene nearly every day, but this was the first time he'd ever seen it in color.

Ansel Adams was a great photographer, but the photo that had hung in Ellis's garage for years didn't begin to do the scene justice.

Standing in the meadow, he felt small and grand at the same time. To experience something of such majesty took his breath away more than the fibrosis ever had. But that wasn't all. Overhead, the vast sky was a cauldron of clouds. Giant thunderheads rolled and billowed, dark and voluminous. The birch trees, whose trunks were stark white lines against the charcoal, green, and purple clouds, swayed in a strong gusting wind.

A flash of lightning arced, and Ellis realized there was something ancient about thunderstorms, some primordial connection to the human spirit. Awe-inspiring by sheer size and power, this had always been at least one face of God.

Thunder cracked, and Ellis felt the bass pass through him, felt it shudder the earth. The effect was amazing, and he couldn't help being thrilled, couldn't help smiling.

"A lot of people think trees are sentient," Pax said, watching the birches sway. "I, on the other hand, *know* they are. And they're incredible. I love being here with them at times like this. Watching them in the wind, feeling what they feel. It's like they're dancing. Showing us what to do—what we should be doing."

"Dancing?"

"Try it." Pax took hold of his hands and began to sway.

Ellis felt foolish. Pax clearly didn't.

Arms outstretched, face raised to the sky, Pax began to twirl as the first raindrops hit them. "You see, Ellis Rogers, I don't just hear thoughts of people. I feel everything—all of it. Every living cell out here. Every blade of grass, every leaf, every flower, ladybug, deer, rabbit, and mouse. I *know* the joy of every parched root rejoicing with nature's gift." Pax pulled off the bowler hat and shouted to the sky, "I just love rain days!"

AFTERWORD

Hollow World is a story I never meant to write. At any given time I have seven or eight novels sitting in a queue waiting their turn, and *Hollow World* wasn't one of them. It started out because of an anthology called *The End—Visions of Apocalypse* edited by N. E. White. Nila runs writing contests on sffworld and wanted to put out an anthology to showcase some new writers. She asked me and a few other established authors to act as anchors in the hopes of a wider readership. I wrote a short story called "Greener Grass." It told the tale of an embittered, angry man who goes forward in time to find a utopia, but since the world he finds is so different than the values he believes in (God and country) to him it's the worst possible future. I won't spoil what happens to him (in case you want to read the short story) but when I had finished it, I realized it really didn't fit the concept of *The End*. I went on to write another short story for that anthology, "Burning Alexandria," and then I had this short story left over.

I showed "Greener Grass" to my wife and a few writer friends, and they all loved it. They wanted more...and I had more to say. Many of the concepts from *Hollow World* were thoughts that had been floating in my head for decades and just didn't have the right place to come out. As I worked on other projects, ideas for *Hollow World* kept coming to me. I'd jot them down in my notebook and try to keep focused on the book I was writing at the time.

The next book on my queue was *Rhune*. This is the first novel in a three-book series: The First Empire, a new set of fantasy stories based in the distant past of the world of Elan (setting for my Riyria Revelations and Riyria Chronicles). My thought was that those books should sell well, as they have an established readership who has already expressed an interest in that plot line. Writing *Rhune* was the smart thing to do. But I'm pretty much known for *not* doing what is smart when it comes to my writing career.

Hollow World was a huge risk. It was in a different genre, and one whose readership had been dwindling over the years. A quick look at the publishing landscape made it clear that the only science fiction books that were selling well were those of an established franchise like *Star Wars* or *Halo*, space opera, and military science fiction. This book was none of those. Not to mention it touched on subjects that people argue over constantly: liberal versus conservative, gay rights, religion, and God. There are plenty of ideologies in this book that people will feel strongly about, and I'm sure many people will hate the book, and possibly me, for some of the things expressed within its covers. But none of that could diminish my desire to write this story.

While we are on the subject of ideologies, I'm sure several people will infer what they believe are my opinions on any number of topics. They're probably almost certainly wrong. As a writer, I spend a great deal of time imagining myself in other people's shoes, and I've been known to argue one side of an argument over a few beers, then once I've convinced my drinking buddy to agree with my position, I turn around and argue the opposite side and bring him right back to where he started. It's an annoying habit, but it can be fun.

In my book *Rise of Empire* Royce Melborn is arguing with Hadrian Blackwater about the notion of absolutes. They are discussing how an object (in this case a dagger) appears differently when viewed from different perspectives. Hadrian concludes that neither perception is correct, but Royce has a different take: that both are right. He goes on to say, "One truth doesn't refute another. Truth doesn't lie in the object, but in how we see it." In other words, two people can have completely different opinions and yet they can both be "right." The problem, as I see it, is that most believe that if they are "right" then the other opinion must be "wrong." I believe in dualities.

But getting back to the writing of *Hollow World*, from a logical point of view, I shouldn't have written it. I knew it would be a tough sell to publishers, and it may never find an audience. But I don't care. I love the way the book came out and if the only people who ever love it are my wife and myself, well then that's enough for me.

After reading the book my agent told me she loved it (okay so that's three, but in some respects she is paid to love my work), and then she said what I already knew, which is it will be a hard sell. If she could get an offer, it wouldn't be for much. No new news there. She sent the book to Orbit. My editor echoed Teri's opinion…"Great book. No market. We'll have to pass…and oh, by the way, why isn't Michael working on the next fantasy series?"

In many ways the rejection was a relief. I had been wanting to do some self-publishing for a while. This isn't to say I'm turning my back on traditional publishing…remember I'm a believer in dualities. And while much of the publishing landscape is waging a religious war between traditional and self-publishing, I probably understand better than most (because I've done both) that there are pros and cons to each. Truth be told, I had every intention on self-publishing The Riyria Chronicles but Orbit's offer was more than I thought I could make through self-publishing, so I signed a contract for it.

So anyway, I had gotten it into my head that I would self-publish *Hollow World*, but there was a miscommunication and my agent had submitted the book to another publisher after Orbit passed. They loved it (that's what, four now?), and made a nice five-figure offer. Robin ran the numbers, and determined that I could still earn more with *Hollow World* through self-publishing so I turned it down.

For those that don't know, I originally self-published the first five books of The Riyria Revelations and then later the series was sold to Orbit. While our self-published books were quality products, they were also produced on a shoestring budget. I did all the covers, Robin was the main editor, and we paid a few hundred dollars to freelance copy editors. We've always had the philosophy that if you are going to self-publish a book, you need to have a product equal to what New York is releasing.

Having published The Riyria Revelations and The Riyria Chronicles traditionally, we had experienced the "New York" process. We wanted to use the same professionals that had worked on those projects (see the acknowledgements for full details), and so we discarded the shoestring approach to have *Hollow World* produced just as if it had come out of New York. We estimated needing about $6,000 for cover art and editing. Having seen several authors successfully use Kickstarter, it seemed like a good way to raise cash to fund the startup costs.

We launched the Kickstarter with a goal of $3,000. The thought being that we would contribute half the money and the readership the other half. Plus I thought $3,000 was a reachable goal but $6,000 would be a stretch. If the funding failed, it wouldn't be the end of the world, we could always get a small business loan or take the money out of our nest egg, but I didn't want to have the failure around my neck like an albatross. It turned out that my fear wasn't warranted as the generous Kickstarter supporters gave $30,857. I can't say enough good things about the people who funded the project—more about them in the acknowledgements.

So *Hollow World* was going to be released, but there were still a few problems. I have had great success in the audio book world and I wanted my fans who "listen" (rather than read) to be able to get *Hollow World* as well. Usually audio books are sold by the publisher as a subsidiary right (keeping 50% in the process...ouch!) but I had no publisher. Luckily my audio book publisher read and loved *Hollow World* (what's that, five now?) and were willing to sign it even without a big-publisher attached. What's more they gave me four times the money as for The Riyria Revelations and I get 100% of the royalty earned rather than splitting with a traditional publisher. Double win!

When it comes to print, traditional publishing has tremendous value that we can't achieve on our own. They get the books in to bookstores and libraries, and their share of profits is much more reasonable than the standard division with ebooks. Plus, the rights revert much more cleanly when dealing with just print. Once all the books are sold, you are indeed "out of print" and the rights revert. What we really needed was a print-only deal.

If you've ever been to an online forum where self-published writers talk to one another you hear this a lot: "I'll never sell my ebook book rights, but if a publisher wants the print rights, I'd sell those." This is a great line to throw out, but unless you are REALLY ingrained in publishing you don't realize just how ludicrous a statement this is. Publishers don't work this way. They know that the biggest share is going to come from ebooks and they aren't willing to settle for just half that pie. They want it all and that means all the contracts are for combined print, ebook, and usually audio as well.

There have only been a few print-only deals, and all of them from authors with a huge number of sales. The first was Bella Andre in October 2012 (just a year ago) when Harlequin paid her seven figures. In December 2012 Hugh Howey got one from Simon & Schuster. Then in January 2013 Colleen Hoover (another huge-selling romance author) got a print-only deal from Atria (imprint of Simon & Schuster). The only other print-only deals I know about were done by Brandon Sanderson who kept the ebook rights to two novellas: *The Emperor's Soul* and *Legion*.

The problem is that each of these authors are *New York Times* bestsellers. They either have sold in excess of one million books, or have exceeded 500,000 sales plus have a major film option (Hugh Howey). I'm NOT in their league. So the chance of me getting a print-only deal wasn't good.

My wife has a saying, "You never know until you try." She knew about Laurie McLean and her new agency Foreword Literary because she represents Tee Morris and Pip Ballantine, two excellent writers who we've become friends with over the years. Laurie's background is in public relations and she started Foreword with an interesting mission. The following is from her website: "We blend the tried-and-true methods of traditional publishing with the brash new opportunities engendered by digital publishing, emerging technologies, and an evolving author-agent relationship." It sounded like exactly what we were looking for.

Robin talked to Laurie about managing the print-only, movie, and foreign language rights. While two of those rights are still being worked, Laurie did land a print-only deal. Tachyon Publications, who is the same publisher who did Brandon's print-only deal for *The Emperor's Soul* will be doing a print-only deal for *Hollow World*. This is great because readers who love print have problems getting access to self-published titles. They are generally not in bookstores and libraries, but because Tachyon is a traditional publisher with an extensive distribution network, these hurdles will be easily jumped. They sold tens of thousands of copies of Brandon's novella, and while my name is not as big as Sanderson's, Robin and I are going to do everything in our power to show Tachyon, and publishing in general, that more print-only deals need to be signed...and not just with the mega-sellers.

So there you have it, a little about how the book came to be. Some may find this boring, but a lot of aspiring authors should find the changes in the industry worth learning about. I do hope you enjoyed *Hollow World*. While it was originally written as a standalone novel I have thought about many more stories that could be told about Ellis and Pax and the world in which they live. As I said, writing *Hollow World* was a gamble and I'd like to be a bit smarter about any future projects in this world. So if you liked it, and want more, please drop me a line at michael.sullivan.dc@ gmail.com, or better yet, take a few minutes to answer the poll at:

http://michaeljsullivan.polldaddy.com/s/hollow-world-feedback. If enough people indicate they want more, I'd like nothing better than to oblige.

—Michael J. Sullivan
July 2013

ACKNOWLEDGEMENTS

Hollow World, more than any other book that I've written to date, is the product of many people. And to each of them I'm eternally grateful. This list is bound to be extensive, but bear with me because if you liked *Hollow World*, then you have these people to thank for it.

First there is Nila White, who ended up planting the seed of *Hollow World* when she asked me to create a short story for her anthology *The End—Visions of Apocalypse*. Nila did a tremendous job pulling together anchor authors and judging entries by new authors as a way of showcasing new talent. This isn't a money-making project for her, and the anthology is often free or sometimes a measly $0.99. There are great stories in there, including a fabulous one by Hugh Howey. Please give it a try.

I had an incredible group of beta readers for *Hollow World* including: Alexander Grevy, Algernon, Audrey Wilkinson, Bobby McDaniel, Cait M. Hakala, Caroline Reiss, Clay Ashby, Elizabeth Berndl, Gary Kempson, Greg, Heather A. McBride, Jeffrey Carr, Jeffery Miller, Libby Heily, Marc Grenier, Marcelle McCallum, Nathaniel and Sarah Kidd, Piero, Sebastian O'Sullivan, Shane Enochs, Shawn Haggard, Sheri Gestring, Simon, Stephanie Van Pelt, William Watson, and a few people who asked to remain anonymous. While I can't call out each and every one of their contributions, they are sure to see aspects in the final book that are the direct result of their feedback. I wish every author had such a conscientious and astute beta group. All of you are welcome to be my beta readers anytime.

I'd like to specifically call out Jeff Miller whose enthusiasm helped convince me of *Hollow World*'s value. Jeff is a fine writer in his own right (if you like well-written mystery/thrillers then check out his *Bubble Gum Thief*, the first in his Dagny Gray series). Jeff provided some exceptional ideas each of which improved the book.

I'd like to thank Marc Simonetti who produced some amazing artwork depicting Hollow World. Not only did it provide me incredible inspiration, but it was the glue to which all my pre-promotion for the book centered around. People saw his incredible artwork and just knew this was a project of the highest quality. His artwork was also used for posters and bookmarks giving an incredible perk to those who contributed to the Kickstarter. I've seen framed and mounted copies of the posters from many readers, and I'm honored that my idea, and Marc's talent, is adorning their walls. For those that don't know, Marc did the covers of my French editions of The Riyria Revelations and has created covers for many other fantasy authors such as Patrick Rothfuss (French editions of *The Name of the Wind* and *The Wise Man's Fear*) and George R. R. Martin's Mexican edition of *Game of Thrones*.

One of the advantages of traditional publishing is structural (sometimes known as content editing). This is an important job done by highly skilled professionals. Structural editors concern themselves with things such as pacing, plot holes, and character development. They are the "reader's advocate," who know from years of experience what works and what doesn't. When I thought I would be self-publishing, I didn't want to skip this important step. Luckily for me, Betsy Mitchell, who was the editor-in-chief at Del Rey for more than a decade, is now offering her services directly. Betsy has over thirty years experience editing science fiction and fantasy and has worked on more than 150 books from authors such as Michael Chabon, Terry Brooks, and many *New York Times* bestselling authors. Betsy confirmed what I suspected, that *Hollow World* was already a good book…then she made it better.

Due to the generous contributions of the people in Kickstarter, I was able to afford not just one, but two exceptional copy editors. Both routinely work for the big-five publishers, including Macmillan, Tor, St. Martin's Press, Del Rey, Putnam, and Ballantine Books. One has two masters degrees (one in English and Writing and the other in Creative Writing and English) and has been nominated for the Nebula, World Fantasy, and Tiptree awards. The other has edited Naomi Novik's *Victory of Eagles*, a number of the books in the *Star Wars* franchise, and two *New York Times* bestsellers for Steve Berry. The two of them saved me from innumerable embarrassments. If Betsy took a good book and made it great, then these two editors made me look smarter and more polished than I am.

Then there was the editing that Tachyon Publications contributed. Jacob Weisman was extremely helpful with feedback, especially in the early portions of the novel, which made the work more focused and faster paced. Another pass by their copy editing staff put another coat of polish that gave it that extra shine.

Of course anyone who knows anything about me and my writing knows that my wife, Robin, is integral to every work that is produced. She is always my "first reader" whose opinion ultimately decides whether a book will see the light of day or die hidden in a drawer...and no she doesn't love "everything" I write. During the writing of *Hollow World* I would discuss in vague generalities various aspects about the book. After many of these conversations she professed how scared she was. You see, Robin is not a science fiction fan, and from the bits and pieces I told her she was far from enthusiastic. In fact, I knew she would have preferred for me to be writing other books that she was already anxious to read. When I finished *Hollow World* I thought it was a good book, but it was only after she devoured the whole manuscript in a day, then requested, "more please," that my suspicions were confirmed.

Robin's fingerprints are all over *Hollow World*. Like Betsy and Jacob, she performed two comprehensive sets of structural edits. She helped organize and coordinate the beta readers, including compiling all their edits and comments into one massive file so I could easily process all their feedback. Then she did that again with edits from Betsy, Jacob, the copy editors, and my agents. She masterminded the Kickstarter, and provided much of the logistical support for it. She worked with Teri to get the audio book contract with Recorded Books and with Laurie to get the print-only deal with Tachyon Publications. There is absolutely no way I could have made *Hollow World* a reality without her tireless efforts. She has always and will always have my love, but she also has my undying gratitude for constantly dealing with all the *business aspects* of my writing and turning my dreams into reality.

Hollow World's audience potential has been greatly increased due to the efforts of two fine literary agents. Teri Tobias, who has also represented The Riyria Revelations and The Riyria Chronicles, and secured the audio book rights. Laurie McLean did the near impossible by obtaining a print-only contract for a mid-list author.

I thank both of them for their efforts and talents they brought to this project.

The audio edition of *Hollow World* will be published by Recorded Books, who did an exceptional job with my Riyria Revelations and The Riyria Chronicles. Recorded Books has an incredible recording facility and top notch voice talent. As indication of their quality, the audio book of *Theft of Swords* garnered an Audie Award nominee for 2013, and that wasn't the only title they were short-listed for. In all, they had six titles selected and the list of awards for their recordings are too numerous to list here, but you can check them out at their website. Recorded Books' acquisition team is picking the best and the brightest in speculative fiction and have produced titles by J. R. R. Tolkien, Diana Gabaldon, Charlaine Harris, Brandon Sanderson, Cormac McCarthy, Gregory Macguire, Marion Zimmer Bradley, James S. A. Corey, Peter V. Brett, Gail Carriger, Joe Haldeman, Connie Willis, Piers Anthony, Daniel Abraham, Ursula K. Le Guin, Kim Stanley Robinson, Ilona Andrews, Naomi Novik, Mark Lawrence, and hundreds more.

The print edition of *Hollow World* is released by Tachyon Publications. They are the perfect example of a publisher who is doing things *right*. In the new digital-age, most publishers are trying to lock up as many rights as possible, whereas Tachyon works with authors to meet their needs. Their willingness to take just a slice of the pie is a smart move, which I hope will be a beacon for the rest of the industry. For those unfamiliar with Tachyon Publications, they have published works by Brandon Sanderson, Charles de Lint, Tim Powers, Peter S. Beagle, Patricia A. McKillip, and anthologies by Ellen Datlow, John Joseph Adams, and others. Patricia's *Wonders of the Invisible World* was a *Publishers Weekly* Best Book of 2012. They have had two Hugo Award nominations in 2013, with a win for *The Emperor's Soul*, plus they have won Nebula Awards in 2006, 2012, and 2013.

Okay, so above are all the people who contributed to the actual creation or distribution process in one way or another. And as I said I'm very grateful to them. But I also want to acknowledge the amazing group of readers who contributed to the Kickstarter project. This was the first time I had ever tried Kickstarter, and since then I've backed many projects (and plan to do more). Kickstarter is changing the way in which products are conceived and delivered, and I love this brave new world they are creating. Backers of Kickstarter projects not only get a product they want, but they get exclusive perks available only to them and the satisfaction of knowing their contributions made a new product possible.

As I mentioned in my afterword, I had estimated a need for $6,000 and so I held my Kickstarter for $3,000 (one-half coming from me and one-half from my readership). As it turned out they funded the project at more than 1000 percent, so when all was said and done, not only did I have money to hire the talented professionals that I had picked out, but I also ended up with what was essentially an advance. This is exactly the way traditional publishing works, but instead of getting the advance from a publisher, I got it from the readers. This really has made me think about the changes in the industry. I know several authors who have shelved projects that they felt strongly about but were either turned down or offered too little to sign. Since these are previously published authors, they already have fan bases and I'm hoping that they'll see *Hollow World* as an example of how they can continue to pursue their dreams by writing the stories they want and finding an audience on their own. So not only did the backers of this Kickstarter make *Hollow World* possible, hopefully it'll provide a template for other authors to follow for their own works.

I thanked each person by name in the Kickstarter edition, but I wanted to once again give them all my heartfelt thanks for their belief in the project, their financial support, and all the amazing reviews and comments they have provided since receiving their books. This book belongs to you just as much as it does to those that participated in the production of the book, and I'm humbled by all that you have done for *Hollow World.*

—Michael J. Sullivan
October 2013

About the Author

After finding a manual typewriter in the basement of a friend's house, Michael inserted a blank piece of paper and typed: It was a dark and stormy night and a shot rang out. Well, he was just eight years old at the time, so we'll forgive him that trespass. But the desire to fill the blank page and see what doors the typewriter keys would unlock wouldn't let him go. For ten years Michael developed his craft by studying authors such as Stephen King, Ayn Rand, and John Steinbeck. During that time, he wrote twelve novels, and after finding no traction in publishing, he gave up and vowed never to write creatively again.

Michael discovered that never is a very long time, and he ended his writing hiatus after a decade. The itch returned when he decided to create a series of books for his then thirteen-year-old daughter, who was struggling in school due to dyslexia. Intrigued by the idea of writing a series with an overarching story line, he created the Riyria Revelations. Each of the six books was written as an individual episode but also included intertwining elements and mysteries that develop over time. Michael describes this endeavor as something he did "just for fun with no intention of publishing." After presenting the first manuscript to his daughter, he was chagrined that she declared, "I can't read it like this, can't you get it published?"

So began his second adventure on the road to publication, which included: drafting his wife to be his business manager; signing with an independent press; and later creating a small press. After two and a half years, the first five books sold more than 70,000 copies and ranked in the top twenty of multiple Amazon fantasy lists. In November 2010, he leveraged his success and received his first commercial publishing contract for three novels from Orbit Books (the fantasy imprint of Hachette Book Group, USA). In addition, Michael reached international status with more than fifteen foreign rights translations including France, Spain, Russia, and Germany, just to name a few.

Michael's work has been well received by critics and readers alike, earning him thousands of positive ratings/reviews, interviews, and articles. He has attributed much of his success to the fantasy book blogging community. Dubbed "the little indie that could" he found his books pitted as the only independent in major competitions such as the 2010 and 2012 Goodreads Choice Award Nominee for Fantasy and the 2009 Book Spot Central's Fantasy Tournament of Books, which he won. His traditionally published edition of *Theft of Swords* was short-listed for the 2013 Audie Award for Fantasy.

Today, Michael continues to fill blank pages and is working on his third series tentatively titled The First Empire.

Contact Information

Website/blog: www.riyria.com
Twitter: @author_sullivan
Email: michael.sullivan.dc@gmail.com
Facebook (author): www.facebook.com/author.michael.sullivan
Facebook (series): www.facebook.com/riyria

THEFT OF SWORDS

If you enjoyed *Hollow World* and would like to read more of Michael's work, you might like *Theft of Swords.*

They killed the king. They pinned it on two men.
They chose poorly.

There's no ancient evil to defeat or orphan destined for greatness, just two guys in the wrong place at the wrong time. Royce Melborn, a skilled thief, and his mercenary partner, Hadrian Blackwater, are enterprising rogues who end up running for their lives when they're framed for the murder of the king. Trapped in a conspiracy that goes beyond the overthrow of a tiny kingdom, their only hope is unraveling an ancient mystery before it's too late.

Stolen Letters

Hadrian could see little in the darkness, but he could hear them—the snapping of twigs, the crush of leaves, and the brush of grass. There were more than one, more than three, and they were closing in.

"Don't neither of you move," a harsh voice ordered from the shadows. "We've got arrows aimed at your backs, and we'll drop you in your saddles if you try to run." The speaker was still in the dark eaves of the forest, just a vague movement among the naked branches. "We're just gonna lighten your load a bit. No one needs to get hurt. Do as I say and you'll keep your lives. Don't—and we'll take those, too."

Hadrian felt his stomach sink, knowing this was his fault. He glanced over at Royce, who sat beside him on his dirty gray mare with his hood up, his face hidden. His friend's head was bowed and shook slightly. Hadrian did not need to see his expression to know what it looked like.

"Sorry," he offered.

Royce said nothing and just continued to shake his head.

Before them stood a wall of fresh-cut brush blocking their way. Behind lay the long moonlit corridor of empty road. Mist pooled in the dips and gullies, and somewhere an unseen stream trickled over rocks. They were deep in the forest on the old southern road, engulfed in a long tunnel of oaks and ash whose slender branches reached out over the road, quivering and clacking in the cold autumn wind. Almost a day's ride from any town, Hadrian could not recall passing so much as a farmhouse in hours. They were on their own, in the middle of nowhere—the kind of place people never found bodies.

The crush of leaves grew louder until at last the thieves stepped into the narrow band of moonlight. Hadrian counted four men with unshaven faces and drawn swords. They wore rough clothes, leather and wool, stained, worn, and filthy. With them was a girl wielding a bow, an arrow notched and aimed. She was dressed like the rest in pants and boots, her hair a tangled mess. Each was covered in mud, a ground-in grime, as if the whole lot slept in a dirt burrow.

"They don't look like they got much money," a man with a flat nose said. An inch or two taller than Hadrian, he was the largest of the party, a stocky brute with a thick neck and large hands. His lower lip looked to have been split about the same time his nose was broken.

"But they've got bags of gear," the girl said. Her voice surprised him. She was young, and—despite the dirt—cute, and almost childlike, but her tone was aggressive, even vicious. "Look at all this stuff they're carrying. What's with all the rope?"

Hadrian was uncertain if she was asking him or her fellows. Either way, he was not about to answer. He considered making a joke, but she did not look like the type he could charm with a compliment and a smile. On top of that, she was pointing the arrow at him and it looked like her arm might be growing tired.

"I claim the big sword that fella has on his back," flat-nose said. "Looks right about my size."

"I'll take the other two he's carrying." This came from one with a scar that divided his face at a slight angle, crossing the bridge of his nose just high enough to save his eye.

The girl aimed the point of her arrow at Royce. "I want the little one's cloak. I'd look good in a fine black hood like that."

With deep-set eyes and sunbaked skin, the man closest to Hadrian appeared to be the oldest. He took a step closer and grabbed hold of Hadrian's horse by the bit. "Be real careful now. We've killed plenty of folks along this road. Stupid folks who didn't listen. You don't want to be stupid, do you?"

Hadrian shook his head.

"Good. Now drop them weapons," the thief said. "And then climb down."

"What do you say, Royce?" Hadrian asked. "We give them a bit of coin so nobody gets hurt."

Royce looked over. Two eyes peered out from the hood with a withering glare.

"I'm just saying, we don't want any trouble, am I right?"

"You don't want my opinion," Royce said.

"So you're going to be stubborn."

Silence.

Hadrian shook his head and sighed. "Why do you have to make everything so difficult? They're probably not bad people—just poor. You know, taking what they need to buy a loaf of bread to feed their family. Can you begrudge them that? Winter is coming and times are hard." He nodded his head in the direction of the thieves. "Right?"

"I ain't got no family," flat-nose replied. "I spend most of my coin on drink."

"You're not helping," Hadrian said.

"I'm not trying to. Either you two do as you're told, or we'll gut you right here." He emphasized this by pulling a long dagger from his belt and scraping it loudly against the blade of his sword.

A cold wind howled through the trees, bobbing the branches and stripping away more foliage. Red and gold leaves flew, swirling in circles, buffeted by the gusts along the narrow road. Somewhere in the dark an owl hooted.

"Look, how about we give you half our money? *My half.* That way this won't be a total loss for you."

"We ain't asking for half," the man holding his mount said. "We want it all, right down to these here horses."

"Now wait a second. Our horses? Taking a little coin is fine but horse thieving? If you get caught, you'll hang. And you know we'll report this at the first town we come to."

"You're from up north, ain't you?"

"Yeah, left Medford yesterday."

The man holding his horse nodded and Hadrian noticed a small red tattoo on his neck. "See, that's your problem." His face softened to a sympathetic expression that appeared more threatening by its intimacy. "You're probably on your way to Colnora—nice city. Lots of shops. Lots of fancy rich folk. Lots of trading going on down there, and we get lots of people along this road carrying all kinds of stuff to sell to them fancy folk. But I'm guessing you ain't been south before, have you? Up in Melengar, King Amrath goes to the trouble of having soldiers patrol the roads. But here in Warric, things are done a bit differently."

Flat-nose came closer, licking his split lip as he studied the spadone sword on his back.

"Are you saying theft is legal?"

"Naw, but King Ethelred lives in Aquesta and that's awfully far from here."

"And the Earl of Chadwick? Doesn't he administer these lands on the king's behalf?"

"Archie Ballentyne?" The mention of his name brought chuckles from the other thieves. "Archie don't give a rat's ass what goes on with the common folk. He's too busy picking out what to wear." The man grinned, showing yellowed teeth that grew at odd angles. "So now drop them swords and climb down. Afterward, you can walk on up to Ballentyne Castle, knock on old Archie's door, and see what he does." Another round of laughter. "Now unless you think this is the perfect place to die—you're gonna do as I say."

"You were right, Royce," Hadrian said in resignation. He unclasped his cloak and laid it across the rear of his saddle. "We should have left the road, but honestly—I mean, we are in the middle of nowhere. What were the odds?"

"Judging from the fact that we're being robbed—pretty good, I think."

"Kinda ironic—Riyria being robbed. Almost funny even."

"It's not funny."

"Did you say Riyria?" the man holding Hadrian's horse asked.

Hadrian nodded and pulled his gloves off, tucking them into his belt.

The man let go of his horse and took a step away.

"What's going on, Will?" the girl asked. "What's Riyria?"

"There's a pair of fellas in Melengar that call themselves that." He looked toward the others and lowered his voice a bit. "I got connections up that way, remember? They say two guys calling themselves Riyria work out of Medford and I was told to keep my distance if I was ever to run across them."

"So what you thinking, Will?" scar-face asked.

"I'm thinking maybe we should clear the brush and let them ride through."

"What? Why? There's five of us and just two of them," flat-nose pointed out.

"But they're Riyria."

"So what?"

"So, my *associates* up north—they ain't stupid, and they told everyone never to touch these two. And my associates ain't exactly the squeamish types. If they say to avoid them, there's a good reason."

Flat-nose looked at them again with a critical eye. "Okay, but how do you know these two guys are them? You just gonna take their word for it?"

Will nodded toward Hadrian. "Look at the swords he's carrying. A man wearing one—maybe he knows how to use it, maybe not. A man carries two—he probably don't know nothing about swords, but he wants you to think he does. But a man carrying three swords—that's a lot of weight. No one's gonna haul that much steel around unless he makes a living using them."

Hadrian drew two swords from his sides in a single elegant motion. He flipped one around, letting it spin against his palm once. "Need to get a new grip on this one. It's starting to fray again." He looked at Will. "Shall we get on with this? I believe you were about to rob us."

The thieves shot uncertain glances to each other.

"Will?" the girl asked. She was still holding the bow taut but looked decidedly less confident.

"Let's clear the brush out of their way and let them pass," Will said.

"You sure?" Hadrian asked. "This nice man with the busted nose seems to have his heart set on getting a sword."

"That's okay," flat-nose said, looking up at Hadrian's blades as the moonlight glinted off the mirrored steel.

"Well, if you're sure."

All five nodded and Hadrian sheathed his weapons.

Will planted his sword in the dirt and waved the others over as he hurried to clear the barricade of branches blocking the roadway.

"You know, you're doing this all wrong," Royce told them.

The thieves stopped and looked up, concerned.

Royce shook his head. "Not clearing the brush—the robbery. You picked a nice spot. I'll give you that. But you should have come at us from both sides."

"And, William—it is William, isn't it?" Hadrian asked.

The man winced and nodded.

"Yeah, William, most people are right-handed, so those coming in close should approach from the left. That would've put us at a disadvantage, having to swing across our bodies at you. Those with bows should be on our right."

"And why just one bow?" Royce asked. "She could have only hit one of us."

"Couldn't even have done that," Hadrian said. "Did you notice how long she held the bow bent? Either she's incredibly strong—which I doubt—or that's a homemade greenwood bow with barely enough power to toss the arrow a few feet. Her part was just for show. I doubt she's ever launched an arrow."

"Have too," the girl said. "I'm a fine marksman."

Hadrian shook his head at her with a smile. "You had your forefinger on top of the shaft, dear. If you had released, the feathers on the arrow would have brushed your finger and the shot would have gone anywhere but where you wanted it to."

Royce nodded. "Invest in crossbows. Next time stay hidden and just put a couple bolts into each of your targets' chests. All this talking is just stupid."

"Royce!" Hadrian admonished.

"What? You're always saying I should be nicer to people. I'm trying to be helpful."

"Don't listen to him. If you do want some advice, try building a better barricade."

"Yeah, drop a tree across the road next time," Royce said. Waving a hand toward the branches, he added, "This is just pathetic. And cover your faces for Maribor's sake. Warric isn't that big of a kingdom and people might remember you. Sure Ballentyne isn't likely to bother tracking you down for a few petty highway robberies, but you're gonna walk into a tavern one day and get a knife in your back." Royce turned to William. "You were in the Crimson Hand, right?"

Will looked startled. "No one said nothing about that." He stopped pulling on the branch he was working on.

"Didn't need to. The Hand requires all guild members to get that stupid tattoo on their necks." Royce turned to Hadrian. "It's supposed to make them look tough, but all it really does is make it easy to identify them as thieves for the rest of their lives. Painting a red hand on everyone is pretty stupid when you think about it."

"That tattoo is supposed to be a hand?" Hadrian asked. "I thought it was a little red chicken. But now that you mention it, a hand does make more sense."

Royce looked back at Will and tilted his head to one side. "Does kinda look like a chicken."

Will clamped a palm over his neck.

After the last of the brush was cleared, William asked, "Who are you, really? What exactly is Riyria? The Hand never told me. They just said to keep clear."

"We're nobody special," Hadrian replied. "Just a couple of travelers enjoying a ride on a cool autumn's night."

"But seriously," Royce said. "You need to listen to us if you're going to keep doing this. After all, we're going to take your advice."

"What advice?"

Royce gave a gentle kick to his horse and started forward on the road again. "We're going to visit the Earl of Chadwick, but don't worry—we won't mention you."